DANGER Lies Ahead!

DANGER Lies Ahead!

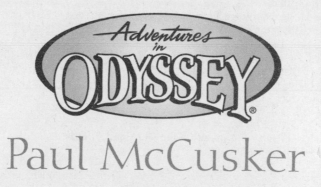

Adventures in ODYSSEY®

Paul McCusker

TYNDALE
Tyndale House Publishers, Inc.
Carol Stream, Illinois

A Focus on the Family book published by
Tyndale House Publishers, Carol Stream, Illinois 60188

TYNDALE is a registered trademark of Tyndale House Publishers, Inc. Tyndale's quill
logo is a trademark of Tyndale House Publishers, Inc.

The books in this collection were originally published as:
Lights Out at Camp What-a-Nut, © 1993 by Focus on the Family
The King's Quest, © 1994 by Focus on the Family
Danger Lies Ahead, © 1995 by Focus on the Family
A Carnival of Secrets, © 1997 by Paul McCusker

A note to readers: The Adventures in Odyssey novels take place in a time period prior to
the beginning of the audio or video series. That is why some of the characters from those
episodes don't appear in these stories—they don't exist yet.

Editor: Liz Duckworth
Cover design: Greg Sills
Cover illustration: Gary Locke
Cover copy: Larilee Frazier

Library of Congress Cataloging-in-Publication Data
McCusker, Paul, 1958-
    Danger lies ahead : four original stories of mystery, fantasy, and family / Paul McCusker.
        v. cm. — (Adventures in Odyssey flashbacks ; 2)
    "A Focus on the Family book."
    Summary: Four stories set in the fictional town of Odyssey follow Mark, Patti, and
other members of the Whit's End gang as they learn of loss, love, and of life.
    Contents: Lights out at Camp What-a-Nut—The king's quest—Danger lies ahead—
A carnival of secrets.
    ISBN-13: 978-1-58997-329-9
    ISBN-10: 1-58997-329-1
    [1. Friendship—Fiction. 2. Conduct of life—Fiction.] I. Title.
    PZ7.M47841635Dan 2006
    [Fic]—dc22
                                                        2005029376

Printed in the United States of America
1 2 3 4 5 6 7 8 9 /10 09 08 07 06

To John G.,
in memory of those wonderful days and nights at Camp W.

To Elizabeth Sarah Duffield,
who heightened my love and respect for the British
by becoming my wife.

Contents

Lights Out at Camp What-a-Nut

Chapter
One

THE BANNER "Welcome to Odyssey Municipal Airport!" stretched across the airline gate, ready to greet the passengers on the approaching plane. Mark Prescott leaned across his mother's seat to get a closer look out the window. Although the pane was dotted with raindrops from yet another late August storm, he could see the banner and felt his heart leap at the name "Odyssey."

"Are you glad to be back?" Julie, his mother, asked.

Mark nodded.

Julie rubbed Mark's back. "I was just thinking how nice it is to be home again. Funny, huh?—thinking about Odyssey as home."

Mark understood what she meant. When his parents separated the previous June, Mark was sure nothing worse could ever happen to him. That is, until Julie moved Mark to her grandmother's house in Odyssey, halfway across the country from his father, Richard, and their home in Washington, D.C. Then Mark *knew* it was the end of the world.

But that was last June.

In the three months since then, he had made new friends, enjoyed Odyssey's gentle charm, and taken part in some exciting adventures (including taking a trip in a time machine and solving a mystery). Slowly, Mark felt less like a stranger and more like a welcome friend. By August, it was as if he'd always been there—and always would be.

Mark and Julie followed the crowd of passengers from the plane to the baggage-claim area. A horn sounded a warning blast, and the conveyor belts loudly whirred to life. Mark stood nearby, grabbing their luggage when it came past. They tossed the cases onto a cart and pushed it to the long-term parking area where Julie had parked the car only a few days before.

Only a few days? It seems longer than that, Mark thought, then said so out loud.

"Did it seem long because you didn't enjoy yourself?" Julie asked as she closed the trunk.

"I guess so," Mark said with a shrug. "It wasn't as much fun as I thought it would be. It's like . . . our house wasn't ours anymore."

Julie nodded her head, a lock of her long, brown hair falling across her face. "I understand. Everything looked the same as it did before we left, but it seemed different somehow. Once or twice, I felt like I was a visitor in a museum." She started the car and backed out of the parking space.

"All my old friends were either away on vacation or they didn't want to see me," Mark complained. That bothered him a lot. Somehow it didn't seem fair that they went on with their lives without him being there to give his approval.

Julie paid the parking attendant, wound up her window, and pulled away. "That's the hardest part. When you go away, you think everyone should suddenly stop in their tracks and never do anything important without you. You think you're the only one who can change and make new friends or have new experiences. And when you come back, it's a shock to find out that their lives kept going—just like yours did."

"Yeah, but Mike Adams is hanging around Tom Nelson! They couldn't stand each other before!"

Julie laughed and said, "Just like you never thought you could have a girl as a friend."

His mom was referring to Patti Eldridge, a girl who had become Mark's closest friend in Odyssey during the summer.

"That's different," Mark replied. He stared out the passenger window thoughtfully. "And I thought you and Dad . . ." He glanced down at his lap uncomfortably.

Julie finished his sentence: "You thought your dad and I would get back together again. I know."

She was right. The reason they had gone to Washington, D.C. in the first place was so that Mark's mom and dad could iron out their differences. But by the time Richard dropped Mark and Julie off at the airport for their return trip to Odyssey, it was clear that wasn't going to happen.

"I'm sorry, Mark," Julie said. "I really thought your dad and I would work it all out. I thought this trip would be the end of our separation. I know you're disappointed."

"Wars have ended quicker than you two getting back together," Mark said as they drove away from the airport.

Julie smiled wearily in return. "You have to be patient. You may not see the improvements, but they're there."

"Then why aren't we together again?"

"Because we're not ready," she answered. "I won't get back with your father until I'm sure we're ready."

"But that's what you and Dad keep saying!"

"I know. But some things came up in our counseling session that we have to figure out." Julie sighed. "You wouldn't understand."

"What wouldn't I understand?" Mark snapped. "Why do you always think I don't understand?"

Julie glanced at Mark, a pained expression on her face.

"I'm sorry," Mark said. "I didn't mean to be so sharp."

Julie acknowledged the apology with a nod, then reached across the seat to touch Mark's hand. "It's all leading somewhere, Mark. You have to trust us. We've needed this time to mend our wounds."

Mark shot her an ornery look, then said, "Maybe you should buy some Band-Aids."

She pinched him playfully and drove on.

Chapter
Two

AT HOME, MARK HURRIEDLY unpacked his case. He was eager to talk to Patti, to tell her everything that had happened. He smiled at the thought of Patti listening attentively to the disappointment and frustration he felt. He imagined her reaction. She would be sympathetic. She would understand how he felt. *In other words, she'll do all the things a friend is supposed to do*, Mark thought. She wasn't at all like those uncaring friends he left back in Washington.

But Patti wasn't home. Her mother reminded Mark that she had left to go to Camp What-a-Nut, a summer camp in the mountains. She'd been gone a week.

"Oh no," Mark whispered. He had forgotten all about it. What was he going to do for a whole week?

The situation got worse when Mark walked downtown to Whit's End. It was an ice cream parlor and discovery emporium for kids, with a library, workshops, and room after room of displays, inventions and play areas. It also boasted having "the largest train set in the county." Mark, like most of the kids in Odyssey, liked going there—not only for the fun, but also because of John Avery Whittaker, the owner. Whit (as he was best known) was a kind, generous, and wise man who used Whit's End as a way to help kids. Sometimes it was enough for kids to simply have a place to play, but Whit often listened to the kids' problems and offered a word of advice. He'd helped Mark on several occasions.

But Whit wasn't there when Mark arrived. He had gone to camp, too. Tom Riley, Whit's best friend, stood behind the ice cream counter and cheerfully served customers. "Howya doin'?" Tom asked Mark in his gentle drawl.

Mark shrugged and answered, "Okay, I guess. Patti and Whit are gone."

Tom tugged at a loose strap on his overalls and buttoned it up again. "Left for camp while you were in Washington, huh?"

"Yeah," Mark replied, cradling his head in his hands sadly. "I forgot all about it."

"Plenty of other people are still around," Tom observed.

"But not Patti or Whit," Mark complained.

Tom watched Mark thoughtfully for a moment, then snapped his fingers as if he had just thought of a great idea. "Why don't *you* go to camp?" he asked.

Mark lifted his head. "It's too late . . . isn't it?"

"I don't think it's ever too late to go to Camp What-a-Nut. Most years they have plenty of room." Tom leaned close to Mark. "I'm sure Whit would be glad to see you. In fact, he was saying just the other day how different the place seems when you're not around."

Mark's spirits brightened. "He said that about *me*?"

Mark found it hard to believe considering the tension between them right before Mark left for Washington. Mark had stayed at Whit's house for a couple of days after Julie left. While he was there, he disobeyed Whit by sneaking into a locked room, where he broke a treasured heirloom of Whit's. Mark apologized and Whit forgave him, but it didn't take away from the surprise of Tom's words.

"Yep, that's what he said." Tom nodded and hooked his thumbs in his overalls straps. One of them came loose.

❧   ❧

"Camp *what*?" Julie asked as she leaned across the kitchen table.

"Not Camp *What*—Camp *What-a-Nut*," Mark corrected her.

"That's a silly name," she said.

Mark couldn't argue. He didn't know where the camp got its name and wasn't sure it was important at the moment. "I was thinking that maybe it would be fun to go . . . you know, before school starts."

He nearly choked on the word *school*—and even felt a tightening in his chest at the realization that summer was ending so quickly.

"But I don't know anything about it," Julie said, spreading her arms. "Where is it? How much does it cost to go?"

Mark pushed a brochure that Tom Riley had given him across the table. Julie looked surprised, then picked it up.

"'Camp What-a-Nut, nestled next to the beautiful Lake Manitou in the Green Ridge Mountains, offers sound moral teaching combined with recreational facilities and large dormitories for the campers. Archery, canoeing, swimming, softball, horseback riding, and a number of crafts are all just a part of the fun found at Camp What-a-Nut . . .'" Her voice trailed off as she continued to read to herself.

Mark shook his leg impatiently.

"Hmm," she finally said.

Mark looked up expectantly.

"Well . . ." she began as she set the brochure on the table again.

Mark stopped pumping his leg.

"If you really want to go, I guess you can."

Mark shouted and hugged her.

Chapter
Three

FROM THE PORCH OF PINE LODGE, Camp What-a-Nut's main cabin, Mark watched his mother carefully maneuver her car past the potholes in the dirt road that led away from camp. He waved, but he knew she wouldn't wave back. She wouldn't dare take her hands off the steering wheel for fear of landing in one of the holes.

He leaned forward and rested his arms on the large, brown log that served as the porch's handrail. From this vantage point, Mark could see most of the camp. Several small cabins, built with the same kind of logs, circled the driveway at the center of the camp like a wagon train under Indian attack. Beyond the circle, a carpet of thick grass stretched toward playing fields, a fenced-in swimming pool, and a large stable. The green carpet suddenly gave way to a wall of trees that covered the mountain like badly combed hair.

To the left, a large, blue lake twinkled in the sun as if someone had thrown glitter all over it. He longed for a closer look. The air was fresh with the scent of pine. Mark hummed softly with the serenity of it all.

Then a screen door slammed behind him.

"Okay, Matt," Mr. Gunnoe, an assistant director of the camp, said.

"Mark," Mark corrected him.

Mr. Gunnoe adjusted his glasses and looked closely at the registration slip in his hand. "Mark. Right. We went over the rules of the camp while your mother was here, we took care of the medical release, we got your tuition paid in full, your suitcase is right here, and—let's see—we'll put you in Wabana."

"Wabana?"

"That's the name of the cabin you'll stay in. Follow me."

"Where is everybody?" Mark asked as they walked across the circle and under the flagpole that marked its center. An American flag flapped in the soft breeze with a sound like birds' wings.

"They're at lunch in the cafeteria—over there." Mr. Gunnoe pointed to a long building just off the circle of cabins. Unlike everything else, the building was made of large sheets of metal bolted together. It reminded Mark of an army boot camp he once saw on television. A large bell in a wooden frame sat in front of the building.

"They ring the bell when it's time to eat," Mr. Gunnoe added. He held open the screen door of Wabana as Mark lugged his suitcase into the dark, cool room. The cabin was filled with bunk beds, lined exactly opposite each other along two walls. Each bed was made, except for one at the very end. On that one, the covers were tossed aside, and clothes were strewn about. It was a startling contrast to the rest of the neatness.

"Disgusting, isn't it?" Mr. Gunnoe said, obviously noticing Mark's gaze. "That's Joe's bed."

Mark frowned and asked, "Joe Devlin?"

"You know him? Too bad for you. Your bed is right next to his."

Mark groaned loudly.

"Sorry, but it's the only one left in this cabin, which is the only one designated for your age group." Mr. Gunnoe pulled a pencil from behind his ear and scribbled on a piece of paper.

Mark dropped his suitcase and glanced again at the disheveled bed nearby. He was genuinely surprised that someone like Joe Devlin would come to camp. More than that, he dreaded the idea of being so close to Joe. They had had several arguments since Mark arrived in Odyssey; one even led to a fight. It wasn't Mark's fault, though. Joe Devlin was a bully.

"The kid's a terror," Mr. Gunnoe said. "We've already reprimanded him once. Twice more and he'll be expelled from camp."

"Good," Mark whispered.

Mr. Gunnoe showed Mark where the toilets and showers were, then gave him a sheet of paper with the afternoon's schedule. It gave Mark the option of taking a swimming, archery, or woodworking class. Mark decided he'd try the archery.

Just like Robin Hood, he thought.

❈   ❈

Until Mark saw Patti walk toward him from the cafeteria, he had forgotten that their last conversation ended with her slamming the phone down in his ear. It happened right before Mark went to see his father. He had been staying at Whit's house, and Patti had called him at the wrong time (just as he was about to solve the mystery of Whit's locked attic door). He was rude to her, and she got mad and hung up.

Now he wondered what Patti would say to him—*if* she spoke to him at all. He stood perfectly still and waited for her to get closer. A tight smile stretched across his lips and froze in place. "Hi, Patti," he squeaked when she was within earshot.

She was dressed in her favorite outfit: faded jeans, T-shirt, and baseball cap. Her right arm was in a cast because of an accident a few weeks before. It was covered with good wishes and signatures. Mark braced himself as she stopped directly in front of him. She tipped the baseball cap away from her forehead. Her eyes burned into his.

"How's it going?" Mark asked.

Patti slugged him in the arm.

"Hey!" he cried out.

"That's for being so mean to me on the phone!" she shouted. "Now apologize!"

"That *hurt*!" Mark whined.

Patti punched him in the other arm. "Apologize!" she demanded.

"All right, all right, I'm sorry," Mark said. He glanced around quickly to make sure no one had seen them.

"Say you're *really* sorry," she insisted, raising her fist.

"I'm *really* sorry," Mark said, then nearly whispered, "*Really, really* sorry, Patti. I mean it."

Mark was sincere, and Patti knew him well enough to realize it. Her tone softened. "Okay. So, what happened to you?"

Mark wasn't sure if she meant at Whit's house or in Washington. Either way, he didn't think it was the right time to explain. "All kinds of things. I'll tell you later. Do you like camp?"

"Uh-huh," she replied. "Did you come up to visit for the day?"

Mark shook his head. "I'm here for the rest of the week."

Mark expected her to be pleased with the news. Instead, she frowned and said, "Oh, really?"

"Yeah. What's wrong with that?"

"Nothing," she said in a voice that meant *something*. She screwed her face up as if she was thinking hard about whether to tell Mark what was on her mind.

Perhaps she would have if they hadn't been interrupted by a tall, redheaded boy who ran in their direction and called Patti's name. He had a lean, athletic build that was well-displayed beneath his muscle shirt and gym shorts. Though Mark guessed he was only a couple of years older than either him or Patti, his voice had already changed to a deeper, more teenage pitch.

"I've been looking for you," he puffed as he wiped the sweat from his brow.

"Hi, David." Patti giggled strangely. "I was just talking to—" Patti stopped, then looked at Mark with wide, surprised eyes. She had clearly forgotten his name.

"I'm Mark," Mark said.

Patti blushed. "Yeah. Mark. And this is David Boyer. He works here. At the camp, I mean. He sets up tables for the meals and teaches some of the classes and . . . oh, he does everything."

"Hi," Mark said uneasily. Patti was acting very weird all of a sudden. If Mark didn't know better, he'd swear she was gushing.

"Is this the kid you told me about?" David asked Patti.

Patti cleared her throat and answered, "Well, uh—"

"You shouldn't have acted like that on the phone," David said to Mark. "It wasn't very polite."

Mark thought of the two punches Patti had given him in the arm and wondered if David would consider *them* polite. "I know," he said.

David turned his attention to Patti again. "We're gonna be late for the afternoon classes."

"You're right," Patti answered with a lilt in her voice.

Mark watched as David and Patti walked away. David apparently said something amusing, because Patti threw her head back and laughed. Her baseball cap fell off, and she bent down to retrieve it. Before she could, however, David deftly snapped it up. He handed it to her in a gentlemanly manner. She shot an uncomfortable glance back at Mark, then went on her way.

I've never seen her act like that, Mark thought. Then it suddenly came back to him. He had. It wasn't long after they first met. She had asked him if he'd ever kissed a girl. And she had carved a heart with their initials into a tree.

"Oh no," Mark said out loud. He hoped she wasn't going through another one of those weird girl things the way she did then. It nearly wrecked their friendship. *And who is that David guy, anyway, to tell me how to be polite?* Mark shoved his hands into his jeans pockets and ambled to archery class.

David was his teacher.

Chapter Four

MARK DIDN'T FEEL MUCH LIKE Robin Hood as he fumbled with the bow, thumped the bowstring as it caught in his fingers, and dropped arrows like a clumsy oaf. He never got near the target.

David was patient. Even helpful. But it was too late. Mark was already determined not to like him, though he couldn't have said why. Patti also took the archery class, but she couldn't do much because of her cast.

"Patti and I like Robin Hood," Mark announced. "We sometimes play it at home."

"Mark!" Patti cried out, red-faced.

"What?" Mark asked.

She sent a disapproving expression his way and shook her head. David didn't seem to notice.

After the class ended, Mark left quickly. He couldn't bear the way Patti gushed all over David. *She'll probably forget my name again*, he decided.

He frowned as he walked. What was Patti's problem? Why was she acting so strange? *I came all the way to camp to talk to her, and she has a . . .* Mark stopped. He was hung up on the word that would complete the sentence. He didn't want to believe it was true.

Patti has a boyfriend?

Mark shook his head. The idea was too new for him to fully appreciate what it meant. And in the back of his mind, he wondered, *Why does she need a boyfriend when she has me?*

It scared him. He pictured Patti spending all her time with David and never having any time for him. *Just like my old friends in Washington.*

Mark determined to put Patti and David out of his mind as he walked beyond the playing fields, past the young horse-riders being led back to the stable by a leather-faced man in a cowboy hat. He went directly to the thing he'd wanted to see since arriving—Lake Manitou.

Under the bright sun, the gentle water swirled like icing on a lemon cake and lapped the ground near Mark's feet. Across the lake, Mark noticed scattered cabins—probably owned by rich tourists. A handful of small boats with sails thrust out like pigeons' chests rode the rise and fall of the current. A large bird appeared, floated above the water, then flew off again. He watched it move gracefully to his left, where it landed on a collection of twisted wood that stuck up from the water and reached out from shore for several yards. *A dock*, Mark guessed. But the wood was old and rotted and probably unable to bear more than a bird's weight.

His curiosity aroused, Mark walked the distance to the edge where the shore met the dock. A large sign warned him to go no farther because the dock was condemned, forbidden. "Stay away!" it shouted. The bird squawked and flew off. The dock seemed terribly lonely.

Lonely, maybe, but Mark wasn't alone. He heard talking—whispering—nearby. He followed the sound around a large pile of discarded lumber and stopped just short of being seen by the gathering of boys there.

"We're not supposed to go near it," one of the boys complained.

"That makes it even better," another boy replied. Mark recognized the voice. It was Joe Devlin. Mark strained to listen more closely.

Joe continued, "An initiation's no good if it's easy."

"I—I don't know," another boy said so softly that Mark could barely make out his words.

"You wanna be in my gang or not?" Joe asked.

No one answered.

"Look, kid," Joe said, "all you have to do is walk to the end of that thing, turn around, and come back. Think you can handle it?"

Mark looked at the dock and tried to imagine the chances of success. It was falling apart, slanted, and slippery from the water that splashed between the wood pilings.

"No sweat," someone said.

Joe laughed. "You think you're so tough, but we'll see. Come on."

Realizing they were going to spot him, Mark jumped back and tried to pretend he was only just arriving. Joe was the first to emerge from behind the woodpile. He was surprised to see Mark and instantly sneered. "Hey! It's Mark Press-snot!"

The group of boys looked at him curiously.

Mark put his hands on his hips and asked, "What're you doing here, Joe?"

"That's for me to know and you to find out," Joe said, poking a finger into Mark's chest. "Unless you're spying on me. You're not spying on me, are you? Or maybe you're playing snitch for your buddy-buddy Mr. Whit's End?"

Mark didn't bother to answer, nor did Joe wait for one. He simply shoved Mark aside and walked on. One by one, his followers did the same. They looked like frightened puppies. *Just the kind of kids Joe Devlin likes to pick on*, Mark thought as he felt anew a deep loathing for Joe. He tried to guess which kid was crazy enough to agree to walk on the dock.

Mark turned back to the wreckage of the old dock. It couldn't be that hard to walk to the end and back, could it?

A bird let out a piercing scream overhead. Mark's skin crawled. *Yes. It could.*

❈   ❈

"Joe's been a real pain in the neck since camp started," Patti said as she stretched her legs and leaned back against a tree. "He's even worse than usual—if that's possible."

"Why?" Mark asked. He sat cross-legged as he plucked a fist-ful of grass and tossed it to one side absentmindedly.

Patti shrugged. "Who knows?"

"But how does he do it?" Mark asked.

"Do what?"

"Get a gang together so fast. He's only been here for two days, and already he has a whole group of kids around him." Mark was genuinely perplexed.

"I guess they attract each other. Kids looking for trouble will find other kids looking for trouble, and so they find trouble together."

Mark looked at her quizzically. He wasn't entirely sure that what she said made sense. But Patti didn't seem to notice. She was too busy examining the signatures on her cast. For a moment he felt a tinge of relief. He was glad he had caught up with her when David wasn't around. She seemed like her old self.

"It's like how I met David," she began.

His feeling of relief quickly disappeared. "Huh?"

She smiled. "I was looking for a tennis ball that I knocked over the fence, and—guess what he did."

"He handed it to you," Mark said dryly, then resumed pluck-ing the grass.

"He handed it to me!" Patti giggled.

She was gushing again. *Maybe coming to camp wasn't such a good idea after all*, he thought. He yanked at another clump of grass and pulled it up, roots and all.

"Mark, have you ever been in love?"

"What!" Mark shrieked. "Snap out of it, Patti! Stop being so weird!"

Patti sat up. "I'm not being weird! There's nothing weird about being in love!"

"In love! With David? But you just met the guy!"

"That's what's so bizarre," Patti said significantly. "It's like we've *always* known each other. Like . . . we were *meant* for each other."

Mark groaned and fell backward onto the grass. "I don't believe it. You sound just like one of those gross black-and-white movies my mom likes to watch on TV. It's disgusting."

"You're just jealous," Patti said.

"I am not."

"I saw how you acted at archery class," she argued. "You acted like you were mad."

"That's only because I was getting sick to my stomach watching you and David make goo-goo eyes at each other."

"You're jealous."

"I am not."

Patti reached over, touched Mark's arm, and spoke with a voice full of honey. "Mark, you don't have to be jealous. If David and I get married, you can come visit anytime you want. We'll still be friends."

"Married!" Mark cried out.

Just then the dinner bell clanged.

Chapter
Five

MARK CARRIED HIS TRAY ALONG the food line and watched with wide eyes as a staff hastily threw scoops of something on the plates and handed them over the counter to each passing camper. It was an assembly line. Only Mark wasn't sure what they were assembling. The food was formless and void.

Patti asked Mark to sit with her and David, but he declined. Her voice was still full of that sickly sweet tone. He didn't want to lose his appetite.

He looked around for Whit but didn't see him. Mark thought it was unusual that he had been at the camp all day without seeing or hearing anything about him.

Mr. Gunnoe blew into a microphone mounted on a makeshift public address system. It made him sound as if he had a mouth full of cotton, and it whistled with feedback when he tried to speak louder. "Testing one . . . two . . . three . . . uh . . ." he said. After jiggling control knobs and readjusting the microphone, he announced that he would say grace for the food and then inform them about the long-awaited camp treasure hunt. A few of the campers cheered.

"Lord," he prayed, "for these and this which Thine hand hath provided, we thank You and ask You to mumphilgreeberhoffas-nagglenasson . . ."

His voice disappeared into a muffled ball of static. The public address system screeched high and loud and then fizzled into silence. Mr. Gunnoe cupped his hands around his mouth and shouted, "Bless this food! Amen!"

Mark found an empty stool at the end of a long, white table. It was the kind of table they could fold up after the meal and stand in a corner.

He didn't realize as he began to eat that he was so close to the very people he wanted to avoid. Two tables away, Patti gazed at David and giggled at nearly everything he said. Farther down Mark's own table, Joe was holding court with his gang. He spoke in a soft, threatening growl while they leaned over their plates, eyes fixed nervously on his every gesture.

Mark looked away and tried to figure his chances of sneaking off without Joe making a scene. It was too late.

"It's Press-snot again!" Joe said derisively. "This is the second time he's been hanging around us. Think he wants to join the gang?"

Tense laughter rippled around Joe's gang.

Mark grimaced and probed his food with a fork.

Joe stood up and came nearer. "I don't think he's tough enough. He hangs around a *girl* all the time."

"Get lost, Joe," Mark said.

Joe squeezed between two campers sitting across from Mark. They watched him anxiously as he leaned forward. "Oh, that's right. You don't hang around a girl anymore because she has a *new* boyfriend."

It was obvious he was talking about Patti and David. Mark clenched his teeth and told himself over and over that he shouldn't slug Joe in the mouth.

"How about it, Mark?" Joe hissed. "Do you think he's a good replacement for you? Does Patti think he *kisses* better than you?"

Mark pushed his fork into the stiff waves of mashed potatoes.

Joe spread his arms and announced to his gang, "Do you see, boys? I try to have a friendly conversation, and he ignores me." He suddenly pounded the table, causing the plates and cutlery to rattle, then walked back to his seat.

That was easy, Mark thought. *Why didn't I try ignoring him a long time ago?*

He glanced over at Patti and David again. They seemed oblivious to the scene between Mark and Joe. Patti spoke quietly to David, then reached across the table and placed her hand on his forearm. Mark felt the scratch of a match against the lining of his stomach. It flickered into a flame that made his face turn red.

Splat. Something wet hit Mark on the cheek. He swiped at it and saw it was a kernel of corn. He looked over at Joe, who had a straw positioned against his smirking lips. It was aimed directly at Mark. Joe's gang laughed.

Mark felt the flame turn into a bonfire and skillfully tossed a scoop of mashed potatoes at Joe. It smacked him in the forehead. The smirk disappeared, and Joe grabbed his entire plate and hurled the contents at Mark. Mark retaliated with a half bowl of withered salad.

An all-out war followed as they both grabbed what they could and hurled it at each other. Soon, innocent bystanders got hit, and they retaliated until it seemed the entire cafeteria had joined in the fight.

Mr. Gunnoe blew into the microphone. It squealed back at him. Through cupped hands, he called for order.

❈   ❈

The four walls of the camp director's office were decorated with odd shapes of mismatched paneling and several antlers of various sizes. A small window was the only break in the vertical sea of brown. A thin, white curtain hung crookedly over it. In front of the window sat a large, gray, metal desk covered with years of scars and coffee cup rings. Mark and Joe sat on opposite sides of the desk in uncomfortable metal chairs. Both were adorned with bits of food from the fight.

If only I could talk to Whit, Mark thought. *He knows how Joe is. He won't let them punish me.*

Like an answered prayer, the door suddenly opened, and

Whit walked in. Mark's heart leaped, not only because of the hope Whit always seemed to radiate, but also because it was the first time Mark had seen him in a week. Whit glanced at Joe, then Mark. The normal twinkle in his eyes was gone, and his bushy, white eyebrows pressed together into a frosty frown.

Oh no, Mark thought as his heart fell.

Whit pushed the door closed. The room was thick with his disapproval as he stroked his mustache for several moments. "I don't know what I'm going to do with you two," he finally said as he walked behind the desk. He didn't sound angry—not as he did the last time he scolded Mark for being disobedient—so Mark felt slightly relieved.

"You're the camp director?" Joe asked, astounded. A small piece of lettuce fell from his hair.

"For this week I am," he said, then hit the top of the desk with his hand. "I haven't had this kind of trouble with even our smallest kids—ever! What do you have to say for yourselves?"

"It was *his* fault!" Joe gestured at Mark.

Mark's mouth fell open. "That's a lie!"

Joe started to argue, but Whit held up his hand. "Quiet! Right now it doesn't matter who started it. The point is, it started. The point is, you two were responsible. So you can plan now to give the cafeteria a thorough scrubbing from top to bottom. Any more trouble and I'll put you both on kitchen cleanup for the rest of camp."

Joe looked as if he might say something, but he lowered his head. Mark and Whit made eye contact. Whit shook his head. For Mark, the disappointment was worse than the punishment.

Suddenly, they heard shouts from outside. The three of them turned to the window, where they saw people running past.

Whit wrenched open the window and shouted at a passerby, "What's going on?"

"The lake!" a young camper replied breathlessly. "Someone fell in by the old dock!"

Mark and Joe joined Whit at the window. "The old dock?"

Whit asked with disbelief. It was as if he couldn't believe some-one would step beyond all the warning signs there.

"Just look!" the camper said, pointing.

They did. Sure enough, people were running toward the dock, where a crowd had already gathered.

Chapter Six

Mark and Joe followed closely behind Whit as he made his way through the crowd. "What's going on? What happened?" Whit asked.

The scene they came upon answered everything. A very wet, very limp boy lay on the ground facedown. David, also drenched, was feverishly pushing on the kid's back, trying to pump water out of him. A red ribbon of blood ran from a gash in the boy's forehead.

"Mouth-to-mouth!" Whit shouted as he dropped to his knees next to David and the boy.

They turned the boy onto his back and, with precision teamwork, applied their combined first-aid knowledge to help him. Every second moved like a minute. Mark wondered how long the boy could live without breathing.

Whit and David kept up the rhythm. They pumped his chest, counting in one-thousands, then breathed into him . . . then counted . . . then breathed.

"Lord, help us," Whit gasped.

How long has it been? Mark wondered.

Count . . . breathe . . .

Mark gazed at the boy's face and realized he had seen him earlier near the old dock. He was one of Joe's gang. Mark looked over at Joe, who watched Whit and David work with a stunned expression on his face.

"Stand back!" Whit shouted before breathing into the boy's mouth again.

"Did anybody call an ambulance?" someone asked anxiously.

"I did," came the answer from the cowboy Mark had seen guiding horseback riders in the afternoon. "They're on the way."

"Go to the front driveway and wait for them, will you, Wes?" Whit said quickly.

Wes nodded and pushed his way through the crowd.

Suddenly the kid coughed, inhaled with a wheeze, then coughed again. Water spilled from his mouth. He gagged and coughed harder.

"That's it," Whit said softly as he turned him on his side. "Get it all out."

The kid retched and heaved for a couple of minutes. His breathing was labored, but at least he was breathing.

"Thank God," someone said. Gentle applause rippled through the crowd.

The boy opened his eyes long enough to say something about the dock being slippery, then passed out again. Whit turned his attention to the bleeding forehead.

"Good work," Whit said softly to David.

"I want a raise if I'm going to do this kind of work," David said with a smile.

"What happened?" Whit asked the crowd.

"He tried to walk out to the end of the dock," a young girl said. "I yelled at him to stop, but he wouldn't listen. Then I saw him fall in, and I ran and got Mr. Boyer."

It took a moment for Mark to remember that Mr. Boyer was David.

"It's a good thing you were nearby," Whit said to David.

David nodded. Mark saw him glance at Patti, whom Mark noticed for the first time standing opposite him in the crowd.

"David dove into the water to get him," Patti offered.

"Why was he out there?" Whit asked.

No one answered.

Mark looked over to see if Joe might say something, but he was gone. Mark quickly scanned the area and spotted him halfway across the field, headed for the cabins. He walked alone, his shoulders hunched, his head hung low.

Off in the distance, a siren wailed.

❦   ❦

The boy—later identified as Brad Miller—was taken to the hospital. Whit followed in his own car. Mark looked back to the old dock and knew what had happened. Brad Miller took Joe's dare. He wanted to pass the initiation to be in Joe's gang. But why was Brad trying to walk to the end of the dock when Joe was with Mark in Whit's office?

"Did you see that?" Patti asked as she walked up behind Mark.

"Yeah," Mark said. "I saw it."

"He would've drowned out there if David hadn't rescued him."

Mark felt a wave of anger wash over him. Why did it seem as though everything centered on David? "I guess he's your big hero now," he said.

"He's *everybody's* hero," Patti replied. She was getting that tone in her voice again.

"He's not mine," Mark said.

"That's because you're jealous," Patti sneered.

"Whit saved Brad. David was only helping," Mark said stubbornly. "And I'm not jealous."

"There wouldn't have been a Brad to save if David hadn't pulled him out of the water first," Patti countered.

Mark didn't have an immediate response, so he simply folded his arms and grunted. After a brief pause, he replied, "Sure, Patti. He's a big hero. Maybe they'll give him a medal."

"This is a waste of time," Patti said.

"It sure is," Mark agreed. "Why don't you go blow-dry his clothes or something?"

"It's more than I'd ever do for you!" she snapped.

"As if I care!" Mark retorted.

"You just wait. One of these days you'll read about yourself in my diary, and then you'll be ashamed!"

"Diary!"

"Yeah. And I'm going back to my cabin right now before I forget any of what happened. Especially what a jerk *you* are when *David* is such a hero."

Mark couldn't get over the statement that Patti kept a diary. "You really write in a diary?"

"Yeah. So what?"

"I just thought sissy girls wrote in diaries."

"Just goes to show what *you* know!" Patti said before marching off.

Mark watched her go. *I always knew having a girl as a friend couldn't work*, he thought.

Chapter
Seven

MR. GUNNOE GAVE MARK a tour of the cafeteria and kitchen—mostly where the garbage bags and brooms could be found. Mark's cleanup duty was to start immediately.

"I don't know where your friend is," Mr. Gunnoe said, "but I'll be on the lookout for him. Avoiding the consequences only makes things worse in the long run."

Mark began to wipe off the tables.

Mr. Gunnoe watched for a moment, then said, "I guess Brad Miller is going to be kept overnight at the hospital for observation."

"Will he be all right?" Mark asked.

Mr. Gunnoe shrugged. "It seems that way. The doctors probably want to make sure he doesn't have a concussion. That was a nasty cut on his head. Must've hit it on one of the beams when he fell. Really foolish being out there like that. Whit called from the hospital and said he wants anyone with information about why Brad was on the dock to talk to him."

Mark wondered where Joe was. *I'll bet he ran away,* Mark thought. *He knows he's going to be in big trouble.*

"Right now, nobody can figure it out, and the kid's not saying," Mr. Gunnoe said. "I sure hope this doesn't put a damper on the treasure hunt tomorrow."

"Treasure hunt?" Mark asked.

"Yeah! Don't you remember?"

Mark didn't.

"Oh, that's right. You just got here," Mr. Gunnoe recalled. "It's pretty simple. Teams of two are picked from the various cabins, and they follow clues from one point to another around the camp. The first to find the treasure wins it."

Mark finished cleaning off one table and started another. "What kind of treasure?"

Mr. Gunnoe looked as if no one had ever asked him that question before. "You know. A treasure. Gift certificates and goodies and . . . well, you know, a *treasure*."

Mark didn't know, but he decided not to press for a better answer.

The screen door at the end of the cafeteria slammed as Joe stepped in. "Janitor Joe at your service!" he announced, then popped a toothpick into his mouth.

"You're late!" barked Mr. Gunnoe.

"Yeah, too bad," Joe said as he sauntered between the tables toward them.

Joe's attitude was so confident that Mark was momentarily confused. *How can he act so cool? Doesn't he realize how much trouble he's going to be in?*

"You sweep up while Mark finishes the tables," said Mr. Gunnoe.

Joe grunted, grabbed a broom, and pushed it around without much enthusiasm. Mr. Gunnoe watched quietly until a phone rang somewhere in the kitchen. He left to answer it. Joe worked his broom around until he stood next to Mark.

"Too bad about that kid," Joe said, using his tongue to switch the toothpick from one side of his mouth to the other.

"His name is Brad," Mark said sharply. "You know that."

"I do?"

"You know you do," Mark said. "He was part of your gang."

Joe laughed and said, "You're out of your mind, Press-snot. What gang?"

"Your—" Mark then realized what kind of game Joe was

playing. Mark also understood why Joe was being so cool. He probably threatened the other kids not to say anything. "You won't get away with it. Brad will tell."

Joe grinned as he said, "I guess that'll make it his word against mine."

Mark replied in a near whisper, "Brad's word and *mine*."

"Huh?"

"Remember? I was down at the old dock," Mark said. "I heard what you said to your gang."

Joe's toothpick twitched. "What are you talking about?"

"When you were behind the woodpile," Mark said. "I heard you dare them to walk to the end of the dock as part of an initiation into your gang."

Joe grabbed the handle of the broom so tightly that his knuckles turned white. "You're lying."

"I am not," Mark retorted. "And if you don't tell Mr. Whittaker why Brad was on the dock, I will."

The next thing happened so quickly that Mark wasn't sure until later what Joe did to him. All Mark knew then was that the wind got knocked out of him. He fell to the floor, clutching his stomach.

"What's going on here?" Mr. Gunnoe said, rushing up to them.

"It was an accident!" Mark heard Joe cry out. "I was sweeping and didn't see Mark behind me."

Mark gasped for air, his mouth opening and closing like a guppy at feeding time.

Mr. Gunnoe knelt next to him. "Take it easy, boy," he said. "Just calm down and breathe when your body's ready."

Mark saw spots in front of his eyes and rocked back and forth on the floor. He saw a drop of mashed potatoes under one of the tables.

"I guess it was the broom handle. It must've jabbed into him," Joe lied.

"Be more careful!" Mr. Gunnoe snapped as he eased Mark into a sitting position.

Mark groaned, making an unnatural sound somewhere in the back of his throat as he tried to take air in. His head spun.

"Go get some water," Mr. Gunnoe commanded.

Joe dropped the broom and obeyed.

"Don't move," Mr. Gunnoe said to Mark.

Moments later, when Joe returned with a glass of water, Mark was sitting on a chair, breathing painfully but more normally. Mr. Gunnoe took the glass of water from Joe and drank it. "Thanks," he said.

Mark started to speak, but Mr. Gunnoe stopped him. "Don't talk right now. Just close your eyes and take it easy."

"Yeah," Joe joined in. "Don't talk, Mark. You'll only make it worse for yourself if you say anything."

Mark looked up at Joe, who grinned at him wickedly.

Chapter Eight

MARK LAY ON HIS BUNK, his arm stretched over his eyes, while the cabin leader—a pimply-faced teenager named Terry—gave a little talk about helping others. "You know, Saint Paul said that sometimes we're the best people to help others, because we can show them the same kind of comfort that God showed us when *we* needed help. It's right here in Paul's second letter to the Corinthians. . . ."

Mark's mind wasn't on Saint Paul or Second Corinthians, but on what to do about Joe. Jabbing him in the stomach with the broom handle was a low trick, even for Joe. And if he thought it was going to *scare* Mark into silence, he had another think coming.

But Mark didn't say anything to Mr. Gunnoe about Joe's involvement with Brad or that Joe purposely hit him. Mr. Gunnoe wasn't the person to tell. Mark had to tell Whit. He was the only one who would understand or know what to do about it.

Mark glanced over at Joe's bunk. *I wonder where he is? Probably torturing other campers. How is he able to stay out later than everyone else and not get in trouble?* Mark rolled over onto his side. Terry was still talking about giving love and comfort to others, even those we don't like.

Mark shook his head. He couldn't imagine ever loving or giving comfort to Joe. He couldn't picture in his mind any time or place when he might care what happened to Joe. Joe was too much of a bully, too obnoxious. How could Mark feel anything other than hatred for him? Especially now that Joe was being exceptionally obnoxious.

Mark remembered that Patti had warned him about Joe when he first came to camp. She said Joe was acting worse than usual. *Why?* Mark mused. *What is it about camp that makes him act like a bigger bully than usual?*

Mark rolled over again and decided the reason didn't matter. Bullying kids was wrong—particularly when one nearly got killed just to be accepted by Joe and the rest of the gang. Whit needed to be told. And since Joe wouldn't tell him, Mark would have to.

Terry stopped talking and the heads of the other cabin members turned as Mark climbed out of bed. He was still dressed, so all he had to do was put on his tennis shoes.

"What are you doing?" Terry asked.

Mark put on his shoes and brushed his dark hair away from his face. "I have to talk to Mr. Whittaker."

"I think you should wait until morning," said Terry.

"I can't," Mark replied as he strode to the door. "I have to talk to him now."

Mark didn't wait for Terry to answer. He stepped out onto the front porch of the cabin and let the screen door slam behind him. The night air was surprisingly chilly. He shivered slightly and walked toward the camp director's office. He guessed that Whit might have a bed near there.

The crickets chirped all around him as he walked up to the dark and apparently empty director's cabin. He knocked gently on the door, but no one answered. Where could Whit be? Mark knew he had returned from the hospital, so he had to be around the camp somewhere. Maybe Whit was making the rounds—just to make sure everyone was all right.

Except for the lights burning in the campers' cabins, where the evening devotions were being given and announcements were being made, the camp was deserted. A clear sky overhead gave everything a blue tint. Mark felt terribly alone. Once again, he was the outsider. He wondered where Patti was. *Not far from David, I'll bet.*

He walked around the main cabin, the dark cafeteria, the chapel, the storage building, the campers' cabins . . . but Whit was nowhere to be found. Mark despaired of seeing him until morning when—*snap!*—he heard the sound of a branch breaking, probably under someone's foot. The crickets heard it, too, and stopped their singing.

Mark's guess was that the sound came from behind a small cabin on the edge of the woods. Unlike the others, no lights burned in its windows. It showed no signs of life at all. Yet he heard another sharp *snap* and knew it came from that direction.

He nearly called out Mr. Whittaker's name but stopped himself. He was afraid of drawing too much attention to himself. He figured he was already in enough trouble for walking out on Terry.

Maybe because he was so determined to find Whit, it didn't occur to Mark that the noise might *not* be Whit. He thought only that Mr. Whittaker was there doing whatever it was camp directors did at that time of night. So he crept along the side of the dark cabin and, at the last moment, decided to stop before stepping around the corner. Instead, he peeked around carefully.

Snap! came the sound again, and this time Mark could see that it wasn't Whit.

He got a bigger surprise than that.

Sitting on his haunches against the rear wall of the cabin, Joe Devlin stared into the black forest and absentmindedly snapped twigs in his hands. It was a particular scene for Mark to witness, because the moonlight struck Joe at just the right angle for Mark to see his face. His cheeks glistened. He was crying.

It surprised Mark so much that he wasn't sure what to do. There was Joe, his worst enemy in the world, completely alone and crying. For a fraction of a second, Mark wanted to step forward and make fun of him. *Look at you! Big, tough Joe Devlin cry-*

ing like a little baby! He wanted to shout it so the whole camp could hear and come out of their cabins to see for themselves that Joe wasn't to be feared.

But Mark couldn't do that. As much as he hated Joe, he couldn't wish on him the humiliation of being caught crying alone in the dark.

Snap.

Mark watched him and wondered why he was crying. Did he feel bad about what happened to Brad? Maybe he felt guilty. Maybe it was something else. Mark couldn't even guess. He simply stood and watched.

Joe suddenly looked in Mark's direction.

Mark retreated into the shadows. As he did, he bumped an old shutter leaning next to the cabin. It banged against the wall.

Joe jumped to his feet and wiped his face with his sleeve as he hissed, "Who's there? What do you want?"

Mark pressed himself against the wall, praying that the darkness covered him.

Joe took a step forward and squinted at the shadows. "Who's there?" he asked again, more nervously than before.

Mark feared that Joe would come investigate, but he didn't. For reasons Mark would never know, Joe spun around and ran.

Mark breathed a sigh of relief, turned to leave . . . and ran straight into Terry.

"There you are," Terry said.

Chapter Nine

ONCE AGAIN, Mark sat in one of the uncomfortable chairs in the camp director's office.

"May I *please* talk to Whit?" Mark asked.

Terry, now occupying the chair behind the desk, glared at Mark. "Whit had to go to Odyssey for the night. He'll be back tomorrow morning. If you had asked me instead of just running out in the middle of my Bible study, I could've told you that. What were you doing behind that cabin?"

"Looking for Whit," Mark answered simply.

"You thought Whit was hiding back there?"

"I heard something and thought . . ." His voice trailed off as he realized how foolish any explanation would sound. Why did he really think Whit would be wandering around behind a dark cabin?

"It could've been a bear," Terry said. "Or something worse. That's why we have rules in this camp, like staying in your cabin after dark. We don't want anyone to get hurt."

"I know," Mark said.

Terry eyed him suspiciously. "You were involved in that food fight earlier today, weren't you?"

Mark nodded and lowered his head.

"I thought so. Well, we have a *three-strikes-and-you're-out* policy here. You now have two strikes. One more and we'll send you home."

"Yes, sir," Mark said quietly.

Terry stood up to signal the end of their meeting. "Go straight back to the cabin and get to bed."

Mark stood, mumbled an apology, and left.

Once again, he thought as he walked across the compound, *Joe Devlin got me in trouble.*

When Mark finally got back to the cabin, he noticed that Joe was in his own bunk, fast asleep.

❧ ❧

By morning, Mark had no idea of what to do about Joe. Part of him wanted to rush to Whit and explain everything. But the image of Joe sitting behind the cabin, crying, haunted him. It wasn't normal, Mark was sure. Kids only hide away and cry like that when something is terribly wrong.

Mark remembered when his parents first split up. He often sat alone in his room and listened to his favorite songs on a tape player . . . and cried.

To his amazement, he decided to give Joe a break. *I'll give him one more chance to confess on his own,* Mark thought.

He sat down with his breakfast tray at a table in the cafeteria and eyed the food warily. He assumed he was looking at scrambled eggs, but they were a questionable shade of orange. He glanced around for Joe but didn't see him.

Patti arrived with her tray in hand. "Okay if I sit here?" she asked.

"If you want to," Mark replied. "But there's only one seat."

"That's all right," she said.

Mark asked her where David was.

"He's helping set up for the treasure hunt," she said before biting into a muffin.

"Oh." Mark picked up something he hoped was bacon.

"Mark, I wish we'd stop arguing so much," Patti said quickly.

Mark tilted his head in her direction. "I will if you will."

Patti sighed and said, "Truce."

"Truce," Mark agreed.

She pushed her tray away. "I . . . I miss talking to you about things."

"Me, too," Mark admitted. He suddenly realized he had never told her about his time with Whit before the trip to Washington, D.C., or how his mom and dad were doing, or even what he knew about Joe Devlin and his gang. Sadly, he realized that if he couldn't talk to her, he couldn't talk to anyone.

"I like writing in my diary, but it's not the same," she added.

He perked up and suggested, "We could take a walk. We always talk our heads off when we walk." He actually looked forward to it. He could tell her everything that had happened.

"David likes to walk, too," she said.

David, Mark groaned inwardly. *Why do we always have to talk about him?*

"I've been wanting to tell you about him," she said, "because he's kind of serious now."

"Serious?"

She rubbed her nose nervously. "I like him in a way I've never liked anyone before. And he makes me feel things I've never felt before. That's why I've been acting kind of . . ."

"Weird?" Mark offered.

"Yeah, I guess," she conceded. "But I'm scared. Camp is going to end pretty soon, and . . . I don't know what's going to happen."

Mark didn't understand. "Happen? Like the camp might be bombed by a terrorist or something?"

Patti ignored the question and turned to face him directly. "If you liked a girl and you were going to leave her to go home after a wonderful week together, would you write to her and be faithful to her?"

Mark looked around nervously. "Why do you have to ask me questions like that?"

"Because you're a boy," she said.

"But I'm not that kind of boy," he objected. "I don't care about stuff like that."

Patti persisted, "But do you think you'd at least kiss her good-bye?"

Mark groaned again and put his face in his hands. *I don't want to talk about this*, he thought.

"What's wrong?" she asked. "Is it wrong to want him to kiss me?"

"How should I know?" Mark answered, his voice full of irritation. "All I know is that they do it in the movies and I think it's gross, okay? Let's talk about something else."

"I can't talk about something else. This is what I keep thinking about. I can't eat, I can't sleep. I just think about him and get all goose-pimply."

Mark put his face in his hands again.

"I think I'm in love," she stated.

"I don't know anything about love," Mark said simply. "And I don't want to talk about this anymore."

"Why not?"

"I told you! I don't know anything about it. You may as well be talking about algebra or gabbing in a foreign language. I don't know, and I don't really care!"

Patti stood up and grabbed her tray. She wasn't angry. She merely looked at Mark with a sad expression on her face—as if she were about to leave for a faraway place and would never see him again.

Suddenly, Mark felt it was true. She was heading into new adventures, adventures he couldn't share because he wasn't ready. Niggling somewhere deep in that part of his heart that would one day grow to maturity was the realization that this experience at camp wasn't something they would later shrug off. It was very real and very permanent, though neither of them knew why.

She walked away.

Mark opened his mouth to call after her, but then he closed it again. There wasn't really anything to say.

The public address system clicked on with a shrill whistle, and everyone turned to look at the front of the cafeteria. Whit, looking tired and disheveled in the gray "Camp What-a-Nut" jogging suit, smiled apologetically. "Excuse me," he said, then adjusted a few knobs on the control panel to get his voice to the right volume. After a moment of fiddling, he asked, "Can you hear me?"

Everyone shouted yes as one voice, and he laughed at the sound of it. It was good for Mark to hear Whit laugh. It seemed as though it had been a long time.

"Are you excited about the treasure hunt today?" he asked.

Again the cafeteria echoed with enthusiastic shouts.

He waved a long sheet of paper at them. "Good, because I'm now going to announce the pairings for the teams!"

A hush fell on the crowd as he proceeded down the list, cabin by cabin, team by team. Sometimes the announced pairings were greeted with laughter, other times with grumbles. When Whit reached Cabin Wabana, Mark sat up.

Mark didn't know his cabin mates very well, but he looked forward to the excitement of the hunt: figuring out the clues, beating the other teams, finding the treasure. *It might be the best thing about this camp*, Mark thought. He looked around eagerly to see whom he might recognize from his cabin.

Whit continued reading the names. "Cameron, Arnold . . . you're with Bob Martinez."

Hoots and howls came from the back of the cafeteria.

Since the list was alphabetically arranged, Whit called out "Devlin, Joe" next. Mark sat up in his seat as high as he could to get a look at who would be stuck with Joe. He turned his head right and left, wanting to catch the first look of surprise when the unknown victim's name was announced. He spotted Joe leaning casually against a side wall.

"Joe Devlin, you're paired with . . ." Whit peered over the sheet of paper, scanned the crowd, and said, "Mark Prescott."

Chapter
Ten

"PLEASE, WHIT. You *can't* team me up with Joe!" Mark pleaded. He had rushed to get to Whit, nearly knocking people over as he pushed against the stream of campers leaving the cafeteria.

"I didn't team you up," Whit said. "That's just the way it worked out. And if I switch you around, I'll have to do it for anyone else who asks. I can't do that. You'll have to make the best of the situation."

"But you don't understand," Mark began to say, but he was interrupted by Joe's arrival.

"Well, ain't this an interesting turn of events," Joe sneered. "Me and Press-snot—together at last. It's a good thing I didn't have high hopes of finding the treasure."

Whit pushed some papers under his clipboard. "Frankly, I think this is the best thing that could happen to either of you. Working as a team toward a common goal will be a good lesson. That's the reason we're doing this treasure hunt."

"It's not fair!" Mark protested.

Whit smiled at him and answered, "Few things are."

"But you don't know about Joe," Mark began, his voice sounding shrill.

"What about Joe?" Whit asked.

"Yeah, what about me?" Joe repeated.

Mark was ready to confess everything he knew about Brad Miller and what had happened on the old dock. Then Whit would keep Joe from taking part in the treasure hunt, and Mark would get a new teammate. He looked at Whit, who watched him closely.

Mark coughed nervously and glanced at Joe's expressionless face—the sharp eyes, the high cheekbones. And Mark once again saw Joe's tears glistening in the moonlight. *Kids only hide away and cry like that when something is terribly wrong*, Mark remembered thinking.

"Well?" Whit prompted.

"He'll be a terrible teammate," Mark answered feebly.

Whit tucked his clipboard under his arm. "Case closed. Come on. Everyone's meeting under the flagpole."

❈   ❈

"The rules are simple," Whit called out to the assembled campers. "Each team should have a sealed envelope. Does everyone have one?" He held up a sample envelope and looked around.

Mark glanced at Joe, who had the crushed envelope in his fist.

Whit continued, "When I fire the starting pistol, you'll open your envelopes for the first clue. If you can figure it out, that clue will tell you where to find the second clue. There are 12 clues in all, and the team that figures them all out should be able to find the treasure. Of course, first team to the treasure wins it. Any questions?"

The air was tense with excitement as Whit looked over the crowd. Mr. Gunnoe stepped forward. "Please don't throw the envelopes on the ground," he said. "You'll be immediately disqualified if you do."

Again Mark looked at Joe. He smirked back at Mark and pretended to puff on his toothpick as if it were a cigarette.

"Is everybody ready?"

The crowd roared *yes*.

Whit raised the starting pistol. "Then on your marks, get set . . ." He pulled the trigger, and the pistol popped loudly.

A mad scramble and commotion of tearing paper ensued as

the teams opened their envelopes. Joe adroitly tore off the top of theirs and pulled out the sheet of paper inside. He held it up and away from Mark.

"What does it say?" Mark asked impatiently as he tried to get a look.

Joe thrust the paper at Mark. It said:
Long box of tin where food for thought
Might get you sustenance, cold and hot.

"Food for thought?" Joe asked. "Does the camp have a library?"

"Sustenance, cold and hot," Mark pondered. "The cafeteria!"

"That's too obvious," Joe argued. "The cold and hot might be talking about the utility shed where the water heaters are kept. It's made out of tin."

Mark watched as most of the other teams raced for the cafeteria. He pointed after them. "See, Joe? The cafeteria looks like it's made of tin, and it's long. Let's go!"

They argued the entire way to the cafeteria. Even when they found the second clue posted on a large sign there, Joe wouldn't admit that Mark was right. He simply grunted and said, "Don't let it go to your head, Press-snot."

Mark ignored him and looked up at the sign. It read:
If you yell these words, they'll make you hoarse,
But the four-legged kind is much better, of course.

"The stable!" Mark whispered to Joe, not wanting the other campers to hear.

"No way," Joe snapped. "That's too obvious."

Mark growled, "That's what you said about the cafeteria. Maybe the clues are easy at first and then get harder."

"Maybe not," Joe said stubbornly.

Once again, the sight of everyone else running to the stables was the only thing that persuaded Joe to go.

Once again, Mark wished Joe would fall off the face of the earth.

MARK WAS RIGHT. The early clues were easy enough, but they grew increasingly difficult. And as the clues got harder, Joe and Mark argued more fiercely. Sometimes Mark came up with the answer, other times Joe did. The "who was right and who was wrong" count was close enough to keep either of them from insisting on having his own way. After a particularly nasty quarrel about clue number six, Mark wondered if any of the other teams came as near to physical blows as he and Joe did.

If this is a lesson about teamwork, then I'm not learning very much, Mark thought.

Fortunately, the other teams were equally baffled about the clues. Within an hour, pairs of campers were spread out all over the greater Camp What-a-Nut area as the teams chased after their guesses. Mark imagined that they would look like maniacal ants if someone could see them from above.

Whit had to rescue one camper from the top of a tree. It was then that Whit made the rounds to assure the teams that clues weren't hidden in any place that might hurt them.

Mark and Joe ran to the dugout by the oldest baseball field at the farthest point from the camp, where Mark was sure they would find the ninth clue. It was there, hanging on a crudely painted sign.

"Told you so," Mark said.

"Shut up," Joe retorted. "I'm trying to concentrate."

Mark looked around. As best as he could tell, they were the first ones to find the clue.

The sign said:

A shelter in a storm, a haven to protect,
The next clue can be found with the deepest respect.

Mark read it again but couldn't figure out what it was talking about.

Suddenly Joe laughed. It startled Mark, because he couldn't remember Joe ever laughing, except when he'd just done something cruel to someone. "This one's easy," Joe said.

"Where is it?" Mark asked.

"Can't you guess?" Joe taunted.

"No, Joe. Don't waste time."

"Shelter . . . protect . . . deepest . . ." Joe hung the words out for Mark to consider.

Mark put his hands on his hips and jerked at his sagging jeans. "If you know the answer, tell me. I don't know."

"The bomb shelter," Joe said.

Mark shrugged. "What bomb shelter?"

Joe nodded toward the lake. "If you follow the shore around to the other side of those trees, there's an abandoned bomb shelter."

"Why would anybody put a bomb shelter back there?" Mark challenged.

"Because there's an old, burned-out house back there, too. Maybe the owner was afraid of bombs," Joe said as he started to walk away.

"I think you're wrong," Mark said.

Joe shrugged and said, "Stay behind if you want."

Mark followed, though it didn't make much sense to him.

The layout was exactly as Joe said. The shore of the lake wound around and disappeared behind a part of the forest that reached down to the water. From the camp, Mark never would've suspected it went on so far.

"How do you know about the bomb shelter?" Mark asked.

Joe chuckled but didn't answer.

They had to trudge through a tangle of wild branches and bushes, some lashing at their arms and legs, until they came to the shell of an old house. It was nestled in the woods and was clearly the casualty of a fire, perhaps long ago. Mark guessed that it belonged to someone who worked with the camp itself. Why it wasn't restored after the fire was anybody's guess.

"The shelter is over there," Joe said, leading the way to the side of the house. Mark stayed a few steps behind.

The place was so desolate and distant from the camp that Mark felt sure they were making a mistake. Why would Whit choose such a remote place to hide a clue?

Joe stopped at the edge of a rectangular hole in the ground. A short stairwell led to a large, steel door at the bottom. The door reminded Mark of the entrance to a bank vault. "The clue must be inside," Joe said as he descended the stairs.

"This doesn't make sense, Joe," said Mark at the top of the stairs. "Whit said he wouldn't hide the clues anywhere dangerous."

"This isn't dangerous," Joe said with a scowl. "I've been in here plenty of times. Don't be such a baby."

"But . . . where is everybody else?"

Joe pushed at the steel door and spoke between grunts. "You said yourself the clues got harder. Obviously, bright boy, we were the first ones to figure it out. Give me a hand."

Mark hesitantly joined Joe at the bottom of the stairs and pushed. The door suddenly gave with a rusty, wrenching sound.

"Nasty, huh?" Joe reached down and grabbed a broken cinder block. "You gotta prop it open or it'll swing shut again."

"I don't like this," Mark said nervously.

"Do you wanna win the treasure or not?" Joe asked as he stepped into the darkness.

"They wouldn't put the clue in the dark," Mark observed.

"Maybe they had a light in here and it went out. You can't expect them to think of everything," Joe growled. He lit a match and added, "I'm telling you it's in here."

"Where'd you get the matches?" asked Mark.

Joe held the match high. "I always carry matches," he said. "You never know when you will need 'em. There. That's what I was looking for."

Mark brightened. "The clue?"

"Nah," Joe replied with a chuckle, "a candle I found in here the other night."

Mark looked around, taking in as much as he could by the light of Joe's candle. Apart from being cold and damp, the bomb shelter was in a state of disarray. Shelves along the walls were broken or hanging loosely at odd angles. Mark noticed a couple of dented cans of food on one shelf and several others that had dropped onto the floor. In the center, a table, tilted from a broken leg, was surrounded by tipped-over chairs—like pins that had been clobbered by a large bowling ball. Two cots with mildewed cushions rested against a side wall.

The scene was the crumbling version of a picture he had once seen in history class. He remembered it from his textbook—a black-and-white photo of a bomb shelter built in the 1950s, when many Americans were afraid the Russians might drop an atomic bomb on them. Mark's uneasiness grew to genuine fear.

"There's no clue in here. Let's go," Mark said.

"Is little Marky scared?" Joe teased.

"I'm going," Mark said as he turned toward the door.

Joe laughed and grabbed Mark's arm. "Don't leave me, Marky! I'm afraid of the dark!"

"Stop it!" Mark jerked his arm away and lost his balance. He clawed at the air for something to grab on to, but nothing was there. His leg lashed out and connected with the cinder block that held the door. He stumbled against the wall and slid to the ground.

"Ouch," Joe said. "Marky fall down and go boom. Is Marky going to cry now?"

Mark leaped angrily to his feet. "I've had enough of you, Joe!" he shouted as he moved toward him with clenched fists.

Joe snickered scornfully and lifted his own fists to defend

himself. Suddenly his expression—so confident and defiant—twisted into one of alarm. "The door!" he cried.

Mark thought it was some sort of trick and didn't look.

Joe sprang past Mark, his arms reaching out. The door slammed shut; the bang of steel against the frame rang in Mark's ears. It was solid and final.

Joe was on his knees, frantically clawing at a door handle that wasn't there. Mark saw it sitting uselessly in a cobwebbed corner.

"Help me!" Joe shouted as he dug his fingers into the thin line between the door and the frame. Mark rushed over and did the same at a higher point. It was no use.

They were trapped.

Chapter
Twelve

SINCE NEITHER OF THEM had a watch, Mark wasn't sure how long they spent trying to find a tool, a blade, a thin piece of wood—anything that might fit between the door and the jamb so they could force the door open again. No success.

After that, they pounded on the door and screamed for help. But they heard only the dead silence of the enclosed room.

Mark remembered another tidbit from his history class: The bomb shelters were generally built airtight, with their own air purifiers to keep radioactive air out. He mentioned it to Joe.

"What does that mean?" Joe asked.

"It means we may not have air for very long," Mark answered.

"Then what are we gonna do?"

"I don't know."

"Great. Just great," Joe said spitefully. "We'll be stuck here forever because you didn't watch where you were going."

"What! I lost my balance because you grabbed my arm!" Mark shouted. "It was your idea to come here in the first place, don't forget. I knew it was wrong."

"I just followed the clue," Joe insisted.

"Yeah, sure. Real smart. Everyone else is digging up the treasure somewhere else while we're stuck in here—because *you're* Mr. Brain Boy who followed the clue," Mark sneered.

"Shut your mouth, Press-snot!" Joe said as he jumped on Mark. They fell to the ground in a tangle of flailing arms and legs, grunts and groans, hits and misses. They rolled into the table and knocked the candle over. It went out.

Unable to see each other, they separated. Mark peered into the thick blackness. It was so dark, in fact, that he couldn't even see his own hand in front of his face. "What happened?"

"You knocked the candle over!" Joe cried out.

Mark tried to sit up but hit his head on the bottom of the table. "Ouch!" he moaned.

"Where is it?" Joe asked.

Mark reached up and felt the rough, splintered edge of the table top. His fingers crawled along the surface until they connected with warm wax. He grabbed it. "Here it is!"

Mark could hear Joe fumbling in the darkness. "I can't find my matches," he said and fumbled around some more. "I can't find them! They must've fallen out of my pocket while I was beating you up."

"You weren't beating me up," Mark muttered.

Joe shuffled around, rubbing his hands against the ground. "Help me find them!"

They crawled on their hands and knees around the shelter floor. The swirling dust made them cough, and the darkness made them bump into each other several times. Mark realized how dangerous their predicament was when something scratched his arm. He screamed.

"What's the matter?" Joe shouted.

"Something scratched my arm."

"Like what?"

"I don't know!" Mark said, rubbing his arm.

"It wasn't a rat, was it?" Joe asked, panicked.

"I said I don't know!" Mark was annoyed.

"I hate rats!" Joe cried out. "Don't move."

They sat still for a moment, listening in the darkness for any telltale signs of life. Nothing happened.

"Okay," Joe said.

They renewed their search for the matches.

"I found them!" Joe shouted after several minutes. Again, Mark could hear him rustling in the dark. There was a sharp scratching sound, followed by a spark and dim flame of the match. "Oh, no. This is my last match."

"Be careful," Mark said as they found the candle again and lit it.

Even in the yellow glow, Mark was glad to see Joe's face. He leaned back and realized what had scratched him earlier. Certainly not a rat. It was a nail sticking out of a fallen shelf.

"You're gonna get lockjaw now," Joe stated.

"I will not," Mark replied as he checked his arm. "It's only a little scratch. It didn't even draw blood."

"It doesn't have to draw blood to give you lockjaw," said Joe. And they spent the next several minutes arguing about the causes and cures of lockjaw.

About the time that Joe was saying Mark would need 17 vaccinations with 12-inch-long needles, the candle hissed and flickered.

"We shouldn't talk so much," Mark said. "I think the candle is flickering because we're running out of air."

They sat in silence, each thinking his own thoughts. Joe's breathing was thick and hard. Somehow it made the solitude more unbearable, so Mark said, "They'll realize we're missing and come look for us. I wonder who else knows about this place?"

Joe shook his head. "Nobody," he said.

"How did *you* find out about it?"

"The old man in the stables told me about it," he responded. "We're pals. He said it was a big secret."

"Great. So nobody else knows about it except the old man."

Joe shrugged and said, "Guess not."

Mark said carefully, "Joe, if it's such a big secret, why did you think Whit would use it as part of the treasure hunt?"

Joe was silent for a moment. "I didn't think of that," he finally replied.

Mark groaned and lowered his head onto his arms.

"I thought it would be a neat hideout for the gang," Joe said, looking around proudly as if he were seeing the shelter for the first time.

"Your gang," Mark said disdainfully. "They're nothing but trouble."

Joe sat straight up and glared at Mark. "Don't you talk about my gang like that."

"Tell me one good thing any gang of yours ever did," Mark challenged him.

"They do lots of good things!" Joe said. "For me."

"I'll bet Brad Miller would argue that," Mark mumbled.

Joe cocked his head. "What did you say?" he demanded.

"Nothing," Mark said.

But it was clear that Joe heard Mark's comment, because he said softly, "I didn't mean for Brad to get hurt. He was supposed to walk on the dock when the whole gang was there—later on. He wasn't supposed to go out there by himself."

"Why did he have to go out at all?" Mark asked.

"For the initiation! If you knew anything about gangs you wouldn't ask such dumb questions."

"Why do you have to have initiations?" Mark persisted.

"Because . . ." Joe began, then realized he didn't have a proper defense. "Because that's how gangs are formed."

Joe spread his arms and continued, "I wasn't gonna make him walk the dock. I just wanted to see if he'd do it. I didn't know he was gonna do something so stupid as to walk alone. Okay?" His voice trembled, and he quickly looked away.

"I still don't get why—" Mark started.

Joe jerked his head around to face Mark. "I don't wanna talk about it. Say another word and I'll pound you good and hard."

Mark frowned and said, "Yeah, that's your answer for everything, isn't it? You'll pound me. We're gonna die in here, and you wanna pound me. Why do you have to be such a creep?"

"Shut up," Joe said.

"In Odyssey—and here," Mark continued. "Why do you have

to be like that? Why've you been so nasty all week?"

"I said to shut up!" Joe yelled, throwing himself at Mark. Again they rolled around on the floor as each one tried to get on top. Again they rolled once too far and banged the table. Again the candle tipped and fell over, going out. The darkness swallowed them.

Chapter Thirteen

THEY SAT IN SILENCE in the darkness. Mark didn't think there was anything else to do. He considered crawling around to look for the candle until he remembered Joe was out of matches anyway. So he sat still. Once or twice, he prayed for God to help them find a way out.

"Help!" Joe suddenly screamed at the top of his lungs, startling Mark. "Help! Help!"

"Joe!" Mark said loudly, trying to be heard above the scream.

"Help! Help! Hellllppp!" He kept screaming until Mark had to put his hands over his ears. Joe's voice eventually went hoarse.

"They'll look for us. They'll find us," Mark said desperately when Joe was quiet again.

Joe didn't answer, and Mark settled into the stillness of surrender.

Mark shifted his position, realizing too late that he'd been sitting cross-legged. His left leg had fallen asleep. He carefully stretched it out and winced as the pins and needles danced up and down his thigh. He groaned.

"What's wrong?" Joe croaked.

"My leg fell asleep," answered Mark. He rubbed it for a moment, then said, "I wish I could stand up."

"Ha. I wish we were out of here," Joe snorted.

"I wish we were out of here and back in Odyssey," Mark

amended. "I wanna be back home, in my own bed, in my own room."

Joe murmured, "At least you have a home."

Mark was puzzled by the statement. Joe had a home. Mark had been there once when he was accused of slashing one of Joe's bike tires. Joe had a father who was a barber, a mother who stayed at home, and a younger brother who was a general nuisance.

The more Mark thought about it, the more he remembered his impression at the time that Joe's home wasn't a happy one. He felt sorry for Joe then, much as he had felt sorry for Joe when he saw him crying behind the cabin. He thought of how the moonlight hit Joe's face in just such a way to show the tears of his cheeks. Even now, he could hear the sniffling.

Mark sat up. The sniffling wasn't in his memory. It was real. Somewhere in the darkness, Joe was crying.

Mark cleared his throat and said, "We'll get out of here, Joe."

Joe didn't reply. The sniffles turned to sobs. The sobs turned to a mournful cry.

The sound tugged at Mark's heart. He felt a mixture of feelings. On the one hand, he couldn't listen to such sounds in pitch black without wanting to cry himself. He feared that Joe was crying because he knew they were truly trapped and were going to die. What else was left to do?

On the other hand, Mark felt a twinge of curiosity. He wanted to *see* Joe cry. He wanted to study it as one might study a peculiar freak of nature.

Mark didn't know what to do or say. It wasn't like the encounter behind the cabin, where Joe would have been mortified to be seen by Mark. Here, Joe was crying openly. There were no secrets in such a tiny place.

He shuffled uneasily. *Do something. Say something*, he told himself. But he froze with the fear of doing or saying something stupid. He was clumsy when it came to other people's emotions. He remembered nights when his mother sat at the kitchen table and cried because of her problems with his dad. Mark never knew what to say to her. Sometimes he made her a cup of tea and slipped away to another room so she could cry in private. Other times, he just sat and held her hand. But there was no tea to be made here, and he wouldn't dare hold Joe's hand.

He took a deep breath and offered up a tiny prayer, asking God to help him. "They'll find us, Joe," Mark said as reassuringly as he knew how.

"I don't care," Joe sobbed.

Mark closed his eyes, as if it made a difference in that darkness. "You don't care if they find us?"

"No," Joe said.

Maybe all that screaming made him lose his mind, Mark thought. "Why don't you care?"

Joe fell silent again.

Mark thought through all the reasons that Joe might not want to be rescued. "Are you afraid of getting in trouble because of what happened to Brad?" Mark finally asked, choosing the only reason that seemed to make sense.

"No." He sniffled and went quiet again.

Mark waited, wondering if he should come up with another idea. Just as he opened his mouth to speak, Joe said, "It's what I said before."

Mark didn't remember what Joe said before.

"About home," Joe explained, as if he knew Mark didn't remember.

"What happened at home?" Mark asked gently. He was suddenly unsure of whether he really wanted to know, but he figured he should follow this to its end.

"My mom and dad," Joe started to say, then got choked up again. He coughed and took a deep breath. "My dad moved out last week, and I think they're going to get a divorce."

Mark looked into the blackness, trying to form the words to say. "I'm sorry," he finally managed.

"I don't want you to feel sorry!" Joe snapped. "It's none of your business anyway!"

Mark normally would have agreed. It wasn't any of his business. Joe was a bully who drove him crazy. Why should he say any more? Why should he listen to his problems? Not long ago, he even told himself he hated Joe. *It's none of my business*, Mark thought.

But he knew in his heart that wasn't true. It *was* his business. It was his business because his own father had left him, and he knew how that felt.

Then Mark heard the voice of a pimply-faced teenager named Terry echoing in his head from the night before. "Saint Paul said that sometimes we're the best people to help others, because we can show them the same kind of comfort that God showed us when *we* needed help. It's right here in Paul's second letter to the Corinthians. . . ."

Mark shuffled in place uneasily. For the first time since he met Joe, he had something in common with him.

"Look, Joe, I know how you feel," Mark whispered. "My parents split up, too, you know."

Mark imagined that Joe nodded in response.

He went on, "It hurt a lot when my dad left. I thought it was the end of the world. In a way I guess it was, because we moved here right after that. All I kept thinking was that I wanted them to get back together."

"Hm," Joe said.

"And I figured it was all my fault. I figured my dad left because maybe I did something wrong or maybe I didn't do enough of something or maybe I didn't do anything at all."

"I've done plenty," Joe remarked.

Mark was sure he had, but he continued anyway. "I figured out that grownups pretty much do what they want without talking to kids."

"You're telling me!" Joe said.

"I learned that my dad didn't leave because of me. It didn't have anything to do with me. He left because of things I couldn't understand."

"Why didn't he tell me that?" Joe complained. "He could've said something to us. Doesn't he care?"

"He cares. He just isn't thinking about it right now. Didn't you ever run away without telling anybody why you were leaving or where you were going?"

Joe was quiet for a moment. "Yeah, a couple of times."

"In a way, your dad's doing the same thing," Mark said. "Except you can't chase after him or make him come back."

"Then what are we supposed to do? My mom's a wreck, and my little brother walks around the house crying all the time."

"You'll have to do what I did, I guess. Just wait and see what happens, because things keep changing whether we want them to or not. All we can do is hang on. Even when you don't feel like it, you have to hang on."

Mark peered into the darkness, glad for it now because he knew Joe's face would have stopped him from saying any more. He added, "See, it's not what happens to us, it's how we react to what happens to us."

Thanks, Whit, Mark thought.

"Yeah? Well, what do you know about it?" Joe said abruptly, as if he'd decided he appeared foolish taking advice from Mark.

Mark didn't get the chance to answer. A sound caught his attention that was unlike anything he'd heard for quite a while. It wasn't the numbing drone of the enclosed shelter or Joe's thick breathing, or even the ringing in his own ears. He thought he heard voices.

"What's that?" Joe whispered.

Before either of them could move or say anything, the door was pushed open.

"In here," a voice said.

"It's so dark," said a higher voice Mark recognized.

"I'll turn on the flashlight. It's a great place. You'll like it," the first voice said.

A blinding light washed out the darkness and Mark's ability to see anything. But he didn't need to. He knew who his rescuers were—Patti and David.

Chapter
Fourteen

"WHAT DO YOU MEAN nobody's looking for us?" Joe asked indignantly after Mark explained to Patti and David what they'd been through.

"Everybody's still on the treasure hunt. Why would they think you are missing?" David asked.

"I don't believe it," Joe groaned.

"How long have we been in here? What time is it?" Mark asked.

Patti glanced at her watch. "It's 11:30."

"No way!" Joe shouted.

Mark was amazed. "We've only been in here for an hour and a half?"

Patti giggled and said, "What did you think, you were in here for a whole day or something?"

"What are you doing here anyway?" David asked, taking charge. "This area is off-limits."

"I didn't know that," Mark replied.

"What are *you two* doing here if it's off-limits?" Joe asked coyly.

Patti blushed, and David was briefly flustered. "We . . . we were making the rounds . . . checking things out."

Joe and Mark looked at each other knowingly.

"What about you?" Patti countered to Joe. "What're those streaks on your face? Were you crying?"

"Get out of my way." Joe suddenly pushed past them and stomped up the stairs that led away from shelter.

Mark lingered for a moment as David and Patti looked at one another awkwardly. "I guess I could use some fresh air," Mark said.

"Somebody should seal this shelter up," David suggested. Mark walked away from them toward the stairs and hesitated at the top.

"Let me see what it looks like first," he heard Patti insist from below.

"I can't *now*," David said sternly. "We have to go back to the camp"—his volume increased as if he was speaking for Mark's benefit—"now that we've finished our rounds."

"Oh. Okay," Patti said, defeated.

As the three of them made their way back to camp, Mark wondered if he had ruined Patti's chance to get that good-bye kiss from David. Judging from the sour expression on her face, Mark was sure he had.

✳　　✳

Back at Camp What-a-Nut, the treasure hunt had just finished. A team from a girl's cabin called Gitchy-Goomy solved the clues that finally led to the Wabana cabin, where the treasure was hidden. They screamed as they opened the box and found gift certificates for free ice cream at Whit's End.

The box was hidden under Mark's bunk.

"Hello, Mark," Mr. Gunnoe said as Mark turned from the crowd.

"Hi."

"Exciting, isn't it?" said Mr. Gunnoe. "I suppose you didn't expect the treasure to be hidden under your bunk."

Mark shook his head no, then asked, "Do you know what the answer to the ninth clue was?" The ninth clue was the one that had sent Mark and Joe on the wild goose chase to the bomb shelter.

Mr. Gunnoe thoughtfully tapped his chin with his finger.

"The ninth clue? Oh, yes. That's the one that said, *'A shelter in a storm, a haven to protect; the next clue can be found with the deepest respect.'*"

Mark nodded again.

"I would've thought it was obvious," Mr. Gunnoe said with a chuckle. "The answer was the camp *chapel*. A shelter in a storm, a haven to protect, a place with deep respect . . . rather poetic, I think. What did you think the answer was?"

"I don't want to talk about it." Mark frowned and strolled away. He headed across the compound toward the cafeteria. More than anything, he wanted a tall glass of lemonade to soothe his parched throat.

On the way, he saw Whit in the distance, talking to David and Patti. Whit shook his finger at them sternly, then spun on his heel and strode in the opposite direction. David and Patti had a brief discussion, then went their separate ways.

Uh oh, Mark thought.

Patti marched toward Mark, then scowled when she saw it was him. "Thanks a lot," she snapped.

"What's wrong?"

"We told Whit about what happened to you and Joe in the shelter. We figured he'd be happy with us because we rescued you."

"He wasn't happy?"

Patti's brow wrinkled into a deep frown. "Yeah, he was happy we found you. But he was mad because me and David were down there at all. He said David knew the shelter was off-limits. Especially for a boy and a girl alone. He said we had no business being there."

"He's right, isn't he?"

Patti glared at Mark. "Of course he's right. He's *always* right. But that doesn't make me feel better."

Mark simply shrugged and said, "Thanks for rescuing us anyway."

Patti grunted and stormed off.

Mark continued toward the cafeteria and spotted Joe under a

nearby tree. Joe was surrounded by his gang. It was clear to Mark that he was telling a very inflated account of their adventure in the bomb shelter. "We dug ourselves out with our bare hands!" Mark heard him say.

Mark grimaced and shook his head. Then, just as he reached for the door to the cafeteria, he felt a tap on his shoulder. He turned to find himself face-to-face with Joe.

"Hey, Press-snot," Joe said, his face now scrubbed to cover any hint that he'd been crying.

"Yeah?"

"Well . . . you know," he said.

"Huh?"

"*You know*," Joe insisted.

Mark said that he didn't.

Joe shuffled his feet and frowned. "Just make me say it, why don't you?" he said.

"Make you say *what*?" Mark asked.

"Make me say . . . well, thanks."

Mark shrugged and said, "I didn't do anything."

"Maybe you did, maybe you didn't," Joe said. "And maybe I can do you a favor sometime."

Mark looked at Joe thoughtfully. "You can do me a favor now," he said.

Joe raised an eyebrow. "Yeah? Like what?"

"Tell Whit what happened to Brad Miller."

Joe cringed. "You're kidding."

"Nope." Mark shook his head. "Tell him."

Joe looked down at his dirty tennis shoes for a moment, then sighed and said, "We'll see."

"And one more thing," Mark added.

"Yeah?"

"Stop calling me Press-snot." Mark then walked into the cafeteria, where he found an ice-cold glass of lemonade.

Epilogue

ON SATURDAY MORNING, campers piled into buses and cars to go back to their homes. Whit kindly gave Mark a lift to save his mom the trouble of coming all the way to camp to get him.

Whit navigated the car beyond the bumpy dirt road that led away from the camp and settled into the smoother main road to Odyssey. Then he spoke. "A curious thing happened last night," he said.

Mark looked up at Whit's round face—cheerily adorned with tufts of white hair on top, above his eyes, and below his nose.

Whit continued, "Joe Devlin showed up at my cabin and said he needed to talk to me."

Mark sat up expectantly.

"He said he had an anonymous tip about why Brad Miller was out on the old dock," Whit said.

Mark squirmed in his seat. "An anonymous tip?"

"Uh-huh." Whit nodded. "He said that Brad Miller was out there as part of an initiation to get into a gang. But Joe wasn't sure what gang."

Mark folded his arms and scowled. *That Joe*, he thought. *A creep to the very end.*

Whit smiled and said, "It doesn't matter. When Brad realized he wasn't going back to camp—and wouldn't have to face Joe—he told us everything."

"Will Joe get in trouble?" Mark asked.

"I doubt it. Officially speaking, he didn't do anything wrong. He didn't *force* Brad to go out on the dock. But unofficially . . . I think I'll have a little talk with him."

Mark grinned and sat back in the passenger seat. *Sooner or later, everybody gets what's coming to him*, Mark thought.

Later, as they drew to a stop in Mark's driveway, Whit said, "You know that I wasn't at camp the other night."

"Terry said you had business in Odyssey—or something like that," Mark said as he pulled his bag from the backseat.

"Something like that," Whit said. "I got to talking to a man and woman—a married couple—and time slipped away from us. Seems like we talked most of the night, in fact. Just trying to sort things out. I think we did."

Mark looked Whit full in the face, trying to figure out why he was telling him about it.

Whit beamed and said, "Go on, Mark. I'll see you later."

Mark closed the car door and stepped away as Whit backed out of the driveway. The screen door creaked open. Mark waved as Julie stepped out. "Hi, Mom!"

Then Richard followed her.

Mark suddenly remembered Whit's words. *Seems like we talked most of the night, in fact. Just trying to sort things out. I think we did.*

Mark dropped his bag and ran to his mother and father. The three of them collided into a crushing hug. Mark could hardly speak, afraid to ask the question, then asking it anyway: "What are you doing here, Dad?"

He smiled and said, "We're getting back together."

Mark looked from his mother's face back to his father's with disbelief. "What?"

"I know you've been waiting a long time," Richard said. "We're finally going to be a family again."

Book
Two

*The
King's
Quest*

Chapter One

MARK WAS SPEECHLESS. His mouth hung open, as if someone had just slapped him in the face. His normally pale cheeks turned crimson. His brown eyes were wide with disbelief.

Across the kitchen table, his parents sat side by side. They watched Mark anxiously as their hands clasped tightly on the tabletop. "What did you think would happen when your father and I got back together?" Julie Prescott asked.

Mark chewed his lower lip. "I didn't think . . . I mean, I never figured . . . you know . . ." He carelessly rubbed the side of his head with his palm, making his dark brown hair stick out.

Richard Prescott leaned toward Mark. His brow was deeply furrowed, as if he were contemplating a particularly difficult math problem. Face-to-face, the resemblance between the two was undeniable; Mark was certainly the younger version of his father. They wore the same expression of thoughtfulness. They shared the same laugh lines around their eyes, noticeable even when they weren't laughing.

"Son," Richard began, "your stay here was only supposed to be temporary."

"But I just got used to being in Odyssey," Mark complained. "And now you want me to leave."

"Your home is in Washington, D.C. It's time to go back," his father said.

Julie nodded and added, "I know it's hard, Mark. But you want us to be together again, right?"

Mark looked down. His fingers were tangled in his lap, little worms that moved nervously back and forth against each other. "It's not fair," he said.

Richard spread his arms as if appealing to Mark. "Can't you just think of it as a . . . a summer vacation? That's all it was. And now it's time to go back home, back to school."

"We'll come visit Odyssey again. I promise," Julie offered.

Mark folded his arms and imagined the packing, the good-byes to all his friends. No more John Avery Whittaker—Whit—with his wild, white hair, bushy eyebrows, and thick mustache that lifted high with his bottomless laugh and bunched up with heartfelt concern. No more Whit's End with its ice cream counter or rooms packed with endless amounts of fun and adventure. No more Patti Eldridge with her freckles and baseball cap pulled down over her sandy hair. No more small-town smiles, friendly handshakes, walks in McAlister Park, or swims in Trickle Lake. No more Odyssey.

"Can't *you* move *here*?" Mark asked his father.

Richard laughed. "And do what? What kind of work would I find in a small town like this?"

"If we thought real hard, I'll bet we could figure something out," Mark said.

Richard shook his head. "No, Mark. Don't even try. We're leaving Odyssey. We're going home to be a family again."

"When?" Mark asked.

"In a couple of weeks," his father answered.

"A couple of weeks!" Mark cried out. "That's too soon!"

"It's the end of the summer," Julie said. "We have to get back to Washington before school starts."

"It'll take that long to make all the arrangements. And that'll give you time to get used to the idea," said Richard.

"I won't get used to it!" Mark pouted as he pushed his chair back and stood up. "I'll *never* get used to it! It's not fair!"

"Mark!"

"No! It's not fair! It's just not fair!" he shouted as the fury bubbled out from inside him like a warm Coke bottle that's been shaken and then opened.

He raced down the hall and out the front door. The screen door slammed like a gunshot behind him, scattering the birds in a nearby tree. His bike lay near the fence. He jerked it up and climbed like a cowboy onto a horse. Up and down, up and down, his legs strained against the resistance of the pedals, then around and around. He pushed hard, gaining speed on the road to downtown Odyssey. The whir of the tires made him pump his legs still harder. He knew where he had to go. He knew what he had to do.

Chapter Two

FROM THE DISTANCE ACROSS McAlister Park, Whit's End looked like a bunch of misshapen boxes and tubes thrown on top of each other. On closer inspection, the boxes and tubes became walls and turrets and even had a section that looked like an old church. There were reasons for the design, Whit once explained to Mark. "Whit's End is simply a very large house that followed a typical Victorian design," Whit said. "Except for the church, of course. It's from an earlier time."

Mark dropped his bike outside and ran into the building. He stopped just inside the door and looked around. Kids played with displays and various hands-on inventions that Whit strategically placed in all corners. It hummed with all the activity but without the chaos of fun houses and arcades.

Mark glanced at the ice cream counter. Parents and children were crowded onto the stools, at the tables, and in booths, licking ice-cream cones or sucking on straws jabbed into milkshakes. A young man Mark didn't recognize happily moved behind the counter, taking orders and answering questions about flavors. Whit often had temporary help. With all the inventing and planning he had to do to keep Whit's End fun and exciting, he needed it. But Whit wasn't there.

Mark quickly walked through the shop, peeking into the many rooms filled with more games, more displays, a complete library, and an enormous train set. Still no sign of Whit. Mark was distressed. He had to talk to him about moving away. He had to see if Whit could come up with an idea that might keep them in Odyssey.

After he exhausted the rooms where Whit was most likely to be found, Mark made his way to the door that led down to Whit's workroom. Few of the kids would have dared enter, but Mark had once worked for Whit and felt he was entitled to go into those special places. He walked down the stairs and stopped at the bottom landing. The room was even more cluttered than when he had last seen it. Apart from the wall-long workbench covered with tools and equipment, the shelves and floor looked like a junkyard of half-finished toys, gizmos, and gadgets that only Whit could identify, including coils and springs, boxes and clocks, electronic wires, and disassembled devices.

In the center of the floor sat a giant contraption that looked like a cross between a telephone booth and a helicopter cockpit. For someone who didn't know better, the machine's dark glass and thick, silver plating made it look as invincible as a bank safe and as threatening as an armored tank. But Mark knew better.

It was the Imagination Station.

Whit had created it so kids could travel through time to learn about the Bible and history. Mark was unsure how it worked or whether it could really move people through time. But he once had an experience of his own in it, and the adventure seemed real enough.

Mark often wondered when Whit would take the Imagination Station out of the workroom and put it where the kids could use it, but Whit always answered the same way: "I still have some tinkering to do with it." And tinkering was the very thing Whit was doing when Mark walked around to the back side of the machine.

"Hello, Mark!" Whit said cheerfully as he tugged at a stubborn bolt with a wrench. "How are you?"

"Not very good," Mark said. "What are you doing?"

"Just trying to"—he grunted and tugged again—"finish a

little program that I"—tug and jerk—"put into the Imagination Station."

"A *new* program?" Mark asked.

The bolt gave up the fight, and Whit spun it loose from the plate. "I've been trying several different ideas," Whit said. He sat back and scratched at his white mane. "What do you mean you're not very good?"

Mark shrugged and answered, "My mom and dad told me we have to move away from Odyssey."

"Oh," Whit said softly.

"You knew, didn't you?" Mark asked, a hint of accusation in his voice. "You knew that if my mom and dad got back together, this would happen."

Whit brushed at his nose with the side of his hand and looked up at Mark. "Yes, I did."

"Why didn't you tell me?"

"Because your parents needed to tell you," Whit said.

"But what am I going to do?" Mark asked, realizing now that the thing he didn't do at home he might do here. He was going to cry.

"Mark," Whit said as he climbed to his feet. "Deep in your heart, you must've known."

Mark shook his head as his eyes welled up. "I didn't. Honest, I didn't."

Whit pulled Mark close. There, in the warmth and comfort of that embrace, Mark released the tears. They came gently at first, then spilled out in hard sobs.

"This is how it is, Mark," Whit said quietly. His low voice resonated through his chest to where Mark's ear was pressed. "We rarely get the good things without the bad. You were miserable when you first came to Odyssey, remember?"

Mark nodded his head yes.

"Your parents had split up, and all you could think about was getting them back together and living in Washington again. Well, that's what happened. Your prayers were answered."

"But it's not fair," Mark sniffled. "I've been here all summer. I like it here."

"And I'm sure you'll come back again," Whit said.

"I don't want to leave," Mark said, crying again. "If I prayed to go, then I can pray to stay, too."

Whit held him for a moment longer, then stepped back at arm's length, his hands on Mark's shoulders. He looked him full in the face and said, "You know prayer doesn't work like that, Mark. God isn't some genie who grants you wishes. Whatever happens to you happens because it fits into His plan for you. It's a plan filled with His love and goodness."

"It's still not fair," Mark declared.

"Maybe it isn't fair. And maybe it doesn't seem right," Whit said. "But I believe with all my heart that, for those who love God, everything happens for the good. Even when we make mistakes, God will turn them around for our benefit."

Within his mind and heart, Mark struggled to believe it. Whit was kind and wise and would never lead Mark astray. He wouldn't say things just to make Mark feel better. Whit was speaking the truth. But Mark's emotions—tangled like weeds around a rosebush—choked off his better sense. *If* God really had some sort of plan, leaving Odyssey couldn't possibly be part of it. God was making some kind of mistake.

"I have an idea," Whit said, and he knelt next to the Imagination Station.

Mark watched him curiously.

"I think this program may help you understand better than anything I could say." Whit reached into the empty square where the panel was removed and set to work.

"What do you mean?" Mark asked.

"You're taking a trip in the Imagination Station," Whit answered.

Chapter Three

THE DOOR TO THE IMAGINATION STATION closed with a deep, resonant boom. Mark settled into the cushioned chair and watched the flashing lights on the control panel. He was struck by how much they'd changed since he was last inside. Whit had been doing a lot of work.

"Are you comfortable?" Whit asked, his voice thin and hollow as it came through the tiny intercom speaker.

"Yeah, I guess," Mark replied.

"Good," Whit said. "If you need anything, just let me know."

"Okay."

The intercom speaker crackled, then Whit said, "You can go ahead and push the red button when you're ready."

Mark looked at the control panel. The red button sat prominently in the center. It flashed at him expectantly. "You mean *this* button?" Mark asked and pushed it.

The power surge took Mark by surprise, making him feel as if the machine were being thrust forward while pushing him back into his seat. *Am I really moving?* he wondered. The Imagination Station whined, rattled, and bounced. Mark wasn't alarmed, but it made his stomach do flips as if he were on a roller-coaster ride.

Through the speaker, Mark heard Whit's voice—surely a recording of some sort—counting backward from 10. As he reached "three . . . two . . . one," he paused and then said, "Once upon a time . . ."

The Imagination Station slowed down, then settled into a soft hum. The door opened by itself.

Sunlight momentarily blinded Mark as he climbed out of the cockpit. He blinked once or twice while his other senses told him he wasn't in the workroom at Whit's End anymore. Gone was the hard cement of Whit's workroom against the bottom of his feet. He had stepped onto a dirt floor, wet and slippery. The smells of moldy straw, horse manure, and rotten wood also accosted him.

And the sounds! He heard a peculiar, metallic rattling, followed by the sharp clanging of steel on steel. Identifying the clanging was easy. It was as if someone were banging a sledgehammer against an anvil. *Ching!* The sound was unmistakable. Mark had heard it thousands of times in old movies. It was a sword fight!

Where in the world am I?

Mark squinted through the bright light and saw he was in an abandoned shack. A wood table and chairs had been carelessly tossed against a wall. No doubt, animals had taken shelter in here at some time. The door, made of wooden boards that termites and rot had long since given up on, hung indifferently from a single hinge at the top of the doorpost. There were no windows.

And abandoned shack, he mused. *But where?*

The constant *ching! ching! ching!* of the sword fight came from outside, and Mark crept to the door. Carefully, he opened it wide enough to get a peek. What he saw took his breath away. Against a backdrop of a green field, grove of trees, and brilliant, blue sky, two men dressed in knight's armor—one suit black, one silver—danced around each other, swords poised for attack.

This isn't Odyssey anymore, Mark knew. Though he had once been to a traveling Renaissance festival that put on pageants, jousts, and battles between knights in shining armor, he couldn't imagine what any of this scene had to do with moving back to Washington, D.C. Maybe Whit made a mistake. The Imagination Station wasn't foolproof. And unlike the sparkling knights of playacting, these fellows weren't shining at all. The armor was dented and dirty.

The knight in black armor threw himself forward with a wide swipe of the blade. The other knight sidestepped and countered with a hard blow to his opponent's back. The movement caused their armor to rattle loudly, and Mark recognized it as the sound he had heard from inside. As the black knight swung around to face his opponent again, the silver knight retaliated with a fierce stab that deflected off the chest plate and struck the black knight's shoulder, piercing the chain mail. The black knight cried out and stumbled backward.

Mark expected the silver knight to follow this thrust with another, but he didn't. Instead, he slumped where he was, as if trying to catch his breath. The black knight swung himself around, allowing the momentum to bring the flat of his sword crashing against the silver knight's side.

The two knights are tired, Mark thought. Not only did they gasp and groan as they struck and parried, but they also held their swords as if each weighed a ton. The armor surely didn't help. It—and the chain mail underneath—covered them from head to foot and seemed to hamper their every move. They looked like a couple of poorly designed puppets in the hands of a bad puppeteer.

Mark then realized that the entire scene seemed to glisten in the light. But it wasn't the glistening of water or dew; the shine came from the blood of the two men. The armor, the chain mail, and even the grass seemed sprayed with red.

"This is real!" Mark gasped.

The silver knight propelled himself forward again—a bad move. His weak legs suddenly slipped out from under him, prob-ably from the wet grass, and threw him onto his back. The black knight lifted his sword high.

"No!" Mark gasped, jerking his hands to his face. His arm knocked against the door, and it creaked loudly as it moved another inch. It was more than the poor hinge could take. Barely clinging to the wood of the frame, it now wrenched free and sent the door falling with a splintering crash. The black knight, startled from his sure victory, turned in Mark's direction. That gave the silver knight the moment he desperately needed. He brought his sword up with all his might and pushed it between two separate sections of the black knight's armor.

The black knight clutched the blade with his metal gloves and cried out. The silver knight pulled the blade out, rolling aside as a precaution in case the black knight had the strength to fight back.

"You will not succeed," the black knight gasped, frozen in place. Then he swayed like a branch in the gentle breeze, fell to his knees, and collapsed face forward onto the ground.

The silver knight looked down at his enemy and jabbed the lifeless body with his toe. Satisfied that the black knight posed no further threat, he turned toward Mark. "Boy! Come out!" he called.

Mark fearfully stepped back into the shack.

"Did you not hear me? I said to come out!" the silver knight shouted. His voice was thick and husky, and he spoke with a British accent. The knight came toward Mark.

Mark retreated farther into the shack, quickly glancing around to see if he had a way of escape. A wooden ladder led upward to a loft. Mark raced for it.

The knight's armor rattled with each step, getting closer and closer while Mark scrambled to the top of the ladder. He had barely made it into the loft—a rotten-smelling, straw-covered platform—when the knight entered the shack. "Boy!" he cried out.

Mark checked all sides and saw there weren't any windows at this level, either. He had nowhere to go. He was trapped.

"Boy!" the knight shouted.

Mark scampered to the farthest point from the ladder and crouched in a dark corner, hoping the shadows would hide him.

Suddenly the knight cried out. Mark heard an enormous clatter and crash of armor, then silence. The knight moaned.

Mark thought it might be some sort of trick and waited a

moment. "Uhhh," the knight continued to moan from somewhere below.

Unable to resist his curiosity, Mark cautiously crept to the edge of the loft and peered over.

The knight had apparently stumbled over the fallen door and now lay still beside it. Whether he was hurt or simply exhausted, Mark couldn't tell. All that mattered, for the moment, was that Mark was safe.

Until the loft collapsed.

Chapter
Four

WHEN MARK CAME TO his senses again, he found himself on a small bed in a room of rough stone walls. A narrow window above his head allowed a shaft of sunlight to illuminate a colorful coat of arms hanging directly opposite. The coat of arms had four crudely painted squares. The first contained a red dragon, the second a roaring lion, the third a white dove, and the fourth a red rose.

He lifted his hand to his aching head, only to feel the coarse cloth of a bandage wrapped snugly there. It took him a moment to remember what had happened, and, once he did, he sat up and tossed the blanket aside. *I have to get out of here,* he thought, certain the silver knight would come clanking along at any minute to hurt him.

The door opened, and a woman dressed like a nun came in carrying a tray. She stopped when she saw Mark was sitting up, muttered something he couldn't hear, then quickly ran out.

Mark seized the chance to escape and sprinted to the door, his feet and head pounding along the way. He made it as far as the doorway before he realized he was wearing only his underwear!

He gasped and doubled back to the bed to grab a blanket for covering. He wrapped it around himself and returned to the door—just in time to be intercepted by a tall, distinguished-looking man with long, gray hair and a tangled beard.

"Well, God be praised!" said the man warmly as he placed a

firm hand on Mark's shoulder and guided him back to the bed. "We feared for your good health, lad, so severe was the fall you took."

Mark sat down on the bed again. The man grabbed a small, wooden chair and pulled it close. Mark noticed he was dressed in a long, brown robe, fringed with a gold and blue design. On his shoulders hung a red cape, which he wrapped around himself as he sat down. A bony foot clad in a sandal emerged from under the robe.

"Where am I?" Mark asked.

"You are in my castle," the man answered with a smile, speaking with the same sort of accent as the knight had earlier.

"But who are you?"

"I am Sir Miles of Brandon, master of this castle and the surrounding lands to the Great River." The man did not move but sat perfectly still and looked intently at Mark.

"Are you the knight who—who—" Mark didn't want to say the word *killed*, but he couldn't think of a good replacement.

Sir Miles shook his head. "Alas, I would that I had the strength and courage of that great knight. In my younger days, yes, but no longer. Sir Owwen is the one of whom you speak. A man of knightly courage and honor. He brought you here."

"He did?" Mark asked, surprised.

"Yes." Sir Miles leaned back and folded his arms across his chest. "Tell me your name, lad, and from whence you come."

"I'm Mark Prescott," he answered. "From Odyssey."

"Odyssey?"

Mark nodded. "Do you know where it is?"

"I fear not," Sir Miles said. "But I suspect it is a great distance by your strange accent."

"*My* strange accent!" Mark said.

Sir Miles scratched his chin, chuckled, and added, "And your clothes."

"Oh, yeah. Can I have them back now?"

"If they are dry, you may," Sir Miles said and clapped his

hands. "Your fall landed you in some very potent-smelling dung. I have asked my servants to wash them."

"Thanks," Mark said.

A different woman from the one who came in before entered. Sir Miles gestured to Mark, and the woman bowed obediently and left. Afterward, Sir Miles smiled and said, "Your raiment has caused quite a disturbance in my household. All the servants want to see your clothes. Your tunic—"

"Tunic?"

Sir Miles plucked at his chest and repeated, "Tunic."

"My *shirt*!" Mark said, proud of himself for understanding.

"Never have I seen round clasps of such strange making. With holes!" Sir Miles said.

Mark figured he was talking about the plastic buttons and said so. Sir Miles repeated the word *button* the way a child might say *Mama*—again and again.

Sir Miles's servant girl returned with Mark's clothes, now dried by the fire in the kitchen, and Mark found himself playing "show-and-tell" with his jeans (which Sir Miles called "leggings") and socks ("very short tights").

After the servant girl left, Mark got dressed while Sir Miles watched. "This is a wonder to me!" he finally shouted. "Must you always work so hard to dress? Do you not have simpler tunics and robes in your land?"

"We have robes," Mark replied defensively. "But we wear them around the house, not outside. May I have my shoes now?"

"Ah!" Sir Miles said and reached under the bed. He pulled out Mark's tennis shoes and held them up reverently in both hands as if he cradled two precious jewels. "Your footwear is white and made of . . . of . . . what is this?" He rubbed his finger against the sole.

"Rubber," Mark answered.

"Rubber," Sir Miles repeated softly. "From whence does this rubber come?"

Mark shrugged and took the shoes. "The factory, I guess. You'll have to ask my mom."

Sir Miles opened his mouth to say something else, but he was interrupted by the arrival of another man. He was as tall as Sir Miles but of a younger, stronger build. His hair and beard were dark and curly and set off his penetrating, pale blue eyes. He wore a large, white vest over black chain mail. On the front of the vest was sewn a pattern of upside-down V shapes in alternating colors of red and yellow.

"Sir Owwen!" Sir Miles shouted happily, leaping to his feet. "How do you fare? Are your wounds dressed satisfactorily?"

Sir Owwen bowed slightly in a gesture of respect. "Sit down, good friend," he said. "My wounds are healing, and I am refreshed thanks to your great courtesy. Thanks be to God that I was victorious over the evil knight who sought my life."

"Praise to God," Sir Miles affirmed.

Sir Owwen turned to Mark and said, "But I would be remiss to mention that victory without saying that it was due primarily to the miraculous and timely arrival of this boy."

Mark was tempted to look behind him, sure that Sir Owwen was talking about someone else.

"You, lad, saved my life and, in doing so, have served our great king in ways you cannot know," Sir Owwen said. "I kneel before you now in gratitude."

Mark blushed and looked helplessly at Sir Miles, who smiled back at him.

Sir Owwen lowered his head and said, "I am your servant if ever you have need of help . . . er, by what name are you called?"

"Mark Prescott," Mark said.

"Of Odyssey," Sir Miles added.

"Mark Prescott of Odyssey," Sir Owwen said, then stood up. "I depart now to continue my quest for the king." He turned on his heel to leave but suddenly stopped. "Odyssey?" he said. "Is that the place from which you come?"

Mark nodded.

Sir Owwen's expression changed to one of amazement.

"Have you heard of it, Sir Owwen?" asked Sir Miles.

"Yes, I have," Sir Owwen replied. He leaned and whispered something in Sir Miles's ear. Sir Miles listened attentively, scratched his chin, then instantly sped from the room. Sir Owwen sat down in the chair next to Mark. In a hushed voice, he explained that the king had told him he would meet someone from Odyssey—a most peculiar thing to say since, to Sir Owwen's knowledge, no such place existed.

"That's weird," Mark said. "How could he know you'd meet someone from Odyssey? I didn't even know I was coming until right before I arrived."

Sir Owwen leaned forward and rested his stubbly chin on the back of his large, callused hands. "In what manner did you arrive? For I searched that shack myself prior to the sudden attack by the black knight, and surely it was empty. You could only have entered through the door, on which I had my eyes set. I didn't see you."

"The Imagination Station," Mark answered.

Sir Owwen cocked his head as if trying to interpret the words, then seemed to give up. "By whatever means you were sent, I can only believe you are a living sign from God in this, my quest for the king. Are you strong enough to travel?"

The possibility of adventure and excitement overtook his better sense, and he jumped up. "Yeah!" Mark said.

"Then let us be on our way!" Sir Owwen shouted heartily. He stood up quickly, knocking the chair over as he did.

As they strode down the long, stone hallway, Mark asked Sir Owwen what exactly their quest was.

Sir Owwen quickly glanced around to be sure they weren't being spied upon, then tilted his enormous frame toward Mark. "We must rescue the Ring of Uther from Slothgrowl!" he whispered.

"Who's Slothgrowl?" Mark asked.

Sir Owwen looked at Mark with disbelief. "Is it possible you have not heard of Slothgrowl?" he asked.

"Honest, I haven't," Mark said. "Who is he?"

"Only the most evil and ferocious dragon in the land!"

Chapter
Five

MARK AND SIR OWWEN walked along seemingly endless stone corridors and down innumerable steps before emerging from the dark and damp castle into daylight. Even then, they were still well inside the fortress walls. Men and women moved to and fro, engrossed in their business. Occasionally someone would stop to notice Sir Owwen or to stare at Mark's clothes. He didn't realize how much he stood out until he noticed that the other men wore brown tunics with a belt, matching leggings, and ragged leather boots. The women wore long dresses and scarves on their heads.

Mark followed Sir Owwen across the courtyard. He later learned that it was called the inner ward and contained the homes of Sir Miles, his family, and servants. It was an odd collection of stone walls and half-timber apartments.

They continued through the inner gatehouse to the outer ward, where guards watched their progress. Mark stumbled once or twice over small children and fleeing chickens who got under his feet when he was staring upward at the gigantic, rounded towers sitting on each corner of the wards.

"I've never been in a castle before," Mark said breathlessly. Mark hoped Sir Owwen would take it as a hint to slow down and let him look around.

Sir Owwen simply grunted and strode on.

At the outer gatehouse, by far the largest in the castle, complete with a drawbridge and moat, they were met by Sir Miles and the two servants Mark had seen earlier. It was clear now why Sir Miles hastily left the room. He had assembled provisions for them—satchels of food and Sir Owwen's freshly cleaned armor (still dented)—all strapped to a packhorse named Kevin.

"Why Kevin?" Mark asked.

"It is the same name as the fiend I drove out of this castle two score years ago," Sir Miles explained.

Mark wanted to hear the story behind that battle, but Sir Owwen interrupted to bid Sir Miles a warm farewell. He took Kevin by the reins and walked across the drawbridge. The sound of Kevin's hooves seemed to bounce in all directions off the castle walls.

"Thanks for everything," Mark said to Sir Miles. Then he ran along the edge of the drawbridge to get a look below. He thought he might see alligators in the moat. Instead, he saw (and smelled) only stagnant water, thick with mud and green slime.

Once they were clear of the drawbridge, Mark and Sir Owwen followed the dirt road through a small village. From homes and shops made of half-timber, wattle (woven sticks), and daub (mud and clay), the villagers came around to proclaim Sir Owwen a "brave knight" and to wish him "godspeed." At Mark, they simply stared.

"They believe you to be my squire," Sir Owwen said as they passed the smiling and waving villagers.

"Squire? What's that?" Mark asked.

"My attendant," Sir Owwen answered.

"*Squire* Mark Prescott," Mark whispered to himself again and again, as if trying it on for size. "Squire Mark. Cool!"

Beyond the village, the road stretched out across the field and disappeared into a thick forest. Mark scanned the panorama and took a deep breath. The colors were so vivid to him; he had never seen so many greens, yellows, and browns. Or a sky so blue or a sun so bright.

"Where are we?" Mark wondered aloud.

"We are departing from the castle and village of Brandon," answered Sir Owwen.

"I mean the country," Mark said.

"Truly, do you not know?" Sir Owwen asked, bewildered.

"I didn't know where Whit was sending me," Mark replied. "He just said to get in, so I did."

"You are in the great country of Albion, blessed by God and favored in His blessings." Sir Owwen beamed.

"Is it real or made up?"

Sir Owwen said indignantly, "Real or made up? Do you question the truth of what I speak?"

"No! But . . . how could this place be real if you have dragons?" asked Mark.

"Stand face-to-face with Slothgrowl and my young liege will know its reality," Sir Owwen said with a chuckle. He went on to add that Slothgrowl was a hideous monster with snakelike skin, except for a patch of scales found just beneath his neck that were said to be made of a substance harder than iron in order to protect his heart. He had talons at the end of each of his four legs. As for his face, it was long and oily with tiny, red eyes, large, cannonlike nostrils, and razor-sharp teeth that were said to bite through the thickest armor.

Mark shuddered, and even Kevin snorted and shook his head, as if scared by what he heard. "So why is the Ring of Uther so important that you'd risk your life trying to get it?"

Sir Owwen patted Kevin on the neck. "That is a great secret which only the king himself can answer. It is enough for me to obey his highness and retrieve the ring, if God so wills it."

"But *why*?" Mark persisted. It was hard for him to understand obedience without explanation.

"Why?" Sir Owwen echoed. "Would I dare offend the king by questioning his commands?"

"You mean you'd do *anything* he wanted you to do?"

"I have sworn allegiance to my king—even to the death," Sir Owwen replied.

"But what if this whole ring business is a mistake?" Mark asked.

Sir Owwen stopped and looked carefully at Mark. "Perhaps *I* was mistaken in bringing you along. The king is a wise and just monarch whom I follow wholeheartedly. Unfortunately, not all in the kingdom agree, and some would overthrow him if they could. The evil knight I defeated earlier is but one of them. He suddenly attacked me as I rode on this quest of the king's."

"How did he know who you were?"

"By my colors and my horse," Sir Owwen said. "Alas, when he attacked, he murdered that good and faithful animal. I suspect the evil knight knew of my purpose and was sent to thwart my undertaking."

Mark shrugged. "Must be a pretty important ring."

"We must be on guard at all times, young Mark," Sir Owwen stated earnestly. "For this quest is not only of flesh and blood, but even more of the spirit! Forces of the darkest kind may be rallying against us. Even sorcery."

"You mean *magic*?"

Sir Owwen nodded somberly and made the sign of the cross with his hand. "We fight not only for our bodies, but also for our souls."

Chapter
Six

By this time, Mark, Sir Owwen, and a wary-looking Kevin had entered the forest. The thick tangle of branches formed a canopy over their heads that nearly blocked out all sunlight. It took Mark a moment to adjust his eyes. A fox ran in front of them, stopped long enough to bark, then fled into the thicket.

"How did Slothgrowl get hold of the ring in the first place?" Mark asked softly, as if his voice could awaken unwanted companions who might be asleep in the many shadows of the wood.

Sir Owwen explained that it was stolen from the king's castle by a shrewd enchantress, who took on the appearance of one of the king's servants to gain access to the treasured ring. Neither the ring nor the enchantress had been seen since. Most people suspected she was in league with Slothgrowl.

"Where is Slothgrowl now?" asked Mark, unable to get rid of the image of the dragon in his mind.

"That I do not know," answered Sir Owwen. "No one knows. Slothgrowl rides on dragon mist and can only be seen by those with the eyes to see."

"Then how are *we* going to find him?" Mark inquired.

"By faith," Sir Owwen replied.

"That's it?"

"The king has given me specific things for which to look," Sir Owwen said. "The first sign was to prepare for the sudden appearance of a mysterious stranger who would speak of Odyssey."

Mark shivered unexpectedly. He still couldn't imagine how he was the first sign in an adventure that he had only just joined. "What was the second sign?" Mark asked.

Sir Owwen said, "It will be the discovery and recovery of the Sword of Scales. It is the only sword that can kill Slothgrowl."

"Great!" Mark said cheerfully. "Where is the Sword of Scales?"

"No one knows," Sir Owwen said sadly. "It has been missing for years, longer than I have had breath in my body. Some suspect that an evil lord is keeping it hidden so Slothgrowl can continue to prowl the land without fear."

Mark cocked an eyebrow at Sir Owwen. "So we're looking for a dragon that no one can find in order to kill him with a sword no one can find?"

Sir Owwen tugged at one of the curls near his ear. "Aye," he said.

They walked on in silence for most of the day, covering quite a long distance, until they heard a sound echo through the woods. At first Mark thought it was the wind in the trees, but then he was chilled to realize it was a human noise. Somewhere a woman wailed, low and mournful, broken only by wrenching sobs. Kevin lurched backward so that Sir Owwen had to yank at the reins to steady him.

"What is it?" Mark whispered. His question was a hope for assurance that they weren't about to encounter one of the dark forces Sir Owwen had mentioned.

"Clearly a woman," Sir Owwen replied as he pressed onward.

They rounded a bend in the road and saw her. She sat upon a log, dressed in rags, weeping profusely with her face in her hands. Her blonde hair was matted and streaked with dirt. She didn't look up as they approached.

"Woman!" Sir Owwen called out. "Pray, why do you weep so that the very branches stoop to mourn?"

She lifted her head slightly and cried, "Alas, sir knight, I am a poor widow of a kind and generous woodsman. He was killed at this very spot one year ago by blackguards in the service of Sir

Cardoc, who desired only our land. They cast my only son and myself out into the woods, where we have wandered, scrounging food from the forest, as our only means by which to live. Until this very day—" She choked on her words and began to weep again.

Sir Owwen directed a wary look to Mark, then knelt next to the woman. "Speak, dame. What events took place this day that should cause you to weep so horribly?"

She mustered her courage and looked fully into their faces. *Under different circumstances,* Mark thought, *she would be beautiful.* He figured she couldn't have been much older than his own mother, which probably meant her son was about his age.

"They took him!" she sobbed. "They took my son!"

Sir Owwen placed his hand on his heart, lowered his head, sighed deeply, and said, "God, have mercy."

"The wicked Sir Cardoc has taken him as a slave to his castle just beyond these woods," she said. "Woe is me, that I should have lived to see such ends!"

"Why don't you call the police?" Mark asked.

Both the woman and Sir Owwen looked at him quizzically.

"Okay, so maybe you don't have police now," he amended. "But maybe we can rescue him!" Mark turned to Sir Owwen and asked, "Can't we?"

The woman gazed at them hopefully.

Sir Owwen reddened and stammered, "My squire is young and ignorant of his words, though his heart be in the proper place."

"What does that mean?" Mark asked.

"That we should counsel one with another before making hasty vows," Sir Owwen said. Then he guided Mark by the arm to the opposite side of the path.

"You don't want to help her?" Mark asked in a hoarse whisper.

"With my whole heart, I desire nothing more," Sir Owwen said. "But my quest is for the king. He bade me to be wary of strangers seeking help, for they might lure me away from my higher purpose."

Mark frowned. "But look at her!" he said. "She's not luring anybody. She just needs help. You're a hotshot knight! You know how to rescue people from castles, don't you?"

Sir Owwen shook his head as he replied, "In the name of justice, I would die trying. But I must remember the king!"

"Are you telling me the king wouldn't want you to help her?" Mark asked pointedly.

Sir Owwen glanced at the woman thoughtfully, then back at Mark. His eyes reflected the inner struggle he waged.

"If you won't help her, *I* will!" Mark announced. He had no idea where all this sudden bravery came from. Maybe it was caused by standing in these thick woods, so full of wonder and mystery. Or maybe it came from this time of valiant knights, dangerous dragons, and damsels in distress. Whatever it was, Mark felt capable of accomplishing anything.

Sir Owwen knelt, bowed his head, and prayed softly. After a moment, he whispered "Amen" and stood up. "Be it folly or valor," he announced, "we will do our utmost to rescue this fair woman's son."

Chapter Seven

IT WAS EVENING BEFORE Sir Owwen and Mark came up with a plan. Borrowing the clothes of the woman's dead husband, Sir Owwen made himself out to be a traveling merchant. Then they covered Mark's "peculiar-looking garments" with an outfit owned by the missing boy and left Kevin and their provisions at the woman's makeshift lean-to in the woods.

"Are you sure this'll work?" Mark asked as he adjusted his tunic.

"By God's grace," Sir Owwen replied. Even in his costume of a rusty brown tunic and patched cloak, he looked imposing.

Yet Mark's heart pounded and his mouth went dry as they emerged from the forest and approached the gate to the great castle of Cardoc. Torches burned on both sides of the open gate, which yawned at them from across the drawbridge and the black moat underneath. Sir Owwen grabbed Mark's arm and jerked him along every step to the gate itself, where they were met by a guard.

"What business have you here?" the guard asked coarsely.

Sir Owwen pushed Mark forward. "What business does any man have being robbed by beggar boys like this? I want justice done by the lord of these lands!" he demanded.

"Justice!" The guard laughed and gestured them through. "Yes, we shall see to justice. Sir Cardoc is in the great hall. Follow me!"

Again Sir Owwen grabbed Mark by the arm, and he led him through the courtyard. It was a dazzling sight to Mark. Unlike the courtyard at Sir Miles's castle, with its shacks and houses, this courtyard was full of booths, carts, and stalls, as if it were the meeting place of a giant market. People milled about, but they weren't idle. They gathered in pockets around men and women who performed by torchlight. Some juggled knives, others played instruments that looked like small guitars and long flutes, while acrobats flung themselves head over heels through the crowd or balanced lances on the tips of their noses. It was like a circus.

Sir Owwen pulled Mark close. "Sir Cardoc is celebrating a market meeting," he whispered. "A better means for our escape."

They followed the guard down a short corridor and through a large arch leading into the expanse of the great hall. And great it was! It stretched almost 100 feet ahead and must have been 50 feet wide. The dark, gray stones reached high up to rafters that disappeared into blackness. Each wall had two or three fireplaces, all burning brightly with huge fires. Tapestries and heraldries decorated other portions of the walls. Tables surrounded by men and women spread lengthwise toward the end of the room, where the largest table of all spanned the hall from side to side. Obviously, the large table—the "high table," it was called—was the place of honor.

As the guard led them past the many tables, Mark saw that the men and women were eating roasted meat on silver plates, but without forks or spoons. They used their fingers and ripped at the brown mutton with their teeth. Drinks were served in pewter cups. Horns of plenty decorated the centers of the tables, each filled with berries.

The floor itself was covered with rushes, and Mark nearly got nipped by the dogs and cats who fought over the odd scraps of food the dinner guests threw to them.

At the high table, the men and women dressed in more-colorful clothes and were obviously of greater rank than their guests. The guard took Mark and Sir Owwen front and center, where they looked up at a thin, sharp-featured man with jet-black hair and piercing eyes. But what caught Mark's attention was the long scar that extended from the man's right temple across his cheek to his chin. This was Sir Cardoc.

"My lord," the guard said, "this merchant craves to speak with you."

Sir Cardoc glanced up from the bone he was gnawing. "What does he want?" he asked.

Sir Owwen cleared his throat and said, "Justice, my lord. This beggar boy tried to forcibly rob me as I crossed your land. I beg you for justice."

Sir Cardoc rested his greasy chin on his greasy hands and eyed them both.

Something's wrong, Mark thought. The plan was for Sir Cardoc to throw Mark in the dungeon—most likely the same place containing the woman's son, since castles had only one dungeon beneath the basement. Sir Owwen would then make as if to leave, but instead he would come later in the night, when it was safe, knock out the guard, and rescue both Mark and the boy. But Mark suddenly sensed, *It isn't going to work.*

"I'll give you justice." Sir Cardoc chuckled low and mean. "Guard?"

The guard stepped forward and said, "Yes, my lord?"

Sir Cardoc gestured to Mark with the bone and said, "Kill the boy."

Chapter
Eight

THE DINNER GUESTS went suddenly quiet.

"What!" Mark shouted.

"My lord?" the guard asked, unsure of what he had heard.

"I said to kill the boy!" Sir Cardoc raged. "We have too many beggars around here anyway. It's bad for commerce."

The guard drew his sword, and Sir Owwen placed his hand on it gently. "Sir Cardoc," Sir Owwen said, "I came only for justice, not an execution."

"You said you wanted justice," Sir Cardoc said. "What did you expect, a beating? A time in my dungeon? It's filled to the brim."

"But my lord, I beseech you. As a humble merchant, I would be stricken to bear the responsibility of this boy's death."

Sir Cardoc laughed. "As a humble merchant, did you say? Is that what you said?" Sir Cardoc roared with laughter, and the guests, relieved, joined with him. Then abruptly, he pushed himself back from the table and stood up. His face turned red with rage, and his scar shone like a stream of blood. He pointed his finger at Sir Owwen and shouted, "You are no merchant! You are Sir Owwen, knight and scoundrel! And now you are my prisoner!"

Sir Owwen cried out to Mark, "An ambush! Quickly!" Even as he shouted, he grabbed the guard by the wrist, twisted it so that the sword dropped free, and scooped up the weapon. One deft stroke took care of the guard, and Sir Owwen spun around to face the rest of Sir Cardoc's men. They rushed from all sides, getting entangled with the confused and frightened dinner guests, who decided it was time to skip dessert and go home.

"Sir Owwen!" Mark screamed, panicked and unsure of what to do.

"Run, Mark! Run!"

Mark did. Past people, between legs, over chairs and under tables, he scrambled for a door. Any door. He found one and pushed through, turning back quickly in time to see a dozen men hurl themselves upon Sir Owwen.

"There he is!" another guard shouted, pointing at Mark.

# #

The door opened into the kitchen—a large, cluttered room containing an enormous fireplace where black pots of varying sizes hung above the flames. Pieces of animals and vegetables littered the tables and floor, making everything slippery for Mark as he ran through. The men and women who served Sir Cardoc's guests were too busy to notice the commotion in the great hall. Or maybe they didn't care.

A guard followed Mark into the kitchen. Mark caught sight of him pushing his way between the tables and past the servants just as Mark darted through another door on the opposite side of the room. It led to a small enclosure crowded with clay pots and jars. Mark quickly looked around for a door or window through which to escape, but he didn't see one.

I'm stuck in a closet! Mark thought as he scrambled around the room, his heart racing like a trapped animal's. He returned to the door and peered out. The guard hadn't seen him leave the kitchen—he pushed over tables and shouted at the servants for not being more observant.

An old woman said something to the guard and pointed to the closet door. Mark closed it and stepped back, glancing around the room for some kind of protection. His eye caught a small, stone edifice in the far corner. It had a wooden covering and a rope tied onto a metal ring.

A well! Mark realized. He lifted the cover and, grabbing the rope, began to lower himself in. He had just disappeared beneath the top when he heard the door crash in and the guard shouting, "Come out, you ratbag!"

Mark continued to lower himself along the rope, wondering how long it would be before he'd touch water. The walls were moist and slimy.

From the noises above, Mark guessed that the guard was knocking over the jars in search of him. He clung to the rope and waited. If the guard gave up and left, Mark could pull himself out.

After a few minutes, the closet above was silent. Mark's arms grew tired, and the moldy smell of the well turned his stomach. He figured he had waited long enough and looked up. All he could see was the ceiling of the room. The muscles in his arms groaned as he pulled on the rope, moving inches upward.

Suddenly the rope jerked. Mark looked up and saw the guard leering down at him. The guard had hold of the rope and was pulling him up!

"Got you, you scamp!" the guard said with a laugh.

Mark frantically lowered himself as the rope was yanked up. The guard was strong, and Mark realized he wasn't making any progress downward. Then his foot bumped against the bucket tied to the end of the rope. Time was running out. Unless Mark let go, the guard would soon have him at the top.

The wet bucket, half filled with water, banged against Mark knees. He looked down at the black emptiness below.

The guard laughed. "You'll be a nice prize for my master," he said.

Mark looked up again at the leering smile and decided the black emptiness wasn't so bad after all. He let go of the rope. The guard fell backward from the sudden lack of weight to pull.

Mark hit the water and sank deeper than he expected. He reached out to the well walls, but his arms flailed freely. The walls were gone. He had dropped beyond the bottom of the well and into a reservoir of some sort. He couldn't feel the top, nor did his feet touch bottom.

He opened his eyes and twisted around, hoping that sunlight might penetrate the darkness. It didn't. He looked up and couldn't see the bottom of the well. He nearly gasped as he realized he didn't know which way to go. His lungs ached.

Pushing himself up with his legs, he kept his hands above his head. They bumped against a cold, stone surface. He carefully felt his way along, praying for a gap of air or another passage. Wet rock met his every touch. His lungs felt like balloons on the brink of explosion.

Mark knew he had to push in one direction or another if he hoped to survive. Froglike, he pumped his legs and stretched out his arms for whatever waited ahead in the dark water. His lungs screamed for air.

He pushed harder, panicking, even though he knew it was the worst thing to do. His ears began to ring, and he felt black bubbles of unconsciousness bursting around his head.

I'm going to drown in the bottom of this castle, he thought. *They'll never find my body. My parents will never know what happened to me.*

His legs continued to pump automatically. His arms began to drop. *It's not so bad,* he mused. *It's kind of like falling asleep. If only I could breathe out and breathe in again.*

He exhaled slowly, the bubbles tickling his nose and drifting upward as they left him. He began to sink farther as the air left his body. *Just like falling asleep . . .*

Suddenly, strong hands invaded the water and grabbed Mark's tunic.

Chapter
Nine

MARK'S RETCHING AND COUGHING brought him to full consciousness again. He was flat on his back, pressed against cold stone, his head turned to the side for the water to spill out of his lungs and mouth. When he could open his eyes, he realized he was on a ledge. His arm was carelessly stretched out, dangling above the water. He wiggled his fingers, allowing them to touch the surface. They made sounds like pebbles dropped one by one into a pond.

"Well?" a thin, scratchy voice asked.

Mark snapped his head around and was blinded by the bright flame of a torch. It was just over his face, held by a stooping figure. Mark blinked to clear his vision and found himself looking up into a wrinkled, haggard old face covered with a thick, white beard and wild, white hair. "Oh," he said, startled.

"How do you fare?" the old man asked. "Can you sit up?"

Mark nodded.

"Well?" the old man demanded.

The demand puzzled Mark until he looked again and realized the old man's eyes seemed a peculiar gray color, as if covered with film. They looked away without seeing. He was blind.

"Yes, I can sit up," Mark said and did, his clothes dripping loudly. "Did you save me?"

"'Twas I, yes," the old man said, clutching the torch.

"But how did you . . . y'know, see me?" Mark asked.

"I didn't see you, lad. I *heard* you," the scratchy voice replied. "After so many years wandering the passageways and corridors of this castle, one knows for what to listen. The well waters do not stir unless there's something in there that does not belong." The old man laughed, then continued, "I thought you were a loose bucket! It is a sign of God's grace in your life that I happened to be here."

"I guess," Mark said. He shook his head and worked his jaw in an attempt to get the water out of his ears.

"Guess? Are you so unsure?" the old man challenged.

"No! I mean . . ." Mark didn't know what he meant and let it go. "Thank you for saving me."

The old man laughed again and said, "But it will be you who saves *me*! You have been sent here. This I know for sure."

Mark shook his head. "Save you? How can I save you?" he asked. "I'm here by accident."

"Accident? There is no such thing!" the old man snorted. "Only fools believe in accidents. You are here by providence!"

"You don't know me or why I'm here!" Mark said. "It was a mistake! Sir Owwen may have been captured, and I would've, too, except I jumped in the well." Mark stood up. "Sir Owwen is in trouble. I have to figure out a way to help him."

"You would not be here unless you were chosen to come," the old man insisted. "You must be the one to free the sword!"

"What sword?" Mark asked.

"The Sword of Scales! Come along with me," the old man said, hooking a bony finger at him.

✳   ✳

They crept along the dark passageways, the old man leading the way with his torch held high. Mark wanted to ask why he needed a torch if he was blind, but he thought better of it. There's no point in offending your only ally.

"The torch is for you," the old man said suddenly, as if Mark had asked his question out loud. "I knew one day you would come and have kept torches at the ready."

Mark was mystified. "How could you know I was going to come? It's just a trip in the Imagination Station. I'm not really part of this."

"You're part of it," the old man said softly. "Even if you don't know what part."

The old man's statement didn't make sense to Mark, nor did he care to pursue it. It was the same sort of riddle Sir Owwen kept saying.

"Where are we going?" Mark asked, changing the subject. "Are we going to get the Sword of Scales? Can we find Sir Owwen?"

"Be patient," the old man said.

"How do you know your way around?" Mark asked.

"A castle like this has many passages that only a blind man could find—because they are hidden behind entryways that deceive your eyes."

Mark persisted. "How did you wind up here in this castle in the first place?"

The old man explained that a long, long time ago, he was a knight who had been entrusted with the Sword of Scales. "But I was captured by Sir Cardoc on the road to find Slothgrowl. He kept me prisoner along with the sword for more years than I could count. Those years of darkness caused me to go blind. With that, I put on an act of insanity so Sir Cardoc and his henchmen might disregard me. As I'd hoped, they eventually did. But tell me, lad, how it is that you are here?"

Mark told the old man that they came to rescue the son of a widow they met in the forest.

The old man suddenly stopped and turned to face Mark. He nodded and said, "Aye, the story is familiar to me. For that same widow lured me from my quest and sent me to this castle for similar mischief."

"But—how?" Mark asked. "You've been locked in here for years. The woman we met was young."

The old man smiled, then continued on his way. "She is really an enchantress employed by Sir Cardoc," he replied.

"Oh, no," Mark groaned. "Then it's all my fault. Sir Owwen didn't want to help the widow, but I made him do it. If anything happens to him . . . it'll be my fault."

The old man held up his hand. "Shh. This is the place." He handed the torch to Mark and pressed his hands against the wall. His fingers moved quickly, finding a gap between two of the stones. "Ah," he whispered and pushed down. Mark heard a soft click—like a latch being lifted—and the old man took the torch back. "Now push."

"Push what?" Mark asked.

"The wall!" the old man replied impatiently.

Mark shrugged but obeyed. He pressed his shoulder against the wall and put all his weight behind his push. To his surprise, the wall swung open like a revolving door.

"Be on the lookout," the old man said as they walked through. "Sometimes a guard comes to check the sword. But the hour is late, and we may hope no one will come."

The room was empty, save for a table and chair with a very old and moldy loaf of bread. Mark started to wonder why the old man had brought him into what looked like a prison cell when he heard a soft humming and saw a glowing light off to the side. He turned in the direction from which the hum and the glow came.

"Oh!" he exclaimed. There on the wall hung the Sword of Scales. The sword pointed down—making the form of a cross—with a brilliant, silver blade that had intricately carved swirls around its edges. At the top, a gold handle bore words that Mark had to strain to read: *Deus Misereatur.*

"Beautiful beyond words," the old man said.

"What does 'dee-oose miser—'?"

"*Deus misereatur* means 'God be merciful,' " the old man said. "It's Latin."

"Let's grab it and get out of here," Mark suggested.

The old man shook his head. "You may try, but you'll do so at your own risk. The Sword of Scales is held to the wall by enchanted chains. Can you not see them? Only the chosen knight may free it. All others will die in the attempt."

Mark looked more closely and saw a gold fastener just beneath the T of the hilt and another farther down the blade. Whether they were really enchanted wasn't his to guess. "So, picking the lock is a no-go, I guess," he said.

The old man nodded and replied, "Indeed."

"So, who's the chosen knight?" Mark asked.

"It's the one who frees the sword," said the old man.

"Oh, I get it," Mark said, not getting it at all. *More riddles*, he thought.

"Do you feel it within yourself to free the sword? Only if you do will you know if you have the calling as the chosen knight."

"I don't feel anything," Mark said, "except that we should get out of here."

The old man tilted his head and said softly, "In this you are surely right. A guard is coming."

Mark heard the footsteps in the corridor and went bug-eyed. "What are we supposed to do?" Mark asked.

"Hide behind the door and hit him with this!" the old man commanded, throwing something at Mark. Then he sat down at the table.

"A loaf of bread?" Mark asked, unsure that stale dough would make a good weapon. He hid behind the door anyway.

The guard lifted the latch and thrust the door open. "What's this?" he exclaimed when he saw the old man at the table. "What are you doing in here?"

"This is my penance," the old man said. Then he shouted to Mark, "Now!"

Mark sprang from behind the door and hit the guard in the back of the head with the loaf.

The guard said, "Oww!" and turned on Mark.

Mark swallowed hard. Bread wasn't made for knocking the bad guys out.

"That hurt," the guard said as he reached for Mark's neck.

With surprising agility, the old man leaped from the chair and grabbed the guard from behind. The guard struggled, but the old man's strength was greater than Mark or the guard could have imagined. In a moment, the guard collapsed to the floor.

"Help me," the old man said, grabbing the guard under the arms and dragging him away.

Mark was too stunned to take any action. "How did you do that?"

"Help me!" the old man said urgently. "Put him in the secret passageway."

Mark grabbed the guard's feet, and they did just as the old man commanded. Afterward, they returned to the room, where Mark was instructed to push the wall closed.

"But what are we gonna do now?" Mark asked.

"Come!" said the old man. "We shall find your friend."

"But we don't have any weapons or even a plan!" Mark complained as he followed the old man out of the room.

"Now you must have *faith*!" the old man said.

Chapter
Ten

MARK WAS SURPRISED they could walk so freely down the halls and stairwells of the castle. "Where is everybody?" he finally asked.

"In the courtyard for the carnival," the old man answered. "But Sir Cardoc isn't. No doubt he'll be in his throne room making sport of your friend."

"Throne room?" Mark asked. "I thought only kings had throne rooms."

The old man waved a hand. "Sir Cardoc imagines himself a king. Such is the pride of the man—a pride that will work to our purposes, Lord willing."

Mark and the old man reached a doorway, where the old man suddenly stopped. "Take my arm," he said.

Mark did and said, "But what are—"

The old man signaled him to be quiet and listen. From inside the room, they could hear voices. Mark peeked around the corner and felt his heart jump. Sir Cardoc sat in a giant chair, with Sir Owwen standing before him. Nearby stood the widow Mark had seen in the forest, wringing her hands anxiously. She wasn't in the simple peasant's gown she had worn in the forest, but in flowing robes that seemed to move with the breeze, though the air was still.

"I have no sympathy for your king or his causes," Sir Cardoc said, his eyes flashing. "And I would not indulge him to receive the Ring of Uther."

The enchantress—if that's what she was—stepped forward and said, "Enough of this nonsense! This knight had a boy with him whom your incompetent guards have yet to catch!"

"What do I care for a boy?" Sir Cardoc asked.

"You will care when he surprises us with unexpected trouble!" she shouted in return.

Mark was pleased to be the source of her concern. He expected it was the only revenge he would ever have for her deceitfulness.

"Where is the boy?" Sir Cardoc asked Sir Owwen. He leaned forward, and his eyes glared viciously. "Did you make some plan to rendezvous?"

"On my word, I do not know where the boy is," Sir Owwen rightly said. "But you must heed me, sir! Even as a fallen knight, you must do honor! I am on a quest for the king. You are duty-bound to free me!"

"Ha! He's *your* king, not mine," Sir Cardoc spat.

"Then, by the traditions of our land, you are duty-bound to allow me a challenge!" Sir Owwen said.

"Fight you? I would not waste my breath or my time!"

Sir Owwen stepped forward. "Confound it! You dishonor yourself, sir! If you will not fight, you must allow me to champion my cause somehow!"

"Perhaps I might make a suggestion!" the old man suddenly shouted. It startled Mark, and he almost didn't hear him add, "Lead me forward, boy."

Mark wanted only to run and hide. "Are you nuts?" he asked.

"Lead me!" he snapped, clutching Mark's arm so tightly that it hurt.

Sir Owwen, Sir Cardoc, and the enchantress were suitably surprised by the appearance of the old man and Mark as they walked toward the throne.

"I warned you!" the enchantress shrieked.

"Quiet, woman!" Sir Cardoc shouted. "He is here with a blind beggar! What harm is it?"

The old man said loudly, "I suggest that the most brave and gallant Sir Cardoc and Sir Owwen might settle their differences in a show of strength."

The enchantress leaned forward. "This is trickery!" she bellowed.

"I said to hold your tongue!" Sir Cardoc growled at her.

The enchantress retreated a few steps. Mark noticed she looked similar to the woman he had seen in the forest, but much older. He wondered how she made herself look so young.

"By what manner do we have this show of strength?" Sir Cardoc asked the old man.

"With swords of choice," the old man cackled. "Both driven into the great stone in the courtyard. Whoever drives his sword farthest wins."

"Wins what? What is the prize?" Sir Cardoc asked suspiciously.

"Freedom, lord. If Sir Owwen wins, we may go free. If Sir Owwen loses, you may do with all of us as you wish."

"Why should I waste my time?" Sir Cardoc snapped.

The old man bowed slightly. "My lord, I do not expect *you* to waste your time. Perhaps you might appoint a strong representative for yourself—to take your place in the contest."

"What!" Sir Cardoc roared. "Let someone else take *my* place in a contest of strength? By my word, old man, I am tempted to strike you down here and now for your insolence!"

"My deepest apologies," the old man said.

"Good sir, you do me great honor speaking on my behalf," Sir Owwen began, darting a glance back and forth between Mark and the old man. "But wouldn't a joust be preferable?"

He's afraid, Mark thought.

The old man said warmly, "Good knight—and in my heart I know you are a *good* knight—take this opportunity."

"Yes!" Sir Cardoc said, jumping to his feet. "I will win this contest, then spend the remainder of the night deciding in what way I will torture, then dispatch, you."

"But I have no sword," Sir Owwen said.

"Incidentals!" Sir Cardoc shouted.

"Our lord Cardoc has agreed that you may choose a sword," the old man said. "Is that right, my lord?"

Sir Cardoc waved his hand impatiently. "Yes, yes," he said.

The old man smiled and said to Sir Owwen, "Then choose . . . the Sword of Scales."

"The Sword of Scales!" Sir Owwen gasped and made the sign of the cross.

The enchantress moved forward, clearly eager to speak but keeping her hand on her mouth.

"It's in a room downstairs," Mark stated. "I saw it."

Sir Owwen turned to Sir Cardoc angrily. "You! You have been hiding the Sword of Scales all these years?"

Sir Cardoc nodded. "Of course," he answered. "And if it is your choice, then I am relieved of my obligation to kill you. Touch that sword, and forces greater than mine will take your life."

"Unless he is the chosen knight," the old man added.

"Are you?" Sir Cardoc asked Sir Owwen.

Mark looked at Sir Owwen's face and wondered if he thought he was.

Sir Owwen lowered his head sadly.

The old man touched his arm gently. "Have faith, my knight," he said.

Sir Owwen lifted his head and gazed intently into the old man's eyes. In a firm voice he said, "I choose the Sword of Scales."

Chapter Eleven

THE ROOM CONTAINING THE Sword of Scales was exactly as Mark and the old man had left it. Mark listened for any sound from the guard in the hidden passageway. All was silent.

The enchantress eyed Mark cautiously. Mark returned her stare until she looked away. It was a small victory.

They stood beneath the Sword of Scales, its hum and glow warm and comforting.

"I am amused that this will settle our conflict without a contest," Sir Cardoc said. "Perhaps disappointed."

"You are a fool," the enchantress said. "They are using your pride to trick you, to force you into disaster!"

Sir Cardoc angrily swung around, striking the enchantress with the back of his hand. She stumbled, then braced herself against the table. She touched the red mark on her chin lightly and glared at Sir Cardoc. Mark expected her to raise her hand and zap Sir Cardoc with a spell or bolt of lightning or something. Instead, she marched out the room.

"I have no toleration for intrusive women," Sir Cardoc snarled. He turned to Sir Owwen. "If you're going to take the sword, take it!"

Sir Owwen knelt where he was, murmured softly, then made the sign of the cross once more. He stood up and turned to Mark and the old man. Mark wanted to shout for him not to do it, to run—all of them—as quickly as they could. If Sir Owwen touched the sword and died, Mark would take the blame for the rest of his life. He hadn't forgotten that it was his fault they were in the castle at all.

Sir Owwen reached for the sword, then hesitated. "Only in the Lord am I worthy of anything," he said.

Sir Cardoc began to laugh.

Sir Owwen grabbed the blade of the sword with his right hand. He clutched it so hard, blood appeared around the edges and through his fingers. But he didn't flinch or look as if he felt any pain. He merely tugged on the sword. Mark was aware that the hum had grown louder, and, unless he imagined it, the sword grew brighter and brighter. The fasteners unsnapped, and the sword tipped forward, as if offering Sir Owwen its hilt. Sir Owwen accepted the hilt with his left hand and held it up.

The sword was free.

"No!" Sir Cardoc screamed as he pulled his own sword from his belt and thrust at Sir Owwen.

Sir Owwen was prepared and repelled the thrust with a quick swipe of the Sword of Scales.

Mark pulled the old man back and watched as the two men lunged at each other. Mark was not so much afraid as he was awed by the ferocity of the fight. At one point, both men fell upon the table, getting tangled as it shattered into pieces. They instantly leaped to their feet again and thrashed at each other over and over. They were evenly matched in their skill, though Sir Cardoc employed one or two dirty tricks to throw Sir Owwen off balance.

The duel went on and on, unaffected by the appearance of guards who looked fearful and kept their distance.

"They fear lest they attack the chosen knight who rescued the Sword of Scales and be smitten by God," the old man whispered after Mark told him of the guards' arrival.

It seemed as if Sir Cardoc had the better of Sir Owwen as he strode forward, hacking away at the Sword of Scales held defensively before him. But Sir Owwen suddenly swung along with one of Sir Cardoc's strokes, spun quickly, and brought the Sword of Scales hard against Sir Cardoc's side. The blow sent Sir Cardoc headlong to the ground, and Sir Owwen was instantly upon him, the pointed end of the sword pressed against Sir Cardoc's neck.

"I yield!" Sir Cardoc cried. "Of your mercy, sir, I yield!"

"You yield now, but what of it when my back is turned?" Sir Owwen challenged.

"I swear to you, good knight," Sir Cardoc gasped, "that a stronger and braver man I have never known. Spare me my life and I will be your man, as well as all my noble warriors and servants!"

Sir Owwen laughed long and hard.

Mark was startled. He couldn't remember Sir Owwen ever laughing so jovially.

"I give you your life," Sir Owwen said, but he held the sword firm.

"God bless you, sir," Sir Cardoc said.

"But I have no use for you, your warriors, or your servants," Sir Owwen said. He turned to one of the guards and commanded, "Sir, if you wish to see your master alive, go on horseback and seek out Sir Miles of Brandon. It is he who will lay siege to this castle!"

"No!" Sir Cardoc cried out.

"Yes!" Sir Owwen said. "You yield to me, and I yield to him. He shall hold this castle until the king himself may minister justice and repay you for your cruelty and treachery!"

Chapter
Twelve

IT WAS DAWN BY THE TIME Sir Miles secured Sir Cardoc's castle, put Sir Cardoc in his own dungeon, and searched in vain for the enchantress. Sir Miles speculated that she used her powers to hide away. Mark, still skeptical about magic, figured she simply left the castle after Sir Cardoc struck her.

The dew still covered the forest when Mark, Sir Owwen, and the old man left the castle. They walked silently for a mile, then stopped at a fork in the path. The old man then announced that he must go on his own way.

Sir Owwen bowed to the old man and took him by the hand. "God bless you, sage," he said. "I owe you my life for your gallant intervention."

The old man placed his hand gently on Sir Owwen. "I did nothing," he replied. "It is your brave heart that saved you. Farewell."

"How can you leave us?" Mark asked. "You were trapped in the castle so long. I mean, isn't it dangerous for a blind man to wander the woods?"

The old man tilted his head back and laughed a hearty, youthful laugh. As he did, his stooped form seemed to straighten so that he was as tall as Sir Owwen. A dazzling light spun around his garment, turning it into a new robe of white. The age and wrinkles seemed to fall from his face like scales. The filmy, gray eyes became a clear blue.

Mark and Sir Owwen stood like statues, unable to move or react—so brilliant was the display. "What is this sorcery?" Sir Owwen finally asked to no one in particular.

The transformation complete, the man (it would be wrong to call him old now) gestured grandly. "It is not sorcery, but the best kind of wizardry."

"But who—what—are you?" Mark asked.

"Do you not know?" he said with a low chuckle. "Sir Owwen knows."

Mark turned to Sir Owwen, who still stood in wide-eyed amazement. "Who is he?" Mark asked.

"He is Peregrine," Sir Owwen said without blinking, "the king's own prophet and worker of wonders."

"Worker of wonders indeed," Peregrine answered with a smile. "For this is a land of wonder and imagination. I was sent by the king to help you. Now I must take my leave."

"But you were waiting for us in the castle!" Mark said. "How could the king send you to help us? We didn't even know we were going to the castle until the widow tricked us."

"Though you were tricked and chose foolishly, God used your choices for the good of His greater plan!" Peregrine replied.

"But—*how?*" Mark asked.

Peregrine held a hand to his chest and said, "You're asking me to explain to you the mysteries of God! I am a tinkerer, not a priest. It is for Him to know the plan and for us to work it out."

Mark shook his head. He couldn't comprehend it.

"Then, kind Peregrine," Sir Owwen said, "might you know the direction we may take so that the Sword of Scales will find its rightful place in the heart of Slothgrowl and we may release the coveted Ring of Uther?"

Peregrine nodded. "Because of your courage and valor, I have one other message to aid you in your quest. To find Slothgrowl, you must go to the Hall of the Forgotten, where the Gold Book is found. You must break the seal and open the book, then do what it tells you."

"The Hall of the Forgotten?" Mark wondered.

"Farewell, and God speed you in your travels, for you shall not see me again," Peregrine said as he turned away from them. "And remember the signs the king gave you!"

Mark watched him move into the sunlit path—a stooped and ragged old man once again.

Sir Owwen knew the way to the Hall of the Forgotten. "It was once a beautiful chapel," he told Mark. "But our legends tell of a day when a handsome young wizard arrived there to be wed to the most beautiful maiden in the land. On the way to the chapel, the maiden was overcome by brutal marauders who slew her and her entire party of bridesmaids. The wizard was so distraught that he placed a curse on the chapel and the road on which the maiden traveled."

"You have a lot of legends, don't you?" Mark asked wryly.

"In a land like this, anything can happen—and often does. Do you not have wonders in Odyssey?"

Mark smiled. "A few. But nothing like this."

They walked another mile until Sir Owwen stopped and gestured. "Here," he said simply.

Mark looked around but saw no chapel or anything that resembled a building; just forest and an overgrowth of thorny bushes.

"Where?"

Sir Owwen pointed at the thorny bushes. "This way."

"You're kidding," Mark said, touching the tip of a bush that pricked his finger.

"These thorn bushes cover the road to the Hall of the Forgotten," Sir Owwen explained. "They are part of the curse."

"And Peregrine expects us to get through there alive?" Mark asked doubtfully.

"Indeed he does. And indeed we will," Sir Owwen said, pulling the Sword of Scales from its sheath. He began to hack away at the thorn bushes. "Stay behind me."

Mark followed Sir Owwen down the path as he laboriously thrashed at the overgrowth. The bushes seemed alive to Mark. No sooner did Sir Owwen cut them back than they reached out again, like tentative fingers, to touch and prick Mark.

"Ouch!" he cried out again and again.

Sir Owwen's breathing grew harder as he progressed down the path. His cuts and jabs became less convincing. He was getting tired.

"Do you want me to do it for a while?" Mark asked.

Sir Owwen shook his head and replied, "Touch this sword and you will die. And I fear that my knife will be useless against these thorns."

"Then can we stop for a couple of minutes so you can rest?"

Sir Owwen nodded, and they sat down in the clearing they had made. The silence was deafening to Mark, and he soon identified the problem. He didn't hear the normal sounds he would've expected from the woods: tree branches rustling or birds singing.

"The curse," Sir Owwen remarked when Mark asked him about it.

They both closed their eyes, allowing what little sun there was to fall on their faces. But as soon as they did, they felt the sting of the thorn bushes again reaching out, threatening to cover them over. Mark sat up and noticed that the path behind them was completely overrun again.

"Sir Owwen!" Mark cried.

Sir Owwen opened his eyes just as the branch of a bush reached out to scratch his face. He quickly chopped it with the Sword of Scales. "We must continue," he said. Then he sighed and stood up.

Sir Owwen continued to slash at the bushes, slower but steadily. Mark helped as he could by using Sir Owwen's knife to chop at the outstretched branches.

For Mark, it seemed like hours before they caught sight of the Hall of the Forgotten. It looked like an old church, as Sir Owwen had said, and it was crumbled and decayed. The ruins stood like chipped and jagged black teeth in a hideous mouth. Sir Owwen and Mark cleared the bushes and stood on a broken stone path leading to the massive, wooden door that served as entrance.

"The Hall of the Forgotten," Sir Owwen whispered. "A place of great desolation."

"Pretty spooky, too," Mark said.

The stones cracked beneath their feet as they approached the door. Sir Owwen pushed it open and stepped in. Mark held back, momentarily expecting something to jump out at them. When nothing did, he followed closely.

The inside was dark and musty. Cobwebs stretched from pillars to fallen beams, glittering in a shaft of sunlight that shone through a hole in the roof. A small bird flew in, ducked, and flew out again.

The Sword of Scales at the ready, Sir Owwen looked to the left and to the right as they walked the center aisle, between the shattered pews, to the altar. There, on a large, wooden stand, sat a golden book that seemed to sparkle in a light of its own.

"I guess that's the Gold Book," Mark whispered.

"Aye," Sir Owwen whispered back. "It was the book of vows from which the priest would have read the wedding ceremony."

"If it's just a wedding book, how can it tell us what to do next?" Mark asked.

Sir Owwen turned to face Mark. "Have you been here so long and yet you still cannot grasp the mystery of this place? There are times to ask questions and times to accept answers without questions. I do not ask now. I am grateful if this Gold Book can serve us on the king's quest."

As they reached the altar, the sun suddenly disappeared behind a cloud. Mark quickly glanced around, afraid it might be some sort of trap.

"Look!" Sir Owwen said as he pointed at the altar.

The Gold Book's cover turned bright yellow, the seal blazing.

Sir Owwen raised the sword high and brought it down with a hard stroke on the seal. It snapped and fell away. Next, as if moved by an invisible hand, the cover flipped open and fell to the side. Then the pages turned.

A harsh whisper—rather, the sound of hundreds of whispers—filled the room. "Have you brought the Sword of Scales?" they asked.

"I have," Sir Owwen shouted as if to be heard above the eerie sound.

"Touch its tip to the bottom of the Book of Gold!" the whispered voices commanded. They seemed to come from everywhere. They sounded as if they were even inside Mark's head. He scanned the room, sure he would see loudspeakers in the corners. He didn't.

Sir Owwen took the Sword of Scales in both hands and placed the tip on the bottom of the book. The book and sword's tip turned red hot as smoke poured upward from the page. It was as if someone had taken a hot iron and branded the altar. It hissed loudly.

Mark retreated a step, wanting nothing more than to run. Like the voices, the hiss seemed to fill every space of air. He thought his eardrums might burst.

Then, as suddenly as it started, it stopped, leaving an echo as its only remembrance. Sir Owwen and Mark stood still for a moment. *Is there something else?* Mark wondered.

Sir Owwen obviously decided there wasn't and moved forward to the altar. Mark followed. They peered at the page together, its gold edgings now scorched black. Words had been burned into the pages that said:

The large door will lead you to the place you seek.
Looking neither to the left nor the right, keep your
eyes straight ahead or all will be lost.

Mark and Sir Owwen exchanged a curious glance, then turned around to face the sanctuary. They hadn't noticed a large door except the one through which they had entered. Surely it wasn't the one. It led back outside to the thorny path. Or did it? They both thought the same thing, for they moved together back down the aisle without saying a word.

Sir Owwen reached down to the door handle and grabbed it as if he thought it might leap from his grasp. With a jolt, he yanked the door open.

The thorny path, the forest, the day—all semblance of the outside was gone. Instead, they stared into great darkness.

"Look neither to the left nor the right, but keep your eyes straight ahead—no matter what happens," Sir Owwen reminded Mark.

Mark nodded that he understood.

Sir Owwen took Mark's hand, and they stepped through the door.

Chapter
Thirteen

THE PASSAGEWAY WAS pitch black. Mark could only guess how Sir Owwen knew where to walk until he noticed a speck of light that seemed to move just a foot ahead of them. Mark wondered if there were walls to each side and thought about reaching out, but he was afraid of what he might touch—or what might grab him. He didn't dare look. His instructions were clear: look neither to the left nor the right, but keep your eyes straight ahead. He obeyed. It was easy, because the passageway was quiet.

Then the silence turned into a house of horrors. From the left came a terrifying shriek that made Mark's skin crawl. Then, from the right, a soul-shaking yell.

"Keep your eyes straight ahead, lad!" Sir Owwen shouted, lifting the Sword of Scales as if it could protect them.

"I'm trying! I'm trying!" Mark called back.

The screams and yells increased from both sides, as if maniacal ghosts were enticing them to look their way. At first, they only made noises. Then a low voice hollered something at Sir Owwen about a fallen knight named Sir Baudwin whom Sir Owwen had slain unjustly. Sir Owwen trembled and cried out that it wasn't true. Voices from all sides began to shout accusations and abuses at Sir Owwen, most of which Mark didn't understand. But Sir Owwen understood and groaned.

Now they're getting personal, Mark thought.

"Mark! Look over here!" a voice screeched from the right. "It's the door to the Imagination Station! You can get out now!"

Another voice chimed in, "You can finish this adventure and go back to Whit's End! Your parents are waiting for you!"

Mark nearly turned his head, if only to tell the voices to shut up. He resisted the temptation and said over and over to himself, *Keep your eyes straight ahead or you'll be lost.*

"We're moving away!" the voice of his mother said. "You'll never see Odyssey again!"

"Be quiet!" Mark yelled.

His father's voice came to him, low and gentle: "Maybe you'll want to stay in the Imagination Station. Maybe you shouldn't ever return."

"No! You're not my father! Be quiet!" Mark screamed.

"I bid you in the name of our Lord to withdraw!" Sir Owwen growled. "Withdraw!"

The voices faded. Sir Owwen stopped where he was and took a deep breath. Mark rested his head against Sir Owwen's back, his chain mail cold against Mark's forehead. Sir Owwen reached around and patted him with a large hand. "By the grace of God," he said.

"Amen," Mark said.

"There—ahead of us—I spy a gray light," Sir Owwen said. "Come!"

They kept their eyes straight just in case they weren't clear yet. But no other voices rose to taunt or tempt them. The low ceiling forced them to crawl by the time they reached the gray light and what appeared to be the mouth of the cave. Only then did they realize *they* had been in a cave and were now crouched at an opening overlooking a larger one. As Mark glanced at the walls of the large cave, he saw other openings—like railway tunnels drilled into the rock.

"Ah!" Sir Owwen gasped and pointed down at the bottom of the large cave. Mark looked and felt his heart skip a beat. The cave was filled with a vast store of treasure; rubies, diamonds, coins, copper, silver, gems, bracelets, and necklaces all sparkled in the dusty light.

"Wow!" Mark exclaimed and jumped from their perch to a ledge below. He carefully balanced himself on the assorted rocks that led to the cave floor.

"No, lad!" Sir Owwen called in a harsh whisper.

"I just wanna look!" Mark whispered back. And in no time, he found himself thrusting his hands into a chest of gold coins. As he played with the coins, he asked, "How in the world are we going to find that ring you want?"

Sir Owwen followed Mark's path. "We must be careful!" he warned. "Don't you smell it?"

Mark hadn't, and now he took a deep breath. It nearly made him gag. The air was filled with something putrid and smoky. "What—"

Mark's question was cut off by an earsplitting roar. Smoke poured out of a black hole at the rear of the cave.

"Hide!" Sir Owwen said, grabbing Mark's arm. "We're in the den of Slothgrowl!"

Chapter Fourteen

SIR OWWEN PULLED Mark by the arm, and they knelt behind a large mound of jewels. The cave grew hotter and hotter until it felt as if Mark and Sir Owwen were sitting next to a fiery furnace.

Slothgrowl emerged from the hole and slithered into the cave. His eyes flamed red, and plumes of smoke drifted from the flared nostrils of his long snout. His forked tongue writhed and his teeth gnashed as a blinding flash of fire flew from his mouth. His long body and slick, lizardlike skin squirmed atop short legs and feet with sharp talons. Under his chin, a patch of scales reached down like a shield to his front legs. He moved his head to and fro, as if searching the cave, then crouched in the center and sat very still.

"I know you are here," Slothgrowl said in a low, gurgling voice that turned Mark's stomach. "Your every movement is known to me."

Sir Owwen signaled Mark to stay quiet.

Slothgrowl breathed heavily, snorting flames. "You are to be rewarded for venturing this far. Few have accomplished as much."

Mark wanted to cough from the stench and smoke, but he covered his mouth.

"Perhaps I will give you part of this treasure," Slothgrowl said. "Answer me three questions—only three—and you shall have your freedom and as much of this treasure as you can carry. Do you agree?"

Mark and Sir Owwen stayed silent where they were.

Suddenly Slothgrowl swiped at the mound of jewels, causing large gems to fall on top of them. "Do you believe you are hidden from me? With one breath I could burn you to cinders! Come out and face me!"

Mark looked to Sir Owwen, who stood and walked out, his hand held resolutely on the hilt of the Sword of Scales. Mark trailed after him. Facing Slothgrowl was more horrifying than Mark could have imagined, and he felt his knees go weak at the sight of the monster.

"Much better," Slothgrowl said. "Now answer me three questions and you will have freedom and wealth."

"We have not come all this way for freedom or wealth, but to return the Ring of Uther to its rightful owner," Sir Owwen said boldly.

Slothgrowl laughed—short snorts full of flame and smoke. "The Ring of Uther, is it? You are wiser to answer my questions and run for your lives than to attempt to capture that ring."

"Say what you will—" Sir Owwen began, but Mark interrupted him.

"What are the questions?" Mark asked. Sir Owwen turned to Mark with surprise. Mark said softly, "Let's stall for time. Maybe we'll figure out where the ring is."

"The boy wants the questions. Do you concur, knight?"

Sir Owwen nodded.

"The first question," Slothgrowl announced, "is simple. By what authority do you come to me?"

Sir Owwen stood tall. "By the authority of the king to reclaim that which is his!" he proclaimed.

Slothgrowl gurgled in what Mark thought was a chuckle. "Very good. For you are a knight of the king and have the right to invoke his name." His forked tongue darted out and back again. "Boy, my next question is for you."

Mark swallowed hard and forced out, "Me?"

Slothgrowl slurped and growled for a moment. "From the

deepest part of your heart, tell me: What is the name of your home?"

The question threw Mark for a moment. It was a trick of some sort, he knew. Sir Owwen watched him carefully, his fingers curling around the hilt of the Sword of Scales. "Do you mean Odyssey or Washington?" Mark asked.

Slothgrowl spat a short flame and roared, "You do not ask me questions! Tell me, from your heart, the name of your home!"

"From my heart . . ." Mark began, wondering how Slothgrowl knew to ask him a personal question and knowing for sure that it was a trick. His home could be in Odyssey or in Washington. How could Mark answer? And then he realized *it didn't matter* whether his home was in Odyssey or Washington.

"You do not have an answer!" Slothgrowl said happily.

"I have an answer," Mark said. "My home is wherever my parents are."

Slothgrowl scowled and stomped his feet up and down angrily in what Mark perceived to be a tantrum. Smoke poured from his nostrils, and fire escaped from both sides of his mouth. But Slothgrowl couldn't deny the answer. He knew Mark was speaking truthfully from his heart.

Sir Owwen placed a hand on Mark's shoulder. "Well done, lad," he said. "Confounding a dragon is no easy thing."

Then Slothgrowl roared out the third question: "How will you kill me? For if you do not kill me, you will die!"

Sir Owwen answered by drawing the Sword of Scales.

Slothgrowl reared back with an expression of surprise, then stood firm with renewed confidence. "That sword is no good to you unless you know how to use it," he snarled. "Do you know?"

"That's four questions," Mark said glibly.

Slothgrowl blasted them with a burst of flames. Mark and Sir Owwen dove behind a large chest of gold nuggets just in time. When it seemed safe, they sprang to their feet and wove their way deeper into the mountains of treasure.

"You cannot hide from me!" Slothgrowl roared. From the

sounds of his shuffling and the crashes that followed, he was obviously searching for them.

"You can kill him with the Sword of Scales, right?" Mark whispered.

Sir Owwen looked worried. "The fiend is right. I do not possess the knowledge to use the sword properly."

"Can't you just stab him with it?"

"I could try," Sir Owwen said, and before Mark could stop him, he scurried over a mound of statues. Mark stood up and peered over in time to see Sir Owwen leap upon Slothgrowl's back. Slothgrowl instantly began to twist and turn to toss the knight off. Before he could, Sir Owwen raised the sword high and brought it down once—twice—three times into Slothgrowl's back. A green slime spilled out like blood. Slothgrowl threw his head back and lurched so severely that Sir Owwen flew into another stack of treasure.

Mark watched as Slothgrowl stopped and closed his eyes. *He's hurt!* Mark thought.

But the hope was premature. While Mark looked on wide-eyed, the wounds on Slothgrowl's back closed, the green slime stopped flowing, and within a minute it looked as if he'd never been stabbed.

"You dishonor your king," Slothgrowl said. "As the chosen knight, you should know how to use the Sword of Scales. Now you will know only death."

Slothgrowl moved toward a stunned Sir Owwen. He was sure to burn him to a crisp.

"No!" Mark jumped to the top of the statues and began to throw the smaller busts, like rocks, at Slothgrowl's head. Slothgrowl turned to Mark. It gave Sir Owwen enough time to throw himself behind another heap of treasure, but Mark wasn't so fortunate. With lightning speed, Slothgrowl flicked his tail at Mark, knocking him head over heels through the air. He landed with a thump onto the hard floor of the cave. The fall knocked the wind out of him.

"This is a tiresome game," Slothgrowl said.

Mark struggled to sit up and leaned against a tall box, clutching his side, gasping for air. Sir Owwen crept toward him, the sword poised in case Slothgrowl appeared.

"I have failed," Sir Owwen whispered. "God grant me a quick death. The Sword of Scales is useless against the beast."

"But I don't get it," Mark groaned. "There must be a way. What's the point of having a special sword unless it—"

Slothgrowl slithered around the edge of the treasure and stood before them. His eyes burned furiously, and a line of greenish drool slipped from his mouth and slid across the scales on his chest. "I will delight in picking your bones," he said.

Mark closed his eyes, but the image of the scales on Slothgrowl's chest hung like a picture inside his eyelids. The scales. They looked like an invincible chest plate, but . . .

Mark opened his eyes and Sir Owwen stood up, ready to fight the monster to his dying breath.

"The scales!" Mark said. "The sword's name!"

Sir Owwen glanced at Mark, then the sword. His expression reflected his understanding, and he shouted loud and mightily— enough to stop Slothgrowl, who looked at Sir Owwen curiously.

"The last herald of defeat?" Slothgrowl asked.

Sir Owwen threw himself at Slothgrowl, the Sword of Scales held forward. Slothgrowl took in a deep breath. *This is it,* Mark thought. *He'll breathe in, then breathe out enough fire to blast us.*

But Slothgrowl's chest, puffed out as it was, made a perfect target. Sir Owwen thrust the sword into the scales, driving so hard that it sunk to the hilt. Unlike the wounds to his back, Slothgrowl felt this, spewing a great flame into the sky and crying so terribly that the ground shook.

Sir Owwen withdrew the sword, then thrust it in again. Slothgrowl reared back onto his hind legs while his front legs tried desperately to claw at the sword. They were too short to reach the fatal instrument. Slothgrowl twisted onto his side and fell over, gasping and wheezing. His head turned upward, and he spat a small flame, then exhaled as his eyes rolled up into their sockets. He was dead.

Sir Owwen collapsed where he was and, on his knees, thanked God loudly for the victory. Mark whispered his own thanks and stood up.

"Now all we have to do is look for the Ring of Uther," Mark said, wondering how they would find it with the glittering treasure all around them.

"It is possible," Sir Owwen suggested, "that the Sword of Scales will assist us." He climbed to his feet, walked over to the slain dragon, and pulled the sword out. An awful smell escaped from the gaping wound and filled the air. Then the dragon began to tremble and shake. The cave echoed with a loud hiss and crackle, like the sound of an egg hitting a hot frying pan. Still trembling and shaking, the dragon's body turned bright red as if burning from internal heat. Then the bloated skin puckered and shriveled, collapsing inward as it turned black. *Pop!* And in a puff of black and green smoke, the dragon was reduced to ashes.

Mark and Sir Owwen approached the ashes warily and looked down. It was as if someone had dropped the contents of a fireplace onto the ground—such was the lasting glory of Slothgrowl's life.

The light caught a glint in the dark remains. Mark thought it was his imagination and nearly turned away. But it sparkled again, and he knelt down to see what it was. "Sir Owwen?"

Sir Owwen also knelt and, afraid to touch the smoldering ashes, poked at them with the Sword of Scales. He found the source of the sparkle and pushed the tip of the sword through the small loop. It was a ring.

"God be praised!" Sir Owwen said with a laugh as he held the sword up. "Slothgrowl kept it with him!"

Mark took the ring from the sword tip and looked at it. It was unimpressive to Mark's eyes: a simple, gold ring with an emerald mounted on top. He handed it to Sir Owwen, who took it reverently and held it close. A tear formed in the corner of his eye.

"My quest is completed," Sir Owwen said quietly.

It took a while for them to find their way out of Slothgrowl's den. There were so many holes and tunnels, it was difficult to tell which one led outside. Eventually, a fresh breeze in one of the tunnels gave them a clue, and they crawled out, emerging in the middle of the forest next to a moss-covered knoll. Through the trees, Mark could see the Hall of the Forgotten.

Suddenly, the ground began to shake violently beneath them. "What's this?" Sir Owwen muttered.

"Do you get earthquakes in this country?" Mark asked.

They clung first to each other, then stumbled over to a large tree and grabbed hold. Bits of debris fell from the trees, and a loud crashing sound drew their attention to the Hall of the Forgotten. The ground seemed to swallow it whole.

The knoll from which they had emerged also collapsed, leaving no trace that it ever existed as an entrance to Slothgrowl's den.

The rumbling stopped, and shortly afterward, birds began to sing in the trees.

"Perhaps the curse is lifted," Sir Owwen said.

Chapter
Fifteen

IT TOOK A FULL DAY, a night, and part of another day for Mark and Sir Owwen to reach the king's castle. From a distance, it shone like a beacon from atop a large hill. And that was only a hint of its magnificence as Mark and Sir Owwen approached. The walls were made of strange, white stone, and the towers and turrets sparkled as if made from diamonds. Men and women dressed in colorful raiment went about their business, calling cheerful greeting to Sir Owwen by name.

"The castle and surrounding village are called 'Carleone,'" Sir Owwen explained. "It is by far the most pleasant of places to be."

At the castle gate, Sir Owwen stopped and told Mark to hold out his hand. Mark did. Sir Owwen placed the Ring of Uther in his palm. "For you to present to the king," he said.

"No," Mark protested. "It was *your* quest! You should give it to him! Besides, I might drop it or something stupid like that."

"It is for you to present," Sir Owwen insisted.

"Why?" Mark asked.

Sir Owwen said, "The final sign."

Mark looked at him quizzically. "There's a final sign? What is it?"

"From boy to king, from the brave to the strong," Sir Owwen recited.

Mark shook his head. "I'm a boy, but I'm not brave," he said. "All I've done is complain and gripe. In fact, I still don't under-

stand why we went through all the trouble for a ring the king
could've picked up at any jeweler's."

Sir Owwen smiled wearily at Mark. "There are things in this
life that are beyond our understanding, things over which we
have no control. Ours is to do what is right and honorable—to
obey our master."

"I'm not worthy," Mark said, blushing as he looked at the gate
again.

"Come," Sir Owwen said, "we must announce ourselves to the
king."

❈   ❈

Mark thought they would go straight in to the king, and he
hastily sweated through the details of how he should act. *What
should I say when I give him the ring?* he wondered. *Do I bow? Do
I kneel? Do I shake his hand?*

But Mark and Sir Owwen were ushered into the king's private chambers and asked to wait while the king took care of some
"affairs of state." As the minutes ticked into an hour, then
another, Mark didn't care whether he should bow or kneel. He
just wanted to hand over the ring and get something to eat.

Sir Owwen stood by a window that overlooked a vast, green
field. Mark suspected he wanted to be rid of his armor and chain
mail so he could stroll in the sunshine.

"Are you glad to be home?" Mark asked.

Sir Owwen continued to stare out the window. "This is not
my home," he said.

"Then where—"

"Home is where my king sends me," Sir Owwen replied, a
hint of a smile forming at the edges of his lips.

"What if the king sends you somewhere you don't want to
be?" Mark asked.

Sir Owwen turned to Mark. " The king could never send me
where I do not want to go," he said. "If it is his desire for me to
go, then it is my desire as well."

The door leading to the hallway crept open. Mark and Sir Owwen watched it expectantly. Mark leaped to his feet and almost dropped the ring.

It wasn't the king. It was Peregrine.

"Hello, my friends," Peregrine said, his white hair and robes rustling as if moved by a breeze, though the air was still.

"Peregrine!" Mark said happily.

Sir Owwen bowed slightly.

Peregrine crossed the room to them and smiled as he said, "Congratulations for your victory over Slothgrowl! The entire land is talking of it!"

"All glory to God," Sir Owwen said.

Peregrine held up his hand and coughed gently. "The king is most anxious about the ring. You *do* have it?"

"Right here," Mark said, holding up his hand.

"Ah," Peregrine said, eyeing the jewel in Mark's palm. "The king asked me to receive it from you for safekeeping."

"As his highness wishes," Sir Owwen said and nodded to Mark.

Peregrine reached forward to take the ring.

Suddenly, Mark closed the ring into his fist and withdrew it. "No," he said.

Peregrine frowned. "What is this?" he asked.

"I can't give it to you," Mark said.

"Be mindful, lad," Sir Owwen said, looking at Peregrine uneasily.

"But I *can't*," Mark maintained.

"Boy, it is not wise to challenge the king's wizard," Peregrine said.

Sir Owwen stepped toward Mark. "Listen to him, lad," he urged.

Mark took a step back. "I can't," he insisted. "You know I can't. The final sign said, 'From a boy to a king.' That means I'm supposed to give it to him personally, right? Peregrine isn't the king."

"Oh, stop quibbling," Peregrine snapped irritably. "The king said to get the ring from you, so give it to me!"

"I beseech you, lad," Sir Owwen said, "give the wizard the ring. It is as good as if the king were receiving it."

"No," Mark said defiantly. "It isn't. That isn't what the sign said. It doesn't make sense."

Peregrine waved a hand at Sir Owwen. "He's your charge, Sir Owwen. Deal with him!"

Sir Owwen looked helplessly at Peregrine, then warned Mark, "I will forcibly relieve you of the ring if I must."

"But it doesn't make sense!" Mark cried, backing away from them. "It's some kind of trick. Maybe the king is testing us. It doesn't fit the sign, and—"

"Mark, please!" Sir Owwen implored.

Then Mark remembered one other detail and pressed himself—and his fist—against the wall. "In the forest, when we said good-bye to Peregrine . . ." he began.

"What of it?" Peregrine growled.

"Peregrine said he wouldn't see us again! Don't you remember, Sir Owwen? This is a trick!"

Sir Owwen looked at Peregrine.

"The boy is wrong!" Peregrine shouted.

"If he is wrong, then I am wrong as well. I remember those very words," Sir Owwen said, and instantly he had the Sword of Scales unsheathed and pointed at the stranger before them.

"No!" the stranger yelled. "It is a mistake!"

"Can you maintain your countenance in the brilliance of the Sword of Scales?" Sir Owwen challenged.

"You are wrong!" the stranger cried in a voice much higher than before.

Sir Owwen brought the tip of the sword closer to the stranger's face. "Am I?"

The stranger backed away, the appearance of Peregrine shifting and changing with each step. "Stay away!"

"Reveal yourself!" Sir Owwen commanded.

The stranger spun around and raced for the door, his clothes transforming from the white robes of Peregrine to the red robes of someone else. Someone familiar.

"Stop!" Sir Owwen shouted. But the figure ran on. Sir Owwen lifted the Sword of Scales and threw it just as the stranger reached the door. Mark couldn't be sure if Sir Owwen did it on purpose, but the hilt of the sword, rather than the blade, struck the retreating figure on the back of the head. It slammed the body against the wall, and then both fell to the ground in a heap.

Mark and Sir Owwen ran to the crumpled figure. It was the enchantress from Sir Cardoc's castle.

"In the name of all things that are good and decent!" Sir Owwen said as he picked up the sword. "Your days of treachery are ended." He stood above the enchantress, ready to run her through.

Mark was certain he would have if the door hadn't swung open and the king himself walked through.

"Guards!" the king called in a deep, warmly resonant voice. Three men entered in response and waited. "Shackle this witch until I decide what to do with her!"

As one man, the three guards moved to the enchantress and carried her through the door.

"On your lives, do not let her fool you with her trickery!" the king added before they left.

The king put his hands on his hips and smiled at Mark and Sir Owwen. He was at least a head taller than Sir Owwen, with broad shoulders and a powerful build evident under the gray chain mail and white tunic with the emblem of a red dragon emblazoned on the front. His eyes danced with hidden secrets, and his face was perfectly smooth except for a salt-and-pepper-colored goatee. His hair, flowing onto his shoulders, had a similar coloring. A gold crown adorned his head.

"My liege!" Sir Owwen said as he knelt.

Mark knelt, too, not only because Sir Owwen did, but also

because it seemed the only thing anyone could do in front of such a man.

"Arise, Sir Owwen! Arise, young Mark!" the king said.

He knows my name! Mark thought excitedly.

"You have had quite an adventure," the king said. "I commend you for your diligence on my behalf and the wisdom with which you accomplished your quest."

Funny, Mark thought. *He sounds a little like Whit.*

Sir Owwen lowered his head and admitted, "We were not always wise, my lord."

The king clasped his hands behind his back and paced around them thoughtfully. "No, you were not," he said. "But still, all things worked together for the good. You acted according to plan, leading to God's ultimate aim."

"Wait a minute," Mark said. "You mean all this was done for *me*? But that's impossible! How could I be part of the plan when I don't even belong here? I just dropped in because of the Imagination Station."

The king stood directly in front of Mark, their eyes locking. "Even *that* was part of the plan. This kingdom—*all* kingdoms—are under God's subjection."

Mark scratched his head. "But what about the ring?" he asked.

"The ring," the king repeated. "The ring is important to me because it was the ring of my father, Uther. With it, my claim to the throne is complete. May I have it now?"

All of Mark's planning for a formal presentation disappeared as he simply reached out and dropped the ring into the king's hand. The king looked at it pensively.

"It doesn't look so special," Mark said. "I mean, not like my grandfather's watch or something like that."

The king smiled and held the ring up. With his free hand, he grabbed the emerald between his fingers and flipped it to the side on a small, secret hinge. "Do you see the king's seal?" he asked.

Mark looked closer. On the ring itself was the emblem of a

red dragon—identical to the one on the king's tunic. It had been hidden beneath the emerald. "Wow," Mark said.

"In days of old, long before I was born, Peregrine wrote my name on the underside of the emerald, lest my kingship be challenged."

Mark squinted to see. Sure enough, the name was there. It said simply, "Arthur."

"You're *King Arthur*?" Mark gasped.

The king nodded and said with a laugh, "I am." He turned to Sir Owwen and called his name.

Sir Owwen bowed.

"As a reward for your obedience and bravery, I entreat you to join us as a knight of the Round Table!" the king said.

Sir Owwen took the king's hand and kissed it. "If it pleases my lord!" he said.

"Indeed it does!" the king answered. "And you, Mark—"

Mark looked up hopefully into the king's face.

"You played your part well," the king said. "You now have learned a lesson I hope you'll remember in the adventures ahead."

"Adventures ahead?" Mark asked, his mind filling with further quests and encounters with dragons and evil knights and—

The king put his hand on Mark's shoulder. "The adventures that await you—and your parents," he added.

Sir Owwen stood again and said, "You have the heart for it, lad. Whatever awaits you, you have the heart." He put his hand on Mark's other shoulder. Mark felt as if he were being blessed somehow.

Then the room went completely black.

Chapter
Sixteen

"I'M GOING TO HAVE to work on it," Whit said as Mark climbed out of the Imagination Station. "It shouldn't just turn off like that."

Mark stretched his stiff arms and legs. "How long was I in there?" he asked.

"Oh, less than an hour, I think," Whit said as he began to tinker with the control panel on the back of the machine.

Mark looked around the workroom, then at his friend Whit as he fiddled with the knobs and levers. None of it seemed real to him. It was as if his adventure were the real world and this was the make-believe. He said so to Whit.

Whit stopped fiddling and looked at Mark. "This *isn't* the real world, Mark," Whit said. "It's a temporary stage, just like those makeshift stages you see at the theater. We're not meant to stay here—any more than you could have stayed in the Imagination Station. It's what the apostle Paul means when he talks about setting your sights on things that are eternal. 'For the things we can see are only temporary, but the invisible are eternal.'"

Mark pondered this idea silently for a moment.

Whit leaned against the machine and tucked a screwdriver into his pocket. "That's why I thought you needed this adventure. So you could see how all we do and say fits into a much bigger plan—an eternal plan that comes from God. Whether you live here or in Washington, D.C., your job is to do what's right—to play out your part—to the best of your abilities."

Mark nodded. He got that message loud and clear. But could he do it? Could he say good-bye to his friends in Odyssey and return with his family to Washington?

Home is where my parents are.

The words echoed in his head.

You have the heart for it, Sir Owwen had said.

"I think I can do it," Mark affirmed.

"It won't be easy," Whit said. "But the great adventures rarely are."

"I know."

Mark hugged Whit and walked out of the workroom, up the stairs . . . and out of Whit's End.

Book
Three

*Danger
Lies
Ahead*

Chapter One

THREE THINGS HAPPENED the first day of school. Mark Prescott left Odyssey. An inmate escaped from the Connellsville Detention Center. And I met Colin Francis.

Okay, maybe I'd better take things one at a time.

My name's Jack. Jack Davis. I live in a town called Odyssey. Somebody once told me it's called Odyssey because the guys who discovered it said it's a town you "oughta see." It's a pretty nice place to live if you like being able to get from your house to the center of town in 20 minutes—on your bike, that is. Which means it isn't as exciting as a big city, I guess, but I kind of like it here. Anyway, back to the three things that happened on the first day of school.

The first one I saw for myself. Oscar—he's my friend—and I walked to school past Mark Prescott's house. There was a big, green moving van parked out front, and two large, hairy men in gray overalls were loading gigantic boxes. I heard one of the men yell, "That's the last crate," and then he spat on the ground like it put a period at the end of his sentence.

Oscar slowed down and tugged at my sleeve. "Look, Jack. There's Patti," he half-whispered. "What's she doing here?"

I craned my neck to look around Oscar, which isn't easy since he's kind of roly-poly and always seems to be in the way when I try to see things. I'm not saying he's fat. He just has a chunky body, which my mom says goes perfectly with his brown hair and freckles. (Moms say that kind of thing.)

"Where?" I asked, still ducking and dodging around Oscar.

Oscar pointed to the open garage. "There! See?"

I did. Patti Eldridge stood just inside with her head hung down so that I couldn't see most of her face behind the brim of her baseball cap. Her hands were shoved deep in her jeans pockets. She looked like she had just lost her best friend. Well, maybe I should say she looked like she was *about to lose* her best friend. All the kids knew that Patti and Mark Prescott had hung around together all summer after Mark moved to Odyssey. I don't know the whole story about why Mark moved here, but I think his parents were going to get a divorce. Mark moved with his mom to his grandmother's house in Odyssey. He hated it at first but got to be friends with Patti. Then his parents decided to get back together, so Mark and his mom were packing all their things up so they could move back to Washington, D.C., where they'd come from. But like I said, I don't know the whole story about that.

Patti lifted her head to look at Mark. She was crying. Mark kicked at a trash can and said something to her just as his mom and dad came out. His dad said it was time to go. Mark's mom hugged Patti, and his dad put a hand on her shoulder. I guess Patti isn't a huggy kind of girl, because she suddenly jumped on her bike and peddled away like crazy. She nearly knocked Oscar and me over. I could hear her sniffling and sobbing as she went past.

I glanced back at Mark and his parents. Mark had moved down the driveway and looked as if he were going to run after her. But he didn't. Just then he saw us and stopped dead in his tracks. I think he was crying, too. He turned around slowly and got into the backseat of the boxy, white rental car.

"That was sad," Oscar said as we headed on to Odyssey Elementary School.

"Sad?" I said. "Are you kidding? The lucky kid! He gets out of the first day of school!"

✳   ✳

I didn't hear about the second event—the escaped convict—until all of us kids met on the basketball blacktop for assembly. We had to get into lines for classes before we marched into the building. Oscar and I scouted around for the sixth grade line and knew we'd found it when we saw the bully, Joe Devlin, pushing his way to the front of the line.

"Joe's back for another try at sixth grade," I said to Oscar.

"Another chance for him to beat us up like always," Oscar said.

"I wonder how old he'll get before they decide to promote him?" I asked.

"Probably older than the teachers," Oscar answered.

Lucy Cunningham-Schultz stood at the end of the line. She was hanging on to her notebooks and shivering.

"Hey, Lucy," I said. Normally I'm not real friendly with girls, but Lucy is different from the others. She knows how to talk about things that boys like. I think it's because she wants to be a reporter when she grows up.

Lucy twirled around and looked at me through her big owl-like glasses. Her mousy hair was sticking out in different places as if she had combed it with an electric brush. Her teeth chattered as she said, "Hi, Jack. Hi, Oscar."

"Are you cold?" Oscar asked her.

"A little bit. It's chillier than I thought it'd be."

"Ha! This is a heat wave!" I said, even though it really wasn't very warm. It was kind of chilly, in fact, but you have to play things tough so people won't think you're a dweeb.

"You wanna put on my jacket?" Oscar offered. He wasn't very good at playing things tough.

"Thanks," Lucy said as Oscar helped her put it on.

I rolled my eyes. I had a long way to go to teach Oscar the ways of the world.

"I guess you heard about the escaped convict," Lucy said.

"Escaped convict?" Oscar gulped.

"Cool! What escaped convict?" I asked.

"The one who got away from the Connellsville Detention Center last night. Everybody's talking about it. It was on a special news bulletin this morning and everything!" Lucy answered. "I think they said he's armed and dangerous."

"Wow!" I said. I wondered how escaped convicts got armed after being in jail, but I imagined he knocked out one of the guards and stole his gun. Or maybe he had a stash of weapons hidden away by his partner.

Oscar looked nervous as he asked, "He wasn't headed for Odyssey, was he?"

Lucy shrugged. "I don't know," she said. "They didn't say where he was going."

I punched Oscar in the arm. "If they knew which way he was headed, they'd put up a roadblock and catch him! Don't you know anything?"

Oscar said that maybe the convict was sneaking through the woods somewhere. Maybe the woods behind the school!

"Maybe he was watching us even at that minute!" Lucy added.

"Cut it out, Lucy," I said. "You're gonna make Oscar break out in hives."

The bell rang, and we whistled the theme to *Indiana Jones* as we marched into the school.

❦   ❦

The third thing happened after we had a first-day-of-school assembly in the cafeteria and Mrs. Biedermann handed out our schoolbooks before leading us to the classroom. I rounded the corner, headed for the door, and bumped into a skinny, blond-headed kid. Our books went flying.

"Watch where you're going!" the kid yelped.

"Watch where *you're* going!" I said.

We stooped to pick up our books, and the kid frowned at me with watery eyes. I thought maybe I'd hurt him, so I said, "Are you new here? I haven't seen you before."

"Why do you want to know?" the kid asked.

"Just wondering," I answered. "Who are you?"

"Who are *you*?"

"I asked you first," I said. This kid obviously didn't know the rules around our school.

After picking up all the books we'd dropped, we stood up. The kid glanced around like he thought someone might be listening in. "My name's Colin Francis," he said.

"Oh. Well, I'm Jack Davis," I said.

He looked at me like he wasn't sure whether to believe me. "Jack Davis?"

"Yeah."

"So . . . what do you want?" Colin Francis asked.

"Huh?"

He squinted his eyes at me. "What do you want? Why are you telling me your name?"

"How are people gonna know who you are unless you tell them your name?" I asked. I didn't understand this kid at all, and I was getting bugged. "Look, forget it. I was just trying to be friendly."

"Sure you were," he said as if he didn't believe me.

I started to answer but stopped myself. I didn't know what to say. It was the first time I had ever felt like I needed to prove I was trying to be friendly.

I was glad when Mrs. Biedermann told us to take our seats.

❈   ❈

I sat down next to Oscar. "What about that kid?" he asked.

"I'll tell you later," I whispered.

Mrs. Biedermann stood at the blackboard and said the kinds

of things teachers always say on the first day of school. She told us her name and explained that we had to fill out a bunch of forms for her files, that she expected us to do our best this year, and . . . I looked around the classroom and wondered if the guy who designed it made a lot of money. It looked like every classroom in every school in every town in every part of the world—from the flag to the pictures of the presidents to the cutout letters on the bulletin board to the portable coat closet that sat on wheels in the corner to the metal desks and hard chairs.

I must have been daydreaming, because suddenly all the students were opening their books. I looked around, not sure what they were doing.

"Page three in the social studies book," Oscar whispered. Somehow he always knew when I wasn't paying attention.

I pulled my books out of the desk and sighed. Summer was over. I really was back in school. Classroom assignments, math, English, history, science, and homework were all I had to look forward to. Count on it. Nothing interesting was going to happen between now and the end of the year.

I shuffled through my stuff and soon realized I had *two* social studies books. *Weird,* I thought. *How did that happen?* And then I remembered the juggling act I did with Colin and *his* books.

"Excuse me, Mrs. Biedermann," I heard Colin say.

"Yes, Colin?"

"I'd *like* to turn to page three, but *Jack* stole my book," he said.

I couldn't believe my ears.

"Oh?" Mrs. Biedermann asked.

"I didn't *steal* his book," I said.

"Look," Colin said as he pointed, "he has two over there."

"Jack?" Mrs. Biedermann asked in a tone that meant she wanted me to explain.

"Yeah, I have two books . . ." I started to say, but Colin interrupted.

"See? And one of them is mine."

"You *know* it's yours," I said. Well, I guess I shouted. "Our books got mixed up when you bumped into me and we dropped them."

"When *you* bumped into *me*," Colin said.

"I didn't bump into you, *you* bumped into *me*," I said.

"That's enough," Mrs. Biedermann said.

"It was just an excuse to take my book," Colin went on.

"What!" I said.

"Just give him the book and we'll forget the whole thing," Mrs. Biedermann said, walking toward me.

"I didn't steal his book," I said.

Colin yelled, "Yes, you did!"

And then I told him he'd better shut up, and he told me I was just picking on him because he was the new kid at school, and I said he was lying because I didn't *care* that he was the new kid, and he yelled something back at me about being a Neanderthal, and I yelled something back at him about his family at the zoo, and Mrs. Biedermann told us both to sit down and be quiet, and we both yelled something at her . . . and that's when she sent us to the principal's office.

Chapter Two

"THIS IS A BAD START, boys, a bad start," Mr. Felegy, our principal, said as he sat behind his desk and shook his head.

Colin sat in the visitor's seat next to me. I glared at him, hoping Mr. Felegy would pick up the idea that I was bugged because it was *Colin's* fault that we got in trouble. Colin sat with his hands folded in his lap and looked calmly at Mr. Felegy.

Who in the world is this kid? I wondered. *Calls me a thief, gets in trouble on his first day in a new school, and then sits like he's waiting for a bus. It doesn't make sense.*

"I'm especially surprised at *you*, Jack," Mr. Felegy said.

"Me?"

"Is this any way to welcome a new student to our school?"

"But, but, but . . ." I sounded like an outboard motor as my mouth got stuck.

"Listen to me, *both* of you," Mr. Felegy went on. "This is it. Your quota for the year."

I asked him what a quota was.

"Four of 'em make a gallon," Colin said.

"Oh," I said and wondered why Mr. Felegy was bringing up milk at a time like this.

Mr. Felegy rubbed his very high forehead. "A quota means you've used up all of your visits to me," he said. "No more trips to my office for the rest of the year or you'll be in *big* trouble. Got it?"

"Yes, sir," Colin said.

"Yes, sir," I said, too.

Mr. Felegy waved at us like he was shooing flies. "Go back to class," he ordered. *And no more fighting.*

I stood up and walked out of his office. A phone rang, and Mrs. Stewart, the secretary, picked it up as I passed her desk. "Yes, Officer Quinn," she said into the phone, "Mr. Felegy is right here. Hold on." She cupped her hand over the mouthpiece and shouted to Mr. Felegy that Officer Quinn from the police department was on the phone.

Probably about the escaped convict, I figured. I imagined him sneaking around the school building and peeking in at the windows. I wanted to hang around to see if there was any big news, but Mrs. Stewart frowned at me, so I left.

In the hallway, Colin suddenly came up to my side. Just before we passed the big bicycle-safety bulletin board, he said, "Are you mad at me?"

"What do you think?" I answered. "I don't guess you have a lot of friends if this is how you act on your first day in a new school."

Colin nodded. "You're right. I don't have very many friends. It's because my family moves a lot."

"How come you move so much?" I asked.

"I'm not allowed to say," he said.

"Why not?"

"Because it's . . . it's a secret."

"Why is it such a big secret?" I asked, though I didn't think it could be *that* big a secret.

"If I told you, then it wouldn't be a secret," he answered.

"Yeah, sure," I said in my best I-don't-believe-a-word-you're-saying voice, and then I changed the subject. "So what's the idea of saying I stole your book when you knew it was just a mix-up?"

"When you've lived the kind of life I've lived," Colin said, "you become suspicious of everyone."

"You're only in sixth grade! What kind of life could you have lived already?"

"I can't tell you."

"Yeah, yeah, it's a big secret," I said. We were almost to the door of our classroom.

When we stopped to open the door, Colin turned to me and said, "*If* we become friends, I'll tell you *everything*."

"Fat chance," I answered with a laugh. "Why would I wanna be your friend after you got me in trouble?"

"You wanna be my friend because you wanna *know* my secrets," he said.

"Ha!" I said.

But as I sat down at my desk, I thought, *Any kid who acts this weird* must *have something interesting going on.*

⊁   ⊁

The rest of the morning, we did some math and wrote a paper about what we had done that summer. At lunch, Oscar, Lucy, and I sat together in the cafeteria. Like every lunch last year in school, Oscar complained about the bologna sandwich his mom had made for him. She always put tomatoes and lettuce on it, and Oscar hated that stuff. Lucy lectured him about eating vegetables. I zoned out and looked around the room. Colin was still in the food line with his tray.

I guess Lucy saw me looking at Colin, because she said, "He's kind of strange, isn't he?"

"Sort of," I said. "I sure can't figure him out."

Oscar peeled the tomato and lettuce off his sandwich and held them at arm's length like he was holding a dead skunk. "Anybody want these?" he asked.

"No, thank you," Lucy said.

"Huh-uh," I said. Oscar walked over to a nearby trash can and pitched them in.

"He gives me the creeps," Lucy said, still talking about Colin.

I shrugged and said, "He doesn't give me the creeps. He just makes me wonder what he's up to."

Oscar came back from the trash can. "Maybe he's the escaped

convict in disguise," he whispered loud enough for half our table to hear.

"Nah," I said. "When I was in the principal's office—"

"On the *first day of school*," Lucy reminded me.

I ignored her and resumed talking. "The phone rang, and I heard the secretary say it was Officer Quinn of the police department. He wanted to talk with Mr. Felegy about the escaped convict."

Oscar's eyes went wide. "Really? What about him?" he asked.

"Hey, it's classified stuff," I said. "Me and Ed—I mean, Mr. Felegy—gotta keep these things under our vests."

"You mean, under your hat," Lucy corrected me. "The expression is: You keep things either under your hat or close to your vest, but not under your vest."

"Thank you, Miss English Professor," I said.

Oscar looked confused. "But you're not wearing a hat, Jack. Or a vest."

"Never mind," I said, then continued real low, "but you want to be real careful today. I think the escaped convict is headed for Odyssey to get revenge on someone who testified against him at the trial. Maybe someone at this school."

"That's crazy!" Lucy said.

"I've never testified against anyone!" Oscar said as if we thought he had.

Bang!

It came out of nowhere and nearly made all of us fall off our chairs. Colin had dropped a book on the table.

"What's wrong with you?" Lucy yelled at him.

"Yeah! Are you trying to give us heart attacks?" Oscar asked.

Colin smiled at them, then at me. "I think this book is yours," he said.

"Huh?" I picked up the book. Sure enough, it was the science book I had signed out earlier in the morning. "Where'd you get this?"

"Must've picked it up by accident when we dropped our books," he said.

"I wish I'd known! I could have accused you of stealing it. Then I would have had revenge on you for saying I stole *your* book," I said, joking.

Nobody laughed. Lucy and Oscar sat there looking at Colin like he had just landed from another planet.

Colin smiled again, and said, "What makes you so sure I *didn't* steal it from you? Our desks aren't locked. Anybody could steal anything around here. This school's not very security-minded."

I tried to guess if he was serious, but decided he wasn't and chuckled to lighten the mood.

"I have to go to the library before the end of lunch," Lucy said suddenly. She grabbed her tray and left.

"You were talking about me when I walked up, weren't you?" Colin asked.

"No way!" I said. "Why would we wanna talk about you?" I snickered as if that were the dumbest idea in the world.

"You haven't been in jail recently, have you?" Oscar asked kind of quietly.

Colin dropped onto a chair and clanged his lunch tray on the table. "What if I have?" he said. "Do you have a problem with people who've been in jail?"

"No!" Oscar said and stood up. "I was just wondering. I . . . uh . . ."

"Where're you going, Oscar?" I asked.

"I gotta go to the library too," he sputtered. "To . . . uh . . . check out some books and . . . stuff."

And he was gone like somebody had set his pants on fire.

"You really have a way with people, Mr. Charming," I said to Colin.

"Why did you lie to me?" Colin asked as he bit into a piece of cardboard-looking pizza.

"What are you talking about?"

Colin slowly turned and looked at me. "You said you weren't

talking about me before I walked up, and you were. In fact, I'd bet a lot of money that Lucy said she doesn't like me. I probably give her the creeps."

I was surprised. "How did you know she said that?"

"Because I know people like you and Lucy," he said. "Why did you lie to me?"

"Because I didn't wanna hurt your feelings," I answered. "Give me some credit for trying."

"You shouldn't have lied."

"What did you want me to say? 'Yeah, Colin, we were talking about you, and Lucy said you give her the creeps, and Oscar thinks you're the escaped convict in disguise.'" I felt kind of annoyed. "It's your own fault that kids don't like you. I think you set a world's record for becoming the most unpopular kid at school in the least amount of time. It's only lunch on the first day, and I'm the only one who will sit with you. Get a clue, will ya?"

Colin didn't seem fazed by what I had said. He just jabbed a fork into some green beans and put them in his mouth. "If we're going to be friends, you can't ever lie to me again," he said as if he hadn't heard me. "We have to be honest with each other all the time." And before I knew what was happening, Colin got up and walked off with his tray.

I watched him hand it off to the cafeteria lady and go into the hall. I put my chin on my fist and tried to figure out what was going on. *Why he is so strange? Why did he act so rude to everybody, including me, and then turn around and talk about being my friend?* I was really curious about him.

While I was thinking all these thoughts, I flipped open my science book. A piece of paper was tucked inside. Oh, brother, that Vicki White had started writing me love notes again! I looked around to make sure nobody was watching and then carefully opened it.

It said, "Watch your back."

Chapter
Three

THE FIRST DAY OF SCHOOL ended with dark storm clouds filling the sky and Mr. Felegy whispering something to Mrs. Biedermann right before the bell rang. She frowned as he talked. I figured it had something to do with his breath. Finally, he left and she turned to us with a serious expression on her face.

"Now, children, I don't want you to be alarmed . . ." she started, which automatically alarmed half the girls and Oscar.

Mrs. Biedermann started over. "I don't want you to be alarmed, but we've heard from the state police that there's a *slim* chance—and I mean, *very slim*—that the escaped convict from Connellsville is headed for Odyssey."

The room buzzed with electric whispering.

"We suggest that you call your parents to come pick you up. Or, if you can't do that, be sure to walk home in groups of two or more. Stay in open, public areas. And avoid shortcuts through the woods. How many of you want to call your parents?"

Hands went up all around the room, including Lucy's. Colin was reading a book and didn't look up.

"All right. Follow me," Mrs. Biedermann said as the final bell rang. She took the kids who had raised their hands out of the room and into the hall.

"Don't you wanna call your parents?" Oscar asked as he came up to my desk.

"Nah," I said, shaking my head. "What for?"

"Because the convict might show up!"

"Let him!" I said, grabbing my books and heading for the door. I glanced back at Colin. He didn't move. He was still reading his book.

Oscar caught up to me just before I got outside. "Aren't you afraid?"

"Why should I be? It's just one convict against the two of us. And I took karate."

"So did *I*. We took *one* class at Kim Lee Weinberg's because it was free!" Oscar griped. "Look, let's go back and call my parents."

"We'll be home by the time they get here!" I said.

"But—"

We heard a roll of thunder. I looked up at the charcoal sky as kids poured out of the building and onto the playground. I started walking.

"Jack," Oscar said, following me.

"I wanna go to Whit's End before it rains." I nearly shouted so he could hear me over another roll of thunder.

Oscar grumbled, "All right. But if we run into that convict, I'm gonna have second thoughts about our friendship."

We cut down a couple of side streets, through some backyards, and over a fence that led to an alleyway that would take us to McAlister Park. That was the park in the center of town. Whit's End was on the edge of it. The sky got thick with more clouds, and everything got darker. No sign of the convict, though.

I angled off to a smaller alley between Beatie's Hair Salon and Willard's Liquor Store. It was the kind of alley that doglegged a couple of times before it opened onto the main street through town. It was always kind of dark, but today, because of the storm, it was darker than usual.

"I don't think we should've come this way," Oscar said.

"You're right," I said.

"I am?" Oscar asked, surprised.

"Yeah. These trash cans smell like booze." And they did. The alley was littered with a couple of large Dumpsters filled to the brim, and there were boxes piled up against the walls of the liquor store. "What a mess! Somebody ought to report this place."

"Maybe we'd better go back," Oscar said.

"Why are you so scared? You think the escaped convict is gonna hang out in a downtown alley where somebody can see him?"

I had just said those words when a stack of boxes fell over right in front of us. Inside the thick cardboard, bottles broke as the boxes hit the ground.

I nearly jumped out of my skin. Oscar shrieked.

"Who's there? Who is it?" he kept saying over and over as he backed away.

A bottle crashed against the wall just behind him, and he leaped forward.

Another bottle shattered on the ground to my right.

I spun around, trying to see where the bottles were coming from. I heard one whiz past my head and break on Beatie's wall.

"Whoa!" Oscar cried out as he dodged another bottle that crashed at his feet.

"Let's get outta here!" I yelled, scrambling toward the end of the alley.

That's when Joe Devlin stepped out from behind a large Dumpster. He had a bottle in his hand, and he laughed in that special way bullies learn in How-to-Be-a-Bully School.

"What a couple of babies!" he said.

"Joe!" Oscar said. I couldn't tell if he was annoyed that it was Joe or relieved that it wasn't the convict after all. To be honest, I didn't think there was much difference between the two.

"You shoulda seen your faces," he sneered. "I thought you guys were gonna have an accident."

"Okay, Joe, real funny," I said. "You had a big laugh. Ha, ha." Then I waved at Oscar and said, "Let's go."

"Wait a minute." Joe stepped in front of me. "Where do you think you're going? You can't go down this alley without paying the bottle-breaking toll."

"We didn't break any bottles!" Oscar said.

"That's why you have to pay a toll. Now cough up some money or face the consequences!" Joe said with a raised fist wrapped around the neck of a bottle.

"But I don't have any money!" Oscar said.

"Yeah," I added. "You gotta get your timing right. We get our lunch money in the *morning*. Trying to get us after school is a bad idea."

"You're telling me you don't have any money?"

I had three dollars in my pocket, but I wasn't going to admit it. "Bad timing, Joe," I said, hoping it wouldn't count as a lie.

Joe pushed me with his free hand. "Then I guess I'm gonna have to beat one of you up instead," he said.

I tried to figure the odds that I could win in a fight against him. They weren't very good.

"Better watch it, Joe," Oscar said. "Jack knows karate."

"Thanks, Oscar," I mumbled. What a pal! I then tried to figure the odds that I could win in a fight against Joe *and* kill Oscar after it was over. They still weren't very good.

Joe looked interested. "Karate, huh? Then maybe you can show me a few moves while I knock you around."

He tossed the bottle aside; it thudded against a box. Raising his fists, he moved forward. I put down my books and took the karate stance Kim Lee Weinberg had taught me during my free lesson. Joe laughed and swung a fist at me. I dodged it and danced to the side.

"So you're Mr. Fancy Footwork, huh?" Joe threw another punch. I ducked the wrong way, and it grazed my shoulder. "Now we're getting somewhere," he said with a smile.

When I'm really stressed out about something, I sometimes have really crazy thoughts. I did then. I suddenly remembered Mrs. Skelton teaching us in third-grade Sunday-school class that Jesus expected us to turn the other cheek in a fight. I always wondered what Jesus *really* meant by that and if He ever got in a fight when He was my age. Then I wondered what Mrs. Skelton would say if she came down the alley right that minute.

Just then, I thought I heard someone farther down the alley. I stupidly turned my head to see who it was just as Joe threw another punch. His fist hit me on the side of my head—right over my ear. I saw a flash of light—or maybe it was lightning. Either way, it made me lose my balance, and I stumbled into some empty boxes.

Joe was coming in for the kill when suddenly a bottle shattered on the ground between us. At first I figured it came from Joe. But when Joe looked as surprised as I was, I thought maybe Oscar had gotten a shot of bravery and thrown the bottle. But Oscar looked surprised, too. Both of them were looking down the alley. I pulled myself forward on the box where I could see what they saw.

It was Colin. He stood in the middle of the alley with a bottle in each hand, looking like he was about to have a duel at high noon.

"You can leave now," Colin told Joe.

Joe's nostrils flared angrily. "Oh yeah?" he challenged. "The new kid thinks he's tough. I eat new kids like you for lunch."

"And maybe you can pick your teeth with glass splinters!" Colin said as he hurled another bottle at Joe. This time it crashed on a Dumpster to the right of Joe. At that point, I got the feeling that Colin had *aimed* at the Dumpster—meaning he could have hit Joe if he had meant to.

I think Joe got the same feeling. "You wanna fight? Put down those bottles and fight," he dared Colin.

"I don't wanna fight," Colin said. "I want you to leave my friend alone. And if I have to hit you with a bottle to make you listen, I will."

As if to prove his point, Colin picked up another bottle from one of the cases.

I watched Joe. He looked down, obviously trying to decide if there was a bottle close enough to grab, and even if there was, if he could grab it and throw it at Colin before Colin pulverized him with *his* two bottles. He realized he couldn't, and he began slowly backing away. "Okay, new kid," he said. "I'll give you this one. But it's the last one you get for free."

"Thanks for being so understanding," Colin yelled back as Joe turned on his heels and took off.

Colin walked up to me. I was still hunched on the box. He held out his hand. I took it, and he pulled me to my feet. Oscar just stood there looking kind of dumbfounded.

"Thanks, Colin," I said.

"Yeah, thanks," Oscar finally said.

"Where are you going?" Colin asked.

"Whit's End. You wanna come?"

"Whit's End? Is that the soda shop place next to the park?"

"Uh-huh," I answered. We started walking down the alley. "But it's not just a soda shop, it's—"

Colin cut me off. "I know what Whit's End is."

"You do?" Oscar sounded surprised.

"I've been in town for a couple of weeks. I make it a point to know the area as best I can."

"Really? How come?" Oscar asked.

"Because lives depend on it," he said seriously.

Oscar and I exchanged uneasy looks. I considered asking Colin what he meant, but I knew he'd say it was a secret.

The storm hit just as the three of us climbed the stairs to Whit's End.

Chapter
Four

"NEAT PLACE," Colin said offhandedly as we walked into Whit's End.

Now, if you've never been there, you need to know that Whit's End is a soda shop like those in old movies. It has a long counter, bright colors, mirrors, old-fashioned straw holders, and all kinds of ice cream. But there's more to it than that. Whit's End is also a big Victorian house that has all these rooms filled with books and displays and games so that kids can have fun and learn something at the same time. It was created by a man named John Avery Whittaker, who is sometimes called Whit, and is probably the nicest adult I've ever known. He's a big guy with white hair and a white mustache. In fact, I remember in school when we studied a book called *Huckleberry Finn*, I saw a picture of Mark Twain, the man who wrote it. He looked a lot like Mr. Whittaker.

Mr. Whittaker came around the corner and smiled when he saw us. "Hi, Jack, Oscar," he said. He looked at Colin, and his smile got bigger as he held out his hand for a handshake. "Who's this?" he asked.

"I'm Colin," he said as he stuck out his hand to shake Mr. Whittaker's.

"Hello, Colin," Mr. Whittaker said. "It's nice to meet you. Are you new in Odyssey or just visiting?"

"New, I guess," Colin answered.

"Then welcome to town—and to Whit's End. Jack, you should show him around."

"I was going to," I said.

Oscar took off. "I'm gonna go check out the train set," he said as he disappeared up the stairs.

"If you have any questions about the place, just ask," Mr. Whittaker said, then turned to take care of a customer at the ice cream counter.

I waved for Colin to follow me. "Come on," I said. I figured he might want to see the train set, too, so we headed that way. I thought about asking him what the "Watch your back" note was supposed to mean, but he spoke first.

"Mr. Whittaker's a sharp man," Colin said. "Obviously he likes you a lot."

I agreed, then asked what he meant in particular.

"He pretended not to know me," Colin said.

I didn't get it. "What do you mean he *pretended* not to know you? How could he know you when you just met?"

Colin smiled, and it was the first time I noticed that when he smiled the corners of his mouth didn't go up like most people's but went down. "I met him the other day when I came in," he said.

"Really?" I said. "Maybe he didn't remember you." But even as I said it, I knew it wasn't true. Mr. Whittaker remembered *everybody*. "Why would he pretend he didn't know you if he does?"

"Probably he didn't want to hurt your feelings," Colin said.

Now I was *really* confused. "What are you talking about?"

Colin stopped just outside the door leading into the train room and turned to me. I could hear the sounds of the trains— the whistles and the metallic skate of the wheels gliding around the tracks. I could even imagine a wide-eyed Oscar leaning over Number 47, trying to make it go as fast as possible without sending it off the side.

Colin had a sad expression on his face. "One thing I've learned is that nobody is what they seem to be," Colin said.

"Huh?"

"People have a reason for what they do. They either want something or they're up to something. But people never do anything just to do it. You can't take anything or anyone at face value. You can't trust anybody." He stopped and looked around suspiciously, then continued, "Like right now, the only reason you asked me to come to Whit's End with you is because I helped you out in the alley. You wouldn't have asked me if we had just bumped into each other on the street, right?"

"Yeah," I had to admit.

"That's called an 'ulterior motive.' It's the reason behind the action," Colin explained. "I remember reading about an ulterior motive in one of my detective novels."

"What's all this have to do with Mr. Whittaker?" I asked.

"Well, I think Mr. Whittaker pretended not to remember me because he felt embarrassed."

"Embarrassed!" I knew that Colin was wrong. Mr. Whittaker never had a reason to be embarrassed.

He went on, "I think he was embarrassed because of what I overheard him saying to Lucy. About *you*."

"Me! They were talking about me?"

"They were talking about how you get yourself in trouble all the time," Colin answered. "Mr. Whittaker said he worried about you. And then Lucy said that the only reason she's friends with you is she feels sorry for you."

"What!" I nearly shouted.

"I'm not finished," Colin said. "She feels sorry for you and then said that your parents asked her to keep an eye on you."

"What's that mean?"

"It sounded to me like she watches you, then reports back to your parents what you do."

I was flabbergasted. It wasn't possible. Lucy, a *spy* for my parents? "I don't believe it," I said. "You didn't hear right."

Colin shrugged and said, "If that's what you wanna believe, go ahead. But I'd check into it if I were you. Does Lucy ever call you when you're not there?"

"Sometimes."

"Then that's probably when she gives your folks the information," Colin said. "It's all a ploy."

I let it sink in for a minute, then shook my head. "No way. Lucy can't be some kind of spy for my parents. It doesn't work like that."

"I heard what I heard," Colin said casually. "You don't have to believe me. But I told you: If we're going to be friends, I'll be completely honest with you. Just see what happens when you get home."

Chapter
Five

THE RAIN HAD STOPPED by the time we left Whit's End. Everything outside was wet and had a bluish tint to it. It suited my mood. As much as I didn't want to believe what Colin had said, it stayed on my mind.

Colin took off almost immediately, saying a quick good-bye at the edge of McAlister Park. Oscar and I walked on in silence.

What a day! I thought. *We have an escaped convict sneaking around Odyssey, and now I find out that one of my good friends may be a spy for my parents.* It wasn't like my parents really needed a spy. But the truth was, I sometimes got myself into situations that my parents wouldn't like if they knew about them. Nothing really bad; just kid stuff. But somehow they always found out. Until I talked to Colin, I always figured my parents knew because parents seem to know everything. It was as if they had eyes in the backs of their heads or ESP or something like that. But now . . . now it looked as if they knew everything because Lucy was a secret blabbermouth.

"How come you're so quiet?" Oscar asked.

I shrugged. I didn't want to tell him about my conversation with Colin, just in case he was in on the whole thing, too.

"I saw you and Colin talking about something outside the train room. Did he tell you something?"

"Just the usual stuff," I said.

"*What* usual stuff?" Oscar asked. "You only met him this morning. What kind of stuff could be usual?"

"Never mind!" I snapped at him. "Just quit asking so many questions!"

We didn't say anything else until we got to his house, just down the street from mine. Then it was only "See you tomorrow" and he left me.

I felt bad about snapping at him like that but it was getting hard for me to know what to say or do. Colin had me all wound up. Maybe he really was wrong about what he'd heard. Maybe he'd misunderstood. *There must be some way to test it,* I thought. As I walked home, I pondered what kind of test would prove or disprove what Colin said. Then I thought of one: I'd wait to see if my parents would say anything about my being sent to the principal's office that morning. They couldn't know unless someone had told them.

I threw open the front door and yelled, "I'm home!"

If Lucy had told my parents about the principal's office, they didn't let on. The time leading up to dinner was as normal as ever. Mom and Dad fixed dinner, talked about their day at work, and got after my little brother, Donald, for leaving a half-eaten bowl of cereal behind the couch in the family room. They didn't ask me about my first day of school at all. That seemed weird. Maybe they were playing *extra* cool to make it seem more casual later. By the time we sat down to dinner, I was certain their strategy was to catch me off guard while I was eating.

After we said grace, Dad reached for the potatoes and said he'd heard that an escaped convict might be in the Odyssey area.

Mom, who works part-time at a bank, said she'd heard the same thing. "I also heard that the schools want kids to call their parents for rides or walk home in small groups just in case the convict was here. Is that right, Jack?" she asked me.

I had a mouth full of pot roast by that time and nodded. I wondered how she had heard.

"Why didn't you call me?" she asked.

I shrugged and tried to say through the food, "I didn't have to. I walked with Oscar. We were safe."

"Don't talk with your mouth full!" Donald squawked. He was five years old and a strict announcer of the house rules. He didn't keep any of them himself, but he made sure everyone else did.

"You probably should have called me anyway," Mom said.

I swallowed my food and tried to sound as normal as possible. "How'd you find out about the school announcement?" I asked. To add to my casual attitude, I picked up my glass of water and took a drink.

"Lucy called for you and mentioned it," Mom said.

I choked on my water and went into heaving gasps.

"That's what you get for talking with your mouth full!" Donald said as Dad slapped me on the back.

"Good grief, Jack!" Dad said. "Be careful!"

"Lucy called?" I asked when I could breathe again.

"Uh-huh. Right after school. Probably while you were at Whit's End," she answered.

I remembered that Colin said Lucy probably called saying she wanted to talk to me, then reported to my parents. How tricky! I knew it would just be a matter of time until they would bring up school and nab me about being sent to the principal's office. I glanced at my mom, then my dad, as they ate so casually—as if they didn't know. I never would have given them credit for being such good actors. Then I realized that Donald was staring at me. Did *he* know, too?

"What're you looking at?" I demanded.

"You have a piece of potato on your chin," he answered.

"Oh." I wiped it away, then realized I was being less than cool.

Dinner went on in silence. I knew they were going to bring it up. I knew it. Any second now and they would say something. The more I thought about it, the tighter my stomach got. How would they throw me off guard? Would Mom start clearing the dishes and just *happen* to mention it? No. They would have a better scheme than that. It would come from Dad. Sure! He would clear his throat and, in that low-key voice of his, casually ask how my first day of school went and if anything special happened.

Then Dad cleared his throat. *Here it comes*, I thought.

He pressed his napkin to his lips and tossed it onto the table. "Wonderful meal, darling," he said to Mom.

"Thank you," she said.

He pushed his plate away and leaned forward on the table with his elbows. So masterfully done! Straight out of a movie!

"So . . ." he began, and I knew what he'd say next.

Mom started to pick up the plates. *Both* plans in operation!

"Jack, how was your first day in school, apart from the excitement about the escaped convict?" he asked.

Bells went off in my head. They knew! Lucy had told them! Colin was right!

"Jack? What's wrong?" he asked. All I could do was stare at him.

What a game, I thought. *There he is sitting so normally like he does after every meal, asking a question for which he already has the answer. What a trick! How should I answer? Should I pretend they don't know, or should I assume they do? Or would it be better to blow Lucy's cover by announcing that I know they already know because of their arrangement with her? Or maybe I should let the game go on?*

"Jack," Mom called as she reached for my plate. "Didn't you hear your dad?"

"You know how my first day was," I said, deciding to blow everything wide open.

"Do I?" Dad asked. He was so cool.

"Yeah. Come on. You know all about it because of your little 'friend.'"

Mom stopped in her tracks on the way to the kitchen with the stack of plates. I must have shocked her with what I knew. She turned to look at me. "Little friend?" she asked.

I laughed knowingly like detectives do in movies. "Okay, if that's how we're gonna play it," I said, talking a lot faster than I meant to. "I got sent to the principal's office 'cause I got in an argument with a new kid and we mouthed off to the teacher."

"Uh-oh," Donald said.

"But you guys already knew that 'cause you have spies, right? I didn't have to tell you. Why are you guys spying on me?" Only then did I realize that I was jabbering in a voice that had gone higher than normal.

"Spies!" Mom said as she set the plates down on the table. They clattered on the hard surface. She looked at my dad and said, "Do you know what he's talking about?"

"I think his conscience has gotten the better of him," Dad said, then leaned toward me. "I want to hear more about this, but first I think you'd better change your tone, Jack. I don't like it."

"And I don't like being spied on," I grumbled, looking down at my plate that wasn't there anymore.

"What's gotten into you?" Mom asked.

"I don't understand your attitude," Dad said.

"And I don't understand why you don't trust me. You can just tell Lucy to mind her own business because her cover is blown!"

Mom and Dad looked at me like I was a one-eyed monster who'd just stepped out of a spaceship. Dad told me to go to my room until I cooled down.

Okay, I have to confess that time in my room made me realize I played the scene all wrong. I should have waited for them to tell me what they knew before blabbing everything myself. I think I was more nervous than I thought. As it stood, I had no idea whether Colin was right about Lucy's being a spy for my parents. I'd wrecked my own test.

Dad came up later and asked me to tell him the whole story about the principal's office. I did, without saying too much about Colin. I concluded the story with Mr. Felegy letting us off without punishment. Dad said he'd do the same—*this time*. But he warned me not to mouth off to the teacher or Mom and him ever again.

I agreed.

He patted my shoulder and smiled the way he always did

when he had to yell at me. "So, do you want to tell me what the nonsense was about spies? Do we have to get stricter about your reading material?"

I shook my head. "It's okay," I said.

"Your imagination got the better of you again?" he asked.

"I guess so."

"You can come back downstairs now if you want to," Dad said, then left.

I moved over to the window and looked outside. It was dark now, and the rain had started up again. It spat at my window, leaving little drops and ribbonlike trails. Lightning lit up the street like a flash camera taking its picture.

I thought about my parents. I had yelled at them that they didn't trust me. But did I trust *them*? What kind of parents would spy on their own kids? Would my parents really do something like that? I'd known Lucy for a long time. Until I met Colin I never had a reason not to trust her. But he said that nobody is the way they seem, and we can't really trust *anyone*. To think of Lucy as some kind of tattletale didn't seem right. But how could I know for sure? As I looked into the night, I tried to decide whether Colin was right.

Suddenly, my heart started to race. I jerked my head to look left. For just a moment, I thought I saw something move in the shadows outside. Lightning flashed again, and I was sure I saw a figure standing next to the tree in our neighbor's front yard.

I waited and looked harder. Was it a man? No, too small. A boy? No, maybe it was too big. I wasn't sure. Another flicker of lightning came, but whatever I had seen was gone.

My heart was pounding now. In my mind, I replayed what I thought I'd seen. I was sure it was the escaped convict and he was watching my house. Then, a second later, I replayed the same scene in my imagination and was almost positive that it was someone else. Someone smaller and younger. Someone like Colin.

Chapter
Six

"So, Jimmy Barclay told Justin Morgan that he heard from Karen Willard that her dad was listening to the police band radio, and they said there was a disturbance in Henry Hecht's garage late last night, and they thought it was the escaped convict trying to get a car or a change of clothes or something like that!"

Oscar was talking in that high-pitched voice he got when he was excited. It was the next day, the day after I'd seen someone in the yard. Oscar and I were having lunch in the school cafeteria. Up until then, it had been a normal kind of day. Everybody was talking about the escaped convict, and I was keeping an eye on Lucy and Colin. Since I didn't know which one I was supposed to trust, I figured it was best to keep my distance from both of them. I don't think either of them noticed.

"We locked all our doors and windows last night. We're not taking any chances!" Oscar said without any sign that he would ever stop talking.

"What makes you think an escaped convict would want to come near your house?" Colin said. As usual, he showed up just in time to make a sharp comment.

Oscar was flustered. "I didn't say he would *want* to come to my house. I just said that . . . Oh, never mind. I think I'll go to the library."

Oscar got up to leave. He looked at me like I was supposed to say something to stop him, but I didn't see any reason I should. It was obvious that Colin made him nervous, so it was probably best that he leave. Besides, I hadn't finished my piece of cardboard apple pie.

Colin sat down, opened his brown lunch bag, pulled out an apple, and took a big, crunchy bite out of it. "You and Oscar been friends a long time?" he asked.

"Since second grade," I answered.

"I guess that means you think you know him real well."

"He's my friend. I guess I know him pretty well."

"Bet you don't know why he keeps going to the library at lunch."

"Bet I do," I said. "He keeps going to the library to get away from *you*."

Colin smiled. "That's probably what he wants you to think, but there's an another reason."

"Oh yeah? Like what?"

"He goes there to meet Lucy."

"What do you mean?"

"Did I stutter? He goes there to meet Lucy," Colin said again.

"Why would Oscar go to the library to meet Lucy? That doesn't make sense."

Colin took another bite of his apple. "It makes sense if you can figure out what they're up to."

I rolled my eyes and said, "Yeah, right, like they're up to something."

Colin shrugged.

"What would they be up to?" I asked.

"Who knows?" Colin said. "Maybe they're talking about you. Maybe that's one way Lucy finds out what you're up to so she can tell your parents."

"Aw, cut it out!" I said and angrily tossed my fork onto my tray. "What's with you, anyway? What's the big idea of saying things like that and writing me notes that tell me to watch my back?"

"It's good advice. I told you: Nobody does anything at face value. You can't trust *anyone*."

"Yeah, I know." I pushed my tray away and fixed my eyes on a bright yellow poster that told us to listen to our safety patrols at the crosswalks.

"You don't believe me? Let's go to the library."

"I don't want to," I said.

"Come on," Colin said as he shoved what was left of his apple into his lunch bag. "Let's see if they're in there."

I don't know why I finally said I'd go with him. Colin had a knack for poking my curiosity just the right way. We walked to the library on the other end of the building.

As we walked, Colin said quietly, "See, you think because I'm the new kid that I don't know anything about these friends of yours that you've known a long time. But I know a lot more than you think. I watch people. I know what they're up to. Everyone has a motive, and once you figure that out, you know how to protect yourself."

"Protect myself from what?"

Colin frowned and said, "Protect yourself so you won't get hurt."

"Yeah? And who hurt you?" I asked.

Colin pressed his lips together. "I can't tell you. Not now."

"I figured you would say that," I said.

"Jack, things are happening right under your nose, and you're too blind to see them." Colin tugged on my arm to keep me from walking into the library. "You don't want them to see you."

He peeked around the doorway. "Uh-huh," he said, then stepped back so I could look.

Slowly I leaned forward and glanced into the room. Sure enough, Lucy and Oscar were sitting at one of the tables. Lucy had an open book in front of her, while Oscar leaned forward on his elbows and was talking in that wide-eyed way he did when he was telling secrets.

I took a step back. "So what?" I said. "They're friends. Aren't friends allowed to talk?"

Colin smiled again. "Sure. So I guess you don't care that they might be talking about you."

"No, I don't care," I said, caring *a lot*.

"And I guess you don't care that there are things your best friend, Oscar, hasn't told even *you*," Colin said.

"No, I don't care," I said. "Like what?"

"Take a look at *how* he's talking to her," Colin said.

I peeked in again, but the scene looked the same as it did before. "What about it?" I asked.

"Oscar has a crush on Lucy," Colin said.

"What!" I said too loudly, stumbling back to keep from being seen.

Colin grabbed my arm and dragged me down the hall. "You didn't know, did you?" It wasn't a question; it was an accusation.

"You're crazy," I said. "Oscar doesn't care about girls. And even if he did, he wouldn't like *Lucy*."

"That's what *you* think," Colin said.

"Not a chance," I said.

"Suit yourself," Colin said. "But if I were you, I'd keep a sharp lookout for them. Not only is Lucy blabbing everything to your parents, but Oscar is blabbing everything to Lucy because he likes her."

I shook my head. I couldn't believe it.

"And you have to ask yourself one more thing," Colin said.

"Like what?"

"Ask yourself why Oscar, the guy who is supposed to be your best friend, has a crush on Lucy and wouldn't tell you."

Everything took a completely different turn after recess. Somebody had been messing around with the desks. Some of the kids started complaining that things were missing from their school boxes and the insides of their desks. My ruler was gone. Lucy complained that some of her colored pens had been taken.

Even Colin was missing one of his notebooks.

Mrs. Biedermann got very upset and lectured the entire class about respecting other people's property. For a minute, I thought she was going to cry.

Oscar sent me a note that said, "The escaped convict did it."

I thought, *Sure, the man's running for his life, and out of desperation, he risked being caught to stop by our classroom and pick up essential provisions like my ruler, colored pens, and a notebook.*

Just then Katie Dutton cried out that Joe Devlin had her calculator shoved in his desk.

All eyes went to Joe. He had a very guilty, maybe even panicked, look on his face. Mrs. Biedermann went straight over to him. "Joe, let me see what's in your desk," she demanded.

"It's just a lot of junk!" Joe said.

"Joe," Mrs. Biedermann said so softly that I could barely hear her, but her threatening tone couldn't be missed.

"I don't know where all this stuff came from!" Joe yelled as he pushed his chair back from his desk. "I don't know how it got in here!"

Mrs. Biedermann pulled everything out of Joe's desk. All the missing things were there.

Nobody was really surprised. We knew nothing was too low for Joe. At one time or another, just about everybody in the class had been teased, picked on, or robbed of their lunch money by Joe. The only thing that didn't make sense was why he'd be so dumb as to steal things and hide them in his desk. I would have given him credit for being smarter than that.

Mrs. Biedermann told us to start our math homework while she personally escorted Joe to the principal's office. I could hear him protesting all the way down the hall.

Across the room, Colin had a funny smile on his face.

Chapter
Seven

ONCE AGAIN, MRS. BIEDERMANN announced the kids should call home for rides or walk home in groups until the escaped convict was caught. The latest rumor was that he had dressed up like the school janitor and was cleaning toilets in the boy's bathroom.

I walked home from school with Oscar, but I felt weird. I wondered if he really was some kind of spy for Lucy. I wondered if Lucy really was a spy for my parents. I wondered if there was really something going on between Oscar and Lucy. I wondered why Oscar wouldn't tell me if there was. I wondered why Joe Devlin decided to go on a stealing binge. I wondered a lot of things.

I guess Oscar was wondering some things, too, because he finally said, "What's going on with you?"

"What do you mean?" I asked.

"You're acting very strange," he said.

"I'm not the only one," I answered.

Oscar hung his head. "You were hanging around Colin all day. And you've been avoiding me ever since lunch. Lucy noticed it, too."

"I guess you'd know more about Lucy than I would," I said.

"Huh?"

"Nothing."

"So, how come you're avoiding us?" Oscar asked.

"I'm not avoiding you," I grumbled. "I'm walking with you right now, aren't I?"

"Only because I chased you down. Lucy thinks you're acting weird because of Colin. I think so, too. He's doing something to you."

I rolled my eyes. "Yeah? Like what? Hypnotizing me? You guys are just . . . just jealous because I've made a new friend. Besides, why do you need me when you've gotten so chummy?"

"Who's gotten chummy?"

"You and Lucy."

"What're you talking about? Lucy's always been my friend. Yours, too."

"Oh yeah? Just a friend, huh?"

"Yeah. What're you getting at?"

"Nothing." We walked in silence for a minute while I tried to figure out how to ask what I wanted to know. I decided the direct approach wouldn't work, so I'd work up to it another way. I started, "I was just thinking about, you know, maybe two people—a boy and a girl—maybe start out as friends. But after a while, things change, and then those two people—the boy and the girl—start feeling something else, like they do in the movies, and they start meeting in secret places—like the library—so their friends won't find out and tease them or . . . uh . . . you know what I mean."

Oscar looked at me for a long time. I didn't look straight back, but I could see him out of the corner of my eye.

"Wow!" he finally said, barely above a whisper. He had that sound in his voice like you get when you see a great-looking sports car or a large-screen TV.

This is it, I thought. *He's going to tell me he has a crush on Lucy.*

Instead he said, "Jack! Are you telling me you *like* Lucy? Wow!"

"No!" I stopped dead in my tracks and turned to face him. "That's not what I'm telling you!"

"You're not?"

"No! I'm not talking about *me*!"

"Oh. Then *Lucy* has the hots for you?"

"No!"

"Then who has the hots?" He furrowed his brow like he does when he's trying to solve a serious math problem. "I know! Colin has a crush on Lucy."

"Oscar . . ."

"Lucy has a crush on Colin! No, wait a minute. She said she doesn't like Colin. Hold on, let me think about this."

I wondered if a whack on the side of the head might snap him out of it, but I decided I'd better not. "Just forget the whole thing," I said and started walking again. "I'm going home."

"Can I come over?"

"Sure," I said, "but Colin's coming over, too. He said he wants to see my baseball card collection."

Oscar looked away and said, "Oh. Never mind. I . . . I have a ton of homework to do."

Colin showed up at my house about an hour later. He looked the same as he did at school—hair combed the same way, clothes and shoes exactly the same. That surprised me. I guess I thought he'd look different sitting on the edge of my bed, in my house, like some adults do when they change out of their work clothes. I remember the time I saw Mr. Felegy at Finneman's Market wearing nothing but an old jogging suit. It looked so weird seeing him without a white shirt and tie. It was embarrassing in a way.

I showed Colin some of my baseball cards. "This is Don Newcombe. He was with the Dodgers. He won the Cy Young Award in 1956."

"Neat," Colin said.

"Did you know that Cy Young had *511* Major League wins?"

"Maybe that's why they named an award after him," Colin said.

"Take a look at these," I said as I flipped through a few more. "I have Harmon Killebrew and Al Rosen and Mickey Mantle and Roberto Clemente and . . . here's Frank Howard. He was with the Washington Senators."

"Cool," Colin said.

"And this is my favorite because it's really rare," I said proudly as I held up an old, yellowing card my dad had given me. "It belonged to my grandfather. There are only a few left in the world. See? It's Ty Cobb. One of the greatest baseball players ever. Did you know that he was the National League batting champ from 1907 to 1919—except in 1916, when Tris Speaker of Cleveland got it?"

"Can I hold it?" Colin asked.

I handed it to him. "Sure. Just be careful."

Colin looked at the card thoughtfully, then looked up at me. "You didn't believe me, did you?"

"What?"

"You didn't believe me about Oscar and Lucy. Did you ask him? He didn't tell you, did he? I'll bet he dodged the question."

"I . . ." was how I started, but I didn't get any further. Come to think of it, maybe Oscar *did* dodge the question by going through that whole dumb routine of trying to guess who had a crush on whom. Then again, I didn't really come right out and ask him, either. "I don't know what to believe," I said after a while.

Colin shook his head. "You have to trust me on this, Jack. I'm the new kid. I'm an outsider. I've *always* been an outsider no matter where I go, and that lets me see things clearer than you. I've trained myself to watch people and know what they're up to."

"Yeah, I know. That's what you keep saying. And you keep saying you have big secrets, too. So what? I don't understand what the big deal is." I sounded more annoyed than I meant to.

"Okay," Colin said. He stood up, tossed the Ty Cobb card onto my collector's book, and walked over to the window. He looked out just like I had during the storm the night before.

I remembered thinking that I saw someone across the street. Maybe it was the escaped convict. Maybe it was Colin. I thought about asking him if he happened to be in my neighborhood last night, then thought I'd sound crazy if I did.

"We're friends, right?" Colin asked.

The question caught me off guard. I hadn't really thought about it. I guess we had become friends—in a way. So I said yes.

"Then what I'm about to tell you has to be top secret between friends. You can't blab to *anyone*—*ever*. Have you got it?"

"Sure," I said.

Colin spun around to look at me. "It's a matter of life and death! Do you understand?"

His voice sounded so urgent it worried me. I imagined myself accidentally telling someone Colin's big secret and a dozen people suddenly dying.

"Do you understand?" Colin asked again.

"Yeah, I understand," I answered. The kid was *my* age. What kind of life-or-death secret could he have?

"The reason my family travels so much," he said in a low voice, "is that my dad is in a federal witness-protection program. Do you know what that is?"

I nodded with my mouth hanging open. "It's when the government hides people because they're witnesses against big-time crooks," I said.

"My dad was an accountant who didn't know he was working for a company owned by the Mafia. When he realized it, he got all the files and computer disks with all kinds of evidence and went to the police. They put him in a witness-protection program. *That's* why we move around so much."

"Good grief!" I said. "You mean they move you all over the country so the Mafia can't . . ."

"Find us and get revenge," Colin said.

No wonder he's such a weird kid, I thought. Suddenly all the pieces fell into place and the bizarre behavior and strange comments made sense. If I were being hidden by the FBI and chased by the Mafia, I wouldn't act very normal either!

"That's only part of it," Colin said and leaned forward on my bed.

"What?" I asked, unable to contain my curiosity.

"The escaped convict is really a hired gun sent by the Mafia to rub out my dad!"

Chapter
Eight

YOU KNOW THE EXPRESSION about your skin crawling, right? Well, mine did at that moment. It came alive and walked all over my bones. I'm not kidding.

"The escaped convict is out to . . . to kill your dad?" I gulped.

"Yeah."

"Then why don't you guys get out of here? Why don't they move you again?" I was so upset that I was ready to help them get on the bus right then.

"Calm down, will you? You're getting loud," Colin said.

I quieted down. "Sorry."

"They *did* move my dad. *And* my mom," Colin said.

"Then what are *you* doing here?" I asked.

"The FBI doesn't want me to go back to my parents until they're sure it's safe."

"Then where are you living now?"

He frowned deeply, as if thinking about the answer caused him pain. "You promise you won't tell anybody about any of this?" he asked.

I raised my hand like I was making a pledge. "I promise."

"Because of everything that's going on, I have to live with my aunt and uncle," he said.

I didn't say anything because I could tell Colin wasn't finished.

"They're not very nice people," he said, then looked down at his fingers and started picking at a fingernail.

I waited for more.

"They . . . drink a lot," Colin said softly. "And sometimes they get carried away and . . . they hit me."

I fell back on my bed. "Oh, man!" I said.

I didn't know what else to say or do. I'd heard about things like that. I even remembered rumors about Freddy Zonfeld and how he kept showing up at school with mysterious cuts and bruises and, finally, a broken arm. Some government social agency took him away from his parents.

"I hope you believe me this time," Colin said, "'cause I'm going to be really mad if I told you my deepest secrets and you don't believe me."

"I believe you," I said. "But you can't stay with your aunt and uncle if they're hurting you! Can't you contact the FBI and tell them to get you out of there?"

Colin shook his head. "No, I can't contact them. They have to contact me when they're ready."

I sat up again. "We have to do *something*! Can't you report your aunt and uncle to somebody?"

"I'm afraid that if I do *anything*, it'll cause publicity, and the Mafia will figure out who I am and where I am and then use me as a hostage to make my dad come out of hiding!"

"Good grief!" I said again while my mind felt like it was on overload. All this news was more than I could have imagined.

"Jack!" my mom suddenly called from downstairs.

Colin grabbed my arm. "You can't tell anybody," he insisted. "You promised."

"I promised," I said and went out into the hall. I leaned over the banister, hoping my parents hadn't heard anything and wouldn't ask me any tough questions. "Yeah, Mom?"

She looked up at me from the bottom stair. "Your dad and I decided we should eat out tonight. Pizza sound okay?"

"Yeah!"

"Tell your friend he can come with us if he wants to call his parents and ask."

I went back into my bedroom. Colin was looking at my base-ball card collection again. He closed the book and glanced up at me with a question mark in his expression.

"Do you want to have pizza with us?" I asked. "My mom said you can come if you call your aunt and uncle to tell them."

"No, I can't," Colin said. "I'd better go home."

"Aw, come on. Don't you like pizza?"

Colin stood up. "I can't," he said. "I have to go home. Thanks anyway."

"But—"

"*I can't*, Jack!"

I held up my hands in surrender. "All right already," I said and went back to the stairs. I yelled downstairs that Colin couldn't go out to eat with us.

This time my dad came to the bottom of the stairs. "If he's sure . . ."

"He's sure," I said.

"Okay. Then come on downstairs and we'll give him a ride home on our way to dinner."

Colin joined me at the banister. "Thank you, Mr. Davis, but I can walk," he said.

"No, you can't," my dad said firmly. "That escaped convict is still on the loose. We're driving you home."

When my dad talked in that tone of voice, nobody but *nobody* could argue with him. We all piled into the car.

☙   ☙

Colin lived farther from my house than I thought. His house was on Mayfair Street in the McAlister Heights section of town. McAlister Heights was where all the rich people lived in houses that were built at the beginning of the century.

"That's the one," Colin said, pointing to a large house with a big porch that wrapped around three sides and seemed to have windows, towers, and chimneys poking out all over.

As Colin got out, I looked around for anything suspicious like an unmarked car from the FBI. All was quiet. The house was dark.

"Thank you for the ride," Colin said. "Good night."

Everybody said good night back to him. He looked at me for a moment as if to silently remind me that I had promised to keep his secret. I nodded at him.

He was walking across the lawn toward the front door when we rounded a corner and I lost sight of him. I leaned my head against the cool car window and thought about everything Colin had said. It gave me a pain in my chest to think of him going home to a drunk aunt or uncle who might knock him around.

"He seems like a nice boy," Mom said.

I tried to think of a way to keep my promise but somehow tell my parents about Colin's aunt and uncle. But I knew I couldn't. It was a matter of life and death, he said.

Dad turned on the radio. Odyssey's all-news station jabbered on. I could barely hear it because of Donald's handheld computer game. Not that it mattered. We always called it Dad's "boring station."

"Put on some music!" I called out.

"Wait. They're saying something about the escaped convict," Dad said and turned the radio up.

The news announcer was in the middle of a report about the escaped convict's background. I didn't understand much of what he said, but I heard that the convict had a string of petty crimes on his record until he turned to larger crimes. He was a known thief and a bank robber, but was probably best known as . . . a "runner" for the Mafia.

Chapter
Nine

I COULDN'T SLEEP that night. My mind wouldn't be quiet. I kept thinking about Oscar having a crush on Lucy and not telling me. Why wouldn't he tell me? Were we friends or not? Maybe not. Maybe the friends I always thought were my friends weren't really my friends after all. How could I consider Lucy my friend when she felt so sorry for me that she became a spy for my parents? What else was going on that I didn't know about? It was as if things were happening right under my nose and I didn't realize it until Colin came along.

Colin. I'd never known anybody like him. He had a dad in the witness-protection program and had to live with an abusive aunt and uncle. What was I supposed to do about him? It seemed like I should be able to help somehow. My parents would know what to do. Mr. Whittaker would have some good advice. But I promised not to tell anyone. And try as I would, I couldn't find a loophole in my promise.

So I tossed and turned until gray light filled my room and the September morning brought a thick, cottonlike feeling to my whole body.

The big news in school was that the escaped convict had *definitely* been seen near Odenton, a little town between Odyssey and Connellsville. And I don't mean seen by somebody's second cousin who had a husband who heard it from somebody who was told by somebody else. I mean it was on the radio and everything. Mrs. Biedermann tried to put a bright face on the news by saying that at least we knew the escaped convict wasn't *in* Odyssey. But Vicki grumbled that Odenton was only a couple of miles away and the escaped convict could have walked to Odyssey by the time the news got around.

It wasn't a good day at school. I felt weird being around Oscar and Lucy. They must have noticed, because they kept their distance from me. They didn't even try to sit with me and Colin at lunch.

We didn't talk about Colin's parents or his aunt and uncle. I guess we both knew it would be a risky thing to do. There was no telling who might overhear us.

I felt lonely. It was like Colin and his secret had put us on an island far away from everybody else. Who could I talk to? It was just Colin and me. And when he left the lunchroom early to finish some math homework he hadn't done the night before, I just played with my food and waited for recess. But recess was no better. I played dodgeball but didn't enjoy it.

Things went from bad to worse when we got back to class and Vicki complained that somebody had taken money out of her desk. Then Melissa Farmer said someone had taken her grandfather's World War II medal that she had brought in for show-and-tell. Colin said he was missing his calculator, pens, and a five dollar bill he had hidden in one of his books.

Before anyone could say anything, Joe Devlin jumped to his feet and said he didn't steal anything. Mrs. Biedermann told him to sit down. Instead, he dumped out everything in his desk as if he wanted the satisfaction of doing it before Mrs. Biedermann did. His stuff fell all over the floor, but none of the stolen things were there. I don't think anyone was convinced. Joe could have hidden the stolen things somewhere else.

Poor Mrs. Biedermann. She looked very confused. She lectured us again about respecting other people's property, and she appealed to the thief to return everything that was stolen.

Nobody moved. Nobody breathed. Nobody wanted to do anything suspicious. Robyn Jacobs said that maybe the escaped convict had been sneaking in and stealing things at night.

Mrs. Biedermann quickly said that was unlikely. Then she said she would talk to Mr. Felegy about the "rampant thievery" (that's how she put it). Meanwhile, she wanted us to turn to page 24 in our history books.

❄   ❄

The bell rang for school to end, and the normal scramble to get out began. Oscar put on his jacket, grabbed his books, and looked at me nervously.

"I . . . uh . . . can't walk home with you," he said. "My mom's picking me up for a dentist appointment."

"Okay, see ya," I said.

Maybe it was just a coincidence, but Lucy walked out at the same time as Oscar.

Colin was instantly at my elbow. "There they go," he said with a smile.

"Oscar has a dentist appointment," I said in his defense, though I don't know why I felt I had to defend him. Oscar and Lucy probably *were* leaving together. I tried not to care—or to feel left out.

"I can walk partway with you," Colin said. I nodded and we left.

We talked about the thefts and compared theories. I figured it was Joe Devlin and he'd found a better place to hide the loot.

"I don't think it's Joe," Colin said.

I was surprised. "Why not?"

"I've been watching him, and I can't see when he got into the classroom to steal the stuff. I think it's someone else. Probably someone the teacher trusts to be in the room when no one else is around."

"Like who?" I asked.

Colin shrugged. "Why do I have to figure everything out? *You* think of someone for once. Who does the teacher trust?"

I thought about it but couldn't come up with anybody. "Maybe Robyn?" I finally suggested.

"Maybe. But think harder. Who's probably trusted more than anyone else you know?"

I went through a mental list of everybody I knew. Finally a name came to mind . . . and a face . . . and I refused to believe it.

"Not Lucy," I said.

"Why not?"

"Because Lucy is . . . *Lucy!* She wouldn't do something like that!"

"Yeah, right. Just like she'd never spy on you for your parents," Colin said.

"I . . . I can't believe it," I protested. "Lucy's no thief."

Colin looked at me impatiently. "As far as I can tell, she's the only one who gets in and out of the classroom whenever she wants. She let me in to do my homework during lunch. She's the obvious suspect."

"It can't be her!" I shouted at Colin. Okay, maybe I felt a little stressed out by everything that was going on.

"Are you calling me a liar?"

"No! But maybe you're wrong!"

Colin looked offended. "Have I been wrong about anything so far?"

"I don't know," I said. "I don't know if you're wrong about Lucy *or* Oscar. I don't know if you're right, either." Boy, was I confused.

"After everything I told you, you don't believe me?"

I shook my head. "I'm confused, Colin," I said. "I don't know what to believe anymore. Everything is so strange now . . . but I just can't see Lucy stealing from somebody. It doesn't make sense."

"You don't know what to believe. That means you don't believe *me*," Colin said quietly.

I didn't answer back. I wished we weren't having this conversation. Finally I said, "The only thing I believe is that the escaped convict didn't steal the stuff." I was trying to be funny. It didn't work.

"Okay, I know how to make you believe me," he said. "But you have to promise not to say a word to anybody."

"*Another* promise?" I complained. "I don't think I can make any more promises. Your secrets are too hard."

"I won't tell you unless you promise."

You probably wouldn't have promised. You probably wouldn't have been as curious as I was. But there's something inside of me that kind of tingles when it comes to a good secret, and Colin was a kid with good secrets.

"All right. I promise," I said.

Colin nodded. "Okay. Everybody's trying to figure out where the escaped convict is, right?"

"Right."

"*I* know where he's hiding," Colin said.

"What?"

"I saw him in an abandoned shack on Gower's Field. I'm sure that's where he's been hiding the past couple of days."

My mouth moved up and down a couple of times, but the words only came out as "No way. You're . . . you're . . ."

"Wrong?" Colin snapped. "Or maybe I'm lying to you?"

"No . . ."

"I'm telling you, I know where the escaped convict is hiding! I've been keeping an eye on him."

"Why don't you call the police?" I asked.

"I tried, but they wouldn't believe me because they said I'm a little kid."

"Then get your aunt and uncle to call!"

Colin frowned. "They're never sober enough, and they wouldn't believe me even if they weren't drunk. Besides, if I can watch the escaped convict, I can figure his routine and find a way to catch him. Then my dad will be safe."

"Let's go to my house and tell *my* parents," I offered.

Colin shook his head quickly. "No, you can't," he insisted.

"Why not?"

"Because I want you to see him first."

"I don't wanna see him!" I said. "It's dangerous. We have to tell my parents."

"You *can't* tell your parents. You promised."

I closed my eyes and wished I would learn never ever to make more promises for the rest of my life.

"I'll make a deal with you," Colin said. "You come see him, and if he's still there, *then* we'll call the police. Maybe they'll believe you more than they believed me. Meet me in front of Whit's End at 7:00 tonight. Can you get away from home?"

"I'll try," I said.

"In front of Whit's End at 7:00," he said again, then turned away to walk down the street leading toward his home.

"Wait a minute," I called after him. "Why's it so important that I see him before we tell the police?"

Colin spun around to look at me. "Because then you'll know who and what to believe. You'll believe *me*," he said.

Chapter Ten

WHAT WOULD YOU have done if you had been in my shoes?

I walked home and kept repeating over and over to myself that I promised I wouldn't tell Colin's secrets. But the three promises were so big that I was afraid I might explode if I didn't confide in somebody. Who could I talk to? Who could I make swear to keep the secrets I couldn't keep? Maybe when we met at Whit's End I could get Colin to talk to Mr. Whittaker about everything. Mr. Whittaker would know what to do.

I felt nervous and excited at the same time. And that's why I nearly screamed like a girl when Lucy suddenly stepped out from behind a tree in my front yard.

"What took you so long?" she asked.

"I got sidetracked," I said and kept walking to the porch. In my state of mind, I didn't dare talk to her.

"Wait a minute, Jack Davis!" she shouted at me.

I turned around.

"Don't just walk away from me like that. I want to talk to you!" she said.

I bit my tongue and sat down on the bottom step of my front porch. "Yeah?"

Lucy walked up to me. "Yeah! I want to know what's going on here."

"Going on?" I asked, getting sweaty palms.

"I can't figure out what's happening to you." She sat down and looked at me through her big owl-glasses.

"Nothing's happening to me," I said.

"You know that's not true," she said. "You've been acting weird ever since . . ." She stopped as if she needed to muster up the courage to say it, ". . . ever since you started hanging around with that Colin."

That Colin. What a funny phrase.

She went on, "I thought we were friends. But now I don't know. Even Oscar feels like you've abandoned him."

"*He's* the one who went to the dentist today," I said.

"That's not what I mean and you know it," she fired at me. "How come you're avoiding us? Why don't you want to be our friend anymore? Why are you letting Colin ruin everything?"

Suddenly I felt like I was being ganged up on: Colin with his secrets, Lucy with her accusations. It bugged me. "Don't preach to me about being friends, Lucy. And quit talking about Colin like he did something wrong."

"But he *is* doing something wrong, Jack!" Lucy cried out. "He's trying to tear us apart!"

I denied it.

"Did he tell you we had an argument today?" she asked.

I looked at her, surprised. "No. When did you have an argument?"

"When he came back to class during lunch—to do his homework, he said. I was working on the next issue of the school newspaper and told him he couldn't come into the classroom unless he had Mrs. Biedermann's permission. He got mad and said he was coming in anyway. I said I was going to tell Mrs. Biedermann, and he said, 'You really are a little tattletale, aren't you? Jack said you were.' Did you really tell him I was a tattletale, Jack?"

"No way, Lucy. I never said that," I said while my mind buzzed like a hornet's nest. "Maybe you didn't hear him right."

"I heard him right. He didn't stop there. He told me that you said I was a tattletale and a know-it-all and that you wished we had never become friends in the first place. I didn't believe him, Jack. I knew you wouldn't say things like that."

Hearing her talk like that reminded me of all the reasons I thought she was all right, even though she was a girl. I turned red. Obviously, she believed in me as a friend more than I believed in her.

"I don't get it, Jack," Lucy said. "Why would he say such nasty things?"

I didn't know. "What happened next?" I asked.

"I went to tell Mrs. Biedermann that Colin was in the classroom, but she didn't care. She said Colin was a good student and could do his homework if he needed to. I didn't go back to class until after recess. I didn't want to be in there with him. He gives me the creeps." Lucy stopped for a moment, then said, "I don't understand what's going on."

Everything I learned over the past few days with Colin suddenly went to war inside my head. Nothing made sense. Somebody wasn't telling the truth.

"Talk to me, Jack," Lucy said.

"Look, Lucy, you're telling me all this stuff, but Colin tells me other stuff, and none of it lines up."

"Like what?"

"Like . . . like you and Oscar having secret meetings behind my back," I blurted out.

"What?"

"Go ahead and deny it. You two keep sneaking off together. I was even thinking that maybe Oscar has a crush on you, or you have a crush on him, and neither one of you would tell me." I started fidgeting with the edge of my notebook, bending the thick cardboard back and forth.

"You're such an idiot! Nobody has a crush on anybody," Lucy said, then sighed thoughtfully. "But you're right about the meetings. I won't deny that."

"Aha!" I said. Now maybe she'd confess everything: her spying on me for my parents and . . .

Lucy looked me dead in the eyes. "The reason Oscar and I keep having secret meetings is that I'm trying to help Oscar with his reading. He's awful at it. He nearly failed school last year because of it."

"You mean . . . you and he were just reading together? But . . ." I stammered, not sure of what to say next, trying to get it all clear in my brain. "Why didn't he tell me? Why didn't he ask me for help?"

"He was too embarrassed to let anyone know. Even you. And considering the way you've been acting this week, I don't blame him!"

The jab hurt, so I lashed back with "Oh yeah? At least *I'm* not spying on either one of you guys!"

"Spying!"

"Yeah! I guess now you're going to tell me that you haven't been spying on me for my parents!"

Lucy squinted with confusion. "Spying on you? Why would I spy on you?"

"So you can tell my parents what I'm up to!"

Lucy's mouth fell open, and she nearly dropped her girly pink-and-green backpack onto the ground. "What?" she shrieked. "Me? Spy on you for your parents? Where did you get such a stupid idea? Why would I do that? Why would your parents *ask* me to do that? Jack Davis, of all the crazy—"

I tried to interrupt, but there was no stopping Lucy once she got started.

"—lamebrained, ridiculous, insane ideas! Even for you, it's a new low!"

"Lucy . . ." I tried again to get a word in edgewise. My suspicions dissolved in front of my eyes. Saying it out loud and hearing her reaction made me realize how crazy it was. But Lucy wasn't going to let me off so easily.

"How, exactly, did you think I was spying on you? Did you think I was carrying secret cameras and video equipment in my backpack?" For dramatic effect, she unzipped the backpack and started digging inside as if she might actually pull out a camera. Instead, she started yanking out other things for a mock show-and-tell. "Maybe a secret microphone in my pencil case? Or a camera in my schoolbook. How about a tape recorder in my lunch bag . . ."

"Okay, Lucy, you made your point," I said.

"Not so fast, Jack," she said and dug further into the backpack until she suddenly gasped. Her eyes went so wide they nearly knocked her glasses off. Her face went white. She couldn't take her eyes off something inside the bag.

"What's wrong?"

"I . . . I . . . oh, Jack!" she cried out and handed me her backpack.

I took it and looked down. There I saw some loose change, a five dollar bill, a calculator, pens . . . and the World War II medal Melissa Farmer brought to school for show-and-tell.

Lucy's backpack contained all the things that had been stolen from our classmates.

Chapter
Eleven

"I DIDN'T STEAL ANY of this stuff! I swear!" Lucy said. Her voice was shrill with panic.

"Then how did it get in your backpack?" I wondered out loud.

"I don't know! Honest, Jack! My backpack was hanging in the coat closet. When school was over, I shoved my books in it and left."

"Calm down, Lucy. I believe you. Maybe it's some kind of practical joke. Maybe Joe Devlin did it to—"

"But *why*? Why would he do this?"

"Beats me," I said as I took everything out of the backpack.

"What am I going to do? If I give it back, everyone will think I was the thief!"

I shook my head. "This is so weird. *Everything* this week has been weird." A new doubt started niggling at the back of my head, but I didn't want to give it a full chance to turn into a real thought.

"We'd better ask your parents," Lucy said anxiously. "They'll know what to do."

"I guess so," I said, then looked over everything that was in the backpack. It was exactly everything that had been stolen. "Looks like everything's here."

"Oh, Jack, this is awful," Lucy said.

"Don't worry, Lucy. We'll figure something out." I glanced inside the backpack to make sure it was empty. But it wasn't. And the niggling doubt suddenly turned into a full-fledged suspicion. I reached into the knapsack and took out a small, flat, rectangular piece of paper.

"Jack?"

Well, it wasn't a piece of paper. It was a bit thicker than a piece of paper.

"Jack, what is that?"

I shook my head and knew beyond a shadow of doubt that I had gotten it all wrong from the beginning. Everything I knew to be true suddenly wasn't anymore. The full-fledged suspicion was now absolutely proved by what I held in my hand.

"Jack! Talk to me! What is that?"

I held up a small, rectangular card, old and yellowing because it had belonged to my grandfather a long time ago and there were only a few left in the world. "It's a baseball card of Ty Cobb," I said. "It's mine. I didn't even know it was missing."

"Did you take it to school?" she asked, baffled by this new twist and what it might mean.

"No. It was in my bedroom."

"Then how in the world did it get in my backpack?"

I frowned. I had a knot in my stomach. My world seemed to turn sideways for a second, then turn the other way, then turn back again.

"Only Colin can answer that question," I said.

Chapter
Twelve

IT FELT LIKE THE TRUTH had exploded, and all I could do was sort through the remains.

If Colin would go so far as to steal my baseball card and put it in Lucy's backpack, he must have stolen everything else, too. And if he was the thief, that made him a liar. So he wasn't just *wrong* about Lucy and Oscar; he *lied* about what was going on, trying to pit me against them, or them against me for reasons I couldn't imagine. Maybe he also lied about his dad, his aunt and uncle—*everything*.

"You have to tell your parents," Lucy said with finality as she left.

I nodded. All bets were off. All the promises I made were based on Colin's lies. I might have been wrong, but I knew that *not* talking to my parents was a bigger mistake than keeping my promises to Colin.

I marched into the house and told my parents everything.

I was surprised by their reaction, or rather their *lack* of reaction. They both looked at me calmly across the kitchen table.

"What possessed you to think we would have someone spy on you?" my mom finally asked. "Don't you think we trust you more than that?"

I hung my head and shrugged.

Then she added, "I really thought you were smarter than that,

Jack. To believe a total stranger over your own common sense and experience . . . What were you thinking?"

Again I shrugged. I felt terrible. "Everything he said sort of made sense," I said. "The way he explained it and everything I saw, all fit together."

Dad put his hand on my arm. "I understand. It's as if his lies had just enough truth to make them believable. That's how it works sometimes."

"Yeah!" I said as my mind ricocheted back to all the conversations Colin and I had ever had. It was almost as if he were playing a game to see how far he could push the truth. I wondered if he goofed up by putting my Ty Cobb baseball card in with the rest of the stolen junk, or if he did it on purpose to see if somebody would catch him.

Dad stood up and went to the phone. "I think his parents should know about this. What's his number?"

"I don't know," I answered, embarrassed. "We always talked at school. He never told me how to call him. I don't even know his parents' names!"

"Or his aunt and uncle—*if* that part was true," Mom said.

Dad dialed Information and asked for a phone number for the Francis household in McAlister Heights. The operator said there was nothing listed. Dad hung up and grabbed the phone book, looking at the list of six Francises in Odyssey. He paused for a minute. "I don't want to call all of these folks," he said. "Maybe we should drive to the house where we dropped him off the other night. Let's go, Jack."

✄   ✄

"There it is!" I shouted and pointed at the house. Dad pulled over to the curb. The house was dark. We walked up to the front door and pushed the doorbell button. I heard the chimes echo inside. No one came to the door. Dad took a few steps to his right and peeked in the front window.

"The furniture's covered with sheets," Dad said. "Nobody's living here."

"This isn't his house? He told us to drop him off at somebody else's house?" I asked.

"Looks that way," Dad said and turned to go back to the car. "What time did you say you were going to meet him at Whit's End?"

"Seven o'clock."

"Then I guess we should go to Whit's End and hear what Colin has to say for himself."

❧　❧

Mr. Whittaker's normally smiling face was wrinkled into his very-serious-for-important-conversations expression. His bushy eyebrows were bent into a single line. His lips disappeared beneath his thick mustache. But his eyes were bright and moved as if his brain was working overtime because of the story I told.

When I finished, he leaned back into his chair—one of the iron-backed chairs in the soda shop part of Whit's End. He folded his arms and looked at me with concern. "I hope you know now that I would *never* talk about you like that, Jack. And I certainly *didn't* meet Colin until he came in with you. The poor boy obviously has a problem."

Dad agreed, and I tried to imagine what kind of problem a kid would have to make up so many lies.

"It's two minutes past seven," Mr. Whittaker said. "Do you think he'll come?"

I had a feeling he wouldn't. "He probably saw us all here and decided not to come in," I said.

"If I'd given it any thought, we should have hidden and let Jack wait alone. I'm not much of a sleuth," Dad said.

Mr. Whittaker sat forward again. "You were meeting him to go *where*?"

"He was going to take me to see the escaped convict's hideout," I said.

Dad frowned at me. "That's another thing, Jack," he said. "Why would you do something so dangerous? What if he was telling the truth about that? Were you going to leave without telling us? What if something went wrong and the convict caught you?"

"I didn't think about all that stuff," I said, blushing. "I . . . I figured we'd go and sneak a peek and then leave. It doesn't matter now anyway. The whole thing was a lie."

"Was it?" Whit asked. "Are we so sure? What if this was one thing he was telling the truth about?"

"You don't really believe that, do you, Whit?" Dad asked him.

Mr. Whittaker rubbed his mustache thoughtfully. "No way of knowing unless we check. Even if it was a lie, maybe Colin's out there somewhere. He might have created a hideout of some sort to impress Jack. Where was he going to take you?"

"A shack somewhere out at Gower's Field," I answered.

Mr. Whittaker locked up Whit's End, and we left for Gower's Field in our car. I didn't expect to find anything there—not a shack, not the escaped convict, not even Colin.

Boy, was I wrong.

Chapter Thirteen

GOWER'S FIELD WAS ON the north end of town and once belonged to a man named Thaddeus Gower. I once heard somebody say that he was 117 when he died. Now the land belonged to his son Thomas Gower, who looked like he was at least 80 years old. I saw him downtown a couple of times. He never said much to anybody, but he made it clear to the whole town that he didn't mind people on his property as long as they didn't hunt or tear up things.

The field itself stretched out in one direction all the way to the bypass, and then the other direction to Rock Creek. That's a *long* way.

From the backseat, I heard Mr. Whittaker explain to my Dad that Mr. Gower only tended the fields right around his house. He didn't bother with the rest of his land. I guess that explained how an escaped convict could hide there and not be seen—*if* he was there at all.

By the time we parked the car beside the dirt road that ran along the south side of the field, Mr. Whittaker remembered that there really was a shack on Gower's property. "It's a shed of some sort," he said as we got out of the car. "If I remember right, we have to go through the woods. It's in a clearing."

Dad found a flashlight in the glove compartment and brought it with us. The drifting clouds blocked out the moon and the stars. The night was pitch black; the woods were even darker. Dad led the way with the flashlight. We had to walk slowly to keep from stumbling.

I don't know about my dad or Mr. Whittaker, but I decided not to talk just in case the escaped convict really was somewhere in the woods. For all I knew, Colin may have set up some kind of trap for us. I didn't know why I thought he'd do such a thing. Then again, I didn't know why he did any of the things he did.

It was chilly in the woods, and I wished I had brought a jacket. I also remembered that I hadn't eaten any dinner. With that in mind, I was just imagining one of Mom's barbecued chicken legs when I ran into Mr. Whittaker's back. He and Dad had stopped; I didn't realize until it was too late.

"Sorry," I whispered to Mr. Whittaker.

"It's all right," Mr. Whittaker whispered back. "We've reached a fork in the path."

"Well?" Dad asked Mr. Whittaker. "Which way do we go?"

"I think the path to the right leads to Gower's house. We'd better go left."

"How far is it?" I asked.

"Maybe a half mile. I'm not sure," he answered.

Dad trained the flashlight on the path ahead. "Only one way to find out."

We marched on and on.

I went through my mental checklist again. I was cold, hungry, and tired. Definitely tired. Why did Colin have to make things so difficult? Why did Colin have to pick *me* to be his "friend"— or his victim? I wasn't sure anymore which category I fit into. The whole thing was crazy. There I was, stumbling through some dark woods, looking for a liar, an escaped convict, or *both*, and all because I accidentally knocked books out of some wet-eyed kid's hands. How could I have known? What warning system in my brain should have told me to stay *far* away from that kid?

Dad and Mr. Whittaker suddenly stopped again, and the way

they did it told me something was up. I could feel it in the rigid way they stood.

"There it is," Dad said.

"You'd better turn off the flashlight," Mr. Whittaker said.

The flashlight clicked off.

I couldn't see because I was still behind them. I couldn't get around them because of the thick brush on both sides of us. "What's going on?" I asked.

Dad turned sideways so I could see.

Mr. Whittaker was right; there was a clearing up ahead. In the center was a shack. I didn't need the moon or the stars to see it, because there were lights on inside.

"I'm a fool," Mr. Whittaker said. "We never should have done this without calling the police first. I guess I didn't believe anyone would be here."

"Maybe it's just Colin," I said. "Maybe he's trying to play some kind of nasty trick on me."

Dad put his hand on my shoulder. "Maybe he is," he said. "But what if he isn't? What if he told the truth and really saw the escaped convict here?"

We were silent for a minute. I wasn't sure what to do..

"I'm an even bigger fool," Mr. Whittaker said.

"You're not a fool!" I told him.

"Thanks, Jack," he said, "but I have to disagree. I brought us in the long way. If I'd been thinking right, we could've parked along the bypass and walked from there. It's half the distance. Where was my brain?"

"It's all right, Whit," Dad said. "You weren't even sure about the shack until we parked and started walking."

Mr. Whittaker was quiet for a moment, and then he breathed in sharply. "I have an idea," he said. "Holloway's Diner is on that stretch of the bypass. How about if I stay here to keep a lookout while the two of you run there to call the police?"

"Good idea!" Dad said.

❈   ❈

Dad and I skirted the edge of the clearing, keeping our eyes on the shack as we passed it at a distance. I was afraid that whoever was in there might see us. Maybe he had a gun. For all I knew, he was watching us with some special night binoculars that let him see in the dark.

Nobody moved inside. The lights flickered unsteadily like a candle flame or a lantern. *Just the kind of thing an escaped convict would use,* I thought. *Or a kid like Colin who might be playing a prank.*

Dad and I had circled part of the way around the clearing and the shack when he tugged at my shirt. "This way," he whispered.

I'm not sure how we saw the overgrown path. Maybe it was one of those kinds of things adults have radar about. Somehow we made our way into the woods, getting a safe distance from the shack before Dad turned the flashlight on again. The batteries were wearing down, and it cast a weak, yellow light.

Dad hit the side of the flashlight with the palm of his hand. "I knew I should have checked these batteries," he growled, then sighed. "Lord, please give us some light."

My Dad prays a lot. It's important for you to know that. And we pray together as a family, too. It's something my parents think is needed in our house, especially with me as their son, I guess.

Anyway, no sooner did Dad say that than the clouds separated and let the moon shine through. I'll let you figure that one out for yourself.

Dad chuckled, and we walked as quickly as we could down the old path. It was littered with bits of bushes and fallen branches. I did a pretty good job dodging them, but Dad didn't. And it was a sneaky branch that caught his foot and tripped him.

"Dad!" I cried out louder than I meant to.

"Ouch!" Dad said. He rolled over on his back and drew his ankle up. He touched it gently. "Ouch!"

"What's wrong, Dad? What'd you do?"

Dad pulled himself up to a sitting position and tried to put his foot on the ground. I reached down to help him up. By propping him against a nearby tree, I got him to his feet. He carefully took a step forward.

"Ouch!" he snapped. "No, it's no good. I must have twisted it."

"Lean on me," I said. "We'll make it."

"It'll take too long," Dad said.

"But . . ." I got a knot in my stomach.

Dad leaned toward me. "You go on, son. Run to Holloway's and call the police. Can you do that? Can you give them directions?"

"Sure, Dad, but what about you?" I didn't like this plan at all, but I didn't want to worry him by saying so.

"I'll either try to make my way back to Whit or wait here until the police come."

My heart beat fast.

"Jack?"

I swallowed hard.

"You can do it, Jack. You're like a deer in these woods. Go on."

"But what if . . ." I didn't finish my question because it was too full of what-ifs—like what if I get caught by the escaped convict? Or what if the escaped convict finds you waiting here? Or . . .

"What if what?" Dad asked.

"What if the police don't believe me?" I asked.

"Make it clear who you are, that you're my son and that Mr. Whittaker is waiting near the shack. Tell them to call your mother if they don't believe you. She'll piece together enough of what's happened to vouch for you. Now, *go!*" he whispered harshly.

I took off, thinking over and over how he said I was like a deer in these woods. I jumped, ducked, dodged, and plowed through the branches, twigs, stones, and thick leaves. With the rhythm of my running, I kept praying that God would let the light of the moon stay just a short while longer.

When my side started to hurt, I slowed down a little and wondered why I was even running. Apart from helping Dad, there was no reason. Colin lied about everything. He lied about the escaped convict being in the shack. I was sure of it. He put that light in the window to trick me. How could I be such a dupe? But Dad needed me to call the police. I picked up my pace to do it.

When I got within hearing distance of the cars and trucks on the bypass, I realized I could hear something else in the woods—the sound of another person running. I hoped it was just the echo of my own feet hitting the ground.

It wasn't.

With a blinding impact that knocked my breath away, somebody tackled me to the ground.

Chapter
Fourteen

"YOU TOLD! YOU TOLD!" Colin said as he whaled at me with both fists. I was on my back, trying to get some air into my lungs, and was helpless against his punches. Fortunately, he swung wildly and mostly hit my arms and shoulders. One or two punches connected with my cheek and jaw. But he wasn't very strong.

"Get off!" I shouted when I finally had the strength to push him away. "Are you nuts?"

We both got to our feet at the same time and looked at each other.

"You broke your promises! You betrayed me!" he gasped.

"Yeah? And *you've* been doing nothing but telling lies all along," I said breathlessly.

Colin took a deep breath but never took his eyes off me. "Who said I've been lying?" he challenged.

"You lied about Lucy and Oscar! You lied about Lucy spying on me!"

"I'll bet *she* said so, right? What did you think she'd say? You think she'd admit it?"

I shook my head. "I'm not arguing about it. I'm not playing your game anymore, Colin. I saw all the stolen stuff in her backpack."

"Aha!" he cried out. But it didn't ring true somehow. "*She* stole everyone's stuff!"

"No, she didn't, and you know it," I said, my voice getting softer. There was no point in yelling. I started to feel sorry for him.

We stayed frozen in place. "What're you talking about?" he asked.

"You stole it, Colin," I said. "You stole everything."

"How can you say that? I thought you were my friend."

"And I thought *you* were *my* friend. You said friends should never lie to each other, but all you've told me are lies. You even stole my Ty Cobb baseball card and put it in Lucy's backpack. What kind of friend is that?"

His silence told me that his brain was working overtime for an answer. He didn't have one.

"Lucy crossed me up. She didn't like me," he finally said. "She deserved to get the blame for stealing all that junk. I thought Mrs. Biedermann would search everything before we went home. It's too bad she didn't. I would have loved to see the look on Lucy's face when everyone blamed her."

"But . . . *why*, Colin? Why did you tell all those lies and steal and try to make us angry with each other?"

Colin was quiet for a minute. Then: "Like you said, it's a kind of game I like to play to see what people are really made of. You and Lucy and Oscar thought you were such great pals, but all it took was a few words from me and you didn't know what to believe. Some friends you turned out to be!" He laughed, but I knew he was sneering in the darkness.

The light that God had been so nice to give suddenly went out as the moon ducked behind some clouds. I braced myself. I thought Colin might try to jump on me again. He didn't. Instead he nearly blinded me with the beam from a flashlight I didn't know he was carrying. Then, while I was still blinded, he ran off through the woods. For a moment, I watched the light bounce up and down along the trees before it disappeared around the bend. I went on to Holloway's, but I didn't need to call the police. Three officers were eating dinner there.

❈   ❈

Getting back to the shack was a lot easier with the high-powered police flashlights lighting the way. They radioed for backups to come toward the shack from the other direction just in case the escaped convict really was there and tried to run.

I wanted to tell them not to make such a big deal out of it. There was no escaped convict at the shack. I figured my talk with Colin was as close as I would ever get to a confession that he had lied about it all. It was just a game to him, he said.

We approached the shack, and the police officers put their hands on their guns when we saw two men at the door. It was Dad and Mr. Whittaker.

Two of the officers walked in opposite directions around the shack.

"Dad!" I yelled and ran to him. Boy, was I glad that he was okay!

"Hi, Jack. Good job," he said and gave me a hug.

"Officer Marsh," Mr. Whittaker said to a policeman.

"Hi, Whit . . . Mr. Davis."

"How's your ankle?" I asked Dad.

"Better," he said. "I think it was a minor twist. I just needed to give it some time before I tried to walk on it again."

"Guess I'd better have a look inside the shack," Officer Marsh said.

"Don't bother," I said in my best detective-wrapping-up-the-case voice. "I ran into Colin in the woods before I called you. He lied about everything."

"Really?" Officer Marsh asked.

"That's not entirely accurate," Mr. Whittaker said.

I looked at him, and he obviously saw the puzzled look on my face. He reached inside the door and pulled out bright orange overalls. On the back was stamped in black letters "Connellsville Detention Center."

My jaw hit the floor.

"The escaped convict *was* here," Mr. Whittaker said.

Officer Marsh rushed inside the shack.

I sat down on the ground in shock. In my mind, I could see Colin smiling devilishly.

Chapter
Fifteen

DAD CALLED MR. FELEGY. It seems he was the only person in Odyssey who knew that Colin and his parents had different last names. Colin's mom was divorced from Colin's dad and was remarried to a man with the last name of Vanderkam. So even if we had called all the Francises in the phone book, we wouldn't have found Colin.

Dad, Mr. Whittaker, and I followed the police cruiser in our car to the Happy Valley Trailer Park not far from Gower's Field. The Vanderkams lived in a long, white trailer that they had tried to make look more like a home by adding a front porch.

Officer Marsh knocked on the front door. Mr. Vanderkam answered it, looking worried when he saw it was a police officer. He invited us all in. Mrs. Vanderkam stepped out from behind the kitchen counter. She began wringing her hands nervously. I thought they both looked really normal, and I felt guilty for barging in on their evening at home. It seemed so calm and peaceful.

"What's wrong?" Mr. Vanderkam asked. They had been watching the news, and now Mrs. Vanderkam rushed to turn down the volume on the tiny TV.

"It's not so much that anything's wrong," Officer Marsh said. "We just need to ask your son a few questions."

Colin's parents exchanged knowing glances.

"Questions about what?" Mrs. Vanderkam asked, still wringing her hands.

Officer Marsh explained about Colin telling me that he saw the escaped convict in the shack at Gower's Field. But the more Mr. and Mrs. Vanderkam asked questions, the more confused Officer Marsh got. Finally Mr. Whittaker suggested that I tell them everything—the lies at school, the lies about his dad being in the witness-protection program and how he lived with his aunt and uncle, the things Colin had stolen from the other kids, and, finally, the events that led up to our going to the escaped convict's hideout. I felt embarrassed telling them the whole story, and I even left out the part where Colin said his aunt and uncle were drunks who abused him.

But then Mrs. Vanderkam asked, "Did he tell you that his aunt and uncle drank a lot and sometimes beat him?"

I blushed.

"Did he? It's all right to say so," she said.

I nodded.

Mr. Vanderkam sighed and said, "It's the same old story."

"What story?" Mr. Whittaker asked. "Has he done this sort of thing before?"

"Yes," Mrs. Vanderkam said, as her eyes got watery.

Mr. Vanderkam jumped in. "Apparently Colin has this fantasy about being the son of a federal witness. I guess he wants a dad who can be a hero in his life. Y'see, his father was the alcoholic who beat both him and his mother. I know Colin has never really liked me, especially after Ruth and I got married. That's when his stories changed and we became the abusive aunt and uncle. I guess it's his way of escaping all the trouble we've had. See, I've been out of work for a long time. It's been hard on all of us."

"Have you tried to get help for him?" my dad asked.

"We tried to get counseling for him, but we had to stop when we moved to Odyssey. We couldn't afford it anymore."

Mr. Whittaker stroked his mustache. "Seems like we should be able to do something about that," he said. And I knew in an instant that Mr. Whittaker would help Colin.

"I'm sorry, folks," Officer Marsh said to Colin's parents, "but

I need you and your son to come down to the station anyway."

"I'd be happy to oblige, but Colin isn't here," Mr. Vanderkam said. "He took off earlier this evening, and we don't know where he is."

Office Marsh looked offended. "You mean you let your son take off without telling you where he's going?" he asked.

"It's not a matter of *letting* him," Mrs. Vanderkam said. "He sneaks out."

"Why don't you call us?" Officer Marsh asked.

Mrs. Vanderkam chuckled and said, "If I called you every time he took off without asking, you'd be down here at least five times a week."

Officer Marsh nodded. He had kids of his own.

Just then we heard a car door slam. Officer Marsh frowned, and we followed him through the door. He put his hand on his gun as he realized someone was sitting in the backseat of his police car.

Officer Marsh walked carefully up to the cruiser and threw open the rear passenger-side door. The figure in the backseat leaned into the light. It was Colin.

"I just heard on your radio that they caught the escaped convict from Connellsville," Colin said brightly. "I guess the evidence in the shack helped them figure out where he was headed, huh?"

"Boy," Officer Marsh growled, "you have a lot of explaining to do."

Colin smiled at him, then looked out at the rest of us. "Hi!" he said.

No one answered.

Colin looked straight at me with clear eyes and said, "I'm Colin Francis! Who're you?"

A chill ran up and down my spine. A new game had begun.

❈ ❈

Dad, Mr. Whittaker, and I sat at one of the tables at Whit's End. Dad and Mr. Whittaker had coffee. I sipped at my hot chocolate. The nights were cooler now, reminding me that September was awfully close to October, which was awfully close to leaves changing and then wintertime.

"I'm going to be blunt with you, son," Dad began. "Don't you *ever* keep secrets like that from us again. If anyone ever tells you the kinds of things Colin told you, come to us right away. Don't even think twice about it. When I think about his stories of an abusive aunt and uncle and you two sneaking off to look at an escaped convict—" He didn't finish. He just shook his head. "Don't you ever do that again."

I nodded. There was nothing for me to say.

Dad took a drink of his coffee, then added, "It really scares me to think of you spending so much time with such a disturbed boy."

"How was I supposed to know?" I asked.

Dad was quiet for a moment, and then he said, "I guess it's tough at your age to figure out who's your friend and who isn't. Maybe at *any* age."

"One thing you can count on," Mr. Whittaker said. "Anyone who would try to pit you against your other friends probably wouldn't be a good friend to have."

I thought about the things Colin said in the woods. I thought about the way he considered it a victory to show how thin my trust in Oscar and Lucy was. I thought about the way he laughed at me for being so easy to fool. I looked down at my hot chocolate and knew I needed to apologize to both Oscar and Lucy the next day.

Mr. Whittaker touched my arm and spoke as if he had been reading my mind. "Don't feel too bad, Jack," he said. "Colin's a smart kid. Probably *too* smart for his age group. He knew how to sprinkle just enough truth in his lies to fool you."

"He was smart about something else, too," Dad added sadly. "He knew that suspicion breeds suspicion if we let it. Look at the world without any trust in your heart and you'll have to suspect everyone. You always have to watch your back. You can never have friends. You can never love."

"What a life!" Mr. Whittaker said. And once again, I knew by that look in his eyes that he would do what he could to help Colin.

"What a terrible life!" my dad said softly, and then he lowered his head like he was praying. Mr. Whittaker did, too.

I sat there with my dad and Mr. Whittaker in a deserted Whit's End and thought about how the place would be packed tomorrow with kids like me having a great time because Mr. Whittaker cared so much about us. I thought about how my mom and dad would keep on loving me even though they were bugged with me for being so stupid. I also thought about Oscar and Lucy, who really were my friends and would stay my friends even after I stumbled all over myself trying to apologize. And for the first time in my life, I thought about how I *could* trust people and believe in them even though kids like Colin might try to make me think otherwise.

What a life! I thought like a prayer of my own. *What a great life!*

Book
Four

A
Carnival
of Secrets

Chapter One

Dear Patti,

How are you? I am fine. Sorry it's taken me a long time to write but I've been real busy since we moved back to Washington, D.C. I was going to call you but Dad said I'd have to pay for the call and I keep spending the money I mean to save up.

The cherry blossoms came out the other day and Mom says she can't believe it's been over eight months since we moved back here. I think she misses Odyssey.

They are getting along. Mom and Dad I mean. They don't fight as much as they used to, and when they do, they make up fast. They are happy. They get all huggy-kissy a lot more now. I think the counselor is helping them.

Most of my old friends are still here and we do things together just like before I moved to Odyssey. We're having a blast. I even like being back in my old school. My teachers are cool. Mr. Nock (he's my math teacher) said that he thinks he visited Odyssey once when he got lost on his way to a convention somewhere. Mrs. Baker (she's my English teacher) read my "What I Did For Summer" essay and said she wished she could go to Odyssey sometime. I will give her your address in case she does.

How is Mr. Whittaker and Whit's End? I told my friends about it and they didn't believe it's real. Maybe one day we'll rent a bus and I'll take them so they can see for themselves.

Sincerely yours,
Mark Prescott

Patti Eldridge threw herself back onto her bed with a heavy sigh. The bedsprings creaked in protest somewhere under the thick, pink comforter. The curved, wrought-iron headstand bumped against the wall with a thud. Patti stared up at the canopy. "Mark . . ." she groaned.

Patti had written to Mark Prescott almost every week since he had left Odyssey. That was last September. Had he written back in the eight months since? No. And when he finally did, it was *this*—a short note telling her how well he was doing.

A car drove past the front of the house. The morning sun hit the chrome, sending a reflection that moved like a white phantom across Patti's forest-green walls. She frowned. Even the walls reminded her of Mark. He had painted her room while she was in the hospital nursing a concussion and broken arm. He'd painted it forest-green because the two of them loved the story of Robin Hood so much. The car drove away. The phantom reflection chased after it, maybe to haunt other houses along the street.

Patti didn't know which was worse, that Mark had sent such a short note after all this time or that he seemed to be so happy. How could he be happy when she was so miserable? How could he go back to his old life and old friends and leave her stuck in Odyssey by herself? It wasn't fair.

"We're supposed to be best friends," Patti said to her empty room. She remembered how Mark had moved to Odyssey at the beginning of last summer because his parents had separated. He and his mom had to live in his grandmother's house. She muttered, "He didn't have a single friend until I came along. I'm the one who took him to Whit's End and introduced him to Whit and showed him around Odyssey and . . ."

He forgot all about that, Patti was certain. *He moved back to Washington and forgot all about me*, she thought gloomily.

Rolling over onto her stomach, she rested her chin on her crossed arms and pouted. She'd never had a friend as close as Mark; not before he arrived in Odyssey and certainly not since he'd left. *No wonder*, she thought. *Who wants to be friends with a tomboy?* The boys didn't like her because she was a girl, even though she liked being outside, playing sports, racing bikes, and riding her skateboard like them. The girls didn't like her because she was too boyish. She didn't have patience for talking about crushes or dresses or makeup like the rest of the girls she knew.

She buried her face in her arms and sunk deeper into feeling sorry for herself. *I'm not pretty either*, she thought. She felt that her blue eyes were too close together. Her sandy hair, normally tucked under a baseball cap, she saw as straight and stringy. She had freckles all over her nose. She'd just entered into a growth spurt that made her arms and legs go awkward lengths. They were too long for her body, she thought. Nobody wanted to be friends with someone like, she concluded.

She was a misfit.

When Mark came to Odyssey, he was a misfit, too—and that's why they became such good friends.

She clenched the letter into her fist and wondered if a good cry might help. Nobody in the world felt as lonely as she did at that moment. She was sure of it.

"Patti?" her mother called from beyond the bedroom door.

"Yeah, Mom?"

The door opened and Susan Eldridge peered in. "What are you doing?"

"Reading Mark's letter," Patti replied as she sat up on her bed.

Mrs. Eldridge looked at the crumpled letter. "Isn't it hard to read like that?" she asked.

"There wasn't much to read," Patti said, then sighed.

"He didn't have much to say?" Mrs. Eldridge asked and smiled sympathetically.

"No, he says he's happy. Nice of him to let me know," Patti growled.

"Terrible, isn't it?" Mrs. Eldridge said as she sat down on the edge of the bed. She wrapped her hand around one of the canopy posts. "Imagine the nerve of him getting on with his life."

"Don't tease me," Patti said.

Mrs. Eldridge rubbed Patti's leg softly. "I know how you feel. It doesn't seem fair that Mark should go back to Washington and be happy. He should be wasting away, miserable without your friendship."

"Yeah!" Patti exclaimed. "He should be. Why should he get to be happy when *I'm* not happy?"

"Is it really so bad for you?" Mrs. Eldridge asked, concerned.

Patti gazed at her mother and realized she was confessing something she hadn't told *anyone* up until now. "He's the only friend I ever had." The words caught in her throat and she fought back the tears that had threatened to come all morning. Patti's mom reached for her, but she suddenly leaped off the bed and prowled around the room. "I'm not going to cry," she said angrily. "I don't *care* if he's happy. I don't care *what* he does."

Mrs. Eldridge watched her daughter for a moment, then said, "Mark is doing the right thing if he's getting on with his life. You should do the same, Patti."

"How?" Patti challenged.

Mrs. Eldridge thought about it for a moment. "That's a good question. Let's think it over and see what we can come up with."

"I didn't say I wanted to turn it into a homework assignment, Mom," Patti said.

"You'd rather sit around and mope?" Mrs. Eldridge asked.

Patti shrugged. "I can't think of anything better to do."

Mrs. Eldridge smiled and stood up. "I can. Your father and I want to take you somewhere to forget your woes."

"Really?" Patti asked hesitantly. "Like where?"

"The spring carnival."

Chapter Two

THE SPRING CARNIVAL had been a tradition in Odyssey for as long as Patti could remember. It came every year to Brook Meadow—a large expanse of land just off of the bypass to Connellsville—when the kids were on a weeklong spring break. With a large Ferris wheel, salt-and-pepper shakers, a merry-go-round, bumper cars, a hall of mirrors, arcades, galleries, cotton candy, and stuffed-animal prizes, the carnival was a welcome relief to everyone after being shut in all winter. As a young girl, Patti thought that spring wouldn't come to Odyssey unless the carnival arrived first.

"It's a shame this'll be the last one," Bob Eldridge said as he handed his daughter a box of popcorn at the carnival later that morning.

"What?" Patti asked, alarmed.

"It's not the last one, Bob," Mrs. Eldridge quickly corrected her husband. "It's just the last time the carnival will be held here at Brook Meadow."

"No. Don't say that," Patti said with a frown. "It's *always* been at Brook Meadow. That's where the carnival belongs. They can't do it anywhere else."

Mr. Eldridge dipped into Patti's box and withdrew a fistful of popcorn. "Sorry, but it's already settled. The government bought Brook Meadow to build some kind of office complex."

"Which government?" she asked, glancing up at the Ferris wheel, which seemed to roll and sparkle against the clear, blue sky.

"Hm?" Her father was preoccupied watching a man trying to knock down milk bottles with a softball. "The federal government, who else?" Mr. Eldridge finally answered.

Patti shook her head. She felt even more depressed at the thought of another change in her life. "I think we should write to the president. Don't they have enough office buildings in Washington? Tell him to leave Odyssey alone."

"I'll sign a petition if you get one started," Patti's father said playfully.

They moved away from the popcorn stand into the crowd. People seemed to crisscross in every direction in front of them; parents tugged at the hands of gesturing children, couples walked hand in hand, teens pushed and laughed at each other. On the Whipper-Snapper, a group of girls screamed as their cab was flung from one end of the ride to another. Patti took it all in, but didn't feel as though their fun had anything to do with her. Her parents tried to coax her onto some of the rides, but she wasn't interested.

"How about the hall of mirrors?" Mrs. Eldridge asked. "You always liked that."

"No, thanks," Patti said.

"You really don't want to shake this mood of yours, do you?" Mr. Eldridge observed wryly.

Patti just shrugged.

He took Mrs. Eldridge's hand. "Well, we're going to have a good time whether you are or not. Let's go." He pulled at his wife's arm and led her toward the hall of mirrors.

"We'll catch up with you later," Mrs. Eldridge said just before they turned to go in.

Alone, Patti stood and ate popcorn, watching the people moving to and fro, the colorful banners and streamers floating gently in the cool breeze, and the rides spinning, twirling, and bobbing. Her eye caught one of the carnival barkers—a large, heavyset man in grease-stained overalls. He rubbed the stubble on his chin and smiled at her. Most of his teeth were missing. She winced and rushed in the opposite direction. His sudden burst of laughter trailed behind her.

The encounter made her aware of all the other ticket-takers, barkers, and mechanics who worked for the carnival. She thought she remembered them as clean-cut young men and women who were spotlessly dressed and polite. But the workers she saw today looked downright seedy. Cigarettes dangled from their twisted lips. Grease and oil smudged their clothes, faces, and hair. They seemed to either leer at their customers or ignore them completely.

Mr. Whittaker had always told her not to judge people by their outward appearances, but with this crew, she couldn't help it. They made her nervous.

"Hi, Patti."

Startled, Patti jumped and cried out. She dropped her popcorn box. Fortunately it was now empty.

Donna Barclay eyed her warily. "Are you all right?"

"Yeah. I didn't see you come up." Patti grabbed the empty box, spied a trash can, and went to put the box in.

Donna said as she followed along, "You look like you're in a world of your own."

Patti nodded. "I'm waiting for my parents. They're in the hall of mirrors."

"My family's on the Ferris wheel," Donna explained. "I don't like heights."

"Oh," Patti said. She dropped the popcorn box in the trash and glanced awkwardly around. She didn't know where the hall of mirrors was anymore. She'd walked further than she had thought.

"Are you going to the lock-in at Whit's End tonight?" Donna asked.

"I don't know. I might be busy."

"Really?" Donna was surprised.

Patti read her surprise the wrong way and snapped, "What's wrong? I have things to do, you know. I have a life away from Whit's End."

Donna held up her hands defensively. "Don't get mad. I just thought that all the kids were going. I was surprised that you might not."

"Well, I'm not sure," Patti said, turning red-faced for getting so annoyed so quickly. She softened her tone. "I'll have to think about it."

"Okay . . ." Donna waited a moment and, when it was clear there was nothing else to say, she shoved her hands into her jacket pockets and started to leave. "Then maybe I'll see you later," she said.

"Yeah, maybe."

Donna hesitated, then said, "Patti . . . y'know, maybe we should do something together sometime. I always see you around, but I don't really know you very well."

"Yeah, sure," Patti said doubtfully. She knew that Donna had her own group of friends, and they'd never let someone like Patti in.

Donna nodded as if they'd agreed on something, then walked away.

She feels sorry for me, Patti thought. *I don't want her sympathy.* She kicked at the dirt, tugged at her baseball cap, and walked on. She didn't know where she was going but simply wanted to get away from anyone she might know. She wished she hadn't come to the carnival. She wanted to go home now. Looking around to see if she could find the hall of mirrors again, she ducked around a ticket booth and nearly ran into another girl.

"Excuse me," they both said at the same time. It sounded like one voice. The girl didn't look at Patti, but Patti caught sight of her face before she strode away. It took a moment, but Patti suddenly realized that she and the other girl looked a lot alike. It was shocking enough to make Patti turn to find the stranger, just to make sure she wasn't seeing things.

The girl was already several yards away at a cotton candy vendor. Patti watched her. *This is really weird*, she thought. It was like watching herself. The girl wore the same style of jeans, sneakers, and sweatshirt. She had the same shape of face and profile as Patti, including the tufts of brown hair that stuck out from under a baseball cap.

The resemblance was so strong that it took Patti's breath away. She could have been a long-lost sister. She wanted to call out to the girl, to talk to her and find out who she was, where she lived, and if they were anything alike. Maybe they were long-lost soul mates who were supposed to meet at this carnival and become friends. Patti had read novels where that happened. Why couldn't it happen in real life?

Patti took a step forward and started to raise her hand to her mouth to call out. Oblivious to Patti, however, the girl grabbed her cotton candy and suddenly disappeared into the crowd.

Patti's heart sunk into a sad, lonely place. Everything seemed to conspire to keep her in a bad mood. She thought of Mark again and felt that urge to cry. Again, she refused. It was one thing to feel sorry for herself; it was another to make a scene in the middle of a carnival. She wouldn't cry.

She made her way back in the direction of the bright, flashing lights advertising the hall of mirrors. Or so she thought. After a moment, she realized she'd gone in the wrong direction and was somewhere on the outskirts of the carnival. The dazzling lights she'd seen were actually for a house of horrors. Grotesque monsters of wax lined the front of the makeshift trailer. A man dressed up as Count Dracula called out to the passersby to come in for the fright of their lives.

Next to the house of horrors, in a small clearing by itself, sat a green tent with faded gold lining and purple tassels over the entrance. A hand-painted sign rested against one of the tent pegs. "Madam Clara," it read. "Your Future Awaits Inside."

Patti looked at the entrance, then the sign, then the entrance again. Curiosity rose up within her. She'd heard of fortune-tellers and clairvoyants—people who could supposedly tell the future. The pastor at her church said that people who practiced such things were wrong and often against God. On the one or two occasions when her parents mentioned them, it was to call them frauds.

Patti wondered about it. Could someone know the future by reading your palm or looking at special kinds of cards? What was her future going to be like? She glanced around quickly to see if anyone she knew was nearby. She saw only a few strangers and stragglers. The crowds were in other parts of the carnival.

Would it be so wrong just to see who Madam Clara was and what she had to say? Patti didn't have to believe anything the woman said. But it would be nice to know if the days ahead were going to be as depressing as today had been.

Patti walked to the entrance of the tent and peered in. Inside it was dark and barren, except for a small table and two chairs in the middle of a dirt floor. A candle flickered on the center of the table. Patti's better sense told her that it would be a mistake to go inside. She should go find her parents now.

"Come in, my dear," an old woman said, stepping out of the shadows at the rear of the tent.

"I think I'm at the wrong place," Patti stammered and retreated a step.

"Are you so sure?" The woman looked just like a gypsy from *The Hunchback of Notre Dame*. She had a scarf tied over her wild, white hair. Her blouse was striped and hung loose beneath a vest of black and gold. She wore a long, black skirt that made it look as if she drifted rather than walked across the ground. She smiled, and her face turned into a series of wrinkles, crow's-feet, and deep lines on deeply tanned skin.

"Yes, ma'am," Patti said quickly. "I was looking for the hall of mirrors."

The woman chuckled softly as if the statement had deep meaning for her. "I have never had my little tent confused with a hall of mirrors. Though there are reflections here that might show people their true selves. But you are early."

Patti didn't understand a word she'd just heard. "Sorry, but—"

"Let me see your face, child," the woman said, and she opened the tent flap farther to let the sunlight in. She gazed at Patti, taking her in from head to foot. Patti thought the woman's expression had changed for a moment, as if she recognized her from somewhere. She said quietly, almost as a secret, "You are in the right place, child. I am Madam Clara, the one you are to see. Come in."

"I made a mistake," Patti began to say, but the woman wasn't listening. She had sat down at the table and crossed her hands in front of her, as if waiting patiently for Patti to do the same. Patti considered running out. But the desire not to be rude mixed with her natural curiosity and led her to the table.

"That's right. Sit down." Madam Clara smiled.

Patti obeyed, but said abruptly, "I don't believe in this stuff. I only came in because I—"

"The less you say, the better. I know why you are here, and it is my role to help you. It's all arranged."

"Arranged?"

The woman leaned forward and whispered, "We know, don't we? You have come to me, and I will help you. Don't be coy, child. Let us not play games. Now, say the words."

"The words?"

The woman nodded.

"What words?"

The woman smiled knowingly. "I see. You don't trust me. Of course, why should you? Here is a strange old woman who asks for your trust. You are wise not to give it until you have proof."

Patti was intrigued. If the woman gave proof of her ability to tell the future, maybe the visit would be worthwhile. "What kind of proof?"

Madam Clara suddenly produced a deck of cards—from where, Patti couldn't tell. The old woman quickly dealt out five of the cards and laid them facedown on the table.

"My father does card tricks," Patti said, unimpressed.

"Does he?" Madam Clara tapped the top of one of the cards. "This is no trick." She turned the card over to reveal a queen of hearts. "This is your card," she said.

"My card?"

"You are skeptical and want proof. This is your proof."

Patti stared at the card as if it might suddenly do something magical. When it didn't, she asked, "How does this prove anything?"

Madam Clara snatched up the card and thrust it at Patti. "Take this card to the shooting gallery and I promise you'll win something special."

Patti hesitantly took the card. "That's my future? I'm going to win something at the shooting gallery?"

"You will indeed," Madam Clara said as she stood up. "The very thing you want. I promise. And then you will believe. Now go. I will not see you again until you are convinced."

Confused, Patti also stood up. "But what about—?"

"No more words. Go, child," Madam Clara said, then walked into the dark shadows of the rear of the tent.

Patti watched her go, looked at the queen of hearts, then strolled out into the sunlight.

Chapter
Three

PATTI WANDERED AROUND the carnival and looked for her parents. When she couldn't find them, she decided to visit the shooting gallery. Her encounter with Madam Clara was so bizarre that she couldn't resist seeing what would happen next.

The man in charge of the shooting gallery was a wiry fellow with thinning blond hair; round, gold spectacles; and a large sweater that obscured most of his body and the upper half of his thin legs. "Step right up! Takes just a buck to try your best against the dancing ducks!" he barked.

The ducks truly did dance—mechanically along the back wall of the gallery. They suddenly appeared on the far left, rose up in Daffy–Duck–like twirls, moving up and down, backward and forward, before eventually disappearing on the far right. Hitting any one of them would be quite a trick, Patti thought. No wonder few people seemed interested in playing.

She eyed the prizes hanging by strings overhead. They included small, cheesy-looking stuffed animals, coloring books, balloons, and one large stuffed bear. The bear—brown, furry, and maintaining a sad expression on its face—was by far the most appealing trophy to be won *if* Madam Clara's prediction was right. A sign pinned to his belly said, "Three in a row to go."

"Are you interested, little lady?" the man behind the counter asked.

"Well, I . . ." Patti wasn't sure what to say. She pulled the queen of hearts from her back pocket and laid it on the counter. "I'm supposed to give you this."

The man's eyes grew wide, then he picked up the card and handed it back to her. "A complimentary player," he said pleasantly. "Not sure what the ducks'll do when no bucks are involved. But grab your gun and see."

Shoving the card back into her pocket, she then grabbed one of the rifles from the counter, lifted it to her shoulder, and took aim.

"Ready?" he asked.

Patti wasn't, but said, "I guess."

He flipped a switch that momentarily stopped the mechanical ducks. A second later, they suddenly came to life. One after another, they emerged on the left, quacking through a loudspeaker as they moved. Patti fired the rifle just as one of the ducks lifted up. She was sure she missed. But she heard a loud "bing" and the duck lit up in a bright red color. "Got me!" it quacked, then slipped away behind a marsh facade.

"Nice shot," the man said.

"Thanks," Patti said as she took aim and pulled the trigger. Direct hit. Again, there was a loud "bing" and the next mechanical duck turned bright red with a loud "Got me!" It fell into the marsh facade just like the other one.

"You're pretty good," said the man.

Better than I ever thought, Patti mused. She took aim again and was just about to pull the trigger when a hand fell on her shoulder.

"There you are," her father said.

Patti turned to him and accidentally pulled the trigger. "Oops," she said. But instantly there was the telltale "bing," and another duck quacked "Got me!" in protest and disappeared into the marsh facade.

"Good shootin', Tex," Mr. Eldridge said with a laugh.

"I didn't know you were a hunter," Mrs. Eldridge added with a smile.

"How did I do that?" Patti asked. "There was no way I could've hit that duck."

"Hit it you did, little lady," the man behind the counter exclaimed as he reached up and grabbed the big bear.

Patti's jaw fell. "I won the bear?"

"Three in a row and he's yours to go," the man said. With a grunt, he hoisted the bear across the counter.

It took both of Patti's arms to carry him. "Thank you," she said happily.

"A prize for the queen of hearts," the man smiled.

His remark stopped Patti in her tracks. She had forgotten about Madam Clara and her prediction. What did this mean? Had the old woman really told Patti's future? Was she supposed to go back now to learn more?

"The queen of hearts?" Mr. Eldridge asked as they walked away.

Patti blushed and shrugged. She wasn't sure it'd be a good idea to tell her parents about Madam Clara or what had just happened. Mostly, she didn't want to get in trouble.

"Are you happy now?" asked Mrs. Eldridge.

"I have a new friend," was Patti's reply.

Mr. Eldridge put his arm around his daughter's waist. "On that pleasant note, maybe we should go home."

Patti sat the bear next to her on the backseat of the car and pondered over a name for him. As her father guided the car out of the makeshift parking lot on Brook Meadow, Patti glanced back toward the carnival. She felt strangely guilty for winning the bear and not returning to Madam Clara. But how could she without explaining it all to her mother and father?

Dust kicked up behind the car and, for an instant, Patti thought she saw her look-alike—the girl she had bumped into by the ticket booth. She nearly called out to her parents to look at the girl. But then the girl pointed in Patti's direction. The shooting gallery man was suddenly at her side, squinting to see the Eldridges' car. They were joined by several other workers from the carnival. One boy even made as if to chase after the car, but Mr. Eldridge had already turned onto the main highway. Patti nervously squirmed in her seat to look out of the back window. The small crowd faded into the distance.

Patti sunk low in the seat and wondered what the fuss was about. Why were they all so agitated? Were they mad because she didn't go back to Madam Clara? Why would they care?

She looked quizzically at her new bear as if he might answer her silent questions. He stared back at her in silence.

Chapter Four

"I'M GOING TO CALL him Binger," Patti announced to her parents when they got home. She pulled the big bear from the backseat.

"Why Binger?" her father asked.

"Because the ducks kept going 'bing' when I hit them."

"Oh. I thought it was because he looks like Bing Crosby," Mr. Eldridge said.

"Who?" Patti inquired.

"The one who sang 'White Christmas,'" Mrs. Eldridge said.

Patti took Binger up to her room and carefully positioned him on the chair to her small study desk. He watched her as she paced around the room, her face pressed into an expression of deep thought.

"Do you believe in fortune-telling?" Patti asked the bear. "I mean, is it possible that I really won you because Madam Clara predicted I would?"

The bear didn't reply.

Patti continued, "Maybe it was some kind of setup. But how? *Why*? Why would they go to all that trouble just to impress me?"

Binger refused to comment.

"Do you think I should tell my parents about it? It was really strange when that girl who looked like me pointed at us as we drove away. And then that guy from the shooting gallery showed up and that kid tried to chase us and . . ." Patti sat down on the edge of her bed. "Maybe I should've gone back to Madam Clara.

I don't believe in all this telling-the-future stuff, but I won you, didn't I? Just like she said I would."

Binger tilted his head thoughtfully for a moment, then slumped completely to one side and fell off the chair. Patti scooped him up and hugged him close on her lap.

"I'm glad I won you," Patti said. "I don't care how it happened."

In another part of the house, the phone rang. One of Patti's parents must have picked it up because it stopped after the second ring. A moment later, Mr. Eldridge called up the stairs for Patti.

"Yeah, Dad?" Patti called back.

"Mr. Whittaker is on the phone for you," he called back.

"Mr. Whittaker wants to talk to me?" Patti was surprised. Mr. Whittaker—or Whit, as he was often called by other adults—was the owner of Whit's End, a popular soda shop and renowned "discovery emporium" filled with room after room of interactive displays, games, activities, books, and all-around fun for kids.

"I think he wants to personally invite you to the lock-in tonight," Mr. Eldridge explained. "He talked your mother and me into being chaperones. Take it on the extension."

Patti was impressed: It was a big deal to get a call from someone as important as Mr. Whittaker. Still clutching Binger, she crossed the hall to her parents' room. The phone was on the nightstand next to their bed. She picked up the receiver and said, "Hello?"

"Hi, Patti," Whit said in a deep, friendly voice. Patti could instantly imagine his round face with its large, white mustache and matching crown of wild, bushy white hair. "I just spoke to your parents about the lock-in at Whit's End tonight."

"That's what Dad said."

"I guess you know that they'll help chaperone. But they agreed only if I can persuade you to come, too. Will you do us the honor?"

Patti hadn't decided about the lock-in since her encounter with Donna Barclay. She hesitated. "Uh, well . . ."

"We haven't seen you at Whit's End much over the past few months," he went on. "Frankly, I miss you. It'd be good to see you again . . . unless you've already made other plans."

Patti couldn't pretend that she had anything else to do. "Yeah—I mean, no—I don't have any other plans."

"So you'll come tonight?"

"Yeah, I guess so."

"Good. We'll see you later."

"Okay." She hung up the phone and only then realized that her mother was standing in the doorway to the bedroom.

"I think you'll enjoy yourself," Mrs. Eldridge said. "You never know what'll happen when you're at Whit's End."

Patti nodded. It was true. Whit's End was the most unpredictable place she'd ever known. But she'd shied away from it over the past few months. She felt as though she didn't have any reason for going anymore. It's not like she had any friends there, apart from Mr. Whittaker. But he was a grown-up, so that didn't seem to count.

"You can even take Binger with you," her mother added.

❋ ❋

"Now I'll finally get to see what happens at a lock-in," Mr. Eldridge said as they loaded the car with sleeping bags, boxes of potato chips, and some cakes and pies Mrs. Eldridge had spent the rest of the afternoon making.

Mrs. Eldridge carefully placed another pie on the backseat. "Our church used to have lock-ins when I was growing up. I wonder if they're the same?"

"Probably," Patti said. "We stay up all night and play a lot of games, eat tons of food, have a Bible study and sometimes a trivia contest, and try to keep each other awake for as long as possible." She pushed Binger across the backseat until he was pressed against the various boxes of goodies. "No sampling the food until later," she warned him.

They arrived at Whit's End just as the sun was going down.

Silhouetted against the darkening sky, the old Victorian building looked like a hodgepodge collection of square boxes, sharp angles, and rounded edges. Patti had learned from Mr. Whittaker some of the history of his shop. The tower, for example, was once part of a church. Another section had been used as the city's recreation center. And there was a maze of tunnels underneath that were put to use by runaway slaves in the days of the Underground Railroad. Mr. Whittaker had also added and changed parts of the building to suit his own needs, putting in a small theater for plays and musicals, a library for the kids to do their homework in, and one room that contained the county's largest train set. Patti knew that Mr. Whittaker would let the kids use all the rooms during the lock-in—and there would be no end to the fun.

Why didn't I want to come? she asked herself.

A couple of girls from school passed by just as Patti pulled Binger from the backseat. "Aw, look," one of them said. "She brought her teddybear to sleep with."

The girls giggled and walked away.

Patti blushed self-consciously.

Mr. Eldridge was suddenly at Patti's side. He scrubbed his clean-shaven chin and peered down his glasses at her thoughtfully. "You know, sweetheart, maybe we should leave Binger in the car. It might look like you're showing off if you take him inside. Few of the kids own such an impressive bear."

Patti looked at her father gratefully. She knew he was giving her a way out of her embarrassment. "Good idea," she said.

"Most bears are still hibernating now anyway," he added as he grabbed Binger by the arms. "I'll put him in the trunk where it'll be dark and comfortable, the way bears like it."

Patti smiled at her dad, even though she felt like she'd suddenly turned back into a five-year-old. *Am I really acting so childish?* she wondered. She thought back to her reaction to Mark Prescott's letter and how she had pouted at the carnival, even doing something as silly as going to a fortune-teller. *Yes*, she concluded, *I'm acting like a baby*. She decided that this lock-in would be the perfect place to start acting her age.

Inside Whit's End, Patti was surprised to find that Mr. Whittaker had set up even more activities than she'd imagined. Tom Riley, Mr. Whittaker's best friend, was sponsoring a table tennis tournament in the Little Theater. Connie Kendall, a teenager whom Mr. Whittaker had hired just a couple of months before, was pulling together volunteers for the water-balloon races. Mr. Whittaker was recruiting contestants for the Bible contest. In some ways, it reminded Patti of the carnival.

At first glance, she figured there were more than 30 kids there for the lock-in—and that didn't count the ones who were in other parts of the building. Many of them she recognized. Jack Davis, Matt Booker, and Oscar Peterson were arguing over whether they should play table tennis first or go upstairs to the train set. Robyn Jacobs and her sister Melanie were in one of the booths finishing ice cream sodas. Karen Crosby, Donna Barclay, and Lucy Schultz stood in front of a display of paintings Mr. Whittaker had set up and seemed lost in conversation about one of them.

Everyone seemed to be with friends—*close* friends. Patti felt her heart sink a little. That's why she'd been so moody after Mark's letter; it reminded her of how alone she was.

"You came!" Donna Barclay exclaimed as she walked over from Karen and Lucy.

Patti shrugged. "My parents decided to help chaperone and I thought I might as well come along."

"Good," Donna said. "I think this is going to be a lot of fun. My parents are chaperoning, too. They're upstairs helping with the Around-the-World game."

"Around the World?"

"Mr. Whittaker set up one of the rooms with displays of various places around the world. You have to guess where they are." She suddenly giggled, "I'm hoping my brother will get lost in the Amazon or get stuck on the North Pole."

"Jimmy's here, too?"

"Everybody's here," Donna said. "I'm glad you came."

Patti eyed Donna carefully. It didn't make sense that she would be so friendly. Did she want something?

"What are you going to do first?" Donna asked as if she didn't notice Patti's silence.

Patti looked around. "I think I'll join the table tennis tournament."

"That's what all the boys are doing," Donna said, rolling her eyes.

"Then it's probably time for some of the girls to show them how to play the game," Patti said defiantly. She walked over to Tom Riley's sign-up table, grabbed a pen, and added her name to the list.

"Good for you, Patti," Tom smiled.

No sooner had she finished than she was aware of Donna at her elbow.

"You're right," Donna said. "It's time to show the boys what's what." She scribbled her name at the bottom of the sheet. Then she grabbed Patti's arm. "Come look at this painting Mr. Whittaker brought in from the Odyssey Museum. Karen and Lucy and I were trying to figure out if it's a boat, a large banana, or a really small lake."

# #

The night spun away in a frenzy of activities. Patti not only made it as a finalist in the table tennis tournament (she was eventually beaten by Mike Henderson), but she finished first in the water-balloon race and was also the first to identify Mr. Whittaker's display for Sri Lanka in the Around-the-World game (she'd had to do a report about Sri Lanka for Mrs. Walker's history class last year).

She never had a minute alone to feel sorry for herself. Donna Barclay was always nearby to make sure she stayed involved. Patti didn't mind. The better she got to know Donna, the more she saw how much they had in common. Though Donna wasn't a tomboy like Patti, she was interested in different kinds of sports, and they shared a mutual hatred of algebra. For that reason Patti agreed to go to Donna's house the next day to work on some math homework together.

It was well past midnight when Mr. Whittaker served up a light snack for the kids, who were beginning to get sleepy. A few had already curled up in their sleeping bags and drifted off in the corners.

To stay awake, Patti volunteered to help clear the dishes. She carried a tray to the kitchen where Connie Kendall was already hard at work with the jet spray. Connie was a teenager in high school (Patti didn't know what grade). She stood just a little taller than Patti and had straight, black hair; a slender, pleasant face; and an energetic manner that livened up her facial expressions and hand gestures. "She's a ball of fire, all right," she heard Tom Riley say at one point in the evening.

"I don't think we've met," Connie said and thrust a soap-covered hand at Patti. "I'm Connie Kendall."

Patti shook her wet hand, then dumped the tray of dishes into the large sink. "I'm Patti."

"I know," Connie replied. "You're the one Whit is so worried about."

"I am?"

Connie frowned, her bright eyes clouding for a moment. "Oh, I don't think I was supposed to say that. Sorry. It's just that he's been talking about you the past couple of days. It was really important to him that you come to the lock-in. He said you had a close friend who moved away last summer and you've had a hard time coping with the change."

"Mr. Whittaker said all that?" Patti was surprised. She had no idea that Mr. Whittaker was paying so much attention to her. It made her wonder if asking her parents to chaperone was part of the plan to get her to Whit's End. Maybe Donna was part of the scheme, too.

"Mark, right? Your friend's name was Mark," Connie continued. With the back of her hand she pushed a stray lock of her straight, black hair away from her forehead. "See, I think Whit mentioned it all to me because he knows I've been having a hard time adjusting to living in Odyssey. I moved here from California because my mom and dad got a divorce and, well, Odyssey's a small town compared to Los Angeles. Do you know what I mean?"

Patti explained, "I've lived in Odyssey most of my life, so it's hard for me to compare it to anywhere else."

"If you lived in Los Angeles, then you'd know what I'm talking about. We had everything there—right around the corner. Good movie theaters and gigantic malls and every kind of store you can imagine." Connie rinsed off a couple of plates and sighed heavily. "I want to go back as soon as I can."

Patti opened her mouth to say something about her own feelings, about being lonely for a close friend like Mark, but Connie didn't give her a chance.

Connie continued. "I'm saving up for a bus ticket—or maybe I'll find a cheap plane-fare. I'll go by boat if I have to. It's been really tough. My mom is happy here, I think. She has relatives in the area. My Uncle Joe, for one. Actually, he's *her* Uncle Joe but I call him Uncle Joe, too, because it sounds goofy to call him my *Great-Uncle* Joe. Do you want to take that bag of trash out back to the Dumpster?"

Patti almost missed Connie's question. "What?"

"The trash," Connie said more slowly. "Do you want to take it out to the Dumpster?"

"Sure," Patti replied, then grabbed the large, green bag. It was heavier than it looked and she had to use both hands to carry it through the back door and over to the large, brown trash container along the side of the shop. It was dark outside. The moon had disappeared behind a thick cloud covering. The yellow porch light flickered unevenly as if the bulb might go out any minute. Patti put the bag down so she could slide the Dumpster's door open. She had just reached for the handle when a hand fell on her shoulder.

Patti cried out as she spun around, stumbled on the trash bag, and fell backward against the Dumpster.

Madam Clara stood over her and said with a crooked smile, "Hello, child."

Chapter
Five

"MADAM CLARA!" Patti gasped.

"I've frightened you. I'm so sorry," the old woman said and helped Patti to her feet. Her hands felt like leather.

Patti glanced toward the back door nervously. "What are you doing here?"

"Seeking you out. I have had a premonition . . ."

"A what?"

"Call it a vision of your future," Madam Clara explained, then held her hand up as if she were making a vow. "Tonight, the cards made it clear that you are not safe. That is why I came to find you."

"How did you know I was here?" Patti asked.

"The cards tell me everything."

"The cards," Patti said warily.

Madam Clara frowned. "You are still skeptical."

"You have to admit, it's a little hard to believe—"

"It is not hard for those who *choose* to believe!" Madam Clara exclaimed. "Was I not correct when I said you would win at the shooting gallery?"

"Yes . . ." Patti admitted. "But that might have been a trick."

Madam Clara threw her hands into the air. "Why would I trick you? I have not asked you for money. I have asked for nothing. I expected only that you would return to me after you won your prize. Was that so much to ask?"

"No . . ." Patti hung her head guiltily.

Madam Clara touched Patti's arm gently and said in an understanding voice, "You were afraid to come back, I know. Perhaps you didn't want anyone to know that we had spoken. You haven't told anyone, have you?"

Patti shook her head. "No. Actually, my parents would be mad if they found out."

"Then do not tell your parents," Madam Clara said. "Tell no one at all. What I must say is for your ears only."

"Why?"

The old woman leaned closer to Patti. "I have said it already. You are not safe. The cards have told me that you are in danger."

"What kind of danger?" asked Patti, still unsure of whether to believe the woman.

"The hearts on the cards," Madam Clara said as if that answered her question. "I have seen them. They spell trouble for you. Things will happen if we do not—"

Suddenly, the back door squeaked as Connie opened it. "Patti? Were you calling me?" She squinted into the darkness toward the Dumpster.

"No, Connie," Patti called back. "I was just talking to . . ." Gesturing toward Madam Clara, Patti turned. But Madam Clara was gone.

Connie took a few steps closer. "To who? Was somebody out here?"

Patti looked around. There was no sign that the old woman had ever been there. "I thought . . . I mean . . ." She didn't know what to say. "Maybe I'm more tired than I thought."

❧   ❧

Patti was bothered by her bizarre meeting with Madam Clara. Had the old woman really come to warn her? What kind of trouble would she be in—except the trouble her parents would give her if they found out she'd spoken to a fortune-teller? Madam Clara used the word *danger*. Why would Patti be in danger? Maybe it was some kind of trick. But why? Why would Madam Clara or anyone at the carnival play a prank on her?

Patti wrestled with these questions while she joined Mr. Whittaker and some of the kids in a middle-of-the-night game of Whit's Golf. The game, created by Mr. Whittaker, involved using large, plastic golf clubs to hit a round sponge-ball from room to room. Each room had a large can that served as a "hole" to hit the ball into. The angles and placement of the holes got more difficult with each room. As an added challenge, each hole also had a question about the Bible that the contestants had to answer for extra points.

While playing, Patti toyed with the idea of talking to Mr. Whittaker about Madam Clara. He'd probably know what was going on—or be able to make a good guess. The only problem was that Mr. Whittaker would insist that Patti tell her parents about it. Patti wasn't ready to do that. Not yet.

The questions persisted. How had Madam Clara known Patti was at Whit's End? Had the cards really told her? Was it possible that Madam Clara really did have supernatural powers? Could she tell the future with cards and visions? She had predicted that Patti would win the bear. And, if that came true, maybe Patti really was in some kind of danger. But what kind—and why?

It was almost 3:00 in the morning when Patti and the other players got to the sixteenth hole in the golf game. Mr. Whittaker had just asked Bruce Neilson a question from the book of Deuteronomy when Connie appeared in the doorway to the library with a worried expression on her face.

"Whit," she said, and gestured quickly.

Mr. Whittaker excused himself and walked over to Connie. All ears in the room strained to hear what she had to say as she whispered in an urgent tone. Only bits and pieces were loud enough to pick up. Patti heard enough to learn that Connie had seen someone outside, wandering around the building.

"At this time of night?" Mr. Whittaker said.

Connie nodded.

"You keep this game going while I check it out," Mr. Whittaker told Connie, then slipped out of the room.

Karen Crosby asked Connie, "There's someone sneaking around outside?"

"Maybe," Connie replied. "I saw someone out there, but it's probably nothing to worry about." Her face betrayed her feelings as her eyes kept darting to the doorway. She obviously wanted to go out and see what was happening.

Patti's knees suddenly felt strangely weak. If anyone was out there, it was probably Madam Clara. And if Mr. Whittaker caught her, Patti would have to explain, and Madam Clara's prediction would come true: Patti would be in *big* trouble.

Connie was just about to reread the question from Deuteronomy when they all heard the small bell above the front door jingle. Mr. Whittaker called out, "All right, what do you want?"

It was like an invitation for Patti, Connie, and the other kids to race from the library into the main soda shop area. Patti's heart galloped as she rounded the corner and saw Mr. Whittaker at the front door, talking to someone. As she got closer, she saw that the mysterious stranger was a man dressed in a dark suit. She breathed deeply with relief.

She crowded in with the kids closer to the door, only to realize that her relief was premature. On the other side of the man stood Madam Clara. Her eyes were alight with anger, and she scanned the faces of the gathering kids as if looking for someone.

"I'm Detective Anderson," the man said as he flashed his badge at Mr. Whittaker. "I was driving past on my way home when I saw all the lights on. They had told me at the station that you were having a lock-in, but I'd forgotten. Then I saw a shadow move across the front porch and caught this woman. She won't answer any of my questions. I assume she's not connected to anyone here?"

Mr. Whittaker turned to Madam Clara. "Are you connected to anyone here, ma'am? Is there a reason you're on my porch?"

Madam Clara's jaw was set. She didn't answer, but continued to look at the faces of the kids inside the door. Patti stepped a little behind Mike Henderson, who was bigger than she was, so she wouldn't be seen. Out of the corner of her eye, she saw her parents come down the stairs and cross toward the group at the door.

Mr. Whittaker then asked the crowd. "Does anyone know this woman?"

Patti's heart jumped. Madam Clara suddenly made eye contact with her. The recognition was instant. "She knows me," Madam Clara said and pointed at Patti.

Everyone turned to Patti.

Hot blood surged through her veins. She felt herself turn red. Her eyes burned.

"Patti?" Mr. Whittaker prompted.

Patti struggled beneath the questioning eyes of her friends and the knowledge that her parents were nearby. Madam Clara locked her in a steely gaze. If she said yes, then she'd have a lot of explaining to do. If she said no, then . . . what? She swallowed hard and felt the panic rise within her. The split section that had passed since Mr. Whittaker's question seemed like an hour. "No," Patti said. "I don't know her."

A buzz—like whispering bees—worked its way through the crowd. Madam Clara's eyes went wide with indignation.

"Let's go," the detective said to Madam Clara. "You can talk to me at the station."

"She's lying," Madam Clara exclaimed in a loud, shaky voice.

The detective put a hand on Madam Clara's arm. "Yeah, right. Tell it to me at the station."

"You do not heed me!" Madam Clara wrenched free from the detective and lunged toward Patti. The kids shrieked and scattered, leaving Patti frozen in her place. Mr. Whittaker and the detective quickly grabbed the woman by the arms and held her back. She strained against them and shouted, "You have betrayed me! You do not believe—and your lack of belief will be a curse to you! Do you hear me? A curse!"

"That's enough," the detective said as he tugged at Madam Clara, drawing her away from the door and toward the front steps.

"A curse!" Madam Clara cried again as the detective led her away.

Patti was aware that everyone was looking at her. She sensed her parents moving from the other side of the crowd. Mr. Eldridge touched her arm. He said, "Patti—"

She dissolved into tears.

PATTI DIDN'T REMEMBER much about the rest of the night. Her parents assumed that she'd cried because of the shock she'd gotten from Madam Clara. The kids turned Patti into an instant celebrity because she'd been singled out by "that crazy lady" (as they called her). And the less Patti wanted to talk about it—for fear that she might slip and prove she had lied—the more everyone was convinced that she had been deeply frightened by the experience.

Mr. Whittaker used the incident to talk to the kids about being very careful with strangers. Patti barely heard a word he'd said. Her mind was racing with the meaning of what had happened. Her stomach was in knots as she wondered what would happen next.

It occurred to her to tell her parents everything: just spill the beans about Madam Clara and the carnival. But the more she considered it, the less she liked the idea. She'd get in trouble on all sides, for going to a fortune-teller in the first place, then lying about it. *What a mess!* she thought.

Then there was the whole business about Madam Clara's curse. Did she really have that kind of power? Did *anyone*?

Mr. Whittaker addressed the kids on the subject as they all had breakfast together. "The Bible makes it clear that there are two kinds of supernatural forces at work in our world—God's and Satan's. God is the most powerful. But Satan gets his tricks in, too. He's the great deceiver and will use lots of means to keep us distracted from God."

"You're going to have to explain that, Whit," Tom Riley said through a mouthful of cereal.

Mr. Whittaker smiled. "Okay, let's consider so-called curses. Can one human being put a curse on another? I'm doubtful. Few, if any, people have truly supernatural powers. Most of the time, people like that are merely using our own superstitions against us. What's the result? We spend our time worrying about Satan and what he's up to—rather than thinking about God and what *He's* trying to do. Satan just loves to keep us confused and distracted."

Connie leaned over to Patti and asked, "Do you believe in stuff like curses and bad luck?"

Patti shrugged.

"I do." Connie nodded toward Mr. Whittaker, who was still talking, and whispered, "Don't get me wrong. I think Whit is really smart, but I don't think he understands how the real world works. There are things we don't know about, like ESP and aliens from outer space and voodoo and horoscopes. Whit doesn't believe in them because they're not in the Bible."

"Don't you believe in the Bible?" Patti asked, surprised.

"Who, me?" Connie folded her arms and looked thoughtful for a moment. "I guess it's a good book. I haven't read it much. It's okay. But I don't think it has the last word about everything, if that's what you mean. For example, I was looking at my horoscope yesterday and—"

"Is there something you want to say to us?" Mr. Whittaker asked Connie.

Connie sat up, blushed, and said, "Uh, no. I was just talking to Patti."

Mr. Whittaker nodded. "So I noticed. Patti, I hope you won't let what happened last night bother you. There's nothing to be afraid of."

"I know," Patti said, but she didn't believe it. It was easy to dismiss curses and bad luck when they happened to somebody else. But now she worried that it was going to happen to *her*.

After breakfast the Eldridges wearily drove home.

"Patti," Mrs. Eldridge said along the way. "Something's bothering you."

Patti squirmed on the backseat. "What do you mean?"

"You recognized that woman, didn't you?" her mother said.

"I saw her at the carnival," Patti said quickly. "But I don't *know* her."

"So you have no idea why she came to Whit's End?" her father asked.

Patti said truthfully, "No, it doesn't make any sense to me."

"Then I wonder why she got so upset with you?" Mrs. Eldridge said. "It's not every day you run into someone who decides to curse you."

Patti didn't have anything else to say. She stared out the window at the passing houses and the townsfolk getting up, starting their Saturday mornings. It all looked so normal. But Patti felt anything *but* normal. She felt as if she'd gotten herself into something bad. Worse, she had no idea what it was.

Once again, she thought about telling her parents the whole truth. Her conscience nagged at her the rest of the ride home, up the driveway, and into the garage. But she rationalized all the reasons it would be better not to.

"Let's unpack the car later," Mr. Eldridge said as they got out. "I'm too old for staying up all night. I need a nap."

Patti's mom agreed and Patti was pleased that she wouldn't have to think or talk about Madam Clara again. In her heart, she wished the woman and her curses would simply disappear.

They stepped from the garage into the house, through the laundry room, into the kitchen, and through to the living room, where Patti's father suddenly stopped.

"Oh no," he said.

Patti's mother gasped.

Patti peered around them and saw what they saw: It looked like a tornado had gone through the place. Furniture was tossed over, books and keepsakes were swept from their shelves, cabinet drawers were pulled out, their contents thrown carelessly on the floor.

"We've been robbed," Mr. Eldridge said and reached for the phone to call the police.

Chapter Seven

IT'S THE CURSE. It's started already, Patti thought as she helped her mother clean up the living room. A couple of policemen had already searched the room for clues, dusted it for fingerprints, and moved into other parts of the house. Every room had been treated the same by the burglars. It looked as if they'd turned each one upside down. Detective Anderson, the same detective who'd caught Madam Clara the night before, was in charge of the investigation.

"They sure did a number on your place," Detective Anderson said as he surveyed the damage.

"The strange thing is that nothing seems to be missing," Mr. Eldridge observed.

"Nothing at all?" the detective asked. "Then they must have been looking for something. Do you keep anything valuable here—like jewelry, negotiable bonds, large amounts of cash?"

Mrs. Eldridge held up a broken statuette. "Nothing like that. Most of what we own has only sentimental value anyway. This belonged to my grandmother," she said sadly.

"Anything else they might want from you?" Detective Anderson asked.

Mr. and Mrs. Eldridge shook their heads.

"It's possible they weren't looking for anything in particular," the detective continued. "Maybe they knew you'd be gone all night and decided to take their time tearing the place apart."

Mr. Eldridge scratched at his chin. "How could they know we'd be gone all night? We didn't even know ourselves until a couple of hours before the lock-in."

The detective shrugged. "Maybe they've been watching your place for a while. Have you seen any strange vehicles or unusual people around?"

Patti's parents looked at each other, then at Patti. They all said no.

"The only stranger we've encountered is that woman you nabbed last night," Mr. Eldridge said. "What about her? Is it possible she's connected to this somehow?"

The detective slid his hands into his coat pockets and leaned against the wall. "It's possible, but not in a way I could prove."

"Didn't you question her last night?" asked Mrs. Eldridge.

"Sure," the detective answered. "But she was tight-lipped. She didn't say much at all. I had to let her go."

Surprised, Mr. Eldridge said, "You didn't arrest her?"

The detective smiled patiently. "You can hardly arrest someone for walking on the porch at Whit's End, even at three in the morning. She was suspicious but did nothing criminal."

"My daughter remembered seeing the woman at the carnival yesterday," Patti's mother offered.

Detective Anderson nodded. "That's ultimately where I dropped her off. She's a fortune-teller there. Calls herself Madam Clara."

"She's a fortune-teller?" Mrs. Eldridge exclaimed, then shot a questioning glance at Patti. "Did you know that?"

Patti stared at her mother for a moment. The burden of her lies weighed heavily on her. She had no doubt that somehow the vandalism of their house was connected to Madam Clara's curse. And the curse was her fault. She didn't know how or why, but she knew it was.

"Yes," Patti said, choking on the word as tears welled up in her eyes.

"Why didn't you say so?" her father asked.

Patti just shook her head.

"Is there anything else you haven't told us?" the detective inquired in a diplomatic voice.

Patti crumbled. It didn't matter how much trouble she got into, she decided, she had to tell them the truth. "Well, there is . . ." she said. And starting with her visit to Madam Clara's tent at the carnival, she proceeded to tell them everything that had happened, including winning Binger at the shooting gallery and her lie at Whit's End the night before. She hung her head in shame when she finished.

"I'm very disappointed in you," Mr. Eldridge said firmly. "You know better."

Patti agreed.

He went on: "I'm especially concerned that you think this fortune-teller has powers like that. Haven't we taught you what the Bible says? The woman is obviously a fraud."

"But how did she know I would win at the shooting gallery?" Patti asked.

"If I may interject," Detective Anderson said. "We see this all the time. The card she gave you—the one she said to show to the shooting gallery barker—was a signal. When he saw the queen of hearts in your hand, he knew to rig the gallery so you'd win. They probably thought you'd be so impressed that you'd go back to her and pay to have your fortune told. Or, better still, you'd take your family and friends back. By winning the bear, you became a walking advertisement for the fortune-teller *and* the shooting gallery."

"That makes sense," Mr. Eldridge said. "But you *didn't* go back. It probably upset her."

"Did it upset her so much that she'd follow me to Whit's End?" Patti asked doubtfully.

The detective answered, "Maybe she wanted the bear back. Their scam backfired, and she got in trouble with the shooting-gallery barker. Who knows? It's also possible that she was a scout for whoever ransacked your house. She was sent there to make sure you didn't leave early to go home."

"Can you arrest her for that?" Mrs. Eldridge asked.

"No. We can't prove anything. It's all circumstantial. It might even be nothing more than a coincidence."

"A coincidence!" Mrs. Eldridge cried out.

"I have to consider everything. But don't worry, I'll certainly question Madam Clara again," Detective Anderson said.

"It's amazing," Mr. Eldridge said. "All this fuss over a fortune-teller."

The detective nodded. "I've been suspicious of everyone who works at that carnival. They're a mangy-looking group. I've got some of my men keeping an eye on them." He gestured to Patti. "By the way—that prize you won. The bear."

"Binger?"

"Where is it now?"

Patti had to think for a minute. Did she leave him at Whit's End?

"He's in the trunk of the car," Mr. Eldridge said.

"I was thinking that I should take him with me," the detective offered. "He might be useful as evidence."

"Evidence? Evidence of what?" Mrs. Eldridge asked.

Patti was upset. "You can't take Binger! He's the only friend I have right now."

The detective held up his hands defensively. "Okay, it was a bad idea. Don't worry. It was just a thought. If he was what they were looking for, he'd be safer with me."

"But why would they go to all this trouble to get a stuffed bear back?" Mr. Eldridge wondered aloud.

"Beats me," the detective said. "I'm just toying with different theories. Forget I mentioned it."

Back in her room, Patti sat down on the edge of her bed. She had a big mess to clean up. All her dresser drawers had been emptied. Everything was pulled out of her closet, the clothes yanked from their hangers. She still couldn't escape the feeling that this was connected to Madam Clara's curse.

Her mother walked in, looked over the damage with a pained expression, then leaned against the doorway. "You know that your father and I can't just let what you did slide. Not only did you visit a fortune-teller—which you knew we wouldn't approve of—but then you kept it from us. And then you lied about knowing Madam Clara. You dug yourself in pretty deep."

"I'm sorry," Patti said. "It's like the whole thing spun out of control. It kept getting worse and worse until I was sure you two would hate me."

"We'd never hate you—not for anything you'd ever do! But that doesn't mean we have to like it when you do something wrong. You'll have to be disciplined. We'll start by making you clean up your room." She paused for a moment and then continued. "You know, Patti, this might not have happened if you hadn't felt so sorry for yourself earlier. Your life isn't so bad. And I think you saw last night that there are kids who want to be your friend. You just have to let them."

Patti agreed, then said jokingly, "It's all Mark's fault for sending me that letter." She glanced around the disaster area for Mark's letter. She'd left it on top of the desk, which didn't look terribly disturbed by the vandals. "Where is it?" she asked after a minute of searching.

"Where's what?"

"Mark's letter. I left it on top of the desk."

"It's probably in the mess on the floor, which is as good a place to start to clean as any."

Patti took the hint and began reassembling her room. Three hours later, she had everything back where it belonged. Some of her keepsakes had been broken and couldn't be fixed. Sadly, she threw them away.

When she was finished, she sat back down on her bed. Her room looked almost as if nothing bad had happened. But she couldn't shake the feeling that her home had been invaded. Did it really have something to do with Madam Clara and her curse, or was it just a coincidence as Detective Anderson said? It was puzzling, too, that nothing seemed to be missing.

Patti suddenly remembered that in all the cleaning up she hadn't found Mark's letter. Where could it be?

She yawned as a wave of sleepiness hit her. She hadn't slept at Whit's End, and it was beginning to catch up with her. A quick nap would be a good idea, she figured. She rolled onto her stomach, dropped her head onto the pillow, and pushed her hands underneath it. Her fingers brushed against something that felt like smooth paper.

She thought, *Mark's letter,* and grabbed the object. Pulling it out, she saw immediately that it wasn't the letter from Mark. It was a playing card: the jack of hearts.

Chapter
Eight

"THIS IS REMARKABLE," Detective Anderson said.

Patti's father had called him as soon as she had found the jack of hearts and told her parents. Careful not to smudge any fingerprints, Mr. Eldridge had picked the card up with a pair of tweezers and dropped it in a sandwich bag.

"Are you sure it's not from one of your packs?" the officer asked.

Patti replied from her place next to her mother and father on the living room couch, "We don't own any cards."

"Even if I did, I wouldn't own them with this design," Mrs. Eldridge added. She was referring to the intricate curls and flowers that were engraved on the back of the card.

Detective Anderson compared it to the design on the back of the queen of hearts that Madam Clara had given Patti at the carnival. It was a different design. "It doesn't match."

"That's too bad," her father said. "Then we'd have proof that Madam Clara's behind this for some reason."

"But why?" Patti asked, echoing the question that had been nagging her ever since they came home to find the house ransacked. "Why would someone leave me that card?"

"I can't even begin to guess," the detective said. The easy chair squeaked as he leaned forward. "Didn't you say that Madam Clara warned you about the heart cards?"

"Yeah, but I didn't understand what she meant. Then Connie came out and she ran away," Patti said.

"Puzzling," the detective said as he looked again at the cards.

Mr. Eldridge pushed his glasses back up to the top of his nose and said, "What about Mark's letter? Why would they take it?"

"You're positive it isn't in your room?" Detective Anderson asked. "You didn't shove it in with your school papers?"

Patti shook her head. "I'm positive. I crunched it up a little, but then I either left it on my bed or my desk."

"It makes no sense to me. Why would they want a personal letter?" the detective mused. Then he said, "By the way, I questioned a few of the people at the carnival. They weren't helpful. Not only did they rudely refuse to answer most of my questions, but they all had alibis for where they were while your house was broken into. Of course, they all vouched for each other."

Mr. Eldridge asked, "What about Madam Clara?"

"She denies that she went to Whit's End to see Patti."

"What?" Patti shouted with disbelief.

"Even after that overdramatic curse business?" Mrs. Eldridge asked.

The detective shrugged. "She said it was all for show. She was playing to the crowd to get them interested in coming to the carnival."

"No way." Patti folded her arms and frowned. What was Madam Clara up to?

"Did she explain why she was hanging around Whit's End at all?" Mrs. Eldridge asked.

"She said she'd gotten lost while searching for a convenience store to buy some medicine. She saw the lights at Whit's End and thought it was some kind of grocery store."

"That's absurd," Mr. Eldridge grunted. "The carnival is miles out of town. There are convenience stores up and down the highway."

"That's what I said," the detective explained. "But she maintained it was the truth. And she said she's never seen Patti before."

"You mean she denied even talking to me behind Whit's End?" Patti asked.

The detective gazed calmly at Patti. "According to her, she didn't talk to you behind Whit's End or even at the carnival."

"What?!?" Patti cried out. "But I have her card. She gave me the queen of hearts!"

Detective Anderson held the card up and turned it around. "Unfortunately, it's a standard playing card. You could've gotten it anywhere."

"Are you saying Patti is lying?" Mr. Eldridge asked.

"I'm saying that this queen of hearts doesn't prove anything. For that matter, the jack of hearts isn't very helpful, either, unless we can match it to the rest of the deck—and its owner."

The Eldridges fumed silently. Then Mr. Eldridge asked, "What about fingerprints on the cards? Can't you check those?"

Detective Anderson shook his head. "I could check, but we probably won't find anything useful," he said. "Patti pushed the first card into her pocket several times, and she's handled both of them. Still, I could have the lab take a look if you insist."

"We wouldn't want to *inconvenience* you," Mr. Eldridge growled.

"Don't get upset," Detective Anderson said. "I believe that something is going on, and I'll do everything I can to find out what it is."

There was nothing more to say, so Detective Anderson left. The phone rang just as they closed the door behind him. It was Donna Barclay.

"Aren't you coming over today?" Donna asked Patti. "I thought we were going to do our math together."

Patti looked at the kitchen clock. It was nearly 5:00 in the afternoon. "I'm sorry. I forgot. Our house was broken into last night."

Donna gasped. "Oh no! Did they steal anything?"

"No," Patti said. "That's what's so weird about it. In fact, the whole thing is really bizarre."

"Look, why don't you come over? My parents are going out to eat, so Jimmy and I are supposed to send out for pizza. You can tell me what happened. Then we can get our math out of the way."

Patti cupped her hand over the receiver and asked her mother. Mrs. Eldridge nodded, then said, "Yes. But we'll drive you over."

"Drive me over? But I can walk," Patti said.

"We'll drive you over," Mr. Eldridge repeated firmly from the living room.

Patti suddenly understood. Her parents were worried about her, but didn't want to come right out and say so.

"I'll be right over," Patti told Donna and, having said good-bye, hung up the phone.

"And you'll call us to pick you up when you're ready to come home," Mrs. Eldridge added.

❈   ❈

"This is really neat," Jimmy Barclay said through a mouthful of pepperoni and extra-cheese.

Donna looked at her brother with a disapproving scowl. "It *isn't neat*, Jimmy. Why don't you go eat your pizza in front of the TV or play Zapazoids in your room or something?"

"And miss this? No way."

The three of them sat in a circle around the pizza box and yanked at the pieces inside. Donna resumed the conversation with Patti. "So they tore your house apart and you don't know why?"

Patti nodded and pulled at a long string of cheese that hung from her crust.

"I wanna go back to that part about the fortune-teller," Jimmy said. "She really put a curse on you?"

"You were at Whit's End. You heard about it," Donna reminded him.

Jimmy said impatiently, "I know, but I wanted to hear Patti say it herself. You were really cursed, Patti?"

"I'm not supposed to believe in curses," Patti said.

"But you do, don't you?" Jimmy watched her closely.

"I don't know," Patti shrugged. "All I know is that everything started to go wrong after I saw her."

Donna sat thoughtfully for a minute, then said, "She told the detective she did the whole curse thing as a performance. So the curse can't really work, can it?"

"A curse is a curse, even if it's put on someone as a show," Jimmy said earnestly.

"How do you know?" Donna challenged him.

"My *Dark Mysteries* comic books," he replied.

"I thought you stopped reading them when you became a Christian," she said.

"I did, but that doesn't mean I forgot everything I read in them before."

"But the curse wasn't for a show," Patti interjected. "She was lying about that. She knew who I was, and she yelled her curse at me."

"So you *do* believe in curses," Jimmy said, a wry smile stretching across his face.

"I didn't say that."

"But you do."

"Leave her alone, Jimmy," Donna said.

Jimmy went on, "But it's important, you see? She gets cursed and then her house gets broken into. It's connected."

"No kidding, Mr. Sherlock Holmes," Donna said, jabbing him.

Jimmy grimaced. "I remember from issue 94 of *Dark Mysteries* that there was this guy who had a curse put on him by some gypsies and later on some things were stolen from his house."

"Why?" Patti asked.

"Because the gypsy who put the curse on the other guy needed something personal to make the curse work."

Donna rolled her eyes. "Jimmy, what in the world are you talking about?"

"It's like voodoo," Jimmy explained. "You know, when they take a lock of your hair or a piece of your clothes and attach it to a doll that looks like you. Then they stick pins in it and you feel the pain."

"Oh, great. Thanks, Jimmy," Patti groaned.

Donna tossed a balled-up napkin at her brother. "You're not helping things."

"I'm just telling you what I read. I didn't say it was true," Jimmy said.

"Then stick to what's true, okay? You're gonna give us nightmares," snapped Donna.

Jimmy reached for another piece of pizza. "I just think it explains why Mark's letter was stolen, that's all."

"You think Madam Clara has Mark's letter stuck to a voodoo doll of me?" Patti questioned him.

"Maybe," Jimmy said, then sipped his soda.

Patti sat silently, chewing her pizza with a worried expression.

Donna glared at her brother. "You're a real pest, do you know that? You're scaring Patti with something we're not even supposed to believe in. Mom and Dad aren't gonna be happy that you're going around quoting old, scary comics."

Patti and Donna went up to Donna's room to do their math homework. "Don't listen to Jimmy," Donna said as they settled down on the bed with their books and notebooks. "He's got a wild imagination."

"Don't worry about it. I don't really believe in that junk," Patti said in as careless a voice as she could manage.

As the evening progressed, however, she found it harder and harder to concentrate on her work. Madam Clara and the curse kept coming to mind. And Jimmy's words kept coming back to haunt her. *That's why they stole Mark's letter*, he had said. It made sense. It was the only thing missing. Maybe there was something magical about Mark's letter that made it more powerful to the curse than anything else. Maybe it was because he was a close friend, or because she missed him so much. The reasons kept going around and around in her mind. Madam Clara's curse seemed stronger than ever. What else could it do to her?

By 8:00, both of the girls were ready to call it quits with their math. Donna offered to put in a video for them to watch, but Patti wasn't in the mood. She wanted to go home. After resisting

Donna's appeals to stay, Patti tried to call her parents to come pick her up. The line was busy. After 20 minutes, it was still busy and she started to worry. Her parents were never on the phone that long. *Something is wrong at home*, she thought. *Something bad has happened.*

"What should I do?" Patti asked as she hung up the phone for the eleventh time.

"Keep trying," Donna suggested.

Ten minutes later, the line was *still* busy and Patti decided she should walk home. She told herself, *if something is wrong, I want to be there.*

"I'll walk with you," Donna offered.

"Are you allowed to leave Jimmy home alone?"

"No."

Jimmy, who had overheard from the family room, came in and said, "Go on, Donna. I'll be all right. I'll call Oscar and ask him to come over."

Donna frowned. "You and Oscar alone in our house? You'll burn it down."

"Thanks for the vote of confidence," Jimmy said.

Patti waved the suggestion aside. "Forget it, Donna."

"But your parents said you shouldn't walk home alone," Donna reminded her.

"It's okay," Patti said. "No point both of us getting in trouble. I'll run. It isn't very far."

Jimmy said, "If you cut through the woods, it's real quick. Just watch out for the creek. It's deeper than it looks."

"I know, Jimmy. I didn't just move here," Patti said impatiently.

Jimmy looked at her for a moment, then scratched at his curly, brown hair. "Boy, Donna, you and Patti'll make great friends. She's starting to talk to me the same obnoxious way you do."

Donna smiled. "You bring it out in people, Jimmy."

"Thanks for inviting me over," Patti said to Donna at the door.

"I'm glad you came. Sorry about all your trouble." She hesitated as if she wasn't sure of what to say next. Finally, she added, "I'd like you to come over again. If you want to. I mean, it's up to you."

"Look, Donna, you don't have to be my friend just because Mr. Whittaker asked you to."

Donna looked confused. "Mr. Whittaker didn't ask me to be your friend. What made you think that?"

"Connie said that Mr. Whittaker was worried about me . . ." Patti started to explain. Donna's expression left her no room to doubt that she didn't know what Patti was talking about. She gave up. "I'd like to come over again. Maybe we can do something better than our math homework."

"We can tackle Jimmy and put masking tape over his mouth."

"It's a deal!" Patti laughed and walked across the porch to the steps. As she made her way to the street, she felt an odd sensation somewhere deep inside. Apart from Jimmy scaring her, she enjoyed being with Donna. It wasn't awkward or forced. They talked about a lot of different things—not just girl stuff—and seemed to have a lot in common. Maybe, just maybe, they really could be friends.

Patti crossed the street and walked down to the edge of the woods. She had made it only a few steps inside when she realized it was a bad idea. The woods were already a wall of darkness, with the trees standing like stark shadows. She imagined that if she were really under some kind of curse, walking through dark woods at night was the last thing she should do.

She glanced back at the Barclay house and wondered if she should go back in and call her parents. *The phone's probably still busy*, she thought. *If something's wrong, I need to get there right now*. Having made up her mind, she strode quickly around the edge of the woods, keeping close to the patchy yellow glow of the streetlights. She hummed softly to herself. At some point in her childhood, she had decided that nothing bad could happen to you if you hummed.

Halfway home, she came upon Wilkins Park, a small grove of

trees with a play area for children. It was almost as dark as the woods—the one or two lamps on the path had burned out—but she knew it was only a short distance. To go around it meant either venturing farther into the woods or jumping the Frazinis' fence and cutting across their backyard. Mr. Frazini was well known for yelling at kids who cut through his yard, so Patti decided to go straight through the park.

She weaved her way past the merry-go-round and the triple seesaws, when something rattled to her right. She glanced over at the swings. They moved gently in the evening breeze as if being ridden by ghosts.

"Stop it," she told herself as she picked up her pace. "I don't believe in ghosts or curses or—"

Suddenly there was a loud *bang!* Patti nearly jumped out of her skin. It sounded like something hard had hit the slide off to the right. This was followed by a *rat-a-tat-tat* as if a rock were skidding and bouncing down the length of the metal board. A branch in the tree above it rustled.

A squirrel must've dropped an acorn, she assured herself as she went from a brisk jog to a furious sprint. Her heart pounded. *Oh, please, let it be a squirrel*, she wished as if the curse had sprung legs and was chasing her.

Subdued panic pumped energy through her body and pushed her to the other end of the park. Clearing that, she raced up a small hillside toward the road and its welcoming light.

"Ah!" she cried as her left foot caught the edge of a rock. Sprawling to the ground, she threw her arms out to try to catch herself. Her math book and notebook flew away. She landed on her left arm, her elbow jabbing into her stomach. It knocked the wind out of her.

The night exploded into pinpoints of light. The pain was excruciating. Patti tried to breathe in, but she couldn't. She rolled onto her back and gasped for air. It was awful. Seconds became long wheezing minutes. The grass was damp and cold and clung to her jacket.

Blinded by the agony and the deep covering of the incline, she could only sense that someone was coming near. She thought it was her imagination at first. But the shadow moved. Not only did it move, but it moved unmistakably toward her from the woods. *Who is it?* she wondered helplessly as her lungs screamed for air. She managed to roll over again to get to her feet. The wet grass was no friend to her tennis shoes, and she slipped, crashing down again.

This is the curse, she thought in her fear. *I can't fight it. I can't even breathe. And now Madam Clara will get whatever it is she wants from me.*

The figure was closer now, bending down, its hands reaching out for her.

Her eyes adjusted and looked into its face. Now she knew she was done for, because the face she saw made no sense. It was all wrong, totally impossible. It absolutely didn't belong here. It was a trick of the curse.

"Are you all right?" Mark Prescott asked in a bewildered tone.

Chapter Nine

"TAKE IT EASY," Mark said quietly as he knelt next to her. "Calm down. Just try to breathe slowly."

Patti eventually worked some air back into her lungs. After another minute she was able to sit up.

Mark leaned close to her. "What happened to you?" he asked.

"I fell down," Patti croaked.

"I figured that much."

Patti took a few more deep breaths. Her vision cleared, but now her head hurt. She turned to face Mark, and for a moment still couldn't believe it was him. But there he was, kneeling next to her. He pushed his dark hair off his forehead—an old habit of his.

"Are you okay now?" he asked.

"Yeah," she replied. Then she punched him in the arm.

"Ow!" he cried out as he fell backward. "What's that for?"

"For scaring the living daylights out of me!"

Holding his arm, Mark stood up. "You're welcome!" he said unhappily.

She reached out her hand for him to help her stand. He grabbed it and, though she expected him to give it a hard yank in revenge for the punch, he merely gave it enough of a pull so she could get to her feet.

"Were you following me?" she asked as she brushed off the back of her clothes.

"I went to your house and your parents said you were at the

Barclays', so I walked over there. When I got to the Barclays', Donna said you walked home. I cut through the woods because I thought that's the way you'd go."

"You didn't follow me through Wilkins Park?"

"No," he said, still rubbing his arm. They started up the hillside to the street. "Are you friends with Donna Barclay now?"

"Kind of."

"You didn't say so in your letters."

Patti turned to him, her eyes narrowing angrily. It was an expression she used only with him. "You mean you've been reading them? Thanks a lot for all your answers. What did I get? One letter. *One* letter! And I got it yesterday! How long have you been gone? Months!"

"I'm not a very good writer," he said sheepishly.

"You sure aren't!"

He said with a hint of annoyance, "Look, if you're going to nag me—"

"You deserved to be nagged," she cut in. "Some friend you turned out to be."

"Hey, I'm here, aren't I? I came to see you as soon as we got in town! You were the very first one. Give me a break." He rubbed his arm again and muttered, "Boy, you punch me, then you yell at me . . ."

In the glare of the streetlight she could see him better. He had grown a couple of inches, though he still had the same slender build. His face had changed, going from round boyishness to the start of the narrow shape of manhood. *He's beginning to look like his father*, she thought. She smiled without meaning to. At summer camp last year, she'd had a crush on a boy named David. That was the closest she'd come to experiencing those feelings. The truth was that she'd liked David because he seemed like an older version of Mark.

"What are you doing here anyway?" she asked.

"I'm on spring break and my dad had to come to Odyssey on business, so—"

Patti laughed. "What kind of business would your dad have in Odyssey? He works for the federal government!"

"That's right," Mark said. "Do you know about that new building they're going to put out at Brook Meadow?"

"You mean . . ."

Mark nodded. "My dad is a consultant on the project—he's helping them to work out the details so they can build it."

"How long are you going to be around?" Patti asked.

"Just this week . . . for now."

"For now?"

"Yeah. If my dad is transferred here after the building's done, then we'll have to move back and—"

"*Move back*? You mean you might move back to *Odyssey*?" she squealed and had to restrain herself from jumping up and down.

"Maybe," Mark replied, blushing at her enthusiasm.

"I don't believe it!" she shouted and, much to their surprise, she stepped forward and hugged him.

He quickly stepped back from her and held up his hands. He looked around to make sure no one had seen it. "Patti, cut it out! What's wrong with you?"

Patti, a little confused, studied him for a moment. "Nothing's wrong with me. I just got excited. Why? Don't you want to move back to Odyssey?"

He shrugged. "I don't know. Everything's happened so fast. It's kind of strange being here."

"Oh, that's right," she said indignantly. "I forgot. You have all your old pals back in Washington, D.C. You said so in your letter. You're Mr. Happy now, aren't you? Busy, busy with your cherry blossoms."

"Patti, what's gotten into you?" Mark asked, dumbfounded.

She tried to wave the question away. "Nothing. I've had a hard day. I'm tired."

"Why did you have a hard day?" Mark asked.

"Didn't my parents tell you what happened?"

They had reached her front porch now. The lights were on

inside the house. Through the front window, Patti could see her parents talking to Richard and Julie Prescott in the family room.

Mark shook his head. "Did something happen?"

"Boy, do I have a lot to tell you," she said and opened the front door.

❈　　❈

Though it was getting late, the Eldridges and Prescotts gathered around the Eldridges' kitchen table for tea, coffee, and cookies.

"How's it feel being back?" Mrs. Eldridge asked as she passed the mugs of hot drinks around. Milk, creamer, and sugar were added, creating a momentary clatter of chinking porcelain and rattling spoons. "Is the house still standing?"

Julie Prescott's mother—Mark's grandmother—had lived in Odyssey. When she died, she left the house to Julie. That's where Julie and Mark stayed when the family had separated early last summer. It was like a second home to them.

"Mr. Wallace is taking good care of it," Julie Prescott said after sipping her tea. Mr. Wallace was hired by the Prescotts to care for the house after Julie and Mark moved back to Washington, D.C. "It's a little strange being back. Things have changed. I noticed they started work on the new mall."

Mr. Eldridge chuckled. "That's Odyssey for you. Always on the march for progress." He turned his attention to Mark's father. "So, Richard, I'm curious about this new government complex. What's it going to be?"

Richard Prescott leaned back in his chair. "I'm not really supposed to talk about it. You know how the government is. I guess you could call it a place for archive storage."

"Like Noah's Archive?" Patti asked playfully.

"Joan of Archive," Mark corrected her. The families groaned.

"Archive storage?" Mr. Eldridge continued.

Mr. Prescott nodded. "Information, papers, computers—a place independent of Washington to keep it all filed."

"Richard was the one who suggested this area," Mrs. Prescott said proudly. "He remembered seeing Brook Meadow during one of his visits here and mentioned it to his bosses."

"I had some local help," Mr. Prescott said modestly.

"Basically you're building a big filing cabinet out at Brook Meadow," Mr. Eldridge observed wryly.

"Something like that," Mark's father said with a laugh.

"Have you chosen your computer technicians yet? You want to make sure everything is hooked up properly," Mr. Eldridge said.

"Not yet. The bids are still coming in," Mr. Prescott replied, then added as a tease, "Why? Do you know a company that's interested?"

Richard Prescott knew full well that Bob Eldridge worked for Parker Technologies, a local computer company. Mr. Eldridge smiled. "I'll tell my people to get in touch with your people."

Mrs. Eldridge pondered the plate of cookies, chose one, then asked, "How do you like being back, Mark?"

Mark shrugged. "It's okay, I guess."

"Is there really a chance you might move back?" Patti's father asked Richard and Julie.

Julie looked to her husband. "Well, Richard?"

"It depends on a lot of different things," he said. "If the building project is successful, they'll want people from Washington to come manage it. I might be one of those people."

"That would be nice," Mrs. Eldridge said.

"Mark doesn't want to move back," Patti suddenly announced.

Everyone looked at her with surprise.

"What?" Julie Prescott asked, then glanced at her son. "He told you that?"

"No," Mark said firmly.

Mrs. Eldridge looked at her daughter, a knowing light in her eyes. "What makes you think he doesn't want to move back?" she asked.

"Because of his letter. All he talked about was how *happy* he is back in Washington."

Richard and Julie nearly choked on their drinks. "Happy?" Mark's father said.

"Now, wait a minute—" Mark started to say.

"He's been *miserable*," Mrs. Prescott exclaimed.

"Mom—" Mark pleaded and held up his hand as if to say something more, but his mother didn't give him the chance.

Julie continued, "He complains that his old friends aren't like his friends anymore and that he doesn't like school and the neighborhood has changed—"

Mr. Prescott chimed in, "'It's not like Odyssey.' Isn't that his pet phrase? Nothing's as good as Odyssey. There's no Whit's End, it's too crowded, there's too much traffic, he has nowhere to play. He never lets up. I had to suggest building the government complex here just to get some peace and quiet at home."

By now Mark's face had turned a deep crimson. His arms were folded and his chin was sunk into his chest.

Patti stared at him, openmouthed. "You're kidding," she managed to say.

"Thanks for the support, Mom and Dad," Mark groaned.

"So you *do* want to move back," Patti challenged him.

Mark's lips were clamped shut for a moment. Then he muttered, "Well . . . I wouldn't say *no*."

Everyone laughed. He sunk lower in his chair.

"I'd like to see that letter," said Julie Prescott.

"You can't," Patti stated.

Mr. Eldridge explained, "It's the only thing that was missing after the house was ransacked."

"That's odd," Richard Prescott mused, his brow furrowed. He absentmindedly pushed his hair back away from his forehead. *Just like Mark*, Patti noted. "The police don't have any clues or ideas?"

"Nothing helpful right now," Patti's father said. "We're certain it has something to do with the people at the spring carnival— Madam Clara, in particular."

Mark's father thought for a moment, glanced at his watch,

then sat up and said, "Look at the time. It's late. We better get to bed if we don't want to miss church in the morning."

They said their good nights to each other. Patti and Mark promised to talk after church about what they would do together next. Then the Prescotts were gone and the Eldridges made for bed.

In her room, Patti felt the happiest she'd been in a long time. She was extremely tired but couldn't stop smiling. Mark was back. He might even come back for good. Suddenly Madam Clara and the curse and Jimmy's comments about voodoo and her fright in the park all seemed distant and powerless. Binger, who was finally retrieved from the trunk of the car, sat contentedly on her bed. "Isn't it great?" she asked him.

She yawned as she pulled open her dresser drawer. Her nightgown wasn't there. She then remembered that her mother had washed it. Pulling on a robe, she padded down the stairs to the laundry room to get it. Somewhere outside, fireworks exploded in the distance. *It's the last night of the spring carnival*, she thought. *They always do a fireworks display.*

She found her nightgown hanging on a rack next to the washer and dryer. As she pulled it off the hanger, she caught her reflection in the window pane directly in front of her. She ran her fingers through her hair and wondered whether she should get it cut differently. Maybe Donna Barclay would have a suggestion. Donna always looked nice.

Patti's reflection blurred abruptly. She blinked, thinking her eyes were playing tricks on her. Suddenly her face was transformed into the face of Madam Clara. The old fortune-teller leered at her through the window.

Patti screamed.

Chapter
Ten

For the third time in 24 hours Detective Anderson came to the Eldridges' house. "I heard the police call on my radio and, once I'd heard the address, I knew it was more trouble," he said.

"We're sorry to get you out so late," Mrs. Eldridge said.

The detective shrugged it off. "A bachelor cop like me keeps all kinds of crazy hours."

"There's no one back there," Officer Stenson informed them as he entered through the back.

"Are you surprised?" Mr. Eldridge asked sarcastically. The three Eldridges were huddled on the couch. Mr. and Mrs. Eldridge wrapped their arms around Patti, whose tears were only beginning to subside, but her body continued to shake.

Patti was vaguely aware of Officer Stenson—who came as soon as Patti's father had called 911—as he signaled Detective Anderson aside. They whispered intensely for a minute. She thought the officer handed something to the detective. Stenson then nodded and slipped out the front door.

"Well?" Mr. Eldridge asked.

Detective Anderson stood next to the couch. His overcoat hung loose and disheveled. *Was he asleep when he heard the call?* Patti wondered for no particular reason.

"Officer Stenson didn't see anyone. But he found *this* on the windowsill outside." The detective held up a playing card by the edges with the very tips of his fingers. It was a 10 of hearts.

"There!" Mr. Eldridge snapped. "What kind of proof do you need now?"

Detective Anderson turned the card around. The design on the back was completely unlike the other two cards. "I still need more than this."

Patti's father grunted. "I don't care if they're identical or different or printed on dollar bills! I just want this harassment to stop! If you won't go out to the carnival and take care of it, then I will."

"You're upset and I don't blame you," the detective said patiently. "But you can't take the law into your own hands. Neither can I. I'll go to the carnival and check things out. I'll talk to Madam Clara again. I'll even have this card checked for prints. But I don't expect to find anything that'll help."

"It has to stop," Mr. Eldridge said more softly.

"Tonight's the last night of the carnival. These characters have to pack up and move on to their next site. Maybe this trouble will move on with them."

"Is that it?" Mr. Eldridge said, mostly as an appeal. "Madam Clara and her pals can harass us and then just skip town? Is that justice?"

"Justice is administered based on solid evidence, Mr. Eldridge, *which* we don't have right now," Detective Anderson said firmly. "Apart from this card, we can't even find evidence that Madam Clara was out there. One could argue that Patti is tired and imagined seeing that face in the window."

"And the card?" Mrs. Eldridge demanded.

"I'm not saying one way or another," the detective said. "Girls Patti's age are often at the mercy of wild emotions. I've seen it again and again. They do things to get attention."

Mr. Eldridge leaped to his feet. "All of this is Patti's attempt to get attention? Is that what you're saying? She tore up the house to get attention?"

"No, Mr. Eldridge, that was real enough. But—"

"But what? Are you a detective or a psychiatrist?" Mr.

Eldridge snapped. "I resent you coming in here and making comments like that. My daughter is perfectly stable and certainly not the kind of person who would resort to *this* to get attention."

"It's voodoo," Patti whispered.

"What?" her mother asked.

"This is all because of the curse. They're playing tricks on me to scare me. It's voodoo," Patti said, then began to cry again.

Detective Anderson gestured toward Patti as if to silently say to her parents, "See? Your daughter has problems."

Mr. Eldridge looked helplessly at his daughter then showed the detective to the door. He apologized for getting angry. "I know you're doing everything you can."

"We'll make sure a patrol car stays in the area for the next few days," Detective Anderson assured him.

Even with a mild sleeping tablet, Patti couldn't sleep. The old woman's face in the window came back to her time and again. "You didn't listen to me," she imagined Madam Clara saying. "You didn't believe in the curse."

❈   ❈

The next morning, Patti went to her parents' Sunday school class rather than her own. She knew the kids were all talking about what had happened, and she couldn't face them. It was better that way for Mark, too. The kids could give him all their attention. Patti barely heard the teacher's lesson. She felt drained and detached. "Be anxious for nothing," someone read from the Bible. "Perfect love casts out all fear," someone else read. Patti picked up on these words because she knew the verses. *God help me*, she prayed.

The Prescotts sat with the Eldridges in the church service. Pastor Henderson made a special mention of the difficulties the Eldridges had been experiencing and led the congregation in a moment of prayer for them. At one point, Mark reached over and held her hand. It took all of her energy to keep from collapsing into heaving sobs.

I'm being overdramatic, she kept telling herself. *I'm making a big deal out of nothing. Maybe I was tired and only* thought *I saw Madam Clara in the window. It might have been my imagination.*

Where Patti would normally stay to socialize after the church service, today she wanted to make a quick escape. Her parents sensed it and ushered her out a side door to their car. The Prescotts followed close behind. Mr. Whittaker was the only one who made a point of chasing them down, and that was to say that he was sorry about the break-in and was praying for them all.

"I hope you'll come see me at my shop," Mr. Whittaker said to the Prescotts while pulling Mark close for a hug.

"We will," Richard Prescott promised.

Mr. Eldridge surprised Patti by opening the trunk and pulling out Binger. He dropped the bear onto the seat next to her and said, "I had a feeling you might need him today."

She hugged Binger, then her father, and promised, "I'll be okay. I'm feeling better now. I'm sorry to be such a wreck."

Her father stroked her hair. "You've had a couple of bad days. You're allowed to be a wreck."

Mark climbed into the car. "Are you okay?"

Patti shrugged. "I guess so."

"You're not too tired?" he asked. It was a leading question. Mark was up to something.

"Too tired? For what?"

"Because me and my mom and dad decided to kidnap your family. We figured we should get you away for a while. We're going up to Trickle Lake for a picnic," he announced.

The two families conferred for a couple of minutes. Mr. Eldridge and Mr. Prescott spoke earnestly about something, then they got into their cars and drove off.

"But I'm not dressed for a picnic," Patti told her parents.

"I put a change of clothes in the trunk," Mrs. Eldridge informed her.

"You knew we were going to do this?" Patti asked, surprised.

"We talked to the Prescotts about it this morning while you

were in the shower. They're very worried about us."

To get to Trickle Lake they had to pass Brook Meadow. The carnival was in various stages of being disassembled. The Ferris wheel looked like an upright pie out of which someone had taken a big piece. The merry-go-round, the games, and the stalls were all being taken down by the workers. *Good*, she thought. *Good-bye and good riddance.* For the first time she was glad the government had bought the land. She never wanted to see a carnival there again.

Mr. Eldridge switched on the turn signal and slowed down.

"What are you doing?" Patti asked, suddenly worried.

"Richard and I want to look around the carnival. He needs to look at the grounds for the building, and I want to look around to see if I can find anything the police missed."

"No, Dad, I don't want to go there," Patti protested. "Please don't."

Mr. Eldridge looked at her in the rearview mirror. "You don't have to," he said. "I'm going to drop you off at the diner just down the road. You don't think I'd really make you see the place again, do you?"

Patti sighed with relief and pulled Binger close.

At the diner, the two dads said good-bye to their families and drove off for the carnival in Richard Prescott's rental car. Mrs. Eldridge pulled a bag of clothes for Patti out of the trunk of the car. "You can change in the women's restroom," she suggested.

Patti stood at the back of the car with Binger in her arms.

"Nice bear," Mark said.

Patti couldn't tell if he was being sincere or sarcastic. "I like him, so watch what you say," she warned playfully.

"Do you want to take him into the diner?" Mrs. Eldridge asked, her hand on the trunk lid.

Patti thought about it, then said, "No."

"Then let's put him inside."

"Poor Binger," Patti said sadly as she gently laid him in the trunk. "He always gets stuck in here."

Mrs. Eldridge closed the lid.

The diner was crowded with a Sunday lunch crowd that looked like an equal mixture of families on their way home from church and truck drivers who'd stopped in for some good, old-fashioned cooking. Mark and Patti and their mothers sat down at a Formica-topped table with chrome siding. The red cushions on the metal-framed chairs were split and cracked, but comfortable. A blonde woman with too much makeup and red-striped outfit took their orders for two sodas and two coffees. Mark flipped over his placemat and began to play a children's "name the states" game on the back. Patti flipped hers over and borrowed a pen from her mother so she could play connect-the-dots. The picture turned out to be a sailboat.

"Is it too early in the year to rent a paddleboat at Trickle Lake?" Julie Prescott wondered aloud.

Mrs. Eldridge smiled. "That's a good idea. We'll see."

Patti was showing Mark her sailboat when her eye was caught by a glimmer outside. A large truck passed by. It was loaded with a ride from the carnival. She followed it until it was gone, then noticed that a stranger was standing next to their car. He turned slightly, enough for Patti to see that it was the man from the shooting gallery. Patti gasped.

Mark leaned forward on the table. "What's wrong?"

"That man," Patti said softly. "He runs the shooting gallery."

"Really?" Mark strained to see. "Are you sure?"

Patti nodded. "How could I forget?"

Susan Eldridge and Julie Prescott were both looking now. "What's he doing out there?" Patti's mother asked.

"Nothing," Mark replied. "He's just standing there."

"Looks suspicious to me," Mrs. Prescott said.

Just then a black-and-white police car pulled into the parking lot. Oblivious to those watching him from the diner—or the man next to the Eldridge's car—the policeman climbed out. He squinted at the sunlight, put on a dark pair of sunglasses, adjusted the belt on his uniform, and strode toward the entrance. The shooting-gallery man saw him and walked away.

"That was interesting," Mrs. Prescott said as relief washed over the four of them.

"Do you think he was going to do something to the car?" Patti asked.

Mark frowned. "Why would he? I mean, how could he know it was your car?"

"That's true. How could he?" Mrs. Eldridge said. "It must've been a coincidence. The carnival isn't very far from here."

Patti suddenly remembered that she hadn't told anyone about the girl at the carnival who looked like her, or the way the shooting-gallery man watched the Eldridges drive away. "He knows our car. He saw us leave the carnival," she said.

"I wish your father would hurry," Julie Prescott said to Mark.

Mark tapped the table excitedly. "I sure wish I knew what was going on. This whole thing is so weird."

"No kidding," Patti said.

Mrs. Eldridge held up the bag with Patti's clothes in it. "Why don't you go into the restroom and change so we'll be ready to go when the men get back?"

Patti agreed, took the bag, and followed a sign with an arrow that said "Restrooms." It led her down a small hallway at the back of the diner. She pushed open the "Ladies" door and went past the three stalls to a large sink on the other wall. Glancing at her reflection, she noticed that she had the start of dark circles under her eyes. *Not enough sleep*, she thought. *Tonight I have to get some sleep*.

No one was in the restroom, so she decided to change quickly right where she was. She kicked off her nice shoes and pulled her jeans on under her church dress. She then unbuttoned the top of the dress, pulled it over her head, and shoved it into the bag. Yanking on the sweatshirt her mother had brought, Patti smiled. *Mom thinks of everything,* she thought. *Trickle Lake is always cooler since it's further up in the mountains.*

Her head popped up through the top of the sweatshirt and she noticed a woman had come into the restroom. The woman turned and smiled at Patti.

Patti thought her heart had stopped. "Madam Clara!" she cried. "Hello, child."

"Don't come near me or I'll scream so loud that the policeman will come in," Patti threatened.

"You don't have to scream *again*," the fortune-teller said gently. "You nearly gave this poor old woman a heart attack when you screamed last night."

"Gave *you* a heart attack! What do you think you did to me?" Patti complained. Somehow this slight old woman didn't seem like anyone to be afraid of. Patti felt anger more than fear.

The woman spread her arms in appeal. "What can I do? How else can I reach you?"

"Don't you have phones?" Patti asked, strengthened by her anger. "Can't you use the front door like normal people?"

"Phones and front doors involve your parents. This is between us, child. It is private. Your visit to me set into motion unfortunate events. For that, I'm sorry. Yet, I've been trying to help you, and you keep making it very difficult."

"*Help* me! You put a curse on me!" Patti said.

"I cursed your lack of faith in me, your betrayal of me when I needed you." The woman grinned crookedly. "It has not been pleasant for either of us, let me assure you. But I'm here now to help you eliminate the curse."

"How?" Patti asked warily.

"By reversing the spell. But you must assist me."

"Assist you how?"

The woman took a step forward, then stopped as if she was afraid Patti would scream. "I need an item. Something personal, which I can use to reverse the spell," she explained.

"I get it. This is like voodoo, right?"

"If you insist."

"You already got that letter from my room. What else do you want?"

"Child, I do not have your letter. How could I possibly get a letter from your room?"

"When you vandalized our house!"

"I did no such thing. It is obviously the result of the curse. But we can stop it. An item, child."

"Like what?"

Madam Clara tapped her shriveled cheek thoughtfully. "Something that is important to you. What do you treasure the most?"

Patti had to think about it. "I have some pictures . . . books . . . presents people have given to me . . . a china ballerina that your curse broke when it trashed my house . . ."

"It must be something larger. Think, child. It must be valuable to your heart."

Finally Patti thought of it. "Binger. My stuffed bear. The bear you made me win."

The fortune-teller cackled. "The bear will be perfect. Bring it to me."

"And you'll make the curse go away?"

"I will."

Patti was suddenly defiant. "What if I don't believe in your stupid curse? What if I said I thought that *you* keep making these bad things happen?"

Again, Patti thought Madam Clara might step closer, but she hesitated. Instead, she pushed her face forward and hissed, "Suit yourself, child. If you do not bring me that bear, I can promise that the curse will extend to you, your family, and your friends. This curse is like a cancer that will spread to all whom you love. A vandalized house and a few broken trinkets are nothing compared to what will befall you!"

"I'm not afraid of you," Patti said, but she was suddenly aware that her knees were shaking.

"Be wise, child. You must do what I say and then you'll be done with it. Bring me the bear or you'll hurt as you've never known it before! And you must say nothing about this—to anyone—or the curse will not be halted! Do you understand?"

In spite of herself, Patti nodded her head. The woman spoke

with such passion that Patti didn't dare refuse her. Images of her parents' death—an accident or a fire—worked through her mind.

"Now, you must bring it to me tonight at the carnival," Madam Clara said.

"Tonight!" Patti said. "Why can't I give it to you now?"

Madam Clara backed toward the door. "Tonight. And then you can live the rest of your life in peace. And . . . not a word!"

The restroom door opened and nearly hit Madam Clara in the back. A startled customer said, "I'm sorry."

Madam Clara glared as she brushed past the woman and disappeared down the hallway. Patti noticed that she didn't go in the direction of the dining room, but the opposite way toward the rear emergency exit. The customer slipped into one of the stalls.

Patti thought she might throw up. *What am I going to do?* she asked herself. She waited a moment to try to get her strength back. She knew she couldn't return to the table looking scared.

The door opened again and Patti's mother peeked in. "What are you doing, dressing for Cinderella's ball? Your father and Richard are back. We're ready to leave."

"I'll be right out," Patti said.

Mrs. Eldridge paused. "Are you all right?"

Patti nodded quickly. "Uh huh. I . . . I just felt tired all of a sudden."

"You can sleep on a blanket up at Trickle Lake. The sun will feel wonderful now," her mother said.

Patti managed a slight smile and her mother left.

What am I going to do? she wondered.

Chapter
Eleven

TRICKLE LAKE WAS even cooler than they had expected, though the sun shone brightly in a blue sky. The paddleboats were still locked up for the winter and wouldn't be brought out until May, according to a sign on the concession shed. The two families had to entertain themselves with Frisbee throwing, a rule-free football game, and the food Julie Prescott brought. It was fun for them all, in spite of their troubles. The only one who seemed unable to shake a dark mood was Richard Prescott. He had seemed preoccupied ever since they left the diner.

Patti fell back onto one of the blankets and, in the golden warmth of sunlight and smells of spring, dozed fitfully. She dreamed of her times at Trickle Lake with Mark last summer. Here they had found a secret cave, which Mark ultimately gave to a group called the Israelites to use as a hideout. Patti nearly hadn't forgiven Mark for that betrayal.

That summer was filled with all kinds of adventures for the two of them. Not all were rough-and-tumble, though. Many affected Patti's heart profoundly and made her realize that she was changing. She was growing up. In just three months she had gone from being a tough tomboy who had given that bully Joe Devlin a good stomping (on the day she met Mark) to being a blubbering girl (the day Mark moved away). She'd never cried so hard as on the day Mark left. It hurt her more than she could have anticipated.

"You'll know hurt as you've never known it before," Madam Clara had said. The words returned in her dreams. Once again, she had been put in the position of keeping a secret from her parents while trying to decide whether to give Madam Clara what she wanted. If she did—if she could sneak the bear out to the carnival site—the nightmare might end. If she didn't—if she refused to believe in Madam Clara and her powers—terrible things could happen.

"Patti?" a voice whispered. "Patti, wake up."

Patti opened her eyes. Her mother was leaning over her. "You were having a bad dream. You were moaning," she said.

"Was I?" Patti asked, then yawned. "I don't remember." Slowly she sat up. Her father and Mr. and Mrs. Prescott were stretched out on various blankets, fast asleep. Mark was sitting nearby, looking incredibly bored. When he saw that Patti was awake, his face lit up and he strolled over to her.

"Do you want to take a walk?" Mark asked.

Patti said "Sure" and stood up. Her head was still fuzzy from her nap. "Where do you want to go?"

"Let's go see the secret cave," he said.

They walked toward the woods. "Be careful in there! You remember what happened last time!" Mrs. Eldridge called out. Last summer Patti had fallen down a mineshaft and broke her arm.

"So what's wrong?" Mark asked her directly once they were out of earshot of the adults.

"What do you mean?"

"Something's been bothering you ever since we left the diner," Mark said.

She thought about it, then decided she couldn't even tell Mark right now. "I'm just tired," she stated simply.

Further up the path away from the lake, they passed a large tree with graffiti carved into it. Neither one of them looked at the tree directly, though Patti was sure she saw Mark glance at it out of the corner of his eye. Patti had carved a heart in the tree with

the words *Patti & Mark 4 Ever*. She did it when she first realized
she had a crush on him but had no idea how to act about it. It
seemed so childish to her now.

Mark didn't even mention the tree and neither did Patti. But
she knew they were both thinking about it.

They reached the secret cave—"secret" because it was natu-
rally hidden from sight by thick underbrush—and had to work
extra hard to push through the thick green curtain to the darkness inside.

It was too dark to see very well. Mark bumped into a wooden
crate. A candle fell to the ground. "Maybe there are matches," he
said and felt around for a pack. He found a small box near the
cave wall. They felt damp and, as expected, had been there too
long to be of any use.

"Well . . . here it is," Patti said, looking into the darkness.

"What happened to the Israelites?" Mark asked. The
Israelites was the name of a group of kids Whit had established
to do "good deeds" around the town.

Patti found the remnants of a glass lantern top. "Whit broke
them up when school started."

Mark shook his head. "It seems like a long time ago."

Sitting down on the upended crate, Patti said, "It *was* a long
time ago. It feels like everything's changed since you left."

Mark turned to face Patti, though they could barely see each
other in the darkness. "I'm sorry I didn't write to you more. It was
so hard being back in my old neighborhood that I figured all I'd
do is gripe and complain. To tell the truth, I didn't want you to
know that I didn't like being back there. I was glad Mom and
Dad were together again, but I wanted them to be together *here*."

"In this cave?" Patti joked.

"Cut it out. You know what I mean."

"Yeah, I know," she said softly.

She suddenly remembered a time when she'd abruptly asked
Mark to kiss her. She wished that he would try to now. But he
wouldn't. She knew that she was just a friend to him, no matter

what he was to her. She wondered what would happen if she blurted out she thought she loved him. He'd probably say she was off her rocker and run out of the cave. She kept her mouth shut. This was one secret she *had* to keep to herself.

Without any light, it was pointless to stay in the cave. They walked back toward the picnic. Near the edge of the woods, Patti sniffed the air and said, "I smell smoke."

Mark said he could smell it too. "Someone must be burning leaves."

"Up here?" Patti asked. "And in the spring?"

Through the break in the trees, they could see smoke rising up into the sky. It came from very near to where their families had been picnicking.

"Come on," Mark said quickly and took off. Patti matched his speed, and they reached the picnic area at the same time. A few yards off to the right was a meadow thick with dried grass and weeds. It was on fire. Patti's and Mark's fathers were frantically hitting at the flames with their jackets. Julie Prescott raced toward the meadow with a bucket of water she'd apparently retrieved from the empty ranger station. Susan Eldridge came from the lake with another bucketful.

"Find a container—anything! Get some water to put out this fire!" Mrs. Eldridge said. "I called the fire department."

"Drench your jacket and use it to hit the flames," Mark shouted to Patti, and then he ran off to the ranger station to find a bucket.

But that'll ruin it, Patti thought as she rushed over to her blanket and grabbed her jacket. A king of hearts fell out of the pocket.

❈   ❈

With flashing lights and blaring sirens, members and equipment from both the Odyssey Fire Department and the Forestry Department fire station arrived within 10 minutes. Five minutes after that, they had the fire under control. It was completely put out no more than a half hour later.

"What happened?" a uniformed fireman named Steve asked as the crews began stowing their gear.

"We don't know," Mr. Eldridge replied. "We were resting over on our blankets when suddenly we smelled smoke. Then we saw the flames in the field. That's when we called you and tried to put it out ourselves."

"Thank you," fireman Steve said. "I'm sorry about your clothes. I'm afraid you'll have a hard time getting them clean again."

"Don't worry about that," Mr. Prescott said.

"Any idea what might have caused it?" Mr. Eldridge asked.

Fireman Steve held up his hands. "I was hoping you could tell me. You weren't barbecuing, were you? Maybe decided to roast marshmallows on a fire?"

"No, sir," Mr. Eldridge answered.

Fireman Steve scratched his balding head. "It's the wrong time of year for a brush fire, so it beats the tar out of me what—"

"Steve!" another fireman called out. He emerged from the woods holding up a large, red gas can. With it was a large rag. "Look what I found!"

"Somebody *set* the fire?" Mrs. Prescott gasped.

"No doubt about it," the second fireman said as he approached. "This one was done on purpose."

Fireman Steve addressed the two families. "Any idea who might've done it? Were you all here when it started?"

"The kids were up in the woods," Mrs. Eldridge said before she realized how it sounded.

"Were you?" Fireman Steve said suspiciously to Mark and Patti. "Doing what?"

"We were exploring in a cave," Patti explained.

"The fire was already going when we walked back," Mark added.

"Uh-huh. Gotcha. Well, I'm going to have to get your names

and numbers anyway for my report. A clear case of arson can't be ignored. And thanks again for being so conscientious." Fireman Steve tipped an imaginary hat and walked away.

Mrs. Eldridge groaned. "Is it never going to end?"

"Do you think your 'friends' from the carnival had something to do with this?" Julie Prescott asked incredulously.

"You can bet on it," Patti's father said angrily.

"But why?" Mrs. Eldridge asked. "What do they want from us?"

Patti knew. They wanted Binger. And they wouldn't stop torturing them until they had him. In that instant, Patti determined what she had to do: anything to stop the curse.

Chapter
Twelve

They left Trickle Lake feeling as if they'd suffered a bad end to what was otherwise a very nice day.

Mr. Eldridge suggested that Patti ride with the Prescotts, then said, "I'll take all our things home, and then we want to go to the police station and talk to Detective Anderson. He has to see that we're in a potentially life-threatening situation. I want police protection for my family."

Patti had never seen her father so angry. It made her anxious enough to consider telling him about the king of hearts in her jacket and the encounter with Madam Clara at the diner. But she didn't. Madam Clara had been very clear with her threat. Patti couldn't tell a soul or there'd be worse trouble. All she had to do was work out the plan.

"I think I want to go home," Patti said. She figured she could move more freely if she was alone. She could sneak off to the carnival while her parents went to the police station.

"No," her father said. "I want you to be *with* someone at all times. I don't know what Madam Clara and her thugs are up to, but I won't leave you alone to find out."

"Can I take Binger with me?" Patti asked.

"Sure you can," Mr. Eldridge replied. The two families parted after Patti got Binger back out of the trunk.

After a stop at the store to pick up some food for an evening meal, Patti returned with the Prescotts to their house—the one

Mark's grandmother left to them. As soon as he had a chance, Mark nearly dragged Patti up to his old room.

"Okay, what's going on?" he demanded in a harsh whisper.

Patti feigned innocence. "What do you mean?"

"Cut it out, Patti. You know what I mean. You've been quiet ever since the diner, and I can see in your eyes that the wheels in your little brain are turning. You're thinking. You're up to something."

"I am not! Why can't everyone leave me alone?"

Julie Prescott appeared in the door. "Are you two fighting again?"

"Kind of," Mark said.

"Just like old times." Patti smiled weakly.

"I want to try to wash our jackets. Maybe we can get all the dirt and soot out," Mrs. Prescott said. "Clean out your pockets and bring them down to me." Then she disappeared again.

"Tell me, Patti!" Mark insisted when she was gone. He picked up his jacket and began going through the pockets.

"I don't know what you're talking about," Patti said, following suit. She lifted her jacket and dug into the pockets. There were tissues and small slips of paper. She pulled them out. The king of hearts fell on the floor.

Mark instinctively bent to pick it up for her. Patti scrambled to get there first. "I've got it," she said.

Her fingers were nearly on the card when Mark stamped his foot down on it.

"Get off!" she cried out and tried to push him away.

He pushed her back, and in the single second it took for her to regain her balance, he snatched the card from the floor. "A king of hearts?" he said quizzically, turning the card over.

"It's mine. Give it back."

"Wait a minute," he said, a light dawning in his mind. "Weren't the cards from that fortune-teller something-of-hearts? Queen of hearts . . . the 10 of hearts on your windowsill . . ."

"Just hand it over."

"Where did you get this, Patti?"

"None of your business," she said. Her hand was still out-stretched for the card.

"*When* did you get this?" he asked.

"I can't tell you," Patti said angrily. "Now give it back."

Mark wouldn't give up. "The diner. Did Madam What's-Her-Name give it to you?"

"No, she didn't," Patti answered truthfully.

Mark tossed the card to her and slumped down onto his bed. "Come on, Patti. I could ask a hundred questions and sooner or later get the truth out of you. I won't give up. You know that. Why don't you save us all the trouble and just tell me now?"

Patti thought carefully. She wanted to tell him, but she was afraid. Then it occurred to her that the only way she could get to the carnival site was with Mark's help. She decided to tell him. "I'll tell you if you promise you won't tell anyone else."

"I won't promise anything until I know what's going on."

Patti had to accept that. "I found the card in my jacket at the fire. I don't know how it got there—or when. But it was a warning to me, or a threat. Both, I guess."

"From who? Madam What's-Her-Name?"

"Clara, yeah. She came into the restroom at the diner when I was changing."

"Patti!" Mark nearly shouted. "Why didn't you tell us?"

"Because she told me the curse would get even bigger if I did."

"Curse! Are you nuts? You don't believe in curses. Did you stop going to Sunday school after I left? Did you give up church? You know better than to believe in curses!"

"I don't know what I believe now, Mark. Call it a curse, call it whatever you want, but it won't stop until she gets what she wants from me. I know that. The break-in, the looking in my window, the fire . . ."

"What does she want?"

"She said she'll reverse the curse if—"

Mark interrupted her. "I don't believe this. *Reverse* the *curse?*"

"Just listen to me, will you? She said she'll reverse the curse if I give her something very personal, something I treasure more than anything else."

Mark paused to eye her curiously. "Yeah? What?"

Mrs. Prescott shouted from downstairs. "I want your jackets now!"

"Coming!" Mark called back. Somewhere in the house, a phone rang. "We're not done with this," he said as he grabbed their jackets to run them downstairs.

Her mind twisted and turned like a roller coaster through her options. She could take Binger and go to the bus stop on the corner. There was a bus to Connellsville every half-hour until 9:00 at night. It went right past Brook Meadow. She could have the driver stop so she could get out and take the bear to Madam Clara. She could walk to the diner and call her parents to come get her. She'd be in big trouble, but she figured she'd be in trouble anyway. At least this way they'd be safe again.

"Patti!" Mark called loudly.

Patti went to the top of the stairs. "Yeah?"

"Come down here, please."

Please? she thought. *Mark said please?* It worried her. She went downstairs and into the kitchen. Mrs. Prescott was putting on her coat. Mr. Prescott and Mark watched Patti with worried expressions.

"What's wrong?" she asked, her eyes moving from one person to another. Richard Prescott sat on the chair in front of Patti so he could see her face better. She thought for a second what a handsome man he was. A grown-up Mark. "What?" she asked him.

"Your parents just called. They've been in a car accident."

Patti felt her knees buckle. Mr. Prescott grabbed her and guided her to a chair. "It's nothing serious," he said. "They're all right. They were on their way here from the police station when the brakes suddenly gave out. They went off the road and into a ditch. They've got some bumps and bruises, that's all. Do you hear me? They're all right."

Patti sat there, stunned and unable to make sense of the news.

Mark's father continued. "The car can't be driven, so Julie is going to get them and take them to the hospital, just to check them over. She'll bring them back here. You're going to stay here with me and Mark while she goes."

"What? I don't understand. Why?"

"Because I think this accident is related to everything else that's happened to you. You're safer here with me and Mark than out on the road." He stood up. "Your parents are okay, Patti. Don't worry. Come on, Julie. I want to check *our* car before you go anywhere in it."

Julie Prescott kissed Patti on the top of her head. "It'll be all right," she said. She and Mr. Prescott went out to the garage.

Patti felt dizzy and nauseated. "I think I'm going to be sick," she said and rushed into the downstairs bathroom. She leaned over the toilet, but nothing happened. After a moment, she turned to the sink and splashed some water on her face. She went back out to the kitchen, where Mark still waited for her alone.

"I have to do something *right now*," she said urgently.

"Calm down," Mark said. "There's nothing you can do."

"But there is! I can take Madam Clara what she wants! It's the only way to stop this curse!" she cried.

Mark shook his head. "You're delirious."

"It won't go away until I give it to her. Don't you understand?"

"What does she want?" Mark asked again.

"Something personal," Patti replied.

"I got that part. But what exactly are you going to give her— a hairbrush? dirty socks?"

"My teddy bear," Patti said.

"All this trouble will stop if you give them their teddy bear back? But that doesn't make any sense!"

"I don't care. Are you going to help me or not?" It wasn't a question; it was an ultimatum.

Mark stood up to his full height. "I sure am! As soon as my dad comes in, I'm going to tell him everything. He'll know what to do." As if on cue, the Prescotts' rental car started up and Mrs. Prescott drove it away.

"No! You can't!" Patti begged. "He'll tell the police, he'll make a big deal out of it, and then things'll get worse."

"They can't get worse if our parents and the police know," Mark said earnestly.

"Wanna bet? This curse is real. Madam Clara is serious."

"And you're crazy," Mark said. "I'm sorry, Patti, but it isn't a curse. It sounds like some kind of blackmail."

"But *why*?"

"I don't know. But we can't handle this alone. I'm going to tell my dad. Are you coming with me?"

She folded her arms and said sternly, "No."

"Okay, then I'm going to do it." He headed for the garage. Patti immediately raced up the stairs to Mark's room to get Binger. She thought she might make it back down the stairs and out the front door by the time Mark and Mr. Prescott returned. She glanced at her watch. It was 8:30. It wasn't too late to catch the Connellsville bus. She grabbed the bear just as a door slammed somewhere downstairs. *Too late*, she thought and considered sneaking out the window.

"Patti!" Mark shouted in a shrill, panicked voice. "Run! Patti—" His voice was suddenly cut off as if someone snuffed it like a candle.

Patti rushed back out into the hall, but didn't call back. Something had happened. She waited. The house was silent. The front door banged open and Patti positioned herself to where she could see it from the top of the stairs. She put her hand over her mouth to keep from screaming. The man from the shooting gallery had grabbed Mark.

Mark bit the man's hand so he had to uncover his mouth. "Run!" Mark screamed.

Another man Patti had never seen before came in through

the front door, glanced around, then started up the stairs. Patti retreated to Mark's room, slammed and locked the door, and tried to think. What should she do? Heavy footsteps pounded up the stairs, then stopped at the top as if the man had stopped to listen. Still clutching Binger, she looked out the window. It led out onto a small section of roof that angled with the gutter into the main section of the house. There was no one below. She opened the window.

The man in the hall jiggled the door handle furiously. Then he banged on the door. Patti was halfway out of the window when the man began to throw his full weight against the door. It was an old house and the door was made of solid wood. It would hold him off at least a minute or two.

Patti carefully crept along the slender section of roof. When she reached the gutter spout, she looked below. All was quiet, even though the man continued to bash at the door. She dropped Binger into a bush, then grabbed the spout for her climb down the back of the house. Her feet soon touched ground and she grabbed Binger. A loud *crack* told her that the man had gotten into the room. There was no time for her to wait.

She pulled Binger from the bush, then turned to escape. But as she did, strong hands grabbed her from behind and dragged her into the shadows.

Chapter Thirteen

PATTI STRUGGLED AGAINST her captor, but to no avail.

"Calm down," Richard Prescott whispered. "It's me. Mark's father."

She relaxed and he let her go. "You scared me!"

"I know. I'm sorry. But I figured if I said 'hi' you'd scream."

He was right, she would have.

"The shooting-gallery man has Mark!" Patti said.

"I know," Mr. Prescott said, then pulled Patti back farther into the shadows. "You need to stay here, hidden. If anyone comes, hightail it out of here."

Alarmed, she asked, "Where are you going?"

"To get my son back."

He was about to step out when someone called for him from the front of the house. "Prescott! We have your son!" Patti recognized the voice. It was the shooting-gallery man.

Mr. Prescott inched his way toward the corner at the front of the house. Patti followed close behind. They both peeked around and saw Mark held fast by the shooting-gallery man and his partner—the one who'd knocked in Mark's bedroom door. They were at the end of the sidewalk by the street. A large, black car with its doors open sat behind them with its engine running.

"You know we don't want to do the boy any harm," the man said. "But we want that bear. Have the girl bring it to the carnival site *alone*. Do you hear? Nobody comes with her. And you better not call the police. When we have the bear, you'll get your son back. An even swap. It's that simple. Otherwise . . . well, we can't guarantee what'll happen to the boy."

The two men pushed Mark into the car and, with squealing tires, drove off. Lights came on in some of the houses around the neighborhood. A couple of doors opened as neighbors looked out to see what all the commotion was about. This was *not* normal behavior in Odyssey.

Mr. Prescott leaned against the house and closed his eyes.

"What are we going to do?" Patti asked.

"They won't hurt him," Mr. Prescott said.

"How do you know for sure?"

He looked down at Patti, then poked a finger into the bear. "Because we have what they want. This bear. And I think I know why they want it so badly."

"You do? Why?"

"I can't say right now."

"But what are we going to do about Mark?"

"That depends," Mr. Prescott said solemnly. "How brave are you feeling?"

❧　❧

The carnival was dark and desolate. Only a few lights were still on at various points around the site. In the dim glow, the rest of it looked like a junkyard of mangled steel, giant crates, and half-dismantled wooden stalls. There was nothing left to indicate that this was supposed to be a *fun* place to be. It was deathly quiet. *It's spooky and dangerous*, Patti concluded. She wanted to be anywhere but here. She had no choice, though. Mark's life depended on what she did next.

Heart pounding wildly, she slowly walked to the center of the carnival. She swallowed hard, hoping her fear might go away. It wouldn't. *God, I know I've been really dumb about this whole mess, but help me now*, she prayed.

She looked around to see if anyone was there. The place was

empty. She clutched Binger tightly, then quickly loosened her grip, worried that she might damage him. Was she anywhere near where she was supposed to be? No one told her where she was supposed to go. Would they suddenly leap out at her? She hoped not. Her muscles were wound tight. If anyone appeared, she'd scream and run, whether she meant to or not.

Madam Clara's tent was the most likely place to go. But she couldn't remember where it was. She scanned the area for any familiar landmarks, a booth or a ride she'd seen before. Nothing looked right. She kept walking and knew she wasn't really as alone as she felt. She suspected that the shooting-gallery man and his accomplice were watching her from somewhere.

Off to the right she saw what looked like the remains of the house of horrors. The monsters were gone, but the trailer still had part of the lettering hanging from the top. It read: *H-USE -F H-RR-RS*, as if whoever took it down decided to pack away the *O*'s only.

If she remembered correctly, Madam Clara's tent was nearby. She stayed far away from the trailer—not wanting to get too close to any building in case someone tried to grab her—and moved around the small clearing next to it. Madam Clara's tent was there. Flickering candlelight poured out from under the tent's sides and front flap. She thought she saw shadows move within the light.

"Hello?" she called out, her voice sounding stark and loud in the dark silence. She called again, "Is anybody here?"

The tent flap was tossed aside and Madam Clara stepped out. She seemed shrunken somehow, smaller and stooped. "Hello, child," she said. "You brought the bear?"

"It's here," Patti said and held Binger up for her to see. "You know, you didn't have to take Mark. I was on my way to bring it to you."

Madam Clara snorted. "You took too long. Some of us are impatient."

"I'm impatient, too," Patti said. "Let's get this over with."

"Bring the bear to me," Madam Clara commanded.

Patti pulled Binger close to her and said, "No."

"No?"

"Bring Mark out and, when I see that you're going to let him go, I'll put the bear down right here." Patti spoke carefully and in a steady voice, as if she'd rehearsed the exact words. It was the performance of a lifetime. She was scared out of her wits.

Madam Clara cackled loudly. "You have a lot of spunk considering your predicament, child."

Patti didn't respond, but waited and prayed. Madam Clara looked at her for a moment. Then Patti realized that she was talking out of the corner of her mouth to someone inside the tent.

"All right, child," Madam Clara finally said. "But if you try any tricks, you'll regret it." She disappeared into the tent, then returned seconds later with Mark. He was gagged, his hands were bound behind his back, and his feet were tied together. Patti's heart skipped a beat at the sight of him.

"You see?" the old woman said. "He isn't the worse for wear."

"Let him go and I'll put the bear down," Patti insisted nervously.

"Put the bear down, walk away, and then we'll let him go," the fortune-teller said. "We want to make sure the bear is . . . *intact*."

Patti swallowed hard. "No. That's not the deal."

"You're not in a position to bargain, child," Madam Clara said. "You wouldn't want another curse put upon you, would you?"

"I don't believe in you or your curses. You made an idiot out of me with all that mumbo jumbo and it won't happen again," Patti said firmly. She pulled a small can of lighter fluid and matches from her jacket pocket. "Let Mark go or I'll burn the bear right here in front of your eyes."

The fortune-teller looked visibly surprised. Again, Patti was aware that she was consulting someone in her tent.

Suddenly the shooting-gallery barker stepped out of the tent and roughly grabbed Mark. "I've had enough of this nonsense!" he shouted at Patti, and then he shouted even louder, "I know you're out there somewhere, Prescott! If you know what's good for you—and these two kids—you'll come out now. Come out!"

Patti waited, her blood turning to ice in her veins. *What am I supposed to do now?* she wondered.

"Okay, I'm here," Richard Prescott announced as he came out from behind a half-disassembled salt-and-pepper-shaker ride. He walked over to Patti until he was only a few feet away from her. "You did a good job," he said softly when he drew near. Speaking even lower, he said, "Get ready to run for cover."

"I want to see that the bear's okay and *then* you'll get your son," the barker said.

Mr. Prescott retrieved the bear from Patti and slowly made his way toward Madam Clara's tent. "You want the bear? You can have it. Here, I'll hand him to you."

"It's a trick," Madam Clara said to the barker.

"Stop where you are," the barker said to Richard Prescott.

"You're going to have to make up your minds," Mr. Prescott said. "Maybe I can help you."

Patti noticed Mr. Prescott's right hand fall to his side. He clenched his fist. Suddenly the world seemed to explode behind her. She fell to her knees, aware that the salt-and-pepper shaker had erupted. In that same instant, Richard Prescott leaped for the barker and Mark. Madam Clara screamed and ran into the tent. *That must be the signal*, Patti thought and dove for the shell of a nearby stall.

Hiding inside, she lay on the ground, panting heavily. She listened and waited. The previous emptiness of the carnival was taken over by loud crackling and whistles. Mr. Prescott must have rigged the ride somehow, or set off a fireworks display. She knew he was going to do *something* but didn't know what. Men and women shouted from every different direction. "Fire! Fire!" someone yelled over and over.

She wondered what had happened to Mark and his father. Working up some nerve, she peeked over the counter of the stall. Mark lay near the tent, squirming against the ropes that bound him. The bear lay abandoned nearby. Two men—Richard Prescott and the barker?—wrestled in the doorway to the tent. They punched, kicked, and rolled until they disappeared inside.

This was her chance to help Mark, Patti quickly decided, and she raced over to him. Reaching him, she pulled off the electric tape on his mouth.

"Ouch!" he cried, then gasped, "Get my pocket knife."

"Where is it?" she asked.

"In my pocket! Where else?" he cried. He rolled so his right pocket faced up.

She dug in his pocket, pulled out the knife, and cut at his bonds. Her hands shook so much that she was afraid she'd stab him accidentally.

Just as she freed his hands, Madam Clara appeared out of the shadows and hobbled quickly toward the bear.

"Don't let her get that bear!" Mark shouted.

Patti, without thinking about the danger, sprinted toward the bear, too. It was a neck-and-neck race but Patti got there first, scooping up the bear. Madam Clara lunged out and grabbed Patti's hair before she could get away. She yanked Patti back and growled, "Give that to me, you rotten child."

Patti gave her a hard kick in the shin.

Madam Clara yelped, but held fast to Patti's hair. By now Mark had cut the bindings from his legs, and he came full speed at Madam Clara.

"Get off her!" he shouted angrily, and an instant later he tackled her with his full weight.

The three of them went down in a confused tangle of flailing arms and kicking legs. Madam Clara clawed at them until they had to roll away from her. Patti was on her knees, clinging to Binger. Mark leaped to his feet.

"I'll scratch your eyes out," the old woman hissed as she got to her feet.

Suddenly the area was filled with a bright, white light. Spotlights hit them from all directions. A voice on a megaphone shouted metallically, "This is the police! Everyone stay where you are! You're completely surrounded!"

Madam Clara shrieked and headed for the clearing behind her tent. A policeman—the same one who'd come to the Eldridges' home—moved toward her from the dark field beyond.

"Not another step," he said to her as he drew his gun.

She swore at him but stopped where she was and held out her arms.

"You know the routine," Officer Stenson said with a smile as he holstered his gun and took out his handcuffs. Then he obliged her by cuffing her hands behind her back.

"My dad!" Mark shouted and ran to the tent.

Just then Richard Prescott came out. His shirt was torn and a trickle of blood slipped from his lip. "I'm all right," he said breathlessly. "But you'll need to call an ambulance for the gentleman inside."

Detective Anderson entered the scene and shouted, "Everyone's going to the police station!" He pointed angrily at Mr. Prescott. "And *you* have a lot of explaining to do!"

Chapter Fourteen

THE INTERROGATION ROOM at the Odyssey police station was too small to handle both the Eldridges and the Prescotts, so Detective Anderson moved them into the squad briefing room. It had several rows of chairs, posters, and charts on the wall about police reports, and a large blackboard behind a podium.

Mr. and Mrs. Eldridge hovered around their daughter anxiously. "Are you sure you're okay?" they asked repeatedly.

She assured them that she was. In fact, she was more worried about *them*. The car accident had left her father with a black eye and her mother with a large bruise on her arm.

"We look like a casualty center," Mr. Prescott said as he pressed an ice bag against his lip to help stop the swelling. His forehead was bruised and the corner of his eye had turned an angry red. Apart from that comment, and a lengthy whispered conversation with an FBI agent at the back of the room, Mr. Prescott had been quiet and subdued.

Mark was also banged up. His wrists were chafed from the tape he'd been bound with. He also had two scratches along his left cheek, compliments of Madam Clara's claws. Julie Prescott stayed attentive to Mark and had found some ointment to put on the scratches. "This'll keep them from scarring," she said.

Mark said he wanted the scars. "It'll make me look cool. Like a pirate."

"You're such a *boy*," Mrs. Prescott complained. "I should have had a daughter."

"They're no easier," Mr. Eldridge said with a wink.

Patti, whose only casualty was a tear in the knee of her jeans, held on to Binger and watched everyone with a feeling of numbness. She was exhausted. But she didn't want to miss anything that was about to happen. Now maybe she would learn some of the answers behind what had been happening to her for the past couple of days.

Detective Anderson burst into the room, letting the door slam behind him. "I'll never work in a small town again. I have a dozen people out there to book and nowhere to put them! And those FBI agents won't even let me talk to them! 'Sensitive material,' they keep saying. I guess Madam Clara and her gang are stumbling all over themselves confessing and trying to make a deal to get off light." He threw his overcoat aside and abruptly snatched up a pot of coffee from a nearby table. Making sure it was warm, he poured some into a plastic mug. "Anybody want some?" he asked.

They'd all had their fill and said no, thanks.

The detective pulled up a chair and sat in front of them. "Do you know how stupid that plan was? You never should have gone out to the carnival like that without calling me first."

"I called you," Julie corrected him.

"Fifteen minutes *later*," he complained. "Somebody could've been seriously hurt."

Patti appreciated the detective's complaint, but everything had happened so fast. After the shooting-gallery man—whose name turned out to be Fred Barber—and his sidekick drove away with Mark, Richard Prescott went back into the house and quickly made some calls. Patti wasn't sure who all the people were that he talked to, but she could tell they were in the government. After getting the okay from them to work his plan, he told Patti that she'd have to take the bear to the carnival, but only if she was up to it. She said she was.

By then, Julie Prescott had returned with Mr. and Mrs. Eldridge. They talked everything over. Mr. Prescott hadn't gone into details then, but was sure he wasn't dealing with killer criminals. They were amateurs, he had said. He was certain they wouldn't hurt Mark or Patti. They just wanted the bear.

"What's so important about that blasted bear?" Mr. Eldridge had asked.

Mr. Prescott had shaken his head and said he couldn't explain. He went on to his plan, which was simple: Patti would take the bear to Madam Clara's tent—they figured that was the most likely place—while Richard Prescott and several agents from an FBI field office in Connellsville followed from various points around Brook Meadow.

"It's somewhat risky," Mr. Prescott had said, "but we don't have many options."

Patti and her parents had agreed to go along with it.

"Just so they get what's coming to them for all this trouble," Mr. Eldridge had said.

It was then that Patti had learned how Mr. Prescott had made a lot of mental notes about the layout of the carnival when he had gone to visit it with Patti's father. That's how he knew the fireworks were stored near the salt-and-pepper-shaker ride. It was a gamble—and fortunate—that the fireworks hadn't been moved during the packing-up process.

The only thing about the plan that didn't make sense to Patti was the very thing Detective Anderson had complained about: Mr. Prescott had insisted that no one call the Odyssey Police until they had a good head start to get to the carnival. That's why the police showed up when they did.

"No offense, detective," Richard Prescott now explained, "but it's *because* this is a small-town police force that I didn't think it was a good idea to involve you from the start."

Detective Anderson was indignant. "Do you know where I came from? Chicago. Fifteen years I've worked as a detective on a big-city force. And let me tell you that if you'd done this in

Chicago, I'd have your rear end in jail. I don't care who you're an agent for!"

"An agent!" Mrs. Eldridge exclaimed.

"You're an agent?" Patti asked, her mouth dropping. She looked at Mark accusingly. "*Mark!*"

"I'm not allowed to talk about my dad's job," Mark replied.

Mr. Prescott held up his hand. "I'm not an *agent* of anything. I work as a consultant with a couple of the intelligence agencies. That's all."

"They must have trained you to be more than a consultant," the detective said sarcastically.

"It's true. We're trained to be prepared for things like this. One never knows when spies and traitors might try something foolish. I just never expected it to happen in Odyssey."

"Spies and traitors!" Mr. Eldridge said. "You better explain yourself, Richard."

Mr. Prescott agreed. "I'll go back to the beginning. I told you that the government complex was going to be a site for archives, computers, and information."

"A big filing cabinet," Patti said, echoing her father's statement from before.

"Right. What I didn't say was *which* part of the government it was connected to. In fact, I still can't say precisely. But it's enough for you to know that it has to do with some of our intelligence and security agencies."

Mrs. Eldridge asked, "You mean the complex was going to hold *top secret* information?"

"Yep," Mark's father said. "It was designed to be an information clearinghouse and think tank for those agencies."

"But . . . in Odyssey?" Mr. Eldridge asked in disbelief.

Mr. Prescott shrugged. "Why not? Their work doesn't require them to be in the Washington area. But the main reason is that Odyssey is in a beautifully *remote* part of the country."

Detective Anderson sipped his coffee, then said, "Okay, so the complex was supposed to be top secret and you're a top-secret consultant. I'm impressed. But that doesn't explain what's been going on here."

"Yeah. Why have these carnival people been trying to drive me crazy?" Patti asked.

"Because they made a big mistake."

Again, they were all surprised. "What kind of mistake?" Patti's father asked.

Mr. Prescott stood up and paced as he spoke. "They let Patti win the bear at the shooting gallery, and she wasn't the one who was supposed to get it. They made a mistake. Rather I should say that *Madam Clara* made a mistake."

"But how did they make the mistake?"

"We're still not sure," Mr. Prescott replied. "For some reason Madam Clara thought Patti was her contact to get the bear. It was obviously a two-step process to keep from getting caught. Madam Clara was supposed to make sure it was the right girl, and then give her the playing card—the queen of hearts. Then the girl was to give the card to Fred Barber as a signal to let her win the bear. Imagine their surprise when they realized that Patti *wasn't* their contact! But she had the bear now, and they had to figure out how to get it back."

Mr. Eldridge asked, "Contact for *who*, though?"

"We don't know yet. In fact, Madam Clara wasn't even sure, which was why she made her mistake."

"So all the trouble we've had has been because of them trying to get the bear?" Mrs. Eldridge asked, amazed.

"Uh-huh."

She looked perplexed, then asked, "But how did they know where to look? Patti never told them her name."

Mr. Prescott turned to Patti: "You said they saw you drive away from the carnival. My guess is that they got your license plate number, had the means to get your address and details, and started after the bear right away."

"So they ransacked our house for it," Mr. Eldridge said.

"And they couldn't find him," said Mr. Prescott.

"He was in the trunk of the car!" said Patti as she suddenly remembered.

Mr. Prescott nodded. "They couldn't know that. They also didn't dare break into your car while you were in public places, like Whit's End, or the church—"

"Or the diner," Julie Prescott said. "Remember when we saw that man by the car?"

They all nodded as the memory came back. Patti wondered if the shooting-gallery man was trying to sneak a peek to see if the bear was in the car itself.

Mr. Prescott continued. "They *did* get something from your house, though. Mark's letter. It had our last name and address on it. People on the inside know that I've been working on this project. The letter was an important link between Patti and me—a bonus for them. They thought they could use it to their advantage."

"I still don't understand something," Mr. Eldridge said. "Why did Madam Clara go to Whit's End—and what was behind that whole business about the curse?"

"I'm sorry to say that Patti set herself up for that." Mr. Prescott glanced apologetically at Patti. "Once Madam Clara realized that her cohorts couldn't get the bear from your house, she had to come up with another plan to get the bear—preferably from you. So she played on your superstition to manipulate you."

Patti blushed but didn't say anything.

"Once she had you believing you were cursed, she let her pals do things to shake you up. I'm sure if you think back to everything that's happened over the past few days—Madam Clara at the window, the fire at Trickle Lake, the brakes going out on the car—you'll see that you weren't cursed. You were simply being followed and harassed. And leaving those playing cards was a shrewd way to remind you of her warning. The more frightened you were, the easier it was to get you to bring the bear to her."

"But she never asked me to bring Binger to her," Patti said, as if it might let her off the hook somehow.

"She didn't? Are you sure?"

Patti remembered back to their encounter in the diner rest-room. She blushed even deeper. "Well . . . in a way she made me think that *I* decided to do it."

Mark's father smiled sympathetically at her. "Don't feel bad, Patti. Madam Clara makes her living as a fortune-teller. That means she's a fake, but she had to be a *good* fake. Which means she has to know how to twist people's thinking around. She played mind games with you from the very start."

"She made me look like an idiot," Patti said sourly. "I still feel like one."

Mr. Eldridge couldn't resist a quick fatherly lecture. "But if you'd been honest with us all along, we could have set you straight. You *know* not to believe in things like bad luck, fortune-telling, or curses. If you'd held on to what you believe from the Bible, you wouldn't have been fooled."

Mark raised his hand as if he were in class. "Wait a minute, Dad. You still haven't told us why they had to get the bear back."

"A very good question, young man," Detective Anderson said. "Why in the world is a stuffed bear so important—and worth taking all these risks?"

"Because of what's inside him." Mr. Prescott gestured to Binger and said, "If we rip him open, I suspect we'll find a few surprises. Does anybody have a knife?"

"I do!" Mark exclaimed, then dug in his pockets. Disappoint-ment fell across his face. "Oh no. I think I lost it at the carnival."

"I have one," Detective Anderson said and stood up to pull it from his pocket. "Hand me the bear and I'll do the honors."

Mr. Prescott reached a hand out to Patti. "May I?"

Patti playfully resisted giving him the bear. "Aw, are you really going to hurt Binger?"

"He won't feel a thing," Mr. Prescott promised with a smile.

At that moment, a man in a suit opened the door. He had the professional look of an FBI agent, rather than one of Odyssey's own police officers.

"Excuse me," he said to Detective Anderson, "but we caught

this girl wandering around the building. She claims she's your daughter."

"Kim is here?" the detective asked, surprised.

The man in the suit stepped aside so they could see the girl. Patti recognized her instantly, though she now wore a smart-looking jogging outfit and her hair was stylishly brushed, not stuck under a baseball cap.

"Kim!" the detective cried out happily.

"Hi, Daddy." The girl looked at the crowd of people uneasily. "I'm sorry. I didn't mean to interrupt. I came down with a snack for you. I put it on your desk in your office."

Detective Anderson gave her a hug. "Thanks. I'd introduce you to everyone but we're a little busy right now. See you later."

"Bye." The girl quickly walked out and the man closed the door again.

"Where were we?" the detective said, then remembered. "The bear."

Mr. Prescott reached to take the bear from Patti.

She pulled it tighter as an odd feeling of doubt came over her. "No, Mr. Prescott," she said very seriously.

He looked at her, puzzled. "What?"

"Something's wrong," she said. Her mind was working fast as the doubt suddenly grew. But she was unsure of where to go with it. She needed a minute to think.

"What's wrong?" Mr. Prescott asked.

"Give him the bear, Patti," her father insisted.

Detective Anderson came over to her, his hand also out. "Let me have it, Patti. We'll put an end to this mystery and go home. It's late." He leaned toward her. The gun in his shoulder holster peeked out from under his suit jacket.

"No," she said more loudly. She sounded panicked, though she wasn't. "I have to think about this."

"Think about what?" Detective Anderson demanded.

Patti looked wide-eyed up at Mr. Prescott. There was something about the girl—who she was and what she said. It didn't line up. Then it clicked. "It's Detective Anderson," she said. "He's the contact."

Detective Anderson turned beet red. "What did you say?"

Mr. Prescott scrutinized Patti. "You'd better explain yourself."

"That girl—I'm not sure, but how can she be his daughter?" She looked to her parents and said, "Don't you remember? He came to the house and said he was up at all hours because he was a bachelor."

Mrs. Eldridge thought about it, then nodded. "That's right. He did."

"A bachelor can have a daughter from a previous marriage, can't he? I'm a widower!" he said emphatically.

Patti hadn't thought of that, but it wasn't the only thing that bothered her. Her voice began to rise in pitch as she spoke. "But that girl. I saw her at the carnival. We bumped into each other. It surprised me because we looked so much alike."

"I was going to say that she looked like she could be your sister," Mrs. Eldridge said.

"The other day she was dressed just like I was and it made her look almost like my twin. Then I saw her later with Madam Clara when we were driving away!" The image was fixed in her mind now—and the truth came clear.

"What does that have to do with anything? A lot of people went to the carnival!"

"Madam Clara thought I was that girl," Patti said to the detective. That was it in a nutshell. Detective Anderson was the missing piece: the contact who was supposed to get the bear filled with whatever secrets it held inside.

Detective Anderson suddenly laughed at her. "This is ridiculous!" he said, but quickly pulled his gun out from under his jacket. "Now stand back," he barked at Mr. Prescott.

Mr. Prescott rolled his eyes in exasperation. "I never would have suspected you."

"But you suspected *someone* on the police force, didn't you?" the detective replied.

"I knew someone with the local police was involved with Madam Clara's gang because they got the license number details so quickly."

Detective Anderson sneered. "That's why you didn't want the police at the carnival right away."

"Now I know why you couldn't seem to help us," Mr. Eldridge added. "You didn't want to."

"You also showed up at Whit's End the night Madam Clara was there," Mrs. Eldridge said, as if she was just catching on to the game of "Accuse Detective Anderson."

"Yes, yes, you're all very clever," the detective said impatiently. "But I can't stick around to listen to the rest of your Agatha Christie impressions. Give me that bear and I'll go." His eyes darted toward the main door, then over to an emergency exit on the opposite wall.

Patti held on to Binger.

Detective Anderson pointed the gun at her. "That bear is worth a lot of money. Give him to me."

"He's worthless," Mr. Prescott said. "You have to realize that we've been compromised. We'll change everything. Whatever information is in that bear is useless to you now."

"Is it? You're going to tell me that the architectural plans for the government complex are no good?" he asked.

"The government complex won't be built. Not here. Not now."

Detective Anderson chuckled. "But these plans aren't for this complex alone. Your design for this building was used for embassies and complexes all over the world. Don't you think that would be worth something? Don't you think there are groups and organizations who'd pay a lot of money to see the top secret designs of intelligence buildings in, say, the Middle East or Russia or South America?"

The blood drained from Richard Prescott's face. He didn't reply.

"Just as I thought," the detective said. He reached down and grabbed Binger by the neck. His gun pointed at Patti, he growled, "Let go."

Patti did.

Keeping his eye on everyone in the room, the detective backed toward the door. He pushed the bar down behind him and shoved the door open. Cool night air blew in.

"You won't get far," Richard Prescott said.

"I'll get far enough," Detective Anderson said. "My daughter's 'message' was her way of telling me that certain things were in place for us to leave. I needed this bear and—"

Suddenly he froze where he was, his face awash with surprise. A voice behind him said, "Freeze. Drop the gun."

The detective obeyed. The gun rattled as it hit the floor. Richard Prescott quickly grabbed it up.

"And the bear," the voice said.

Detective Anderson handed the bear to Mr. Prescott.

"Now, get down on the floor, facedown, with your arms and legs spread. You know how it's done."

Again, the detective obeyed. As he did, the door swung open wide and John Avery Whittaker stepped inside. He wasn't holding a gun at all. He had pressed a large pen against the detective's back. He blew on the end like an old cowboy who'd just won a gunfight, then slipped the pen back into his shirt pocket. "Imagine my surprise when I was walking past the station and saw Detective Anderson waving a gun around. I thought, 'Now that's strange. What could he be up to?'"

"Thanks, Whit," Mr. Prescott said. "Bob, would you get Agent Cooper in here?"

Mr. Eldridge nodded, then rushed into the hallway to bring in the FBI.

From the floor, Detective Anderson groaned. "I want my lawyer!"

"In time," Richard Prescott said. He handed Whit the bear. "You better get this out of here before anyone else decides to try for it."

"Okay," Mr. Whittaker said and took the bear.

Expressions of disbelief fell like shadows across every face around the room.

"*You* work for the government, too?" Mark cried out.

Mr. Whittaker shrugged and smiled. "It's a hobby."

As quickly as he had appeared, he disappeared back through the door.

Chapter
Fifteen

IT WASN'T UNTIL THE NEXT DAY, when the Eldridges and the Prescotts reunited for lunch, that Richard explained to them about Mr. Whittaker. "He's given me the okay to say only this much: He's worked as an analyst and researcher for the government off and on for years. Because he was local, I was instructed to ask him to find out what was inside the bear, then hold on to it for safekeeping—or to make certain that it's destroyed. He came to the station to get the bear. Fortunately, he came when he did."

Patti shook her head. There was still so much she didn't know about Mr. Whittaker.

"What will happen to Detective Anderson, Madam Clara, and the rest?" Mr. Eldridge asked.

"The FBI has them all in custody. They'll go to trial and, hopefully, will be prosecuted as the traitors they are. You won't be asked to testify in person, by the way. They'll videotape your testimonies."

Patti was genuinely surprised. It hadn't occurred to her that she might have to make a court appearance.

"We'll do anything we can to help," Mr. Eldridge said.

"Thank you," Mark's father said. "And I hope I don't have to say too strongly that you can't talk about any of this. To anyone. You have to pretend like it didn't happen. If word got out, there'd be no end of problems."

They all agreed soberly.

Mr. Prescott looked uncomfortable for a moment, then said, "I got some other bad news, though. Julie and Mark don't even know about this."

Everyone waited with hardly a breath between them.

"As I suggested in the confrontation with Detective Anderson, as far as the government is concerned, the site has been compromised. They said we'll have to draw up new plans and choose a different place to build it. Now they're saying they want it *closer* to Washington, D.C."

"Oh no," Patti said as she realized what that meant. Mark wouldn't be moving back to Odyssey after all. Patti exchanged sad glances with Mark. He then sat quietly and stared at the table.

That wasn't the end of it. "I'm really sorry, but I have to go back to Washington right away," he added.

"Today?" Julie Prescott asked.

"I have to give a full report about what happened and pull together the teams to discuss our change in plans." He looked miserable and said again, "I'm sorry, everyone. I didn't expect this to happen."

Lunch was ruined for Patti and Mark. They ate quickly and quietly.

"We could let your father go home and fly back later in the week," Julie Prescott suggested to Mark.

"No," he pouted. "I don't want to be here if we're not moving back. Why torture ourselves?"

Later in the afternoon, when Patti was alone with Mark on her front porch, she said, "You know, you're getting a little too big to pout like that. You could've hung around for the rest of the week. We could do things together, have fun."

Mark shook his head. "I know it sounds crazy, but if I stay and have fun and get used to going to Whit's End and . . . and being with you . . . then I'll be miserable when I have to go back to Washington. Maybe I'm being a brat, but I don't know how to have a good time here and then be happy back there."

Patti thought about it for a few minutes as they looked out at the beautiful spring day. Somewhere, someone had started a lawnmower. A bird sang nearby. "We have to try harder, Mark."

"Try *what* harder?" Mark asked.

"Try to get used to where we are," she said. Her mother's words came back to her. "We have to get on with our lives."

Mark frowned at her. "That's easy for you to say. You're living here in Odyssey."

She frowned back at him. "What makes you think it's easy? For a long time after you left, I didn't like Odyssey. I hated it."

"How could you hate Odyssey?" he asked incredulously.

"Because *you* weren't here! Are you completely clueless? I *miss you*, you clod! You're the closest friend I've ever had, and I hate it when you're not around. But I have to try. *We* have to try. It's wrong to be miserable."

Mark sat quietly for a moment. "I miss you, too," he finally said softly.

"I love you, Mark," Patti whispered quickly before she lost her nerve.

He didn't look at her. He stared at his fingers as they folded and unfolded nervously on his lap. "I love you, too," he whispered back.

Patti didn't know if he understood what she meant by those words, or if he understood what he meant when he responded. She didn't dare press him. She left the moment alone.

The Prescotts were ready to depart later that afternoon. Mark reluctantly hugged Patti before he left.

"Maybe we'll come back this summer!" Julie Prescott said hopefully.

Then they were gone.

That evening, Patti climbed onto a stool at Whit's End and dejectedly asked Mr. Whittaker for a soda.

"Mark's gone again, huh?" he asked as he handed her the drink.

"Uh-huh," she said. She had decided to try to get on with her life, but she knew it wouldn't be easy.

"I have something that might help you whenever you miss Mark," Mr. Whittaker said, reaching under the counter. He lifted up Binger and handed him to her.

"Mr. Whittaker!" she exclaimed, her breath taken away. Binger looked at her with the same melancholy expression he'd always had. Except for a tiny stitch along his back, he looked unchanged.

"I tried to be careful when I worked on him," he said. "I hope you still want him."

"Are you kidding? Thank you, Mr. Whittaker! This is great!" She hugged Binger tightly and swung back and forth on the stool.

Mr. Whittaker observed, "He can never replace a real friend, but he might be nice to have around."

Patti smiled. "He'll do just fine."

"I'm sure he will—until something better comes along," Mr. Whittaker said with a smile and a knowing tone. Then he looked beyond Patti to the door.

Donna Barclay had just walked in. "Hi, Patti," she said. "I just called your house and your parents said you came here. I was wondering if you want to go up to Trickle Lake with me. I have to collect leaf samples for a project that's due next week. But only if you want to."

Patti glanced at Mr. Whittaker, then back at Donna. "Only if I want to? I'd love to," she said.

FOCUS ON THE FAMILY®

At Focus on the Family, we work to help you really get to know Jesus and equip you to change your world for Him.

We realize the struggles you face are different from your parents' or your little brother's, so we've developed a lot of resources specifically to help you live boldly for Christ, no matter what's happening in your life.

Besides exciting novels, we have Web sites, magazines, booklets, and devotionals . . . all dealing with the stuff you care about.

Focus on the Family Magazines

We know you want to stay up-to-date on the latest in your world — but it's hard to find information on entertainment, trends, and relevant issues that doesn't drag you down. It's even harder to find magazines that deliver what you want and need from a Christ-honoring perspective.

That's why we created *Breakaway* (for teen guys), *Brio* (for teen girls), and *Clubhouse* (for tweens, ages 8 to 12). So, don't be left out — sign up today!

Breakaway
Teen guys
breakawaymag.com

Brio
Teen girls
briomag.com

Clubhouse
Tweens ages 8 to 12
clubhousemagazine.com

Weekly Radio Show
whitsend.org

Phone toll free: (800) A-FAMILY (232-6459)

BP06XTN

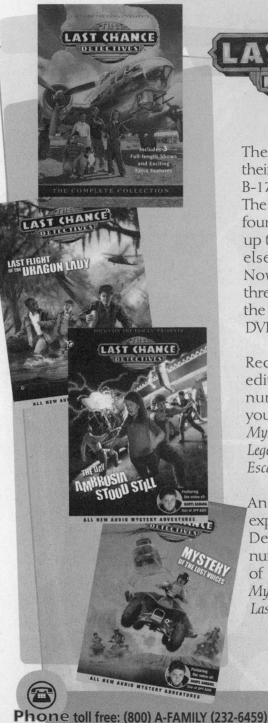

THE LAST CHANCE DETECTIVES ®

Their town is Ambrosia . . . their headquarters is a vintage B-17 bomber . . . and they are The Last Chance Detectives . . . four ordinary kids who team up to solve mysteries no one else can be bothered with. Now, for the first time, the three best-selling episodes in the series are available in one DVD gift set.

Request this collector's edition set by calling the number below. And see if you can crack the cases of *Mystery Lights of Navajo Mesa*, *Legend of the Desert Bigfoot*, and *Escape from Fire Lake*.

And for the latest audio exploits of The Last Chance Detectives, call that same number. Request your copy of *The Day Ambrosia Stood Still*, *Mystery of the Lost Voices*, and *Last Flight of the Dragon Lady*.

Phone toll free: (800) A-FAMILY (232-6459)